ASH AND RUIN

ASH AND *RUIN*

THE PALADIN OF SHADOW CHRONICLES

BOOK TWO

by
Michael Eging
and
Steve Arnold

Taylor & Wells

Chardon, Ohio, USA

Taylor & Wells Publishing
11525 Taylor Wells Rd.
Chardon, OH, USA 44024
www.taylor-wells.com

First Print Edition

Cover art created by Ina Wong

Printed in the United States of America

ISBN 978-0-9887099-8-0

The guilty conscience take thou for thy labor,
But neither my good word nor princely favor,
With Cain go wander thorough shades of night,
And never show thy head by day nor light.
Lords, I protest my soul is full of woe
That blood should sprinkle me
For now the devil that told me I did well
Says that this deed is chronicled in hell.

—*William Shakespeare*

Prologue

THE BURDEN OF THE LORD

The city remained alive, even with the winter sun long descended over the western horizon. Residents hung lanterns to disperse encroaching shadows—for this city, center of the great grinding wheel of Roman dominion, knew no sleep. In these days, the *polis* rested safe behind thick fortified walls that had seen many sunsets since Constantine had chosen these hills for his city, his *Constantinople*. Decades later, Theodosius II had erected another layer of defense: mighty ramparts that stretched for miles in stolid might to ensure many more seasons would pass, fulfilling ancient pagan prophesies of a thousand-year Roman rule.

Yet this was a Christian city, so intended by that same Constantine who had lent it his name—he who had united the empire and given the religion imperial sanction within these walls. At nearly every corner, an edifice to the One True God stood regally above the populace, many of whom, even at this late hour, straggled into evening prayers and devotion. Nobility wore the ermine-fur and foxtail-trimmed cloaks that had been conveyed by merchants and adventurers from distant Slavic lands north of the Black Sea. Said nobility also brushed elbows with homespun common folk who struggled to eke out a living among the warren of streets inside those mighty walls.

Constantinople lay astride the crossroads of the world. The greetings, the farewells, the challenges and the gossip in Greek, Germanic, Latin, and more exotic tongues could be heard amid the gathering darkness.

And through this cosmopolitan air, a young man named Dylan hurried along the Middle Road, clutching a sack to his chest.

Every time he glanced over his shoulder, Dylan's steps faltered, causing him to stumble into people. He murmured apologies in halting Greek, then continued his flight, threadbare garments rustling at his ankles. Mercifully ignored by price-haggling shoppers, pleading beggars and distracted government officials, he pressed through the masses toward the tall Charisius Gate that would lead him from the city proper into the outlying suburbs. He prayed no one would stop him.

Chilly air swept into his lungs as he huffed past massive buildings. He who had once been a farm boy, studying in far-off Canterbury, now fled headlong down the Mese, the wide thoroughfare stretching the length of Imperial Constantinople, from the Xylokeros Gate all the way to the grand square fronting both the emperor's palace and the *Hagia Sophia,* the Church of Divine Wisdom.

At the Cistern of Aetius, one of the expansive wells that watered the city, Dylan paused, clutching his side. He scanned the Mese yet saw little more than a thinning crowd of nameless faces and the calm surface of the reservoir, sprinkled with lantern light from the neighborhood.

Despite his being only twenty and four, Dylan's blond hair was thin about his crown, his temples streaked with premature gray. He rubbed his eyes, strained from searching the shadows between buildings and over the broken roofline. His feet throbbed, not only from running but from the long hours searching for anyone who might assist him. From learned citizens in the great library to richly robed priests who thronged the royal courts, none spared a concerned glance at the ragged Briton, who was not quite a priest himself.

Since disembarking from the Sicilian merchant ship two days ago, Dylan had not felt safe anywhere among these streets and alleys. Northward from the cleric, however, across the block walls of the cistern, the *Prodomos* of Petra, a monastery, rose above the tiled roofs of the surrounding buildings. He prayed that once inside those consecrated walls, whatever had been pursuing him these last many months would be stymied for a time.

Dylan crept toward the cistern's shimmering waters. He clutched the sack tighter to him, the circular edge of the cup within creasing his chest. The reservoir's low stone wall had absorbed the coldness and the shadows of the night.

Then one of those shadows peeled off toward an alley.

That was when Dylan ran, his garments flapping. Something flashed, then whistled through the air and tore at his skin, leaving a red trail across his cheek. If it was a warning, he didn't wait to find out. He shouted to a clutch of merchants closing a nearby shop, but only one looked his way, then waved him off. He ignored their disregard, sprinting toward them, breath burning in his chest.

"Please . . ." he panted in broken Greek, "someone is after me!"

A hearty-looking fellow with a blond, gray-flecked beard responded to his call and searched back up the street.

"Maybe you outran them," the man said, voice heavy with a northern accent.

Across the Mese, people gathered around a small fire burning in a grate. Beyond the cistern, scattered travelers and residents hurried along the surrounding garden paths for the warmth of shelter. Everything appeared benign as any other night for the last two centuries.

"It was here," Dylan insisted.

He swiped at his cheek, drawing blood across his hand. Something had pursued him—of this he was sure.

"Where are you bound, lad?" asked the bearded man.

"There," Dylan said. He pointed across the cistern toward the lights on the other side.

"The monastery?"

"Yes, yes. The monastery."

"The monastery?" the man responded, thumping him on the shoulder with a meaty hand. "They take care of travelers?"

Dylan nodded wordlessly. The older man pressed a pair of bronze *half-follis* coins into the younger man's cold fingers.

"They'll give you a better bed for this, I'm sure," he said pleasantly.

The young man closed his hand on the coins.

"I cannot . . . I cannot repay you," Dylan stammered.

"Tch . . ." the merchant clucked. "Get a warm room for the night. And don't let the thievin' priests rob you blind."

The moon rose, shadows of barren limbs reaching across the cistern's smooth waters. Dylan scuttled through the gardens toward the glowing monastery lights, picking up his pace even more when those lights began winking out with the monastery's curfew. With each step he could sense the presence that had pursued him through the city.

His scamper became a trot, then a full sprint, until he vaulted up the steps to the hefty iron-bound door. His breath was ragged as he pounded on the stout oak planks. The sound was quickly quelled, absorbed within like hot ash in lye.

But then a voice replied from behind the thick portal. Dylan pressed his ear to the cold wood. Between his poor language skills and the thickness of the door itself, the words were difficult to make out.

"Salve?" Dylan huffed in Latin, the universal language of Mother Church. "Hello!" he called again, louder. "I'm . . . I'm from a distant land. Please, it's cold. And I've no shelter!"

He waited, the chill reaching into his chest and clutching at his heart. At least he hoped it was only the cold.

"Yes, yes . . ." a voice replied from within. "The monastery is closed for the night. Come back tomorrow."

"Please," Dylan pleaded. "Shelter! In the name of Christ our King, I need shelter. I have a few coins . . ."

Moments went by, marked only by the throbbing of his heart. He placed his back against the door and fervently traced a cross on his chest.

"Dear Jesus, God . . . be with me," the youth whispered, his words trailing from his mouth in a trail of vapor. "Be my strength though I face certain death . . ."

The cup's edge cut into his beating chest. A simple carpenter's vessel, smooth and unadorned, it fit easily into his clenched hand. He had borne the cup willingly, dutifully, ever since that fateful night when his entire world had plunged into ruin on the words of a long-dead pagan magicker.

The door lock clicked, then the bolt slid against the wood. The young man pressed closer to the door.

"Please, let me stay the night . . ." Dylan pleaded. *Oh, please give me shelter, for I am alone in the valley of death.*

The door opened a hair's breadth, a sliver of light cutting into the night.

"And who is requesting respite?" asked the gravelly voice from within in fluent Greek.

Dylan took a moment to decipher the question.

"Come now," the voice snapped.

"Please, I come from far away," Dylan replied, again in Latin. "I just disembarked from a ship."

"This is not an inn," the voice said, this time in Latin as well. "This is a house of holiness, a house of orders."

"Of course, holy Father," the young man replied, his voice deferential. "But I have no place to stay. I am a student, Father. A student of the Lord."

"And where did you say you were from?"

"Britannia. Albion, as we call it. An island once ruled by Rome. I was a lector at Canterbury."

The door opened a little wider.

"I only just happened to be walking by," said the voice, "when I heard your knock."

"Please do not leave me out here," Dylan pleaded. "The night is cold. And wet. I've not been someplace warm since I was aboard the ship."

That was not a lie, either. He had run out of coins when he'd paid the ship's captain for his passage and had been on the streets since. Oh, in truth, the night of his departure was likely the last time he'd truly felt

6

warmth. Syracuse had seemed like the center of the world to him, fresh off another boat from the coast of Gaul back in the waning days of summer. Cosmopolitan, it was the very center of German rule and Roman culture on the Isle of Sicilia. But, just like every other place he'd sheltered in since fleeing Canterbury so long ago, the city had become unsafe. This last ship had spirited him away on a rainy night from under the eyes of the city guard searching for a killer. A killer who had ripped out the throats of a family that had given him employment and shelter.

The door creaked closed.

"Please . . ." Dylan pled. "I have coins."

The creaking stopped.

"Show me."

The young man reached into the folds of his garments to produce the two bronzes the shopkeeper had given him. A narrowed eye examined them.

"The poor have many needs."

The monk thrust a pudgy hand through the door. Dylan snatched the coins back.

"Only once I'm inside," he hissed.

The monk shrugged, then opened the door, revealing a poorly lit interior, but Dylan stepped in quickly.

"Close it—close it," he stammered.

"Yes, yes . . . all right, then. Patience is a virtue," the monk admonished, shoving the portal closed, then ramming home the bar. He looked the young man up and down. "So. You are not from around here? I see many different people, you know. Oh, indeed I do. Why, we even see barbarians from the frozen reaches of the north, we do."

"Yes, I am sure," Dylan replied politely, rubbing his shoulders and stamping his feet. "Thank you. I may have frozen tonight."

"Sure, you might. Not much to your name, I suspect," the monk observed, holding out a hand for the coins.

Dylan dropped them into his palm even though he had been put off by the man's manner. He was just glad to be within the walls of the monastery.

"Most of what I had lies across the world," he admitted.

The monk shook his head, blew his nose into a cloth, and pointed to a rough-hewn bench against the wall.

"Wait there," he snorted. "I shall fetch someone who can find you a blanket and corner in a cell."

Inside the chapel, oil lamps gave off a flickering light, illuminating ash-smudged walls. The abbot knelt at the altar, his balding pate shining with beads of sweat. A priest allowed Dylan inside, then gestured for him to keep silent while the abbot's evening devotions whispered through the air. The priest shut the door behind Dylan.

"And as we watch the relics of devotion, O Lord," the old man intoned, "we pray for the strength to stand with the saints in the face of sword and death. For a martyr's crown, we cry the truth to heathen ear, O Lord of Hosts, that we may shed this flesh and ascend to thy throne . . ."

Dylan bowed his head, his eyelids heavy while he attempted to absorb the words. Within his cloak, his hands clutched the cold metal cup—a constant burden since the first time he'd touched it. That fateful night was many years ago, far across the known world. And between then and now, there and here, was a shallow grave, deep in a silent Gallic wood, where the torn body of his friend Cedric lay with his heart pierced by a willow spike, head severed and wrapped in a canvas bag. He had since been without any companion.

The abbot's words finally trailed off. Dylan cracked open his eyes, then squinted against the flickering lamplight. The abbot rose from his knees with a visible creak of his aged body, braced himself against the altar, and met Dylan's eyes with rheumy orbs that appeared ethereal in the candlelight.

"A stranger to the city?" he murmured with a thin smile that refused to reach his eyes.

"Yes, holy Father." Dylan dipped his head respectfully. "I seek shelter."

The older man took a few limping steps toward Dylan, searching the youth's face in the dim light. The abbot's eyes seemed to grow sad, almost resigned.

"You are being hunted, my son. But you know that, I suppose."

"How did you . . . ?" Dylan sputtered.

The abbot sighed, the sound of his breath a bare rattle.

"This is an old city. A land populated for a thousand years before Constantine pressed his boot on the Golden Horn. A thousand years of survival for the living . . . and the dead."

Dylan clutched at the cup inside his garments, then whispered, "I do not understand."

"We are a people who stand in God's light. But centuries of, shall I say, *accommodations* . . . aye, that would be the word, accommodations have kept this city and its people alive. Accommodations that have allowed us to live together."

A chill crawled up the back of Dylan's neck.

9

"Us . . . who?"

The abbot shifted to one side. Just over his shoulder, in a dark recess of the shrine, a shadowy form unfolded. A personage emerged, tall and slender. It stepped forward into the light of the lamps, revealing a young man's pale visage framed by oily black locks. Though wearing the garments of a cosmopolitan nobleman, the man moved with a primal hunter's grace. Dylan backed away until he felt the solid planks of the door against his back.

"What is this?" he rasped. "Father, I seek the sanctuary of the Church!"

"And yet you bear a great burden," said the pale newcomer. A crooked smile touched his lips. He inclined his head to one side, like a serpent sizing up its prey. "We can lift that burden."

The abbot crept to Dylan's side, raising his hands, palm before him.

"Please, my son. This is for your good."

The pale man glided closer as well, his eyes like deep dark pools.

"You are ignorant of our sensibilities," the creature hissed. "Within the City, we seek only accommodation. The Greek and the Persian trade silks and spices in the markets even as they war in distant deserts. Gothic longships deliver wheat and furs, though their kings covet the City's riches. There is much wealth to be had—wealth that can buy indulgence for a lifetime or several lifetimes. Enough exotic diversions to satisfy the most jaded of creatures that easily tire of a common existence. The living and the dead seek much the same in this City, and peace ensures we all prosper in our own spheres."

"This is Christ's house!" Dylan bleated at the abbot. "I seek sanctuary from these very monstrosities—"

"Oh, foolish child." The pale man laughed. "I seek not your life. Not here. Those are the terms that permit me to stand in this place. No violence. Sanctuary is inviolate. But outside?" His tone grew intense, eager. "Give me what I seek, and you may even remain alive when you depart these doors."

With an offended scowl, the abbot turned on the creature.

"I'll have none of that here, Demonithus! Not in His house!" the abbot said, touching the points of the cross on his breast. "What would you have of him? He's but a poor pilgrim with nothing to steal."

"Old blind man! He bears one thing of immense value." The pale man's finger was long and gaunt when it stretched toward Dylan. "Oh, come now, lad. You know of what I speak."

The cup felt heavy in Dylan's grasp.

"I cannot surrender anything to the unclean, the—unholy."

"Oh, I'm not unholy, my friend. Look," the pale man said, spreading his hands. "I stand on sacred ground. I can care for your burden—I can release you from it!"

The creature's hands thrust toward Dylan again. The abbot cleared his throat, his expression still puzzled.

"Be prudent, Demonithus," the holy man warned. "Your time on the Lord's ground is limited."

"Yes," the creature hissed, his eyes fixed on Dylan. "Give me the cup, boy, and this will all be over. You have no need of it for your sacraments. It cannot bring you wealth or fame. Give it to me. We can protect it. Keep it safe."

Bile rose in Dylan's throat, for the creature's words ripped open a floodgate of memories—from the dangerous flight from Canterbury to the shores of strange and exotic Francia, then across the known world. A world awash with blood and horror.

11

"It is of no consequence," Dylan insisted. "A peasant's traveling cup. Nothing more."

"On the contrary," Demonithus said, the corners of his mouth curling up and revealing yellowed canine teeth, "it is a fount of life. I will keep it for you that it might be put to good use."

"*Ex hoc malo protegat Deus tuus,*" Dylan shouted. "*Jesus dominus supra omnia mea sanctificabunt!*"

The creature shrank away with a snarl, then shook itself to regain its composure. When it finally spoke, undead breath plumed across Dylan's skin.

"Give me the cup. Or I swear I will drink you!"

The abbot lumbered sideways, interposing himself between the beast and Dylan. "There will be no violence here," he said. "You know the terms."

There was a long moment in which the two old adversaries glared into each other's eyes, each daring the other to make a move.

"We honor the pact," Demonithus finally spat, jabbing a long finger past the abbot's shoulder into Dylan's face. "But know this, boy. We will not have eternal patience. I will possess the cup if I must tear these walls down to get it!"

With that, the creature faded into the shadows until the door of the chapel creaked on its ancient hinges and he was gone.

The abbot visibly sagged. "This item you bear . . ." His face cragged with lines of worry while he spoke. "Is it worth a war between the living and the dead? Is it worth the chaos that could be unleashed if I provide you shelter?"

He clutched at Dylan's shoulder with his blue-veined hand, searching the young traveler's face with his weak eyes.

"I am sorry, my son," the abbot continued. "But I can only offer you what remains of the night and the day tomorrow. Beyond that, you must leave."

"But where . . . where will I go?" Dylan asked, uncertain in a world of *accommodations* that permitted the Lord's own sanctuary to host profane horrors that shouldn't even exist. "I spent my last to reach this place. I've nowhere else."

His hand felt along the door for the latch, but the abbot's skeletal fingers clung to his shoulder. "We tolerate them, that is all," the old man murmured. "Appearing in the very sanctuary—never has one of their kind even dared such. Please know we do not condone their ungodly preying on innocents."

"But you *tolerate* it," Dylan accused.

The abbot pursed his lips. "There is one whom they would never dare disturb," he stated, his voice dropping further while his eyes darted about. "Four Roman miles beyond the Charisius Gate lives a holy man . . . Daniel is his name. You'll find him atop a column carved by the hands of the pagans. Seek him."

The abbot withdrew his hand and hung his head.

"I wouldn't know where to start," Dylan stammered, releasing the cup from his grasp and allowing it to settle once more in the pocket inside his garments. "I've only just arrived—I barely found this abbey."

The abbot motioned him to follow into a dim corridor. "Come the morrow, Brother Titus will lead you to the gate and set you on the road. For now, rest and sleep."

As if I possibly could, Dylan thought.

Dawn blossomed over the Bosporus, light finding once more the alleys and warrens of the great city. A certain cold darkness, however, remained stubbornly in Dylan's bones. Daytime allowed him mobility, yet that was only a guarded freedom. The living minions of the damned had tracked him under the sunlit skies. His skin crawled with the memory of the cold trek through Gaul with his companion Cedric. Through the forests and fens, the unwashed and savage servants of the Higher Dead had trailed them beneath the brilliant orb of light, to be replaced by their implacable undead masters when night returned.

Dylan withdrew the cup from his garments and held it up to the brightening winter dawn. A simple vessel—not the grand chalice of an emperor but the rough cup of a carpenter's son, a man accustomed to the company of commoner, outcast, and sinner. Despite the cup's plainness, the power emanating from it kept Dylan trekking ever eastward toward the land of the Apostles and the blessed Lord in Palestine. The green-tinged metal lent him strength and hope when he should have curled up next to Cedric's stiffened body, cradling his friend's severed head to await the ravens.

The monks stirred for early morning devotionals, their voices a whisper outside the door of the small traveler's cell. Dylan put his feet on the cold floor, then tucked away the cup. He tugged on his well-worn boots, grabbed his cloak, then pushed against the stiff door hinges.

The hallway beyond was a flurry of ecclesiastical activity. Clerics hurried to the chapel while novices finished up more menial tasks about the chambers before following to morning prayers. Dylan breathed in the comforting familiarity of it all while following the constrained chaos toward the main chapel. This structure was much larger and grander than the abbot's personal chantry. Pausing at the chapel threshold, Dylan allowed his eyes to rise to the clerestory windows that lined the upper interior. The glow from the rising sun cast beams of light across the vaulted ceiling.

Fingers folded around his arm, startling him.

"You must be the traveler who visited us last night," a voice said in smooth, melodic Greek. A diminutive face caught Dylan's attention, features pale and gaunt, bounded by dark, close-cropped hair, a tonsure shaved at the crown.

"Yes . . . yes, that is me," Dylan replied, his own grasp of the language halting. He pulled away from the monk's hand. "You're Brother Titus?"

"Yes . . . yes, that is me," the monk mimicked with a crooked smile. "The abbot asked me to show you the path to find Daniel." Then, in response to Dylan's blank look, he offered, "Daniel the Stylite?"

"I do not understand," Dylan said. "Who is this Daniel? And what is a Stylite?"

Titus clapped Dylan on the back, steering him down the hallway away from the chapel.

"Oh, where would one start with Daniel? He is a legend, no? But I see from your eyes that's not a legend at all in your homeland. Where was that? Far-off Albion?"

"Yes," Dylan admitted. "I studied at Canterbury."

"Well, a name unknown to me," the monk admitted, leading Dylan into warmer passageways where scents of newly baked bread tempted his nostrils. "Daniel, he is a different sort of monk. Many, many years ago, he arrived outside the city and took up residence on a column of stone, vowing to remain alone on that rock. He believes his devotions allow him to become closer to God by shedding the dross of this world. Pilgrims travel from all over the world for his counsel.

Emperors have humbled themselves at his feet. If the abbot intends for you to meet Daniel, there must be a reason. And I for one would not question his judgment."

Bile rose in the back of Dylan's throat when events of the previous night flooded back into focus. "But this monastery, this city . . . so much evil."

Titus guided Dylan into a large kitchen larder.

"Come, gather what you need," he urged, rummaging through cluttered shelves. With a grunt of satisfaction, he pulled out a small canvas sack into which he stuffed loaves, vegetables, and dried meats. "You know, life thrusts us amid evil. But we can choose not to be evil. Or even as Daniel—to rise beyond its touch."

Dylan grabbed a puckered apple from a barrel.

"How long have you been here? In the monastery?"

"Me? Very long," Titus replied, counting with a twitch of his cheek. "Since I was nine summers old. Almost forty years."

Dylan took a bite of the apple. "Then you know not of what you speak."

The monk's cheeks drooped. "How so?"

Dylan held up the apple, displaying the bite he'd taken deep into the soft flesh. The interior was not white and fresh—it was already turning brown.

"You can't live in it without it taking a bite and infecting your insides."

Titus did not reply, but simply finished filling the bag before handing it to the young cleric. Dylan murmured his thanks while following the monk through another doorway that led back to the main hall where he'd entered the night before. The corridor echoed with the ethereal chorus of resident monks and novices, their morning prayers drifting through the airy interior of the monastery. Titus paused at the great doors, bowed, and murmured his own prayer. He pulled the hood of his cloak up over his head, motioning for Dylan to follow him outside.

Constantine's city appeared starkly different in the light. The young Briton marveled at the sophisticated architecture revealed in the sun's cold, golden rays. Now, after years fleeing through the wilds of Gaul and the Germanic frontier across the Rhine, the city appeared less sinister than fascinating. Though those lands had promised some measure of safety in their very lack of habitation, he eventually came to know that the answers he sought wouldn't come from the lips of the heathen. Thus he'd crossed back into civilized territory to seek wisdom in scattered islands of learning among the monasteries and libraries of Ostrogothic Italy. But the Higher Dead had found him once more, and he had been forced to flee, this time to the city where the learning of the ages had been collected.

Dylan grimaced. Despite all his efforts and trials, the dead had found him before he'd even had a chance to borrow a book or query a scholar.

The two monks emerged from twisted alleys by the deep blue pool of the Cistern of Aetius. Even at this early hour, residents carried buckets to dip into its waters. Brother Titus navigated the side streets until they reached the Mese, which ran straight to the looming wall and the Charisius Gate.

Once at the gate, they fell into a crowd of travelers who'd already braved the early morning hour to await the daily opening. Dylan shifted from foot to foot, his eyes nervously darting about. Many of the faces close to him remained shrouded by shadows in the slanting light.

They could be here still, the wretched minions of the Higher Dead—hunting him on the edge of night and day, wolves to his sheep.

Try as he might to avoid contact, his gaze met eyes deep inside the folds of a hood barely an arm's length away. An ominous chill crawled up Dylan's spine and his foot shuffled backward. But the packed crowd made flight impossible. Fear clutched his breast. He couldn't breathe. Of course, they would find him. They would find him and they would slaughter him, here in the street, where he presumed himself unnoticed by this cultured, distracted crowd before a great Roman gate.

His escort's name froze in his throat. The brothers of the abbey already had blood on their hands and now led him to the slaughter to appease the demons.

"Roderic!" someone called. "Roderic!"

The man pulled the cowl from his face, revealing craggy features that softened when he called out, "Marta!" And, of course, this Marta appeared across the way with a small child in tow.

Dylan's heart relinquished its fear, but only for a moment. He raised his face to the sun. A horn blasted from the wall's heights, then the thick iron bolts that had held the gate in place began moving. Beyond the massive portal lay far-sprawling suburbs. Titus pointed a gnarled finger to the northeast, where the road curved up into distant hills.

"Go with God, brother," said Titus. "The answers you seek lie beyond the city. The Stylite will guide you."

With that, the monk turned back up the street toward the abbey. He did not look back.

Hours passed after Dylan cleared the Charisius Gate. He trudged through those endless suburbs until city streets eventually gave way to open farmland. Though well past noontime, he expected a shadow to leap from the edge of a tree or hollow of a ditch. And despite the hour, the wind bit through Dylan's threadbare cloak. He clenched his teeth and forced himself to press onward.

Atop a distant rise in the road, a handful of travelers congregated around the old Greek ruins protruding from a hilltop like the ribs of the Colossus. They were pilgrims, a mixture of exotic colors and bland habits, a true cross section of humanity. Rich and poor shuffled toward the broken columns, heads bowed as much against the wind as in deference to the holy site where Daniel the Stylite dwelt. Dylan held the cup to his chest and shuffled on until he fell in with the supplicants.

Day bled into evening and shadows reached once more from the broken columns across the road. In those growing hours, Dylan reached the singular column whereon sat the hunched figure. Most of the crowds had scattered to take shelter in nearby inns. Still, he waited as, one by one, those before him ascended the rickety ladder to the top of the column, asked Daniel their questions, and stretched on tiptoes to hear his reply. Occasionally the sainted Stylite stretched forth his hand to touch an upturned brow before the supplicant descended back into the deepening dark.

Then the line of supplicants moved up by one, and the process repeated.

The cold had numbed Dylan's limbs by the time he finally stood alone at the foot of the old column. Without the sun's illumination, the ladder appeared to vanish above his head into the sky. He grabbed the rung, then froze. While atop the column the dead would come after him—of this he was certain. He would be trapped with no escape. His fingers slipped from the frozen wood.

Then a voice whispered, almost heaven-soft. Dylan craned his neck to see a shadow silhouetted against the stars. His heart leapt. Again the voice spoke, only this time loud enough for the cleric to hear.

"Climb the stair."

Dylan laid his fingers on the ladder rung. Cold wood bit at his skin. But with his jaw set, the young cleric grabbed the rung and lifted himself into the starry sky. With each ascending step the world below fell away into darkness and cold. After a few steps, Dylan pressed his body to the ladder with a sudden wave of fear and nausea. His foot slipped, pain shooting up his leg from the impact with a rung.

He gasped for breath.

Run, said an inner voice. But his breath halted in his lungs, his body like stone. Demonithus would surely make good his promise to bleed him right here at the foot of the mystic's broken column. Dylan pressed his forehead against the ancient ladder, suddenly too exhausted to climb and too terrified to descend.

There it was—he was consigned to his fate. He had run the length of the civilized world, and in the shadow of hope that quest would end.

Then the whisper spoke much closer to his ear. "Move!"

Tears stung his eyes and Dylan blinked them away. "I cannot," he sobbed. "I am afraid."

"Move!" was the only reply.

Through his burning, wet eyes, the broken top of the column still appeared so far away. But he move he did, stiff fingers and protesting arms grasping higher toward the firmament. Finally, he reached out his hand to the jagged stone lip. Cold fingers snapped around his wrist. And suddenly, with that frigid touch, the young cleric's body thawed.

Legs and arms burning with renewed strength drove him past the ladder's peak to the broken top of the column. Dylan placed his other hand over the monk's, surprised to feel only bones and skin beneath his touch.

"They are coming for me," Dylan panted.

The Stylite rolled onto his back, raising his arms like willow shoots to the sky. Wild hair obscured his face.

"Oh, my Lord God . . . He has brought you to this place. At long last."

Dylan knelt beside the old man, lifting his head from the cold hard stone.

"What do you mean?" the young man asked. "I need your help. Please!"

The Stylite touched Dylan's face—his fingers bony beneath the parchment of his skin.

"No, my son—listen," the monk sputtered. "*You* are needed. Not I."

Across the broken landscape, the shadows crept closer to the single broken column.

"I cannot stop them," he admitted to the Stylite. "They will take the cup. Don't you understand? I came to you for help!"

Daniel struggled to sit up. His breath sounded in his chest like the rattling of knucklebones.

"I have come so far!" Dylan pleaded.

"Yet the path soon ends," the Stylite assured him. "There is always an end."

The ladder creaked and jumped against the stone column.

"You must stand," Dylan urged. "I can't do this alone."

Daniel's hand dropped from Dylan's face.

"Time has arrived . . . you have been worth the wait."

A head rose above the column's edge, hair dark and glistening in the moonlight.

"What, no warrior of God charging from the sky to save you?" Demonithus snarled, exposing long vicious teeth. "Fortunately, I feel generous. Now give me the cup, and you may yet survive."

The Stylite's eyelids fluttered.

Dylan unfastened his cloak, rolling it into a ball to pillow the ascetic's head. He stood to face the fell creature that dared to stand on holy ground without sanction.

"The cup!" Demonithus commanded, extending a clawed hand. "Just give me the cup and all this can be over!"

Dylan reached inside his tunic, withdrawing the cup he had borne since that long-ago day when he and Cedric had violated the crypt beneath Canterbury's altar. The cup weighed more than the metal of its making in his hand.

"Come now," the creature cooed in the fluid Greek of ancient poets. "We will care for it. Keep it in this sacred city—home of mystics, stoics, and ancient learning. Why, pilgrims will travel from the far reaches of the world to study the cup and learn more of its powers."

"No." Dylan trembled now, rattling the cup against the stone.

Demonithus advanced another step up the ladder, words slithering from his lips. "You cannot deny me. Look, look around you."

And Dylan did.

From the darkness, through the broken bones of the ruins, flowed a stream of creatures. Each moved with purpose toward the broken column. And in that moment, he could hear the whispers of the damned threatening to drink his still-warm blood. They congregated at the bottom of the column and the stone stirred. The undead pressed their shoulders to the ancient Greek column, heaving against it like the waves of a dark malevolent sea.

"I should not have to say it," Demonithus intoned, "but your journey is over. Give us the cup."

Dylan stood, shaking with the desire to flee yet having nowhere to go. He stood over the Stylite, gripping the cup tightly before him.

"This is holy ground," Dylan said, his Greek halting. "This is not—"

"Oh, but it is. Even your holy man hasn't the strength to repel my legions."

"*Deaus Carus—*" Dylan began in Latin. "Father, Son, and Holy Spirit! Protect this place with Thy power!"

The undead creature laughed. "You, the coward with the cup, believe you can command the power of God?" Demonithus cackled, stepping from the ladder to the rough stone. "The power fades from this place, and I will have what I've come for."

Fingers clamped around Dylan's ankle. Energy burst up his skin to the crown of his head, an ethereal heat that burned back down his arms to the ends of his fingers.

Demonithus grinned, his teeth yellow and long. "Too late," he hissed, then lunged.

Dylan threw out his hands and, with a jarring impact, met undead flesh. He toppled backwards, the monstrosity landing atop him. But Dylan did not release his grip, even with Demonithus' weight crushing him against the stone. Beneath Dylan's touch the beast's flesh sizzled, filling the air with the smell of rancid meat under a summer sun.

The undead creature shrieked.

"By the power of God, be gone!" Dylan cried, his hands tightening on Demonithus' shoulders. *"Be gone from this holy place!"*

23

Fire erupted from the cleric's fingers, sweeping over Demonithus' back. Dylan twisted away to shield the aged monk against the blistering heat. Holy fire consumed the beast. Demonithus grasped at Dylan's robes, the creature's limbs wrenching in unnatural ways. Its head snapped back. Demonithus' shrieking threats were consumed in a howl of rushing wind sweeping down from the sky. The fiery torrent of living flame burned the master of New Roma's Higher Dead until all that remained was ash and bone.

At the base of the column the dark minions scattered before the threat of another divine touch, leaving Dylan alone atop the column, cradling the dying Daniel in his arms.

Chapter One

⚬⚬⚬

BLOOD ON THE WATER

The towering white cliffs of Albion quickly faded into the night when the *Pagan Dancer* swept into the Litus Saxiconum, the channel between Albion and the continental Gaul. The crew scampered up the rigging of the single-masted *corbita*, hurrying to set the wide canvas while Captain Kulo's rotund bulk stalked the deck to check knots and direct the angle of the single-canvas sail. A mad prophet of the sea, his beard whipped wildly in the wind, spittle flying with each bellowed command.

The mate hustled Erik and Thelwyn below decks. The knight from Birkenshire led the way, staggering down the narrow ladder against the ship's pitch and roll. He grabbed at a beam to steady himself, but the bucking ship was not his only challenge—his head pounded against the voices warring to speak through his mind, the bitter voices accusing him, taunting him, and hurling threats after the fleeing vessel.

Their flight from the hidden warrens of the Council of the Dead had ignited a war among the higher examinates in Londinium. Though

Erik understood little of what had unfolded in Flavia's enclave, he'd grasped enough to foresee a conflagration that would tear at ancient bonds of hunger, fealty, and a twisted version of undead family. Bonds built through centuries of *Pax Romana* that had kept Britannia free of barbarian incursions while the rest of the Roman carcass was consumed by the Germanic lions.

Bonds that had kept mortals slumbering peacefully so the wolves could hunt undisturbed among the fold.

Erik sank to his knees, his head falling into his hands. Those blood-soaked immortals had stripped him of his own family, hauling him trussed up in chains from the chaos that had engulfed Caer Baen. Upon closing his eyes, those very memories engulfed his mind. The dead had opened Hell itself around the small hamlet, which hadn't seen such carnage in hundreds of years. His father and sister, his friends, all snuffed out like candles—some needless excess to a mad god's plan.

Thelwyn rustled in the darkness, pulling together a wad of blankets for bedding. The old man's aura glowed amid the near absolute blackness in the hold—a blackness sealed by the pitch lining the interior and the mold that thrived where the crew could not clean. But the mage emanated enough energy to illuminate each motion of his body. Though of a different type of vision, he could follow the movements of the restless fox—his own familiar—that clung to the inside of the old man's robes.

Across the crowded hold, creatures skittered among the crates and bales of cargo. The knight pushed himself to his feet. *Rats. Fleas. Certainly, the ship carries them from port to port.* He felt a prickle on his leg.

"Sit." Thelwyn extended his hand, flames sputtering from his fingertips. "There's not much night remaining."

Erik grabbed the nearby ladder, his knuckles barely whitening despite his desperate grip. He found himself constantly mindful of the new perimeters of his existence, bound together by the setting and rising sun.

"Air," he murmured. "I will return once I get some air."

With his words but barely spoken, he understood the irony of his own comment—for he needed no breath. Regardless, the knight climbed the ladder once more onto the pitching deck, avoiding as best he could the crew securing the last of the cargo. Above his head, the sail swelled against the wind, causing the mast to creak and the lines to groan. He secured a place at the rail. There he willed himself to see the still-far-off outline of Germanic Gaul. But beyond the ship's bow lay only gray water and more darkness.

A sailor, high above on the masthead, called warnings to the tiller-man while the portly captain marked the scattered stars above, barking adjustments to their southeasterly course.

Erik leaned hard against the rail, his cloak pulled up about his features. Horrific memories rioted in his mind. He sucked in the salt air, but the tangy stuff did little to clear his head or invigorate his body.

And his heart beat too slowly.

One . . .

Two . . .

Three . . .

Someone cleared their throat and Erik turned.

"So, you're the body we contracted to steal away in the night?" Kulo said with a chuckle, leaning his bulk over the rail. "If it were not for the coin—some very old Roman coin carrying more gold than what they put in 'em these days—I never take the *Dancer* out at this time of night."

27

"Impeccable timing," Erik replied with a nod.

"Well, yes—of course," the captain said, wheezing from deep within his barrel chest, his thick fingers tugging through tangled beard. "That fight on the docks. Put a fear of God into my crew. Not good, lad, not at all. Do you happen to be the queen's condemned lover?"

"The queen's? No," Erik replied. "Just a traveler to points east, I fear."

No sooner had he spoken than a smudge of light warmed the distant eastern sky.

"Another moment, and whoever hunted you on the pier would have caught you—and my ship," Kulo observed, his dark-shrouded eyes remaining fixed on the knight. "And I brook no threat to my *Dancer*. So this better be the last of them. I have enough to worry over between here and Ostia."

In all fairness, Erik was certain this band of cutthroats contended with pirates and marauders during their voyages. The rough-and-tumble sailors scrambled across the deck and up the mast. However, the knight reckoned that, if it came to a scrape, the captain would praise whatever saint watched over this wallowing tub for the extra sword.

"I pray this remains a quiet voyage," Erik offered.

The captain thumped his shoulder with a meaty paw and laughed. "Do that, lad, and you will have my gratitude for it!" He called out to a nearby sailor to re-secure a sliding bale of furs. Then he strode the deck to inspect his domain. Sunlight splashed over the rail. Erik pulled his cowl further over his features. A chill crawled up his spine with each spear of early dawn.

No sense tempting the boundaries of the curse, he mused, staggering across the deck to the ladder below.

The guts of the vessel creaked and groaned with each toss of the sea. But when he stepped from the ladder, he once more felt the desire to climb to the upper deck. Caught between sunlight and water, the curse ensured he would constantly war with himself. Clenching his teeth, he found a perch near the mage's still form and settled there, pulling his cloak tightly around him.

The hours will pass slowly, he thought. *Much too slowly.*

Like his heartbeat.

Four . . .

Five . . .

Six . . .

Muted sunlight filtered into the hold, lending the clutter a grayish cast. Thelwyn stirred and stretched. Curled nearby into a tattered cloak like a cocoon, Erik sat still against the crates that creaked with each movement of the ship. The knight's face was hidden within the shadows of the hood.

Thelwyn scratched at his robes. The fox moved within.

"So, you awaken," the mage observed when he stood and tested his legs. "Well, we have put a stretch of sea behind us. Should be able to proceed without as many prying eyes."

Silence was the only reply, punctuated by the noise of the crew on deck.

Thelwyn shrugged and took in his surroundings. The ship's hold was stuffed with heavy crates of tin and copper plates, barrels of northern liquor, bales of skins, and stacks of planked old-growth wood to supply southern craftsmen. The *Pagan Dancer* represented quite a haul of goods for ports along the coasts of Gaul and Italy.

"Still a few hours to night." He paused near the ladder, holding his hand up and rolling his fingers in the gray light. "We should be able to see the coast of Gaul this evening—if the sky permits."

Still, Erik replied with silence.

Thelwyn took his perch once more against the crate.

"My boy," he began, "this world is part of a fabric that most mortals will only observe from their own narrow, fraying thread. Humans exist oblivious to the works of the whole tapestry. And that tapestry? Well, it extends into the past and the future at once, each thread the telling of the mortal and the immortal—each interwoven with others and locked into the weave of the whole. Remove a thread, cut it short or let it dangle loosely and the whole is altered. Kings and peasants, warriors and priests, nobles and thieves—none of us are free from the flow of the tapestry. There are consequences for every action."

The knight remained gravely silent, and, feeling awkward, Thelwyn rubbed at his nose. He drew a deep breath and continued, convinced the young knight was listening.

"My people are seafarers. Much the same as your mother's northern folk. An ancient nation who braved the deep to Albion. The trade winds have taken them along the folds of the tapestry in all directions, their threads woven into the lives of mortals and immortals alike. Humankind has many names for my kin. The People of Danu, or the Tuatha dé Danann in the old tongue. Some call them Dark Ones, though they are not evil. Rather they keep to their own purposes. Your people still recall tales of elves who seek truth and knowledge among the forests and glens of a distant land. Those stories recount how my people abandoned Albion long ago after the advent of iron weapons, leaving men to fend for themselves."

He fished in the pouches about his belt to produce a pale, wrinkled lump of something, from which he broke off a piece. Then he pressed the morsel to the fox's muzzle before nibbling the remainder himself.

"You may not know this, but long before Roman banners flew over Albion," Thelwyn said, "human kings frequently traveled the seas between your land and mine. Alas, most ventured the dangers to ask favors, with little more desire than to defeat a rival or steal the heart of a forbidden love. Magic abounded in my people, and we granted boons too freely."

He turned the food over in his hand for a moment. When he continued, his voice became lost in a distant memory.

"When I was young, a bare lad, my master become involved with a king—a man who ruled through his passions and lusts, much the same as Uther Pendragon generations later. This king had stolen my master's daughter. He held her surrounded by his warband, and those armed with iron weapons. This *king* offered to return her in exchange for another weapon powerful enough to seat himself securely on the thrones of his rivals. You see, the desire to unite all of Albion under a single ruler extends through ages, stronger than religious ideology or even carnal passion."

Erik stirred at last, though his visage remained lost in his hood. "What does this have to do with me?" he growled.

"Well, that really is where the story begins, isn't it?" Thelwyn replied. "The Gray Lord has struggled in much the same way to exert his influence over the land of the living. Often that struggle was mirrored in Albion's fortunes and those of her inhabitants. A divided kingdom is easier to control, and easier for a god of waning influence

31

to draw in followers from the discontented and the dying. Once the People of Danu barred his way, but alas, they were driven back to the west. Then Rome's legions offered brutal, efficient order. As that rule spread, the Gray Lord's influence dimmed. The isle's inhabitants fled the sacred groves to worship the deities of the empire."

Erik stretched beneath his tatters. Even the faintest motion indicated, faintly, that he engaged with Thelwyn's words.

"The Gray Lord remains one of the most powerful of the Old Gods," Thelwyn said after a moment. "He is a master of the afterlife, and every aspect of this realm affects him. He is a jealous god to be sure, almost as much as your eastern deity. He fought tooth and nail against incursions from other gods and their adherents into Gaul. Yet his greatest struggles fell in Albion. But the tide of the Caesars eventually overwhelmed even divine resistance. This was before the coming of Magnus Maximus, the Spanish general crowned *imperator* by his troops in Londinium. Now, *this man* was an ireful beast, given to violent fits of madness."

"We all know of the Magnus," Erik replied sullenly. Flavia's declaration of his lineage had left a bitter gall in his stomach, for it connected his family to the wicked state of affairs in Londinium.

"A kingdom united had always thwarted the Gray Lord," Thelwyn said. "Arthur fought a combined army of Higher Dead, wily dark elves, and renegade humans to secure his throne. But only in stealing Arawn's great cauldron could the High King finally overcome them. To wrench Albion from the Gray Lord's grasp, Arthur then deployed the graal of the eastern god to rally his people. Once these threats were resolved, the Lady of the Lake bestowed upon him the mystic Excalibur, the Sword of Light. With it, he drove the Saxons to the sea and restored Roman order to troubled Gaul.

"The Magnus, though, was a far different character," Thelwyn recalled. "Brooding. Savage. A man quick to the wineskin and hungry for power. I had occasion to deal with him when he resided in Albion." He paused once more, knitting his woolly eyebrows while sifting memories. "But one cannot exist without the other—*salvation* and *ruin*, that is. Thus forged in the same fires as Excalibur was her dark sister.

"My master did not fully understand the wild forces unleashed by that anvil. Unknown to him, his work of necessity crafted a fell blade of black steel tempered in a godling's blood. The completed weapon was then dressed in sacred woods and precious metals. My master thought he could hide the dark sword from prying eyes. But power-mad men found him out and stole it away to Albion, where it caused havoc for centuries. The Magnus learned of the sword while a lowly centurion in Spain. As he rose through the ranks, he sought it in every dark crevice of the empire."

"And this sword?" Erik pressed. "The very one Flavia spoke of— seems oddly opportune that we should be after the same artifact."

"All roads lead to Rome, as they say. I suppose there are only so many ways to kill a god," Thelwyn said, still stroking the fox's fur—his eyes engaged beyond the shadows to cull his thoughts. "The Magnus' journey was terribly harrowing. I shan't belabor the details. Suffice it to say, he found the sword guarded by ghoulish undead that could not wield it. Upon dispatching those unfortunates, Magnus found *he* could wield the weapon with vicious effect. But, as a mortal man, he never fully penetrated the darkness *within* it. If he had accessed the sword's full powers, then Constantine's legions could never have stopped him. The Gray Lord prospered in Albion under Magnus because the Spaniard left bloody chaos in his wake. In his lust for power, Magnus nearly destroyed the Roman order on the isle, and the minions of the dead erupt now because of it."

"Did it have a name, this dark sword?" Erik ventured.

"Demonbane," Thelwyn said in a hushed voice. "Steel forged as black as the deepest cavern. And yet in battle, soldiers who survived the wars claimed the sword sang when Magnus wielded it."

Above them, men scampered about the deck, the ship's rolling creak settling into a more regular rhythm.

"It has taken me centuries to piece this all together," Thelwyn ventured. "As a mere lad, I had no dream of the implications of this work."

"Tell me more of this sword and your master."

"First, I need to prepare some brew for your appetite."

Thelwyn hopped from his perch to rummage in his pack. The rarer ingredients in his concoction could only be had in his former homeland, and there would be no returning there. He prayed for Danu's grace that his meager supplies would last the entire journey—and that his own strength would not fail him. He began crushing the ingredients and steeling himself for the drain on his essence soon to follow.

That night, the ship anchored near the coast of Gaul—a land steeped in ancient heritage, now infused with fresh beginnings by the Germanic people who ruled in place of the Caesars. The native-but-Romanized Gauls still lived, worked, and died much as they had when the Eagle's legions stood watch at the Rhenus River. Only now, long-haired Franks held sway over most of the land.

The *Dancer's* crew kept a wary eye on the brooding wood along the shore. The Breton raiders who held this stretch of coastline would just as happily snatch up a merchantman as they would cut the purse from a Frank clergyman along the highway before stealing the poor friar off to the slave markets.

From his perch in the ship's prow, Erik could sense activity among those trees. This supernatural sense unsettled him. He stood motionless, forcing himself to understand the world into which he'd been cast by this curse of heart and soul. He closed his eyes. And in that state, he could feel the press of *her* lips to his—something he'd dreamed of for so long, only for the dream to be dashed upon cold razor teeth.

His eyes snapped open.

One of the sailors stood nearby, scanning the shore—a scruffy cutthroat with a short stiff blade thrust into his belt. Even with Thelwyn's potion, Erik could almost hear the blood running through his arteries—a call to his deep hunger.

The crew would fight over his possessions and toast his passing, said a voice.

The knight pushed the stray thought back and swallowed the hunger until the man finally trudged along, dodging around the crew sleeping on the deck until he finally made his way aft. Erik remained alone at the rail.

Or not. Someone, or something, crept along the deck with a padding scrape. Without casting about with his eyes, he knew it for what it was—the fox had at last ventured from the secure folds of Thelwyn's robes. Eyes flashed sharp in the starlight. It sniffed at the air, hackles bristling. A snarl curled back its lips, exposing sharp teeth. The knight leaned against the rail and rubbed at his forehead, his gaze resting on the defiant beast.

"What would you have of me?" he muttered.

Not since his Anglan companion and mentor, Merrovaine, had perished under the slavering teeth of the hellhounds had he wanted to entangle another being in his cursed life. He'd sacrificed his beloved steed to ensure that no harm would come to another. Caer Baen still smoldered in his memories, a reminder of those who dared be entangled in opposition to Annwyn's will.

The fox's sharp dark eyes bored into him.

"We should reach some sort of accommodation," Erik said finally, his voice low. "It would be a long swim back—and neither of us wishes to take *that* plunge."

He knelt, holding out his hand, palm forward. The fox bared its teeth again.

"You know, she who made me was accompanied by a great black beast. A dire wolf of the most vicious sort. And me—a very knight of the realm? I have you." He flexed his fingers before continuing, "Well, it appears we both face the unexpected. Neither of us asked for this union. No easy path for you and me. But we may as well walk it together."

The fox nosed forward, but its feet remained in place. Dark eyes flashed, its hackles rising even higher. The knight reached into his pouch, where he found a petrified crust of bread left from his days of mortality. He pinched it between his fingers, then held out the morsel.

The creature took a hesitant step, tentatively placing a paw closer as it sniffed at the knight's extended fingers. It snapped the crumb, then darted back into the deeper shadows.

"Good enough," Erik muttered. "Do not worry. I will not scratch your ears or anything."

Days in the ship's damp hold merged into nights above deck while the ship visited one inlet after another along the Gallic coast. During those nights, Erik remained aboard, pacing the length of the ship, never taking to the ship's boat bobbing across the waves to the land for provisions. On occasion, Thelwyn pulled an oar with the shore parties to gather some herb or root for his concoctions. But as far as the crew were concerned, Erik remained a shadowy eccentric passenger seeking the care of an expert physician in Rome, and they willingly followed Kulo's dictum that he was not to be disturbed.

Eventually, Gaul's verdant coastline gave way to distant purple mountains and a more open landscape as the ship plied further south. This was Iberia, once the home of Magnus himself, now the kingdom of Visigoths who jealously guarded these northern reaches of the Pyrenees to discourage the Franks from expanding to the south. Likewise, armored horsemen patrolled the dun-colored beaches to discourage the pirates and reavers that frequented the southern waters from making their own incursions.

Then late one night, Captain Kulo skirted a soaring rocky height that rose above both the surrounding landscape and the surface of the sea, the imposing *Gates of Heracles*. The wide-hulled ship ran silent in the warm breeze that whisked them into waters where the Romans had once smugly declared *mare nostrum*—or simply *our sea*. From that hour, Kulo's stolid silhouette moved about the aft deck, where he vigilantly scanned the southern arid coast that was once the old Roman *Dioecesis Africae*. In this region, any settlement could harbor the low-slung Vandal galleys that had plagued shipping now that Roman fleets were bottled up in the eastern reaches near their capital at Constantinople.

Progress remained slow, for *Pagan Dancer* had been built for the rough seas far to the north, where only a stout wide-beamed vessel could withstand the bluster that oft tossed her between Cymru and the trading villages of the Saxons and Danes. In these seas, however, the waters tamed easily before the ship's broad-breasted bow, and the listless wind caused the sail to flutter and tug halfheartedly.

Below the gently rolling deck, Erik paced back and forth, hidden away from the sun beating mercilessly against the wooden boards above his head. Heat radiated from those planks, softening the pitch used to chink the ship's hull. Thelwyn had escaped the rising temperature long ago, shedding even his cloak and woolen garments to bustle about in his linens like a shameless toddler. Erik jealously regarded the pile of clothing by their packs.

Nothing to worry about there, Erik supposed, for even the rats sought refuge further below the lower deck, nearer the *Dancer's* waterline. But the water, the rats, and even thoughts of the Grey God became a more distant concern, for the deck above remained the only shield between the cursed knight and the sun.

A footfall creaked at the nearby stairs and Kulo came to rest on the steps, his eyes narrowed. He mopped at his brow with a stained rag, then wrinkled his nose from the moldy stink in the hold.

"So, you'll not take any relief on the deck then?" he asked.

Erik shook his head. "No. Not until we put into port at Ostia."

The captain's eyes narrowed. "Well, we wouldn't want you peeling like some fish on the beach now. For what they paid for your berth— well, you have the right to keep bolted up down here. But for the life of me, I have never understood you nobles and your maladies."

"My mother's side of the family, God rest her soul." Erik touched the corners of the cross on his breast with his right hand.

A sailor called out. Kulo craned his neck back up the ladder to the deck.

"What?" he bellowed. "By Saint Brendan's bones, what is it?"

Without pausing to excuse himself, he bolted up the ladder. Once he was on the main deck, the boards creaked under his great strides. In his wake the crew scrambled in a flurry of feet, a marked change from their more lackadaisical rhythm. Another, lighter creak of the ladder announced Thelwyn returning below deck.

"Something afoot?" Erik asked.

"Sails have appeared to the south," the healer said. "The captain intends to run north to seek shelter closer to Goth lands."

Erik reached up and touched the beam stretching above his head. The ship's bones trembled with the course change. Amid the scrambling, Erik heard the men unsheathe their motley assortment of cutlery.

"Then those sails belong to no fishing boats," Erik concluded.

He strode across the hold to his gear, pulling his spatha from its scabbard. He examined the length of Roman steel, then drew his finger across the finely oiled shoulder. While he knew the *Dancer*'s crew was comprised of capable cutthroats, facing multiple reaver crews would jeopardize not just the ship and her valuable cargo but also the very quest intended to hurl Arawn back into his pit.

"You cannot go up there," Thelwyn protested, scrambling down the ladder and hurrying behind him. "My potions will not protect you!"

Erik shrugged off his cloak. His mail coat, battered breastplate, and cavalry helmet, with all his knightly accouterments, now appeared to him as scraps of tarnished junk but also as a reminder of the new equipment he had borne on the fateful day he had left Caer Baen with Merrovaine.

Saint Michael, find my lost soul and strengthen my own arm in the battle to come, he thought.

"How long before they catch us?" Erik then asked.

Thelwyn wrinkled bushy eyebrows. "There was talk of only hours. Not enough to elude them when darkness falls."

"Then we must fight," Erik declared. He glanced about the ship's hold. "And you will help me."

Dancer rolled over the water with much less grace than the two low-slung vessels pursuing her, their triangular sails catching the wisps of warm wind luffing at the merchant ship's expansive square canvas. Kulo stood near the rudder, exhorting his crew with threats of death and demons. They responded by jumping about the rigging and scampering along the deck with bundles of weapons and buckets of sand and water. He pulled reflexively at his beard, his keen eyes searching for a weakness in the reaver ships—anything his crew could exploit in the battle to come. But the sinking weight in his chest only grew heavier, for the Vandals bristled with steel and men expecting to digest the *Dancer's* cargo and spit out its bones.

The Vandal ships drew apart in a flanking maneuver, all while steadily bearing down on the merchant.

A commotion broke out amidships. A dark figure emerged from the hold. His form, from boots to helm, was covered in tar-smeared steel and twisted leather.

"God of Heaven and Earth," Kulo prayed. A smattering of vapor seemed to waver from the knight's body and diffuse in the air, smelling of burnt flesh.

Kulo ambled across the deck to his passenger. A cold chill crept up the back of his neck and sweat beaded his brow. He had faced raiders in the Middle Sea before and, the gods willing, he would survive to face them again. But this was not the time for such defiant foolishness.

Keep the casualties to a minimum had always been the ship master's credo.

Passengers were the greatest prize, fodder for ransom or slave markets across Africa and the Levant. While he always appreciated the extra coin from wealthy patrons who paid well for their berth, the money was not worth dying over.

"I do not want a war!" he called to the knight.

The tar-blackened helmet faced him. Kulo's great bulk stopped in its tracks, for the knight's eyes were veiled by thick swaths of canvas and tar. That seemingly blind gaze unnerved the captain.

"No need for heroics," Kulo insisted. "Leave this to me."

"Trust me," Erik replied. "You will not see heroics this day."

"Get back below," Kulo snarled.

The reply was a scrape of steel against leather. The spatha flashed in the evening sunlight, slicing the smoke issuing from the armor.

The first of the Vandal pirates hove to alongside the *Dancer*. Sunburnt faces crowded the rail, their broken skin surrounded by motley beards and locks of various hues under rust-mottled steel caps. In the bow stood a tall lanky man beneath a mail hauberk. His homespun surcoat bore a crude black raven device that from a distance was little more than a splotch on his chest. Squinting, the pirate scanned the *Dancer*'s deck until he saw Kulo and the adjacent figure overshadowing him.

A grin broke across his face, and he shouted in northern-accented Latin, "Stand down. Prepare to be boarded!"

"You heard the man," Kulo spat. "Put that thing up. There are upwards of thirty armed men on that ship. If we tangle with them— they will strip *Dancer*, then fire her to the waterline!"

"And if you do not, they truss us up and seek a ransom," the knight hissed.

"They want the furs, the amber, and the mead. We can give them that and all get out of this alive."

Erik's fingers adjusted on the spatha hilt. "You are a poor liar."

Kulo held up both hands to the Vandal captain but whispered to Erik, "What would you have me do? We cannot take them both."

"I will take this one. You prepare for the second."

The Vandal raider scraped against *Dancer*'s hull, and grappling hooks bit into the rails. Grinning, the reaver captain tugged a line to ensure it held before his men bent their backs to pull the two vessels close. When they thudded together, a black smudge arced from the *Dancer*'s deck over his head to land with a *bang* amidships, sending his men scrambling to get out of the way.

On that pirate ship, Erik straightened amid the chaotic deck, pulling his oval shield close to his body and hefting the spatha in his other hand. Long and slender, the spatha was a butcher of a weapon from a more gallant age. Sunburnt men stumbled open-mouthed at the shock of his arrival but after a heartbeat recovered to charge the interloper. The spatha flashed. A pirate dropped to the deck, blood spurting from a deep gash across his face.

Erik's senses struggled against the sunlight, now blurring his ability to track the living. Then the fox-familiar scrambled from beneath his cloak, darting through the feet of the crowding Vandals. Suddenly images from the beast's eyes flooded his mind, giving him bearings, ranges, openings. *There*—the spatha darted out, steel exploding through another Vandal's neck. The remaining pirates lunged to press Erik's guard but met lightning ripostes that severed fingers and arms and sent heads tumbling over the bloodying planks.

"So, what in the hell might you be?" the Vandal captain roared, sauntering across the deck as if the damage done to his crew was of only passing interest. "You are no Roman!"

He brandished a battle-axe and closed in a fighting stance. Erik advanced likewise, trailing wisps of smoke, to engage the Vandal's heavier blade. They paced forward, backward, a thrust here, a block there. The fight ebbed and flowed, but Erik fought two foes as each motion threatened to open gaps in his protective cover. Every inch of his body thus exposed screamed in agony from the sun that sought to incinerate him into unholy ash.

Across the chaotic deck, the fox leapt onto a perch upon a keg where he could see the fight without obstruction.

"Have you no words?" the Vandal roared, lifting his weapon. "My wolves! Let us finish this!"

Erik surged forward but the men pressed close, slowing his progress and thrusting with spear, sword, and knife. He shrugged through them toward the rail, his own sword whistling in the air. Roman steel sliced deep through sinew and bone. He felt the tip of a spear tear the flesh beneath his arm. The unfortunate bearer quickly choked, then fell when Erik opened him at the midriff, slicking the deck with his entrails.

In his ears Erik heard cries of *"Demon!"* and *"Hellspawn!"* to which his sword provided the only reply.

Color drained from the Vandal captain's swarthy face. He scrambled through his men for the higher ground of the sterncastle. Near the helm stood a figure in a simple cleric's habit. His tonsure glistened with sweat, and he clutched at the crucifix hanging from his neck on thick silver links.

"Stantes coram Deo, in Christo conforta bellatores tuos!" His voice cracked.

God stand before us, he'd shouted, *strengthen thy warriors in Christ!* The irony of the words was not lost on Erik when he staggered beneath a Vandal axe battering his shield. But the blade bit deeply into the splintering wood and Erik heaved against the pirate, twisting the weapon out of his grip. Another quick thrust and the Vandal stumbled into another, arm squirting crimson and sending both raiders to their backsides. Erik drove the shield's ragged edge into the first man's chest and stepped over him, crushing his boot onto the neck of the second. Then he moved on.

Under the persistent weight of Erik's onslaught, the crew melted away. He howled in the bloodlust that drove him on. He became a fluid shadow that stood against the daylight powers of Sol, meting out death and dismemberment. Tar ran in thick clots.

Screaming for his men to stand their ground, the pirate captain pushed even the priest into the grinding melee. The cleric held his crucifix before him, yammering urgently while around him men stumbled, splashed his garments with dark fluids, then dropped to the deck. The priest was left to face the specter alone. Erik stumbled when the holy symbol exploded in a blinding flash. Seeing that his devotion had slowed the monster's impetus, the priest straightened, and a wolfish grin spread over his bearded face.

"Ite, et revertimini in lacum, in infernum pariat!" His spittle flew with the words—*Go back to the pit, hellspawn!*

The priest sought support from his captain, but the seawolf cowered among the dead. The crucifix wavered but a moment.

"I *am* a Christian!" Erik growled, slamming the priest with his splintered shield. The man flew flailing into the sea.

With his back to the transom, the pirate captain stood and roared with renewed vigor, raising his axe over his head. Erik easily parried the following downstroke and his father's blade rang along the axe's haft. Severed fingers arced away. The axe clattered to the deck. The captain retreated beneath the knight's assault, urging on the few remaining reavers to stand firm.

A length of steel bit Erik's leg and searing pain shot through the limb. He stumbled, the spatha slipping from his grasp.

Through the familiar's vision, a gap-toothed Vandal crouched beneath him, dagger frozen in the tear he had punctured in the knight's trousers. It was through that tear that the sun's deadly kiss now burned. Erik yanked his foot away, then smashed the heel into the man's face. He kicked once more, bones crunched, and the Vandal howled, slumping to the greasy deck.

An older, much more massive man now struck. Without his spatha to block the attack, the mate's single-edged seax plunged into Erik's throat. Pain seared his chest and gore flooded his mouth, the sun seeking every breach in his defenses. Vapor steamed from his wounds, carrying the acrid smell of burnt flesh.

"Foul beast!" the older man spat, snatching at Erik's helm to pull the covering away. "Let God see your face!"

Erik's mailed hand shot up and clenched the man's throat, fingers tearing through flesh, crushing bones. The Vandal released his weapon, clawing vainly at Erik's fingers. Ignoring the fires burning his flesh, the knight growled defiantly and squeezed until blood bubbled between the man's lips.

Images from the familiar fluttered through Erik's senses. He shunted them aside and jerked the seax's long blade free, then used it to rend strips of cloth from the mate's tunic, stuffing them into the gaps in his coverings. He smeared clots of tar about the patchwork for additional protection before grabbing at the ship's rail to pull himself to his feet. The surviving crew crowded near the bow as far as possible from the dreadful vision in smoldering armor.

The familiar burst out from under a shattered shield and alighted on the rail near the knight.

Chaos erupted about the *Pagan Dancer*—the second raider ship had grated alongside. Germanic warriors leaped over the rails to press the crew with violent fervor. Then, to Erik's surprise, the heat shimmers rising from the gory deck faded and a gust of welcome, cool air blew across the water. Coalescing amid the azure sky, a massive cloud boiled upward, crackling with energy. A brilliant bolt struck the pirate ship's mast, the wood exploding in a deadly shower of massive splinters that felled men in a wide, screaming arc.

His body burning from wounds of steel and sun, Erik gritted his teeth, scooped up the familiar, and leapt across the water toward the *Dancer's* deck. He plunged downward, trailing vapors and flailing an arm. With a horrific *boom*, the knight hit the side of the ship, then scraped downward toward the water. He clawed at the clapboard hull, desperately seeking purchase. The familiar scrambled onto his shoulder and leapt upward toward the deck. The sea hungrily churned up blue waves for Erik, his boots scrambling against the side of the ship. One hand hooked over the rail and he dragged himself upward, his boots sloshing with sea water.

By the time he crawled onto the deck, the raiders' attack had stalled. *Dancer's* crew fought with renewed vigor, emboldened by the shattering bolts from above, now roasting Vandals in their own melted armor. The Briton knight plunged into the raiders' rearguard to begin the final reaping. Ignoring the cries of the fallen, the Vandals dropped their weapons, scrambling and tripping back to their ship. Those with presence of mind hacked at the lashing-ropes, but the dark-swathed juggernaut followed them over the gunwales, trailing caustic vapor. The sword swung relentlessly while night spread across the waters, putting a quick and brutal end to their efforts.

The familiar leapt for the stump of the mast, the animal's sight flooding Erik's senses once more. But the images were confusing. Erik failed to mark a spear-toting ruffian who exploded through his mates, a wordless cry on his lips and spittle flinging into the air. With muscles rippling across his arms, the Vandal drove the spear into Erik's side, rending armor with a shriek of metal to bear the knight to the deck. Foul ichor oozed from the wound. Erik desperately clamped his gloved hand around the spear, not so much to stop the gore as to seal out the remaining threads of light threatening to incinerate his flesh. With a wild snarl, the familiar darted past and leapt at the Vandal spearman.

"No!" Erik shouted.

The German kicked at the woodland beast like a ship's rat. Erik wrenched the spear from the Vandal's hands, then swung his sword in low. The edge bit the warrior's boot, sending the pirate stumbling.

Anxiously sifting through the jumble of images in his mind, Erik triangulated the familiar's sight with his own undead senses, drew back the spatha, and struck again. Roman steel caught the warrior under his chin and exploded through the man's skull, ripping his helmet from matted locks of hair.

Erik wrenched the blade free and staggered to his feet. He snapped off the spear haft still protruding from his side, ignored the remainder extending from his back, and turned to the last few raiders in the ship's prow.

The knight from Albion stepped over the wounded and the dead— it was now only a matter of time.

***

Not long afterwards, Erik stood on the low foredeck of the foundering ship with a heap of bodies at his feet. With the setting sun, the butcher's bill would soon be obscured in darkness. *Dancer* drifted nearby, grappling hooks trailing cables in the water, its surviving crew crowding the rail. Bloodied linen bandages were wadded around Kulo's face. He leaned his great bulk on a sailor's arm for support. Fear hung thick in the air, for all had seen the destruction Erik had wrought upon the Vandals.

Setting his sight on a clear patch of deck near the ship's bow, the knight leapt with measured effort across the short span back to the ship. When Erik's feet thumped the oak planks, the ship's mate raised an axe, then, with a quick stroke, severed the last grappling line to cast the reaver ship adrift. A gruff word followed from Kulo. The sailors peeled themselves from the rail. Some bent their backs to toss the dead overboard while others scrambled to work the rigging. The single sheet thumped against the mast, gathering scant wind.

Kulo's tentative smile smoothed away the horror that had moments ago lived on his face.

"I thought you just an old cavalryman. Capable of fighting in a pinch, though in your condition..." His voice trailed off. Erik's performance revealed the lie that was the knight's story of maladies and infirmities. "Understand, I did not want to risk losing my ship or my men. A good crew. Why, they're worth their weight in— well, copper at the very least."

Grinding his teeth at the agony racking his body, Erik rushed the captain. He clamped his fingers around the man's fleshy throat, crunching chain mail. There was a scrape of steel and a collective gasp. Erik had to credit them with being willing to fight after what they had just witnessed. Thelwyn pushed through the clot of men, his face an appeal for calm. But the hunger coursed through Erik's body, tempting him to rip off the tarred helm that had shadowed his vision and to feast on the men around him.

"And the coin you'd have saved on our account?" Erik's voice rasped, barely audible.

"I have never transported passengers such as you. I swear. Usually, your kind stay below in boxes—never wandering the deck." The captain's voice strained with each syllable. "You paid in good coin, so I stand with you. Please—please, I beg you."

Erik released his grip.

The captain raised both hands.

"Thanks be to you," he wheezed, rubbing his throat before he hacked spittle onto the deck. He turned a foreboding eye on his men. "What the hell are you waiting for? Get us underway. Quickly now!"

Without protest, the crew tipped yet more bodies over the rail and set to work for the remaining voyage to Ostia, the coastal port of Rome.

Erik ignored their stares. He focused on the western horizon and counted the time that crawled past much too slowly.

Like his heartbeat.

Seven . . .

Eight . . .

Nine . . .

Chapter Two

AT WIT'S END

Londinium, the grandest of Albion's cities, boasted many nocturnal creatures that hunted in the city's alleys and crevices.

Since the collapse of Roman imperium in the west and the abandonment of the outlying provinces, the city had grown in status as the economic gateway to the northern lands. With that increased stature, the dregs of humanity had soon followed to feast on the people's waxing and waning fortunes. Other shadowy denizens had in turn followed them, feeding much more literally, if with equal voracity, on their lifeblood. These horrors, outcasts of God's original creation, maintained familial organizations through untold centuries, and each of their noble houses were represented in a ruling body known simply as the *Council of the Dead*.

Once of Aquitaine—and mortal wife to the usurper Magnus Maximus—Flavia remained their ever-ambitious matron. Yet on this night, the Mistress of the Coven was much agitated following the chaos on the docks along the Thames. And her discontent did not bode well for Ganelon, patriarch of an undead clan in his own right and the current Presiding Speaker of the Council.

Flavia stood in her personal audience chamber, taking in the shrouded Roman battlements on the city's edge. Beyond the confines of her own long-dead flesh, she read the pulse and flow of human life throughout this city. With a pale hand traced by fine veins no longer carrying her own blood, she stroked the sculpted musculature of the statue of *Mithras Slitting the Bull's Throat* that dominated the lower part of the room. She listened with inhuman acuity when Ganelon's calfskin boots beat a determined rhythm down the corridor beyond her door.

That rhythm stopped at the portal, and the iron-bound ebony wood shook with his characteristic firm rap.

Flavia knew, of course, why he was here. Such was the reason for her disquiet, made all the worse by the fact that it was mostly her own fault.

"Enter," she croaked, fixing her gaze on the city below.

Ganelon creaked open the door. A tall, sleek, hawk-nosed man stepped in. This higher dead creature had lived as a Roman patrician in mortality, though centuries before Flavia's mortal span.

"Coven Mistress," he responded with a flourish of his hand.

"It seems that you are here with a purpose, Ganelon," she said.

"Oh? Am I so transparent?"

His voice held a hard edge on this night, not at all his usual political detachment. Recent events had apparently burrowed beneath his skin, and that worried her. She fought the urge to meet his eyes with her own.

"I know why you are here, Ganelon," she cooed. "Let me get right to it. What purpose would be served keeping the knight here? Better to have him seeking a solution."

"You helped him escape before seeking sanction from the Council. And nearly killed Kraken in the process."

"Kraken is nothing but a perpetually starving animal—mindlessly dangerous," she retorted.

"He is one of ours, Mistress. And a sitting member of the Council." His voice remained diplomatic, though his patience with her visibly waned. "His words must be heard."

"He inserted himself where he did not belong," she said, eyes flashing dangerously.

Ganelon, however, remained unflappable. Despite her frustration with him, Flavia had to admit his appointment as Council head had been the right decision.

"You divided the Council with your insistence on following this Merlinite prophecy. Destroyed the trust we enjoyed pursuing our desires—yours and mine. Do not forget that I supported you from the beginning in resisting Arawn's encroachments in the mortal work from his perch within the Celts' own underworld. Some now question just how far you will go to stay out of the Grey God's grasp."

"As far as needed," she replied sullenly. "You know that."

"To the point of sacrificing other Council members?"

"If it must be!" she spat. "What is our alternative? To live out our eternal existence under the thumb of a— a— *foreign* god?"

"This was Arawn's land originally, Flavia," Ganelon replied dryly. "You know that."

"Don't play with me. I will not have it from you!"

She swept across the chamber from the statue to her throne that loomed deeper in the shadows. Torches sprang to life as she passed, illumining a lithe body forever in its sensual prime and offering artificial warmth to her cold ivory skin. She climbed the steps and sat with a flourish, crossing long alabaster legs and regarding Ganelon down the length of her perfect nose. Her hands trembled slightly.

"You know yourself that most of this land remained Roman for centuries," she murmured. "Have you not yourself claimed to be present when Caesar crossed the channel to Albion, as well as when he broke the Druids at Anglesey? This Arawn, this Grey God of the Celtic dead, is no more a deity to our kind than *Yeshua* from the east, and weaker still, to be trying to usurp *that* one's power for himself."

"You play a dangerous game. Kraken is not one to be trifled with."

"Kraken is a jealous child," Flavia retorted. "A child blinded by envy ever since I appointed you as Proconsul."

"He commands a powerful brood," Ganelon observed. "Even you had to beg him to retrieve the abomination when we finally realized who and what he was—when we saw the Huntsman also on the boy's trail. Only Kraken possesses that strength."

He crossed the room to position himself squarely in front of her seat. Flavia sullenly met his eyes with her own. Unable to bear the tension between them, she launched herself down the few steps to stand before Ganelon, pressing her body close. She reached up with tenderness to stroke his cheek, breasts pressing against him.

Her eyes, however, betrayed her anger.

"Yet he trembles before the Grey God," she said, "the very same who has not the strength to claim his own. We have no need for one of so little resolve."

Ganelon snatched her hand away. "We must stand together against Arawn. But now I fear he threatens to betray us to the Grey God."

"You know this of a surety?" she asked.

"He has not been seen since the incident."

"Probably still licking his wounds," she said with a coy smile. "Oh, Ganelon—we should not fight so."

She loosed her hand from his grasp and sauntered back to her customary position by the statue, stretching herself along its length in a repose that had been the last pleasant thing seen by many mortal men.

"But we must give the Council something," Ganelon pressed.

"Something of what?" she purred.

Ganelon balled his fists at her obstinacy. "If we are going to resist Arawn, we need the means to do so. We must have a plan!" He barked the words, but his frustration caused his left cheek to twitch. "And this Erik of Birkenshire—you believe him to be of your stock? We do not even know if he can wield the blade. Even if the Council crawls to the cliff's very edge with you and accepts that this weapon possesses the power to defeat our adversary, can it be found?"

She straightened with an elegant, seductive motion of her body, then strolled out to the balcony on the far side of the gallery. The breeze played at her gossamer gown.

"So many questions," Flavia mused. "But yes, it can be found."

"*Will* it be found?" Ganelon challenged.

"One of my blood shall bear the blade," she countered. "Merlin himself foretold it. The youth is the last, ergo—"

"But will it be found *in time*?"

Flavia hesitated for the barest moment too long.

"As I thought." Ganelon pounced like a predatory feline. "The Council worries, Flavia. If Arawn regains control of Albion, we must

55

either join with him and accept whatever scraps he deigns to leave us—or perish."

"The stakes have not changed. I understand the imperative."

Ganelon stepped up behind her, grabbing her arm to twist her around and face him. He took her cold face in his hands.

"Then help me," he pleaded. "Help us. If this mad quest of yours fails . . ."

Flavia pulled away and paced in tight circles, arms folded, fists clenched.

"It won't. Ganelon, you know it is a waste of time debating before the Council," she snorted. "All they do is squabble for their own advantage or their own amusement. Because we do not die, I fear we do not truly understand what it means to run out of time."

"Without the Council's blessing, we will fight our own as well as Arawn," Ganelon warned.

She thought for a moment, her face softly aglow in the moonlight streaming in through the open windows.

"All of this is like herding feral cats. Admit it," she said, furrowing her brow. "No, *we* must solve this. You and I—it falls to us."

Ganelon threw up his hands and retorted, "Well then, Coven Mistress, how do you suggest we begin?"

Flavia sighed dramatically. An unnecessary gesture, but useful to communicate her frustrations.

"Arawn moves in Albion," Ganelon offered. "Mere vision and revelation cannot track his every machination. He may have even found a source of power to replace the Cauldron."

"One either stolen or schemed away from another."

"But he has limited use of it." Ganelon leaned in impatiently. "Have you an idea what this source might be?"

She lidded her eyes coyly.

"Out with it, Flavia!" he screeched. "I thought we had no time for games. Or is this acceptable because it's *you*?"

"Oh, very well," she huffed. "You have always been an impatient sort. It's Yeshua's blood."

Ganelon's eyes widened before he caught himself to regain his undead disdain.

"The eastern god? From the Levant?"

"Do you know of another Yeshua?" she snapped back.

"Well, it is a very common name in that region. But that damnable mage, Merlin, hid it up, did he not?"

"Apparently a pair of reckless novices in Canterbury stumbled into secrets that should have been left alone."

He regarded her with narrowed eyes. "How do you know this?" he asked.

"I have many progeny." Her words were thoughtful. "I watch them all."

"You did not tell me this before," he pressed.

"Because I watch them *all*, Ganelon," she said, a little wearily. "Generation upon generation. Yet some news was just uncovered very recently. I am agreeing with you. Let us leave it there. But you are right in urging for an alternate plan. This has troubled me since Erik and his dark elf companion left us. I promised to tell Erik more of that damned sword, but Kraken's attack—well, there just was no time. Then he was gone."

"So he knows naught of what he seeks," Ganelon said.

"We can now only rely on Merlin's foresight," Flavia admitted. "And hope he learns what he needs while upon the journey."

Ganelon rubbed his brow, looking frustrated. "My dear, such an assumption may well doom us all. Our reserve plan could become the last remaining option."

"Do not be too cross with me," she purred with doe eyes.

From beneath his steepled fingers, Ganelon returned her look. "Your hurt will be nothing compared to the despair loosed upon us all if Arawn is victorious. We need to deal with the Grey God and this usurped power—however little use he gets from it."

"Yet before we think about that, we must uncover his works through the Veil," she said.

She graced Ganelon with her most endearing gaze. "Come, my fickle lover and stolid friend," she urged with both her words and a gesture.

The two higher undead navigated hallways, then descended twisted stairwells leading below the Council chambers. Cut and dressed stonework gave way to living bedrock, carefully carved and polished, until tall double doors appeared from within a deep arch. Ganelon grasped the well-oiled bronze handle and heaved.

The room beyond was large, several dozen paces in each measure, and stacked to the high ceiling with shelf upon shelf of scrolls, codices, and clay tablets, ancient learning sequestered here in the temperate subterranean climate. Across its marbled floor was an inlaid map of Albion, Cymru, and Hibernia, illustrated in multicolored thumbnail-sized tiles in a Roman-style mosaic.

Flavia stepped onto the blue marble that made up the *Oceanus Brittanicus*. She thrust her hands onto her hips to accompany a withering glare she directed at Ganelon.

"You have been scheming this whole time," she said, jabbing a finger at his chest. "You manipulated me into coming down here!"

The barest of a thin-lipped grin grew on Ganelon's face. "Hush, dear Flavia. Would you have walked with me otherwise? You have never shown much interest in the centuries of learning that can be gleaned from other than your own minions."

"That is not totally true," she murmured. "I am lost here among the learning of old. And finding anything takes far too long. Much easier just to ask you."

"Perhaps," he said.

"So you do have something?" Flavia shot back with a pout. She drew her toes over the blue as if playing in the surf. "You know me too well, I fear. That does not import good things to come."

Ganelon shook his head. "We have been through too much together, you and me. There is naught to fear. I would not want to be responsible for your brood anyway."

"What does that mean?" she demanded.

Ganelon shrugged, then stepped away to a nearby alcove where he lifted a large silver ewer from a pedestal. A dark viscous liquid sloshed within.

"However, I will correct you," he said. "I *might* have something to share with you."

He carried the vessel carefully out over the southern coasts of Albion to the Cornish peninsula, then set it down. He knelt beside it, looking northward over the map at the Môr Hafren.

"When Kraken did not return after your encounter . . ." he began, but her expression became stony. He cleared his throat. "Well, I started to think—"

"Always a dangerous proposition for someone as ancient as you," she interjected.

"I began to *suspect* both his motives and his subsequent actions," he blandly began again. "Of course, you and I have been over this map trying to find evidence of Arawn's movements, but he has so far been able to hide his hand. Now, though, I feel that hand being forced. His dealings with the Huntsman, for instance. What if Kraken found something for which he could treat with the Grey God himself? Surely he must have left evidence of his search to contact Arawn."

"My dear Ganelon," Flavia said dryly from behind folded arms, "you are the master of setting the stage, but please arrive at the point."

He lifted the ewer and swirled the contents. "The blood in here is too fresh to have been used by me last. It would have clotted over by now. It has been replaced."

"So he has been looking," Flavia replied in a low voice.

"*Someone* certainly has. They activated the magicks."

"Damn you, please just tell me. Did he find anything?"

Ganelon's lips curled ruefully, then he replied, "The magic itself leaves no traces."

Flavia threw her hands in the air, stomping one delicate foot with a thump. She snorted. "This is all you can tell me?"

"I did not bring you here to demonstrate my failures," Ganelon replied wryly. "I do have a modicum of pride remaining in this old carcass. We know he was here looking. So there must be something to see."

He hefted the ewer, slowly pouring the blood out onto the floor. Wherever it touched, the tile shimmered and became transparent. Then the topography of southern Cymru came into view as if from an aerial perspective. As night was falling, the image was dark. But with their augmented senses as rulers of the undead, they could focus on the details of the coasts, the rolling waves, the green hillsides, and the ebb and flow of life.

Ganelon set the empty ewer down to kneel near the edge of the image. Flavia stepped close, leaning over him, and rested a hand on his shoulder. Together, they studied the landscape for some time until a frown tugged the corners of Flavia's lips.

"I see nothing," she said. Flavia let her hand slip from him, and she paced the room, fingers knit behind her back. "But we know Arawn operates in Cymru . . ."

"He took the princess from here," Ganelon said, pointing to the region north of Caerleon.

"And Erik traveled westward when he encountered Blaine."

"Did you ask him where that occurred?" Ganelon asked.

"There was no time," she said. "*Someone* wanted a vote."

Ganelon ignored the barb. "What about the dé Danann?" he asked. "He must have seen signs."

"Kraken had him trussed up and under guard the whole time he was here," she recalled. "Of course, Kraken might have learned something from him. Did he let slip anything with you?"

Ganelon scowled, examining the map more closely. "There was an encounter here." He gestured toward another circle of stones—squat rough-hewn chunks. "It might have been Blaine. There's enough residual power left. You can see traces here." He pointed to faint green tinges in the miniature landscape.

"That's not a dé Danann circle," Flavia noted, narrowing her eyes.

"Probably Fenni tribe, I would imagine," Ganelon mused, methodically scanning the vision.

Flavia nodded. "A poor substitute for true dé Danann work."

"Making do, I gather. If it was the old wizard."

His finger swept across the landscape, only to hover over a small village awash with the unnatural green hue. "And then Caer Baen, here," he said, his finger trembling slightly over the region.

"And then we had them."

"And then they were gone over the seas in search of the blade," Ganelon said, turning accusatory words toward Flavia.

She made a point of ignoring him. "So what exactly did Kraken seek? There is nothing here we didn't already know."

"He *tortured* something out of the dé Danann," he countered pointedly. "And now all of them are gone, and in the end, *we* have *nothing*."

The disappointment still on Ganelon's face rankled her. "Enough. What would you have me do? We cannot recall Erik—he is beyond our reach."

"Flavia, all I want is for you to help me!" Ganelon exclaimed. "The Council will bicker among themselves until Arawn rolls over them all. No offense, Coven Mistress, but I am reluctant to rely on your champion. We must act."

"No, I understand," she said.

"I must examine all possibilities." Ganelon stood and paced around the shimmering view. "Perhaps Kraken remains true. He might have gone to ground to lick his wounds, like you said. Some unfortunate but unconnected mishap may have befallen him. Say—if he is gone, as Coven Mistress you take control of his brood!"

"I would need a formal declaration of assent by the Council. You know this."

Ganelon waved a dismissive hand.

"Easily done," he huffed. "He has been gone long enough. I can convene the squabblers for a vote."

"But the threat remains," Flavia stated flatly.

"Correct," he said, even as his hand gestures became increasingly animated. "I still need the gate, the breach, the rift Arawn used. Even your champion will need it if he is to succeed."

"One crisis at a time, Proconsul," Flavia said with a soothing tone. "All possibilities, yes? A gate, a breach, a rift. It takes real power to open a gate."

She cast her eyes down, scanning the map once more.

"Or make a breach?" Ganelon suggested. "And Arawn has been weak since he lost his Cauldron."

"An accidental passage between worlds," Flavia postulated.

Ganelon snorted. "I have only heard of such things in Delphi."

Flavia scowled at her lack of knowledge of such mystical things. She always hated depending on others. "How is it possible in Greece?"

"There are intersections of powerful ley lines . . ." His voice trailed off, though his eyes lit up. "The convergence of forces rends the Veil!"

Animated by new energy, he bounded across the room to a small door and disappeared within. After a few moments clattering around, he returned a moment later with an ornate urn.

"A crematorium?" Flavia asked.

"You know I am a collector," he said, holding the gold-chased vessel up with a grin on his face. *"Clinicius Scipius Aeschilius, Legatus, Legio III Cyrenaica."*

Flavia pursed her lips. "A general, no less."

"Let us hope he has the influence to grant the insight we need."

He carefully opened the lid, reached in, and removed a handful of ash. The scholar scattered it wide over most of western Albion. The

63

fine particles settled slowly. Here and there, images of the ley lines sparkled in the milky eddies, spreading across the landscape. A few intersected here and there, these crossings marked by stone circles.

Flavia frowned yet again. "Are we to be stymied at *every* turn?" she demanded. "None of the larger lines cross *anywhere* west of the Marches."

She kicked at the slowly settling dust, stirring it up yet again and making the markers glow all the more mockingly bright.

"Very well, then," Ganelon said in frustration. "This gets us nowhere."

He slammed the lid on the urn and shoved it away. Flavia's expression darkened.

"A *gregari* would have done better," she snapped at him.

"Common soldier or not, the ley lines are what they are," he said dispassionately. "Part of our problem is we don't know enough of that part of the wild. The map only reflects what we've put into it. We need someone who's been there."

"Gods damn me, and I let Erik go." Ganelon had been correct, she realized, about her choice throwing them all into uncertainty. "There must have been others tracking the princess. There's too much ground to cover for one knight. Besides, the High King, her father, he would not leave his daughter in the hands of an untested youth. Others would have been sent."

"Few men would be so foolish," Ganelon agreed. "So how would we find such men?" He paused, eyebrows rising hopefully. "You have spies all over, even out there, apparently. Could you find their names by next Council session?"

"By next—you would have me fly through the night?" Flavia asked.

"It is but a request for your particular graces." He flashed her a very disarming smile.

"My dearest friend. I simply have no words for you," she said.

She patted his cheek gently, once, twice, then a third time with a crack—hard enough that he winced. A reminder for him to remember who was in charge.

"But if I find this out for you and you locate any of Mattheus' errants," she mused in a seductive voice, "you must leave them intact when we get the information we need. This king is intimately connected to all this, and I expect we may need his aid before all is finished. We cannot have his knights' blood on our hands when we shake his."

"As you wish, Coven Mistress." Ganelon at least had the aplomb to maintain a straight face.

"If you can name those who accepted these missions," he replied with a surety in his voice, "I promise you that all our spies—yours, mine, the Old Man's, even what's left of Kraken's—will be watching for them."

His smile broadened. "If they surface *anywhere*," he said, "we will find them."

Chapter Three

⊸⊶⊷

ECHOES OF EMPIRE

The broad bow of the *Pagan Dancer* plowed over starlit waves as the ship lumbered on toward Ostia. The Port of Rome finally appeared, rising over the shoreline and radiating a glow from lamps designed by ancient engineers to wash out the stars so delicately capering over the swells. Silhouetted against the glare, ships of every description lay at anchor, waiting upon the city's Ostrogothic masters to pass them into the expansive man-made harbor of the Claudian Basin, a great stone and rubble wall that allowed approach to the city without navigating the treacherous Tiber River estuary just to the south.

Kulo stood by the helm where he could watch ship, crew, and shipping traffic. He bellowed the order to shorten sail. The *Dancer* slowed until it bobbed like flotsam in the shadow of the ancient lighthouse that stood at the apex of the harbor.

He barked another curt command. This time the crew heaved the anchor over the side. Kulo turned his attention to the lighthouse—an immense pile of stone and finish work that had for centuries guided ships to the empire's central harbor. Near the structure's base, a flickering light ignited, bobbing up and down on the water's edge before inching out over the ripples.

Kulo cursed under his breath.

Of course, the authorities monitored the waters about the harbor during the night hours. But he'd hoped to pass unnoticed at this late hour, granting them time to be rid of unwanted cargo.

"Take the skiff and row for shore. Leave now," he hissed at Erik when the young warrior stepped up beside him. "They will station men on us overnight to ensure we do not unload before they collect taxes and bribes. Damn, the harbormaster is a greedy son-of-a-bitch."

Kulo tangled his beefy fingers through his beard, studying the stained deck that still bore witness to the battle against the Vandal pirates.

"And finding the likes of you aboard would raise many, many questions," he concluded.

"No need to draw more attention to your fine vessel," Erik replied with a curt nod.

"The skiff is even now over the side," Kulo prompted. Then he added, "Please, do not a-come looking for us when you need passage back. We will not be here."

Erik hefted his pack. Thelwyn had already clambered over the seaward rail into the bobbing boat. Erik quickly followed. He'd had enough of the sea, and the prospect of dry land underfoot beckoned to him. The knight lowered his bag into Thelwyn's hands to keep his armor from clanking, then followed with equal stealth.

When he planted his feet on the craft's flat bottom it tossed unpredictably, making his skin crawl. Surrounded by the *Dancer*'s thick hull for the weeks and months of the voyage, Erik had been able to push fear of water into the back of his mind. But the sheer intimacy of the sea always sent a quiver through his undead flesh.

Desperate for distraction until the boat settled down, he knotted torn pieces of canvas around each oar to muffle the locks. At the same time, he focused on the corona of the city that threw the lighthouse into glowing relief. This would be a silent run through scattered shadows to the shore, and this illumination, even though distant, could be their enemy.

They pushed carefully off from the ship. Erik settled the oars into the locks and pulled with long, deep strokes against the waves. Thelwyn crouched in the stern thwart, raising his arms above his head as if in supplication. His foreign words drifted across the boat—a low singsong sound that barely reached the knight's ears. The mage then waved his arms in a sweeping circle. At his beckon, tendrils of mist rose from the water to wrap the boat in a cold, moist embrace while the lamp of the lighthouse master's launch reached the *Dancer*.

After a time, the boat grated onto the rocky beach north of the city. Erik shipped the oars while Thelwyn leapt into the surf to pull them more firmly up onto the shore. Once the flat bottom had firmly grounded, Erik clambered over the last lapping swells and trudged up the gravel to face unseen Rome lying eastward across several more miles. The countryside stretched before them, nearly as dark as the sea behind. The brow of a hill blocked much of Ostia's radiance.

Once upon a time, all the world's roads had led to this nexus, the Imperium of Rome. But those days of iron-fisted Caesars were long past, and the light of the ancients did not reach as far as it used to. Erik hefted his pack, glanced at Thelwyn waiting patiently, then stepped off on the next leg of their journey.

Erik's eyes fluttered open, his cheek brushing dank stone. The sun had finally sunk over the world's edge beyond the cellar's walls, allowing him to venture forth. He had slept through the day surrounded by slabs of smoked meat and wrinkled vegetables whose combined smell offended even his altered senses. Sojourning in the open countryside would be a welcome reprieve from the encroaching closeness of earthen walls and wooden bulkheads.

Across the cellar, tucked between kegs of ale and sacks of onions, Thelwyn held the cup he used to mix the potions that suppressed Erik's murderous urges. The old magicker raised a hand over the steaming brew, lowered his head, and mumbled unintelligible words in a melody that made the gibberish at once soothing and powerful. From within the mage's sleeve a light began to pulse, flickering in time with Erik's sense of Thelwyn's heartbeat. That throbbing beacon of power flowed down his outstretched fingers and dripped with liquid glow into the cup.

In time the quiet chant ceased, the dripping essence halted, and Thelwyn's shoulders sagged. When the mage set the cup on the floor, his hand visibly trembled.

"That is not a simple tincture or tea, as you often made it out to be, is it?" Erik asked in a tone more accusatory than intended.

Thelwyn leaned against the cellar wall, face gaunt in the shadows. A wan smile spread across his lips.

"Keeping the curse at bay has been quite a task," he said. "In Albion, one can tap the ley lines with ease for additional . . . powers, shall we say. Even passing down the coast of Gaul, primal energies remained near at hand. But here, well . . . this is a different land. These ley lines do not appear to permeate *Italia*. This faith of Christ, its adherents don't seek the strength of the earth like their ancestors once did. The channels flow to where they are used, and here they have long since atrophied. We will likely travel many days before finding enough energy to infuse the next brew."

That explanation caught Erik's interest. His head already throbbed with the returning blood-craving that he'd fought so hard to deny. Thelwyn's elixir helped to mask the raw hunger, but the remaining ache in his chest was a constant reminder that he was no longer the young knight of Birkenshire. Rather he was an instrument of death, a dark creature that had stood upon the blood-washed deck of a Vandal vessel and roared defiance at the sun.

"So by drinking you," he stated, his stomach twisting, "I am a leech."

"No, no. Of course not," Thelwyn replied. "My people absorb primal energy as a matter of course from everything around us. It can be replaced throughout the day by going about my daily activities. The ley lines channel power toward me continuously. But we currently traverse a desert."

Erik stood but was forced to duck under the low ceiling. Close at hand, thin slivers of light stabbed through cracks in the cellar door. Erik pressed a hand to the weathered wood, avoiding the straws of fading light, and pictured the scene—sensing the crawl of the sun and the sky. And that sky would most certainly be the dizzying, cloudless azure of the middle sea rather than the comforting close gray slop of his native land. Even without the curse he would have found that deep, dizzying expanse to be a bit disconcerting.

Thelwyn shook out his hand, flexing his fingers.

"But still, I have replaced swilling blood by sipping on your life force." Erik's revulsion dripped from the words.

"By no means—it is energy from the earth. I loan you strength from the living source of my power. This world holds ancient magicks that can be accessed by the living. I merely collect it, then use it to keep you infused with life. If that energy is drained from you, the hunger will consume you, and simple concoctions of herbs and roots will not suffice."

Erik sank to the floor. "This curse—I must end it. I cannot wade through blood again . . . like on that ship."

Thelwyn placed the cup in Erik's hands. "Then we must find the sword—stop the dead from breaching the boundary from Annwyn."

The healer's eyes appeared to lose focus when Erik took the cup.

Reluctantly, Erik drank. The concoction burned through his mouth and down his throat into the center of his being. He fought a shiver against this newest understanding, then handed the cup back.

But Thelwyn did not reach for it.

Erik held it for a moment longer while the mage stared off into space, then nudged the mage's arm with it.

"Eh? Oh." Thelwyn took the cup and packed it away.

"We should go," Erik urged, stooping to collect his things. "The sun will be gone very soon."

The rising moon cast an otherworldly glow over the countryside when Erik and Thelwyn finally emerged from the hole at the rear of the home where they had sheltered. Flickering lamplight shone through the house's open windows while the occupants settled in for the evening, oblivious to the dangers resting beneath their feet through the day.

The companions crept between rusting plows, worn pitchforks, and broken fences into an orchard overgrown with brambles. Before them lay a track through undergrowth that had been pushed aside by wheel tracks—a rough path, but one that allowed them to move quickly while paralleling the road leading along the Tiber to Rome. In the distance, a pack of feral dogs let out a howling chorus, and they hastened their pace.

Erik moved from shadow to shadow, his hand dropping to the pommel of his spatha. And then there was Thelwyn. Healer, mage or whatever he was, who kept to himself secrets that Erik could not fathom. The mysteries of this quest unnerved the knight. He squeezed that pommel, as the wood and bone were the only things solid and knowable in his grasp.

After many hours, the farmland began giving way to clusters of stucco huts and walled manor homes. Erik and Thelwyn skirted the edges of these burghs, clinging to shadows while canine howls marked their passage.

Eventually, successive ranks of stone arches rose to cross their path like a bridge. But these arches reached from hills far to the north to pass high over the road and run onward to the suburbs of Rome, just barely visible in the light of the westering moon. Erik stood at the base of one massive buttress and placed a hand against the cool surface, looking up at the superimposed vaults. The enormity of the structure was beyond anything that the knight from Birkenshire had ever seen, and he could not fathom its purpose.

Then his fingers sensed something high above that chilled his tormented flesh.

"Water up there," he said.

"Yes," Thelwyn said, rubbing his chin. "These are Roman built. Man-made rivers that drain from highland lakes to fill bellies in the city. We have them in Albion as well. Though not on this scale."

"But they have a river." Erik waved in the direction of the Tiber.

"Yes, they do," Thelwyn conceded. "But remember that for centuries this city held more souls than roamed all of your homeland."

An unexpected thought came to Erik. "How many died in the construction?"

"Only the Caesar who built it knows," Thelwyn said. "And I expect he did. The Romans were obsessive about details like that. Expenses, you understand. But come along."

They hurried off the road beneath the soaring arches. Thelwyn surveyed the high path of the aqueduct while Erik's gaze wandered above the roll of hills scattered with tiled rooftops that halfheartedly reflected the dull moonlight. This celebrated land had been forced to endure the scourge of Huns, Vandals, and more bloodthirsty mercenaries than one could count. Burnt out. Burnt over. Long ago, the courts of power had fled across the peninsula, leaving behind glorious bones to be brawled over by the cutthroats and the desperate poor who lacked the means to leave. And brooding in the distance, once-mighty walls drew together the cobbled roads like the empty husk of a great spider in a dusty cobweb.

In the decades since the final child emperor had sat upon his unsteady throne in distant Ravenna, the Eternal City had wasted away to nothing more than a tarnished bauble in the tin crown of remnant empire. Yet somewhere within the remains, the city could still contain those obsessive records of which Thelwyn spoke. Tallies and reports of the day-to-day commerce of the Caesars—somewhere in the moldy documents lay a clue for a sword that had been stripped from the body of an upstart general who would have been emperor. A sword forged in fae fires and lost thereafter among men.

But first they had to gain the city, and not be seen doing it. Thelwyn gestured upward toward the heights of the aqueduct river above them.

"We may be able to avoid the earliest merchants?" he suggested.

Erik ran a hand across the stone blocks, still precisely squared and tightly fitted despite being covered beneath centuries of dead ivy and bramble. He tugged at the vines. They held. Far above, the water rushed into the city, open to the air.

"If we must," the knight said.

He reached up, grabbed a fistful of vines and, without looking back at his companion, he climbed.

The vines flexed and curled within his fingers. Erik pulled himself up, scrambling to find footing among dead leaves. When his right foot caught a stirrup of support, he stretched to clench another leafy fistful. Those dry vines tore into fragments, pulling away from the stone. He flailed, fingers grasping at shredding stems.

Then something moved within his suddenly desperate clutch.

Dead strands rustled, regaining lifelike pliancy. Stalks grew higher and thicker on the pier to reach past the lowest arch, then the next rank of arches, and the next, carrying Erik aloft like a horse regaining its feet beneath his rider. A familiar power flowed through the vines' explosive reach toward the flowing river at the top of the aqueduct. While clinging to the growing stems, Erik glanced down through the emergent leafy green to see Thelwyn standing with both hands pressed to the cold stone. Generative power flowed from the old man's body. Not waiting for the growth to stall, Erik scrambled upward on his own.

By the time he topped the second rank of arches, Erik could see Rome's walls winding through the rolling landscape like a crenelated serpent, a stone dragon encircling the city. Beyond the ramparts, scattered lights flickered through the general dark. At the upper edge of the aqueduct, the stone was smooth and firm under his hand. He reached with his other, but water splashed across his skin, and he reflexively jerked away. He nearly lost his balance, but Thelwyn's hand, calloused and strong, clamped over his wrist.

"Thank you," Erik managed to murmur, slumping onto the narrow rim and drawing his feet up from the water. "You never mentioned being able to do that. Magic yourself up here, I mean."

"I would have needed time for that climb," Thelwyn answered breathlessly. "And time is against us. Come, I am all but exhausted."

With that, he turned and splashed toward the city, his skin crawling once more from the closeness of the fast-moving stream that gurgled about his feet. Fortunately, the passage from Albion had somewhat tempered that supernatural horror so that Erik was able to grit his teeth and hustle along behind the mage. But as the last few hours of night swept past, Thelwyn's shoulders sagged, his pace flagging. Soon he stumbled a few steps at a time by leaning a hand on the channel wall. The days at sea had been long and arduous, forcing the mage to draw on his reserves far too often without the benefit of rejuvenation.

Erik grabbed him about the waist, for the proximity of the morning sun to the horizon burned already in his bones. Thelwyn fell to his knees. Erik hefted him up once more, but the narrow channel hampered his ability to keep up the rapid pace.

"Go," Thelwyn puffed. "You must reach the walls—there is no time to drag an old man."

75

Erik took another step, then another, but Thelwyn dropped out of his grip.

"No. This will be for the best." Thelwyn sank against the wall. "Run. Find a safe place in the shadows. When the sun rises . . . well, by then I will have rested. The orb's rays lend me what they can."

"I will not leave you behind . . ." Erik declared.

Thelwyn patted his hand. "This is an easy route into the city," he assured the knight. "I will be along presently."

Erik looked up at the stars that even now began fading in the east.

"I will find a hole or something just inside the wall," he said. "The sewers, if I must."

"I found you once—just let me gather my strength," Thelwyn replied, waving a hand for the knight to move on.

"Gather it quickly," the knight said.

Erik scooped up the fox, tucking it into his shirt. The creature fussed, then settled against his skin. Erik slapped his arming cap onto his head, then ran—ran as if the hellhounds of Albion nipped at his heels, trying to outpace the sun.

The Mediterranean light danced on the upper edges of the gate towers that had once made Rome the impregnable city of legend. Erik picked up the pace beneath the protection of the tall rim of the aqueduct's channel, but those daggers of light reflecting off the high clouds already lit his body with pain.

Plunging onward, he grabbed his gloves from his belt and strapped them on. He shielded his face, then climbed the channel wall to scout the way ahead. Not more than a few hundred steps away, the great block-like gate lay across the Tiber Road—the immense stone and oak portal one of the great Aurelian gates that had kept the city safe for centuries.

Desperate, he slipped back into the channel and ran. Above him, slivers of light became shards, shards became rays, and rays became beams along the city's distant hills. During their lengthy voyage aboard ship, he and Thelwyn had spent hours tarring the seams of his armor, using sailcloth and old garments to build layers between him and the sun. Even then he had slowly burned beneath the coverings. The walls drew closer, but this also brought the risk that passersby on the battlements might hear him dash through like a horse in a ford. Finding a hiding hole inside those walls consumed his mind, shutting out everything else while he threw his body into a singular sprint.

Then, at last, he reached the point where that channel pierced the wall.

His boots slipped on an irregularity in the slick stones at the junction. He clutched at the channel walls, terror of falling into the water briefly overriding that of incineration. Recovering his footing, he scanned ahead for an exit. But while stonework channels forked off in several directions, none were large enough to admit passage, and the main channel continued arrow-straight for hundreds of paces further. With nowhere else to go, and with the dawn reaching the channel's rim, he climbed to the top, straddled the edge of the structure, and sought escape to the shadows on the ground.

The sun burst over the horizon, fire erupting in Erik's veins.

In desperation, he clawed himself over the side of the upper stones.

Light seared his eyes.

Light burned his skin.

Light set his hair ablaze.

The knight fell, his arms and legs flailing for purchase that was not there and dropping through alternating light and shadow until he hit the ground. And then the darkness swallowed him.

Chapter Four

THE END OF THE ROPE

The grizzled farmer once again bent his back between the green rows of his muddy plot, hurrying to finish weeding before the sun set. A gust of wind laden with the promise of rain blew in across the fields. And he did not want the weeds to gain any further foothold.

The wind also carried the stinging dust of the old Roman road running along his patch of vegetables. His grandfather had worked this same patch when the proud Eagle had marched those Gallic stones for their campaigns, until the Franks had finally put an end to their rule. But judging from the stories that the Gaul could remember, the new rulers were but a pale shadow of the old. Even more so were these newly arrived Bretons who had once sailed from the lands across the channel that separated his own northern fence-line from Albion. They brought with them devotion to their eastern god and his crucified son, causing no end of uproar among the people with their proselyting and their criticisms of the Old Ways.

He heard the pounding of heavy hooves and the anxious creak of a loaded wagon. He permitted himself a moment's respite to straighten his back for a look. Galloping up the Roman pavers was a ponderous rig dragged along by massive geldings that in an earlier age would have towed a consul's baggage train. The great beasts, not sleek enough to have served in the *equites*, charged like either the Morrigan herself pursued them or a despised foe fled before them. The wagon drew close, and he noted with idle curiosity the large cage enclosing the human cargo within.

Slaves, he thought. *Poor bastards.*

Then he caught sight of the odd-looking drivers dressed in motley-colored garments and his mood grew foul. *Foreigners.* Between the Franks and the Bretons, he'd had enough of their kind.

Good riddance to wherever they're bound, he mused. *And don't bother coming back.*

The farmer bent his back between the green rows once again, then hurried to finish his clearing work before sunset.

Aldonzo, scion of the House of Septimania and heir-betrothed to the throne of Mattheus, High King of Gwent, hunkered down into the stale straw. After tossing and turning, he gave up trying to find a comfortable position. The overloaded wagon bounced mercilessly down the washboard road, shaking to its trucks with every rut and hole. The driver cracked his whip madly over the frightened horses. His every joint hurt from the rattling.

He sniffed at the air. Judging by the smell, they would all soon be drenched as well. His only remaining pleasure was the downtrodden expressions on his captors' faces. They had had a rough scrape a few miles back. Apparently, the line of slave-wagons that he had stumbled upon after coming ashore was more a collection of independent interests rather than a single train. During a stopover at another market, a dispute had erupted among its members, which had escalated to a fracas, then erupted into a brawl. Aldonzo's party had managed to escape the violence, but only just, and now they fled with abandon. Clearly, the road to Brest's slave markets was not an altogether collegial route. Aldonzo wondered how many times he might expect to change hands before finally getting to the auction block. He was reminded of the vision he'd had while captive aboard the pirates' dromond—being hawked from market to market, his price dropping at each successive venue.

His bitter smile quickly became a yawn. But an escape into sleep was not to be his. The wagon crested a rise, rounded a bend, and the rain found them. Not a raging torrent, but rather large, scattered drops that drove through Aldonzo's thin linen tunic in a staccato that left him soaked and annoyed.

Raking the tangle of hair from his face, he allowed himself the pleasure of cursing his fate yet again. Dismay welled up within him, by now an old friend. His mind wandered wistfully to long-ago days that extended into forever and the dreams of little boys, even princes, that oft steered the actions of men . . .

She could read, really read, and her lips did not move when she read to herself.

Over the years of his childhood and youth, his father had spared no expense on his son's education. Longinus of Septimania possessed one of the most extensive libraries in southern Gaul—books, codices, scrolls, there were sixteen in all! But Aldonzo's favorite had always been the book of stories, with pages full of tales about valiant warriors and frightful beasts.

"There, Nana, what does that say?" Aldonzo asked yet again.

He thrust a pudgy finger at a colorful drawing that made the page appear magical, knowing full well the answer but wanting to hear it anyway, since he had not yet mastered his letters.

"That, young sir," Nana gently replied, straightening her posture to orate like a Greek thespian, "is the noble warrior reciting his creed before departing to slay the Giant. To succor the weak, to champion the right, to defend the defenseless, I pledge my sacred honor—"

The door slammed behind them. Aldonzo twisted in Nana's lap, straining to see around her bosom.

"Father!" the lad exclaimed.

Longinus had returned at last from campaign, still covered in dust from the road.

"Aldonzo, come here, boy!" he called.

Aldonzo threw himself into the older man's arms. "Nana's reading to me, Papa," he blurted.

"Is she now?" his father said. "And what is she is reading to you?"

Nana stood and curtsied sheepishly. "Children's tales, my lord," she said.

Aldonzo fairly squealed with his knowledge of the tale. "The brave warrior is going to suckle for a week!" he more or less recited, clapping with delight.

Longinus laughed in spite of himself. "Oh, those stories again, is it?" he snorted.

Nana bowed her head and replied, "His favorite book, my lord."

Longinus set the lad down and plucked the volume out of Nana's hands. His voice had a disappointed edge to it.

81

"Yes, I know it is," Longinus conceded. "I should sell it. If anyone would buy it. Aldonzo."

"Papa?" the boy asked, looking up at his father with wide eyes.

"What say you and I see what's in the kitchen?" he said, hefting the child up into his arms. "Instead of filling your head with silly tales, how about I tell you some real adventures?"

"Will you tell me how you beat back the Franks again, Papa?" the boy asked.

"I will tell you how your father outsmarted those cheating northerners at their own game. Come now, we must charge the larder!"

Longinus carried his son toward the door, and Aldonzo reached out his left hand to push it open.

Aldonzo caught himself lifting his left hand.

He passed off the motion by making a study of the stump of his ring finger. The remaining flesh had begun festering a few days ago, and the slavers had been obliged to cauterize it. At least they had some medical skill, particularly when the merchandise could be damaged. He tucked the hand back into his armpit, lifting his dirty face to glower at the rain.

To succor the weak. To champion the right. To defend the defenseless.

All the silly ideas he had learned from the pages of stories retold to him time and again by his nana. Within the pages of those old tales, a romantic journey had always unfolded for the brave knights. But he had since learned that the world, in truth, was much the opposite. Such had been his fortune since his mission to rescue Marianna had come to such a bloody and miserable end. There would be no riding proudly at the head of an avenging army for him. Marianna had not been at the castle, and now his entire party lay slaughtered on the damp stones of that miserable heap. Only God knew now where she had been spirited to. And, despite his best efforts, since then he'd been battered by one crisis after another.

He rolled over to hide his face from the wind.

The girl across the wagon quickly looked away. Fair-skinned she was, with butternut hair that betrayed pale blond highlights when the sun caught it right. Her eyes, the dark blue gray of early dawn, looked right through him when he caught a stolen glance. A few years younger than himself, he reckoned. Beside her clung her ever-present shadow, a little girl of not more than six years of age. Their linen shifts were simple but finely woven, and their hands lacked the calluses of field hands. Household staff who had once lived a life of privilege, their former owner likely forced to sell them on when fallen on hard times.

A few more miles rolled beneath the wagon's wheels before Aldonzo noticed something very odd about these two that somehow had escaped him during these several days in their company.

They wore *torcs.*

Centuries ago, the Celts had been known to fashion these rigid circular neck adornments. Though less popular now among their Christian descendants, torcs were still viewed as a symbol of status, though the ones worn by the girls appeared to be of heavily tarnished bronze and of a style rather different than those Aldonzo had seen in Albion.

And then there were the slavers.

One drove the wagon while the other faced the load of slaves with a bared axe, boredom finally beginning to glaze his eyes. They were foreigners, by the look of them, Avars from beyond the eastern empire. Without intimate knowledge of this region, they had probably dismissed the torcs as slave collars, little different in intent and appearance from the heavy iron appliances borne by the rest of their stock. But to Aldonzo, the torcs implied these girls had come from the service of an important family, most likely on the Armorican peninsula.

Well, he thought, *then they may know the lands about.*

He lifted his shackles, giving them a shake, then glanced back up to the Avar with the axe, who now watched him. Aldonzo smiled, offering the cutthroat a half wave. The slaver huffed spittle into the straw and returned to watching the horizon for any sign of pursuit.

The wagon continued bouncing and jolting along the ancient paving stones until well past midnight. Finally, they drew the horses to a frothy halt, well off the road amid a stand of crooked trees. By now Aldonzo's joints throbbed, and he was sure daylight would reveal bruises in places better left unseen. Judging by the moans of his companions, no one else fared any better. But Axe quickly quelled the murmurs with an angry rap of his weapon against the bars.

At last, the driver, whom Aldonzo had taken to referring to as Whip, opened the cage long enough for each slave to be taken out in turn to relieve themselves some distance from the wagon. Aldonzo knew there was no respect of human dignity wasted in these two—they simply didn't want the smell to spoil what remained of the night.

Now that he had realized something notable about the girls, Aldonzo focused his attention on their behavior. The younger, like any small child, bounded about in endless wonder, refreshingly unconcerned with her plight. The older carried herself with a calculating aloofness that appeared to the prince like she was quietly biding her time.

The slavers barked orders in broken Celtic while packing their human cargo back into the wagon. They thrust loaves of coarse bread and water skins into outstretched hands. Once the cage was locked, Axe took up his watch-post nearby. His comrade settled into a dirty wool blanket for his turn to sleep.

No fire was lit this night.

Aldonzo watched the girls out of the corner of his eye. They ate their meal quietly, conversing in hushed tones.

He leaned back against the bars to consider his options, narrow as they were between the bars and the chains. Thankfully the rain had stopped, though now the straw remained damp. High above, stars peeked out through a ragged sky. Somewhere in the darkness, hounds bayed in a doleful yowling that echoed from distant hills with an oddly ethereal quality. The younger girl fought back a whimper. Her sister pulled her close, gently stroking her hair.

Aldonzo plucked at the straw when an idea flashed into his mind. Grabbing a fistful, he began twisting and bending the pliant stems into a rough shape. After some time, the effort did not take the shape he'd hoped for, yet expediency demanded he keep at it. He pulled strands of linen from his tunic for bindings. When the thing unraveled in his hands, he was sorely tempted to toss the whole thing in frustration. But he quelled his irritation with the uncooperative straw to try once more.

Finally, he rubbed a tired fist into his eye. In his other hand lay a small, roughly shaped doll. When he looked up, the little girl lay curled in her sister's arms, staring off into the night. He hobbled across the cage to sit beside them. The older girl looked at him suspiciously, but he ignored her.

This mission, he decided, *will take diplomacy.* Inside his head, he imagined his father's voice urging him. *Exploit the weak link.*

He offered the girl the doll. For a long moment she stared at it while Aldonzo held his breath. Suddenly she wormed a hand free of her protector to grab the offering.

"My name is Aldonzo," he said. "What is yours?"

The girl looked up, startled, like she'd only just then noticed he was there. She retreated deeper into her sister's embrace, her eyes growing suddenly wary.

"I hope you like it," he said as cheerfully as he could muster.

He offered her a benign smile, then retreated to his corner.

It was a start, he determined, and that was all he would need. He bedded down in the damp straw and slept.

The next morning Aldonzo opened his eyes to find the wagon already rolling over the ruts and holes on the road. Overhead, the cloud cover had broken into thin wisps that caught the bright cheery rays of dawn. Birds sang and fluttered in the trees.

Much to Aldonzo's surprised relief, the older girl leaned close, examining him with those piercing eyes.

"Good morning?" Aldonzo started. He skittered back until his shoulders pressed against the bars.

"Sorry?" Her voice was deeper than he had expected, the tone suggesting she was a bit put off by his withdrawal.

Nothing can be gained by scaring the prize away, he told himself.

"You just . . . well, you surprised me, that's all," he replied.

She handed him his morning crust of bread and water skin.

"Thank you," he said.

He allowed her to drop them into his hands. With a disinterested look, he tore off a chunk and stuffed it into his mouth.

After a moment, she murmured, "I wanted to thank you."

Across the wagon, her sister played with the dirty straw doll.

He took a pull on the water skin, washing the crumbs down his throat. "You are welcome," he replied benignly.

"You do not hail from around here," she declared, like she thought he might benefit from this little piece of truth.

"What makes you say that?" he asked innocently, drawing her into further conversation.

A tentative smile touched her lips. "Your accent. Your name. *Aldonzo?*" she said, cocking her head to one side. "Are you a Roman?"

He snorted almost by reflex.

"Frankish, then." She tried again.

Aldonzo shook his head slightly.

"Then where?" she pressed.

Aldonzo remained acutely aware of the Bretons' general dislike for Goths of any stripe.

"Knowledge can be dangerous," he observed. "Why should I tell you?"

She bristled, sat up straight, and slid herself back across the floorboards to her sister.

Damn it, Aldonzo thought.

The prince of rags knew he would need to allow this conversation to recede with time. Yet he was also acutely aware that time was not passing in his favor.

The wagon trundled along the rutted road beneath the clear blue sky. Whip and Axe appeared to worry less about pursuit and once again become mindful of damage to their stock from driving recklessly down a rutted highway. Though each evening they continued the journey into the darkness, at least they no longer clattered along at the breakneck pace that rattled teeth and bones. Rather, the slavers meandered from town to town, picking up fresh supplies, tending to injuries, and keeping an eye out for new stock. Such a pace slowed any real progress.

Aldonzo spent this long day making a point of looking away from the girls while trying to catch them staring at him. With a childish sense of delight, he decided he was the better master of the quick glance, since he had caught them more than they had him.

The sun set, the moon rose, and the stars wheeled in a splash of twinkling light across the heavens before at last they made camp. Once again, the ritual was repeated—the slavers marched them one by one to a convenient location for bodily functions, returned them to the cage, and handed them their rations. Aldonzo made a point of appearing eager to drain his bladder, even if he felt a fool for dancing back and forth. This, after all, was the artful side of the strategy, and he wanted to return to the wagon before the others.

The dramatic performance succeeded. He regained his place when the older girl was led away. When she returned and food was tossed to her, he snatched it out of the air, holding it long enough to force her to look at him before handing it over. But he did not release her gaze.

"I am sorry about earlier," he offered. "Septimania."

"I was close," she replied smugly.

She planted herself next to her sister. The prince took the liberty of placing himself with them, calculating his distance. The little sister shoved bread into her mouth, scattering crumbs that would attract starlings later.

"We used to live in Arree!" she piped up.

"Hush, Fainche!" the older girl snapped sharply.

Arree, Aldonzo mused. *A mountain range in central Armorica— on the road to Brest. We may pass the very place.* Aldonzo stored that away in the back of his mind. Their family would be Bretons, and there was no love lost between the Goths and their people.

"So, Fainche, is it?" he began. "Now you know my name, and I know your name."

He nodded at the older girl.

"Elaetha—" Then she caught herself and continued with irritation in her voice. "I know, *it's a beautiful name*, isn't it?"

And there was the chink in her armor, Aldonzo thought.

"Just because a liar once said that doesn't make it less true."

His response caused her to avert her eyes. For the slightest moment, she appeared vulnerable. This young woman had kept a brave face throughout their journey to the slavers' block, and for just a moment he'd taken that away from her. It made him oddly uncomfortable, for he admired her courage.

"It was our grandmama's name," Fainche blurted out. She continued as if she'd just found a fascinating bug under a rock: "What about your name? *Aldonzo.* Where is Septey . . . Septey . . ."

"Septimania," Aldonzo finished. "Far south of here, between the Romans and the Franks."

"Are you named after your grandmama?" Fainche asked, leaning closer as if he would tell her a secret.

Elaetha stifled a laugh, and her aloof facade snapped back into place.

"As a matter of fact, I was!" he whispered conspiratorially to Fainche and breathed a sigh of relief to himself.

"Was she pretty?" she asked, her child's eyes widening, a dimple creasing her cheek. "Ours was! I saw her in a painting."

A *painting*... The torcs could have come from their previous owners, but family portraits are the sole province of the wealthy. Trouble indeed had crossed their path somewhere in their past.

"Mine was not so fortunate," he replied. "She was a horrid old crone."

"Did you see her painting?" Fainche asked with a giggle.

"No. I saw her face!" Aldonzo said, screwing up his own face in mock dismay. "A painting would not have switched me on the arse with a willow branch!"

"Do not talk about your grandmama like that!" Fainche exclaimed, clapping her hands over her mouth.

"I suppose you are right," Aldonzo murmured.

As on the previous night, the distant hills echoed with the otherworldly baying of hounds. He cocked an ear, trying to mark their movement through those hills, but their bearing eluded him. Meanwhile, the darkened farmland around them had gone deathly silent. The other slaves appeared to be holding their collective breath as well.

A whimper escaped Fainche's throat, and Elaetha covered her ears.

The surreal quiet lasted a few moments longer, until a branch cracked and fell off a tree. As if released from a spell, the normal sounds of the wood returned.

Axe rapped on the side of the cage. "Sleep!" he groused.

Knowing better than to defy him, the slaves rattled around the cage, found their respective places, and settled into the mildewed bedding.

Aldonzo pressed his face against an iron bar. Under the pale light of the quarter moon, a range of mountains brooded in the distance. Aldonzo focused on them, trying to picture in his mind the maps he had studied as a boy and calculate their progress.

Pieces are falling into place, he admitted to himself. *Now to get free of this cage.*

Chapter Five

BLOOD'S ALLURE

The darkness crawled, whispers of formless movement. Somewhere nearby, water rushed in great torrents. A memory came to him of a stone channel atop arches stacked to the very sky. Something scraped against his cheek, gritty and cold. In this vision, he rolled over. Above rose a white flame. It was painfully pure, rising from nothing, consuming no fuel, and dissipating into the stygian dark. Nevertheless, that flame refused to illume the creatures he could sense surrounding him.

Erik rose, stretching a hand to the flame. He could mark the outline of his limb easily enough in the searing brilliance, but the dark stubbornly clung to its domain beyond and refused any details of its inhabitants.

"Why am I here?" he asked. Or thought—he wasn't sure.

The flame flickered dramatically in response, but there was no voice. Not that any was needed, for Erik knew who waited beyond the flame—Arawn.

He who had stalked Erik the breadth of Albion, had sent the Huntsman to hound him through wretched forests and had dispatched a legion of shambling dead to his beloved Birkenshire. The Lord of the Underworld—the King of Annwyn, he who had been worshiped by Erik's Briton ancestors until Roman hobnailed sandals marched onto the isle's beaches.

Erik, Sworn Knight of the United Britons under High King Mattheus, drew his spatha and stepped into the pillar of flame to be consumed.

Erik cried out when dark hands lifted him and carried him through the shadows. The only noises were the shuffling of feet—no labored breaths and no voices whispered in the absolute, palpable, drowning darkness. With his vision useless, Erik sought to detect the lifeblood, but there was none. Just the *slap, slap, slap* of leather soles echoing off fluted pillars that stood mere inches to either hand. Erik found he could detect those columns by their reflected sound as readily as if they'd been lit by torchlight—even to their uttermost reaches supporting the vaulted Roman ceiling high overhead.

Stolen into the darkness by the higher dead. Like Caer Baen all over again. The thought chilled his dead body.

He found himself at the edge of the surf on a fog-shrouded beach. A dream, he knew, for his body remained distant from him. Broken.

He wandered from the water toward the ancient trees that had been twisted by violent gales thrown against this shore. On the beach ahead, a stooped and hooded figure beckoned to a young boy emerging from the boughs, unsteadily bearing a long and narrow bundle. The lad's face was almost delicate—almondine eyes with protruding ears like pikes. Fae folk, the Tuatha dé Danann.

To seaward stubby curraghs took form in the mists, bobbing on the waves. The bent figure threw back his hood and frowned. Men with iron weapons in their belts vaulted the gunwales to wrestle the cumbersome crafts through the foamy wash onto the sand. Erik studied the old one. Long gray hair, silver-shot beard, ears sharp like the boy's, eyes bright but narrowed in deep worry. The old fae laid a hand on the lad's shoulder, whether for reassurance or support Erik could not tell, and with a quick admonition stepped forward to confront the newcomers.

One of the men, short frame rippling with energy and dark shoulder-length hair tamed by an iron band, waded through the waves to meet him. His bearing distinguished him as leader of the motley warband. He stopped short before the fae and placed his fists on his hips to glare into the old one's eyes.

"Do you have the sword?" he spat.

The fae drew himself up to a surprising height, his face shedding the appearance of burdens too long borne.

"What is the meaning of this, Conchobar?" He crackled with indignation. "You bring iron to the very Immortal Kingdom. Perhaps I should have Oberon run you out!"

Conchobar stepped forward, fixing the fae with his gaze.

"Tch—there will be no calls to your precious king, Gordennan. We both know that would raise too many questions. Now give me the sword!"

The fae merely looked down the length of his nose at the man.

"What?" Conchobar demanded. "Are you afraid I have not kept my part of the bargain? I see it in your accursed eyes. Well, here then."

He gestured to his men. They pushed forward a pale-skinned girl whose eyes betrayed burning hatred—her cheeks smeared with streaks of tears. While Conchobar scowled impatiently, Gordennan remained frozen in place, eyes fixed on her.

"Now you!" the king demanded.

Creases deepened across Gordennan's face. But he motioned with his fingers to the boy, who struggled with his bundle until Conchobar snatched it away, tearing open the wrappings like a beggar skinning a rabbit. The intricate workmanship of the hilt, revealed for the first time to human eyes, gleamed in the misty light. Though it fairly pained Erik to look, he could not tear his eyes away. The design, at once delicate and powerful, was very familiar to his Briton sensibilities.

Excalibur.

Conchobar's face split into a vicious grin when he drew the rest of the blade clear of its wrappings. The folds and welds in the virgin edge hinted at immense skill with the forge. The blade shone, refracting the meager dawn through power embedded in the steel. Conchobar hefted the weapon over his head, brought it down with a flourish, then absently used it to wave his men to him, as if it were a common farm implement.

They thrust the girl roughly forward, then clustered around their king. She faltered, regained her footing, then stumbled into Gordennan's arms. He clutched her tightly, speaking comforting words while stroking her hair. But his eyes remained fixed on Conchobar, who appeared very pleased with himself.

"Tell your smith he has done well," the king exclaimed breathlessly. Gordennan snorted. "I will inform him of your approval."

The human king lifted the sword over his head again, his voice triumphant. "Let that bastard Connacht defy me now! He will surely taste the steel of a king!"

The warrior slapped his thigh and howled, but Gordennan's face remained stony. Conchobar turned back to his boats, ordering his men aboard.

At the rail he turned back to shout, "It is almost a shame, is it not?"

"What do you mean?" Gordennan asked in a voice heavy with trepidation.

"That there is not another like it!"

With a parting smirk, the human king leapt into the boat before the crew shoved off. Gordennan remained on that lonely broken strand for a long time after, holding his daughter and watching empty waves throw themselves unimpeded upon the sand.

Erik cried out in agony when his bones were pulled apart, then jammed back into place. A dry tongue clucked with a sharp, odd sort of sound. Gnarled fingers gripped fractured bone before another jerk of his limbs sent shockwaves through his body.

Someone, or something, laughed—a cackling that sounded like the shaking of bones in a tin cup.

Dark smoke wisped from the ancient forge. Erik watched from the shadows, for all purposes a very part of the stage on which his pain played the dream. A smith, his back to Erik, reached tongs into a steaming vat to extract an exquisitely wrought blade. At first it appeared to be the sword given to Conchobar—but the weapon was not the famed Sword of Light that would find its way to Arthur's court and thence into legend.

96

No oil had tempered this forging. Rather, the black swill in the vat clung like clotted blood that reluctantly beaded off to reveal steel the color of the new moon. The weapon throbbed with an unnatural vitality that could have bred shadows at midday. The smith examined the line of the steel, then grunted with satisfaction, gripping the blade with a cloth from his belt and carrying it to his workbench.

Next came the cross guard in the shape of a two-headed dragon with eyes of flashing garnet. The smith tapped it down the tang to the blade's shoulders, bit off his glove, then caressed the metal like it was a prized staghound. Blue flame dripped from his fingers into the seams, welding the guard into place. The pommel was similarly secured. The fine-grained wooden grip he pinned and wrapped with a flap of odd-looking skin of a liquid gray hue, this last bound with wire that glittered like a spiders web in the morning dew. The smith was singularly intent on his craft. The only eyes in the chamber that noticed the young interloper were those glowing red garnets of the sword—they moved, those eyes of the dragon.

At last, the smith held up his handiwork, casting his critical eyes along the length of the blade for any remaining imperfections. He found none.

"All the Light that could be mustered," he said, "created a sword worthy to guide future kings."

His pursed lips sagged into a frown.

"But alas, to gather such, one must find a place for the Darkness that remained in the balance."

He wrapped the weapon in soft lambskin and gestured to the young fae, the same youth from the beach, now watching from the doorway.

"Master Keenan," the youth offered with a nervous bow.

The smith turned—his face visible to Erik at last. Wide-set, bulbous eyes glittered in the ember's light, bushy brows and red beard braided with leather bands, a single tusk protruding from a lopsided jaw. Erik had never heard tales of such a creature—even those ancient legends recounted by elders in Caer Baen. This Master Keenan caressed the wrappings one last time before placing the bundle into his apprentice's hands.

"Take care no one sees you," he warned the youth. "Do you understand? No one must ever know of it!"

The apprentice fearfully bobbed his head, then crept out of the smoky forge. Through the open door, Erik and Master Keenan watched him scamper into the dark wood beyond, the skeletal tree limbs yet untouched by the encroaching dawn.

Something hard pressed into his mouth. He bit down—and the fingers found his shoulder to wrench it back into place. Pain engulfed him, hurling Erik into the darkness once more.

He stood before a rough-hewn timber citadel that squatted amidst a sun-blasted desert. A hot breeze stirred with the fetid smell of decay. Tromping feet drew close from behind him, and he turned to look.

Cresting a barren hill, a mass of soldiers beneath shredded banners marched in a loose formation past Erik, away from the outpost, toward a temple swathed in gaseous vapors.

In a blink of an eye, Erik found himself within that temple and, from this vantage, he watched the soldiers tromp in—a beaten, undisciplined mob. The troopers sported a hodgepodge of armor and weapons that spanned the leagues and the decades of the empire's existence. They crowded the center of the temple floor where a gaping hole vented sulfurous vapors, feet crunching over dead animal carcasses great and small that littered the tiles like autumn leaves. Stairs led down and, despite obvious trepidation, they formed a single file and made the descent. At the bottom, they came upon a scum-slicked pool that drained through a rusted wrought-iron gate. From what source the pool was filled, Erik could not tell, but beyond the drain he thought he could hear the rush of water and the hiss of voices.

None tried to drink from the vaporous water, for death emanated from this place.

One veteran, heavily scarred from untold battles, pushed to the edge. He hefted a bundle above his head.

"Mithras!" he shouted in a voice cracked dry from weeks in the desert. "We have done what you have required—this task entrusted to us by our master! Free us from this cursed thing and Maximus' soul from its grasp!"

The soldier pulled back the coverings, exposing the black sword with its red dragon-eyes. He held it gingerly, warding himself with the wrappings, and waded into the pool. Around him, the soldiers beat weapons on their shields. He reached the gate, then strained with one hand to heave it open. Again and again he jerked at the iron bars, cursing, until the gate gave way. But his footing slipped at that moment and the blade fell from his other hand. He snatched instinctively at the dark weapon and his bare hand touched the exposed blade. He dropped instantly dead into the vapor.

Without hesitation another leaped forward into the water, hands covered by a legionnaire's thick cowhide gauntlets. With one glove over his mouth, he bent to feel for the sword. The others stood breathless while he snatched it from the swirl, then plunged through the gaping portal.

Something deep within the earth erupted, scattering stone shards and debris. Men screamed and fell. In his dream state, Erik staggered when the energy passed through him, tearing the vision to shreds—

—reality and visions mixed with a terrible stab of pain that caused him to shriek. Something seared his skin with the smell of burnt flesh.

Then, one final time, darkness wrapped its arms around him.

He opened his eyes.

It was dark.

But that darkness hid noises—skittering claws, feet shuffling across stone, sticks dragging over leaves. He attempted to focus his supernatural senses on the sounds, but either the creatures were too far distant or he was not yet skilled enough. This surprised him, for in the forests of Albion the presence of wildlife had been overwhelming. Yet this was different.

He shifted, and the slats tied about his leg ground into his flesh. Agonizing moments passed before he could assume a position of comfort once more. When he moved again, pain shot through his ribs.

He alerted at the sound of cackling laughter. A wisp of light appeared. From the far side of iron bars, a skeletal hand held out the dusty stump of a candle. When the dust ignited, the light flared erratically.

"Better, this?" hissed a voice.

Erik squinted his eyes. Pain disturbed his undead senses so he could not see through the shadows. But the light showed him a grotto carved out of solid stone, secured beyond an iron grate.

"Come now," the voice continued. "I found you baking in the morning sun—broken. Laid out most unnaturally. Hours it took to put all aright."

In the wavering of the candlelight, a skeletal visage appeared, skin stretched taut over sharp bones. Wavering shadows framed piercing, wicked eyes. Wisps of hair clung to scarred and grotesquely elongated ears like nests of gray spiders. A twitch of the mouth revealed sharp canines glimmering in the dim flame.

"As unto Icarus who tried to fly too close to the sun and fell to his death in fiery failure," the creature mused, leaning closer to the bars. Its voice chilled Erik's skin like the kiss of frost across a winter morning in distant Albion. "Walk we in the footsteps of Deity to eternal life! Yes, we rise from the grave and live."

It cackled in its blasphemy.

"Who are you?" Erik finally managed.

"Why, a humble disciple of the Christ," it replied in a much more even tone. "My mother—I think she was my mother—she called me Florian, she did. But the gods of Olympus yet ruled the Eternal City then. My brothers in the desert called me by a new name—Hilarion."

"That cannot be," Erik protested, his voice dry and cracked. "He was a holy man. A saint."

"Oh, yes, he was indeed. Sitting in a dusty little cell in Palestine. But am I not a saint? Look around you!"

He held up the candle. Beyond the iron cage in which the knight was imprisoned, corpses shambled aimlessly about, bodies ranging from freshly dead in costly robes to ragged skeletons dragging themselves around on the stumps of missing limbs.

"Saved them, yes, I did!" Hilarion exclaimed. "Saved them all from the grave. Gave them purpose in seeking those who need my ministrations."

He leaned close with the candle again, the corpses fading into the shuffling dark. "Those like you!"

"You enslaved them," Erik blurted out in response.

Hilarion's face screwed up in rage. He flung the candle against the bars. Wax spattered to the floor, but the stub of wick remained lit, defying the darkness.

"Resurrected them. I did that! And I mean to free you," it hissed, stabbing a crooked finger at Erik's face. "Enslaved by the flesh, you are—by mortal desires. I will free you of that corruption, carry you across the threshold of death into life eternal."

With a pointed tongue, it licked its lips.

"I have no desire for your ministrations unless you can *lift* this damn curse, not make it worse," Erik said, leaning back against the cool stone. "I owe you thanks for pulling my bones back into place."

Hilarion's eyes narrowed with a viper's calculation. Erik returned that stare, malice for malice, until the creature shrugged like a barnyard chicken ruffling its wings. It kicked the smoldering candle away, the feeble light tracing the length of the prison cell until it came to rest behind a column.

A song then broke from the creature's lips, dripping with the very blasphemy that perfused this Hilarion—this creature of darkness lurking beneath the glorious ruin that once was Rome.

What new mystery then is this?
The Judge is judged and holds his peace;

The Invisible One is seen and is not ashamed;
The Celestial is laid in the grave and endureth!
What new mystery is this?

The ghoulish once-holy man swept his rags around his thin frame.

"You will be saved, boy. Not by the demons that pursue from your wretched uncouth land—but by my hand, in the Name of the Lord! When you give over to the Mystery, I shall welcome you into Life Eternal!"

The candle stubbornly flared, then gave out, plunging the catacomb back into darkness.

Erik shifted himself higher against the cool stones. He tried moving his toes, found them responding, then tested other joints to assess where damage had been done. Perching atop the aqueduct near the Aurelian Gate was the last he recalled when the sun rose above the horizon. Thus the creature had spoken the truth about him flying like a burning Icarus. Until he slammed to the stone far below, where his body had shattered as any mortal's would from such a height.

And yet he did not die.

Between dream and reality, he was no longer certain of which horrors could rip him bodily apart and which would merely frighten. Shuffling noises in the dark recalled the brief sight of Hilarion's animated carcasses. But he could just as easily see once more the faces of the troopers in that shrine of the damned, despondent, and lost. The dead stood between him and escape from the catacombs. But they appeared more like a herd of cattle blocking the barn door. The legionnaires, though decades gone, harkened him to a path that he must tread. And that path required that he escape this prison.

He shook his head, the motion tugging painfully at the muscles and nerves in his neck. He ignored the discomfort, fighting to keep the

103

name of the dead lord from his mind. There was power in that name, great and horrible power. The very utterance, even in thought, could gain a purchase in Erik's mind. Dreams he could deal with, but the power of a distant god was not to be risked while in the clutches of this mad monk.

Something rustled in the darkness. The shambling of the undead had drifted off when Hilarion slithered away. This was the scratching of paws on stone, a skittering rat or subterranean creature. Undead or not, the young knight did not look forward to being gnawed on. He swung his splinted arm into the darkness, hoping the motion would scare the creature away. But pain exploded in his shoulders, causing him to collapse back against the wall.

Eat on, then, he thought. *I have not the fortitude to fight you.*

The scratching stopped.

He ignored the piercing lance of pain between his temples and focused his undead senses on finding the fox, wherever it had got to, and his surroundings jolted a bit more into focus.

We dead are nothing if not creatures of darkness, he thought.

The fox-familiar brushed his leg. Then paws landed on his chest. A warm, wet nose pressed against his cold skin.

The familiar's memories flooded Erik's mind. Darkness, weightlessness, fear. Torn flesh igniting in the light. A terrified leap from the flames engulfing Erik's clothing, impact with the ground, then confusion. Cold, foul-scented men with milky eyes shambled upon them, then hauled the knight into a thick canvas sack. The fox dashed into nearby bramble when they hefted the sack to shuffle into the shadows within the inner walls. With its nose elevated against the rotting scent, the fox trailed them into a nearby building where rows of holes lined the floor. One of the holes was broken open and the creatures that once had been men clambered in with their load.

Compelled to follow the dead things, the fox padded along dripping tunnels, deeper and deeper into a maze of columns and vaults until they reached a lonely cell.

Pain exploded through Erik's head when the familiar broke the contact, the woodland creature collapsing into his lap.

"*Et tu, Brute?*" Erik murmured, leaning back against the stone once more. "Come to bring me horrific visions as well? I can conjure enough of my own, you know."

He knew the diminutive beast to be reluctant in their relationship, as was he—possibly even more so, for it certainly had no affinity for Erik's undead condition.

"What more have you seen?" he murmured.

That thought died on his lips as his body sensed the rising of the sun far above the deep hole that hid Hilarion's own Hell from the world of men—a world now awash with light. In that moment of transition, the hunger rose in Erik's gut, that consuming desire he feared would eventually drive him to slake his thirst in blood. And yet at this same moment, the sun conspired against him, for with Thelwyn's potions he could remain conscious into the daylight hours. But without the draught, he succumbed to the cold embrace of sleep.

Tap. Tap. Tap.
Something scraped across the iron bars like claws on slate.
Tap. Tap. Tap.
Tap. Tap. Tap.

Erik stirred.

The stiff chill of the nightly rigor mortis yet frosted his bones even as the sleep of the damned dissipated. His mind whirled, his body twitched, then suddenly his frame revived. Once more aware of his surroundings, he saw the splint on his arm was gone, and he could move with less agony than the night before. But the stiff, cracking movement of his face told him that his skin remained scorched and encrusted with scabs. However, nothing of his condition concerned him at that moment, for his jailor's features vividly appeared in his mind even before he opened his eyes.

"Very good, young one. Very good indeed." The creature cackled, grinning a wicked grimace punctuated by sharp fangs.

Erik cracked open his eyes. The dungeon remained dark, but he could hear the scuffle of the wandering dead, the constant muddle without glow of lifeblood. Just beyond the bars loomed Hilarion's face, the prince of the catacombs among his rotting minions. The creature reached into the cell, stroking Erik's face, causing the knight to recoil.

"Yes, your faculties return," the mad monk continued. "Some flight from the aqueduct. I doubt God accepts the spirit of those who walk our path if they suffer such a death. No. No. The heavens are not for such as we."

His finger stopped on one of the bars and *tap, tap, tapped* again. He eyed Erik with a conspirator's wink.

"Ahhh . . . ours is a far more glorious resurrection!" Hilarion said, his hands wringing together with his words to mimic the snapping of a twig. "We must *break* Death's bonds and become gods ourselves!"

Erik flexed his fingers. While his arm remained sore, he began straining against the splint and the linen rags used for binding it to his limb.

"You are nothing more than a leech," he snarled.

Hilarion's form blurred, then ice-cold fingers shot through the bars, digging claws into Erik's throat. Red eyes flashed in the deepest dark.

The priest's words spat against his skin. "You speak of what you cannot comprehend . . . blood must bathe your throat. A life offered for a life—a heart stilled that another may live forever."

"No . . ." Erik forced through his crushed windpipe. "I will not drink a life. Not for you. Not for anyone."

Hilarion's bloody orbs narrowed, his black pupils boring into Erik.

"Given the right to make choices, by God's grace," the ancient monk grumbled. "So it is. I leave you to choose. Yes, I leave you to drown in your own choices."

Hilarion released Erik's neck with a shove, dragging gnarled nails across the knight's skin and leaving deep gouges in his flesh that oozed thick blood.

"I have defied the very Lord of the Dead," Erik choked.

Hilarion's face twisted in the pained scowl of a parent whose patience has been spent. There was a crackle like dry leaves on stones and, in a quick distortion of darkness, he was gone. Then even the shambling dead filtered off deeper into the catacombs, leaving Erik, finally, alone.

Not quite alone, though. The fox's pulse thrummed against his sore ribs. He reached into his shirt to lift the animal free.

But what he heard next caused him to struggle upright and search the darkness. Another heart pounded at the edge of his ragged senses. Not the rapid vibration of the fox, or even a rat, but the steady *th-thump—th-thump—th-thump* of what could only be another human.

Each elevated pulse sent hot blood coursing through veins to feed body and limb, stimulating Erik's thirst.

"I know you are here," he challenged, first in his native tongue.

Whatever or whoever it was, it remained silent.

He repeated the query in the schoolbook Latin of his childhood studies, the common language of the empire since the barbarians occupied Rome. Silence remained the only answer. However, his sharpened hearing caught a sniffling sound, then what could only have been a hand wiping at skin. He strained to focus on these sensory shreds, ignoring the brokenness of his own body. He listened to the darkness more deeply until he caught it—a rasping of air being drawn into a living body.

"Who are you?" he tried, this time gentler, in common Latin.

The breathing stopped but the heart rate increased, blood racing through the veins of this new cellmate almost as if it were his own. Erik shifted toward the sound, but pain shot up his leg. He gasped—a deeply ingrained mortal reflex. The knight sank back.

"I will not hurt you," he whispered. "Whatever that beast has done to you, I am not like him—or even as those other things."

His cellmate stirred slightly.

"We have to find a way out," Erik pressed.

There was another draw of breath.

"*Non est . . . non est exitum,*" the voice said, barely a trembling whisper, high-timbred and faint. "There is no way out. The priest . . . he has eyes everywhere."

Erik remained still until the pain subsided, allowing him to clear his mind. He reached deep within for those supernatural senses, those that allowed his kind to become the predator that lurked in the unrelenting darkness. But beyond the cage, only tiny feet skittered in and out of the holes that permeated the walls of the ancient catacombs.

"Rats," Erik murmured. "Nothing but rats."

"No, the priest," the voice coughed.

"You are ill," the knight stated.

Silence greeted his observation.

"Yes," Erik agreed belatedly. "The priest. He is a monster."

His cellmate chuckled, a cracked sound that broke once more into a cough, and Erik realized with a start that his companion of the dark was a woman.

"In the last days," she murmured, "the seals will be broken, and the very demons of Hell will be loosed upon the earth. We are caught up in the last days . . ."

"We are caught in a spider's web," Erik corrected. "And we must escape."

"They will pounce on us if we get too close to the bars."

"Then we fight them," he said.

A sob countered Erik's declaration.

"You have no idea the beast that is this—*vrykolakas*," she said, shifting into Greek to give the beast a name.

"I have some idea," Erik noted.

"No, you cannot," she said. "We were ambushed! Our guide promised to take us to the catacombs of the earliest martyrs. To view the chambers of the Apostles themselves. The creatures—they tore the poor man apart. We ran, but some treacherous wind blew out our torches. The priest must have conjured it. Then in the dark—oh, dearest Mary, Mother of God, they hunted us. We were less than game of the forest, for . . . we could not see them."

Bile rose in the back of Erik's throat. Surely Blaine and his minions had been just as cruel to Marianna's retainers on her pilgrimage. But they had been soldiers, armed and trained. At least they had stood a fighting chance, dying to fulfill their sworn duty. This girl sought nothing more than a manifestation of faith—and instead had found an epiphany of the purest evil.

"Yours is not the only tale of pain at the hand of these creatures," he murmured. "The one named Hilarion surrounds himself with those he slaughtered. Those creatures took me from inside the gates during the daylight."

She shifted closer. "Who *are* you?"

"A knight from Albion," he replied. "Erik of Birkenshire."

"Britannia, you mean?"

"Yes. We were once under Rome's rule."

"A . . . *knight* . . ." She rolled the unfamiliar word around the tongue. "I've not heard such a word. What is a knight?"

"Well . . ." he started, hoping this girl, with her proper Latin and knowledge of distant territories, would understand *Patavinus* that described the Germanic term. "You might call me something akin to *equites cataphractarii*. A cavalryman. We are mounted warriors who keep the peace since the Romans departed Albion."

"I see. But Erik . . . is this a German name?"

"Not where I am from."

"This city *is* ruled by Ostrogoths." Her voice took on a condescending tone. "Are you an *auxilia*? Isn't that how a German carries Roman rank?"

"My mother's father was named Erik. His family sailed to Albion from Scandia. A land of rock and ice. He settled there after the Romans snatched away their legions to leave us undefended. My father was a Briton, descended from citizens of the empire."

He again heard her limbs sliding across the stones ever so slightly.

"Why are you here?" she asked. "Were you on a pilgrimage?"

"No," he replied. "I seek something that was lost—a family relic of sorts."

"So you are a man? A mortal. Not *vrykolakas*. And you know Greek?"

He could sense fear in her words, causing the nape of his neck to tingle. She was afraid yet did not realize she was caged with a hungered beast.

"As a child, my family hired a scholar from your lands," Erik said. "I learned somewhat of the ancients, and even the saints. We are a devout family."

He grabbed the bars, rust scale rough beneath his skin. He twisted them, shook them, and the whole cage rattled.

"You will draw them back to punish us," she warned. "Stop. Please, stop."

Erik's hand fell away. He lay back against the bars.

"He is a monster," she croaked. "Born of the deepest pit . . . he ripped open my cousin's throat. Gnawed him like he was meant to be food. I— I can still hear the sound of that monster slurping Julian's blood. I— I just wanted to see where the Apostles walked . . ."

Her voice trailed off into muffled sobs. Then after a bit of rustling, she continued. "Now my family and friends walk as his acolytes, those dead things around him."

"In my village," Erik said, forcing the edge out of his voice, "we fought creatures like these. They overwhelmed us."

111

The sounds of that night, the sobs of the dying and the screams of the living, echoed between his temples until he *thumped* the back of his head against the cage.

Then he finally said, "You are not alone in your loss."

Something touched his neck.

Erik jerked away. The young woman shrank into the darkness of the cage. His supernatural senses remained unfocused, his head pounding now.

"He hurt you as well," she whispered.

"I fell. And how do you know, anyway?"

There was more rustling, then undaunted fingers found his face again.

"I saw you in the candlelight," she said, her voice low. "He keeps us alive that he might feed on us, you know."

"Oh, Saint Michael's bones . . ." he hissed through his teeth, for it suddenly dawned on Erik what the mad priest intended.

Caged and healing his broken body, the time would soon arrive not when Hilarion would feed, but rather when Erik would rip out the throat of his cellmate to lap her blood. Hilarion meant to force his transformation.

"We must escape," he said.

The fox stirred in his shirt. Erik could sense the pain in the creature's body when it tentatively stretched its legs. At that moment, though, by their brief contact, the young knight formed a plan—and communicated it to the animal.

"My name is Cassandra," the young woman whispered. "My home is in Thrace—a town called Germen. My family serves the empire."

Her fingers reached for his arm, as if to make certain Erik really had substance in the darkness.

"But for now, I must rest," he lied abruptly. "Don't stray too close to the bars."

The fox crept up Erik's legs to his chest. Hot, shallow breaths brushed against his cheek. Erik inclined his head to the fox's, then a flurry of chaos erupted inside the knight's mind. Erik was sucked into mashed memories of woodland serenity and undead uncertainty. In the deepest of the blackness, the knight looked at himself, body slumped against the wall, eyes closed, through the red-tinged vision of his familiar. Man and beast crowded their curse-linked souls together, and therein was the blending that made the fox truly familiar with the undead knight.

The creature's combined sight now cut through the darkness more clearly than Erik had been able to achieve through its eyes alone, even in daylight on the ship. The familiar augmented its own night vision with the curse and could thus see the girl huddling in rags in the near corner.

The fox-familiar lifted its head, drawing in the cloying stench of death that hung in the air.

Faint sounds from distant chambers reached their perked ears.

The quest through the warren of catacombs had been a fight for the woodland creature, but the union infused the *familiar* with strength and healing. Deep within that union, the familiar realized that this effort drew on the undead knight's flagging reserves and only hastened the rise of Erik's own hunger.

The familiar plunged through the cage bars.

The surrounding tangle of catacombs had once provided refuge to the earliest Christian saints who'd fled from the horror of imperial pogroms. Many of those refugees had scratched a crude record across the rough-hewn walls, recording their passage alongside marks left by earlier generations of fleeing slaves and black-market gangs. In contrast, twisted and moldering bones scattered among the nooks and grottoes marked the movements of the undead.

The familiar padded quietly along the twists and turns with urgency, nose lifted to each stirring within the subterranean maze. Its eyes flashed over piles of neatly stacked skulls—telltale signs that Hilarion curated the rotting lichyard. Finally, in those moldering depths, the familiar caught the barest hint of a scent apart from the accumulated layers of death—a wisp of fresh air that brought memories of springtime days after rain in distant Albion.

From a nearby tunnel, there was a shuffling, scraping noise.

In the depths of the catacombs, tucked into the deepest wells of rock, were ledges where corpses rotted and moldered, leaving bones and cobwebs after the carrion of the underworld had picked the rest clean. The familiar scrambled up onto a ledged alcove until it found a vantage point among the protruding ribs of a Roman patrician. Within a few breaths, a herd of Hilarion's minions shuffled into view, ankle deep in a chaotic wave of rats that nipped and tore at their heels. The familiar held its breath while their stiff-legged march carried them past its hiding place as if beckoned by some mystical piper.

The sound of flesh and bone then issued through the darkness.

Once they'd shuffled beyond the scope of the familiar's keen sight, it took a tentative step, then another. When nothing appeared to challenge it, the creature picked up its pace to close upon the parade of the dead. The trail proved easy to follow, for it was littered with scraps of flesh and blotted with old, rot-scented blood.

Then a sound halted the familiar. Its blood chilled. Something scampered across the corridor behind it.

The familiar crept to the wall, pressing against the cool stone. Two red pinpricks glowed in the dark passage they had just quit. How long this other had been shadowing the fox-familiar's steps, only God knew, but losing it in the labyrinth now became the priority.

The wiry familiar leaped into motion. Its paws dug at the flagstones for balance, then it bolted around the nearest corner. Claws scraped in pursuit, while ahead more feet skittered closer and closer. The familiar skidded into a torn gap in the rock wall and plunged down a twisting channel into a connecting tunnel that switched back and dropped the familiar into another corridor.

It slid onto its haunches, efforts at breathing labored. Ears quirked up, the familiar listened. All around, the chattering of rats grew louder, filling the darkness with noise. The familiar stood up on two legs, leaning a paw against the wall, and extended its nose upward, searching among the scents of many, many bodies.

Centuries of decay and dust stirred, but they carried the faint, reassuring hint of Thelwyn's presence somewhere above. Yet the rats continued to converge on this spot. Amid the long-tailed vermin pouring from cracks and crevices were a pair of glowing red orbs, those knowing eyes that could only be another familiar. Floating embers against black canvas, burning with hunger.

The fox-familiar bolted.

The rodents packed together in an undulating mass, skitter-scurrying ahead like dirty gray surf. The familiar barreled into them, driving deep into their unorganized ranks. Chitter-chattering wailed through the darkness with flailing claws and teeth that drew blood along his legs and ribs. Undaunted, the familiar scrambled up the side of the wall, gaining an acrobatic purchase, and leaped. Below, its monstrous rat adversary plowed through the verminous tide. The fox-familiar alighted on the rodent-familiar's back, plunging its teeth into its neck.

The plague of rodents squirmed around them while the combatants spun, front paws gripping, rear claws slashing—a proxy for a struggle between the knight of distant Albion and the mad monk of Rome.

Blood flooded the fox-familiar's mouth. Yet it drove its teeth deeper into flesh, into veins, and across bone. The rat-familiar's eyes glowed brighter then, and the other rats crowded to rend the fox-familiar. The canine violently threw its head back and forth, tossing the rat-familiar's body from side to side. But the rat-familiar fought back, scratching and twisting. Yet its strength ebbed in the chaotic melee until it at last crumpled to the ground. The fox-familiar shook the now limp body until there was an audible snap.

Hilarion's swarm bubbled over the rat's carcass, and the fox-familiar dashed clear of the fray. In the confined distance, a whisper grew to a wordless scream, then to a deafening howl that echoed through the catacombs.

The rats scattered.

The fox-familiar staggered for a moment. Its torn ear perked once more, listening until the incessant squealing and chittering began to fade. With singular focus, the creature ignored the pain of its battle wounds, stepped over what was left of the rat-familiar, and ran onward into the darkness.

Relentless darkness blanketed the twisting, turning tunnels. The familiar's eyes pierced the subterranean night while its swiveling ears searched for any guiding sound. Though its nose lifted defiantly, life ebbed from the familiar with each beat of its heart, leaving sticky paw prints on the stone.

Each step required an immense effort of will that strained the supernatural union between cursed knight and woodland beast. Finally, sounds of scuffling mixed with moans and incoherent cries led the fox-familiar down a corridor with a well-worn floor. There, at the end in a large room, Hilarion flailed about, rags hanging from his body and hair in an unrestrained tangle.

"*Pater noster . . . pater noster . . . qui fecit hæc Omnia?*" the creature slurred in an accusatory tone. "Father! Who? Who? Who?"

With wild ferocity, the mad monk's hooked fingers raked at his own face. He stopped, then, to reach those same hooked fingers out before him—to clench at nothing. His eye sockets were empty, fingers dripping with gelatinous gore.

"You!" Hilarion shrieked.

Beyond ceiling-high towers of skulls, the monk's rotting devotees twitched with agitation.

"I smell—the stink of your blood!" he continued. "Yes! Yes! My *rattus* you killed. My *rattus* . . ."

The *vrykolakas* lunged and the fox-familiar darted out of reach.

"But you are not long for this world!" the priest cackled. "You cannot survive being trapped in that body when it dies! No, no, no . . . And it will! It will!"

117

He clawed at his eyes again. The familiar slunk around Hilarion's writhing form, dragging its feet back toward the corridor. Bloody fingers grabbed the familiar by the scruff. Hilarion threw it into the twitching mass of undead.

Beneath the haunting gaze of the stacked skulls, the familiar twisted in the air to land on all fours amid the dead herd. For an instant they ignored the creature, but then a horrific gurgling noise erupted. One dropped to the ground, groping for the warm body. Another tripped over the first, then another and another, until feet kicked and hands clutched in a tumultuous mass of limbs, bones, and gnashing jaws.

The familiar scrambled between thrashing bodies. A horrific rotted face chomped air as the familiar dodged another corpse's stomping foot that crushed through the first's worm-ridden skull. The herd responded to the scent, the fresh blood left by the familiar dragging itself across the rough floor, like moths after a flame.

A hand caught the familiar's tail and dragged it backwards until it bit through fingers. A tangle of feet and legs formed a scrum through which the familiar darted back and forth. Hilarion's shrieking whipped the herd into a frenzy. At last, the fox-familiar emerged from the squirming limbs to plunge once more into the darkness beyond the mad monk. But the creature ran into something solid—a bar of iron protruding up through the floor. It skirted quickly around two other bars to find itself in the relative safety of an iron cage.

The familiar panted for breath before realizing someone lay huddled nearby, clad in a homespun cloak smelling of the earthy western marches of Albion.

Thelwyn.

The old druid did not stir.

118

With chaos erupting about the cage, the familiar scraped across the floor, trailing sticky blood. It nosed at the torn cloak until it reached Thelwyn's face. The scent of infection barbed the old man's shallow breath. His skin burned with fever.

The familiar yowled aloud, for, deep within the combined man and beast, Erik gave way to despair.

Beyond the bars, the undead hungrily gnashed their teeth and groped through the bars. Hilarion's dry gibbering raised the familiar's hackles with the realization that the undead would not stop until they had supped on the flesh of the living within that cage. The familiar thrust its head against Thelwyn's face and barked. Corpses threw themselves against the iron bars until the metal groaned. The fox-familiar squared up its body to face the dead. Even as the creature's strength ebbed, its eyes glowed a hellish red, seething with anger, teeth bared for the fight.

The monstrous tangle crashed once more against the bars, sieving like lard the foremost bodies and dropping flopping limbs to the bottom of the cage.

A hand, hot with fever, clamped over the fox's head, and an explosion of light speared the darkness.

Then there was nothing.

Only one word rang through Erik's mind.

Thelwyn!

When the link to the familiar shattered, darkness and vertigo engulfed the knight. Erik lurched upright against the wall, eyes open. The woman's trembling hands pressed each side of his face.

"You cannot be dead," Cassandra's voice whispered in the dark. "Please, Emmelia, Macrina, and Theosebia, I beg for your intercession. He *must not* be dead!"

When he moved beneath her hands, she pulled them away.

"Dear sweet Jesu," she said, "you were dead—your flesh cold. I thought you had died of your wounds."

Erik's eyes urgently scanned the chamber about the iron-barred cell.

"Where . . ." he began.

He flexed his fingers and toes, then reached with one hand to tug at the knots around the remaining splints. While not fully restored, the ability to move his limbs signaled advancements since he'd merged with the fox. He searched the dark for the woodland beast, but the shadows remained still, devoid of living warmth.

Thelwyn.

The fox remained in the poison-iron cage encircling the mage.

"We must go," Erik croaked, bracing a hand against the wall to regain his feet.

"But you cannot," she replied. "Your wounds . . ." Her fingers probed the darkness once more, then tightened around his forearm. "They will find us. Kill us."

"We must move now," Erik said. "Or we will surely die here."

The cursed knight took a tentative step. Nothing would keep him constrained while Thelwyn remained a caged prisoner. He searched for something to use against the bars, but his own discarded splints were the only tools within reach. A pair of hands groped at him from the darkness, rattling the bars with a thunderous racket. Erik fended off the fingers, then drove a splint deep through the eye into the brain beneath. The shambling dead dropped to the ground.

120

Erik grabbed at the bars, testing them one at a time. He gathered up the bits of rope and torn cloth that had held the splints, knotting them together to form a kind of short rope.

"Can you help me?" he asked Cassandra.

He heard only aimless shuffling noises. Erik cursed himself as a fool and grabbed her hands, twisting the wrapping into her hands.

"Pull straight," he said. "Keep pressure on it."

The bar groaned ever so quietly when she tugged. The splint leveraged between the bars, then, after a tug or two, shattered in his hand. The tension slackened on the wrap.

"Again," he growled.

And once more the bar groaned against the strain. Erik likewise pulled and twisted against the primitive welds and anchoring cement. When Cassandra sagged again, he redoubled his efforts until his finger joints cracked from the strain.

Cassandra's breath caught at the sound of motion she could not see.

"*Erik—*"Her voice broke when the iron snapped.

"We must go," he urged.

Chapter Six

PARLEY

Mattheus ap Jordanes Emrys, High King of Gwent and Unifier of Cymru, surveyed the deep night sky that was layered with distant stars. The waxing crescent moon had long since set, yet hours would pass before a frosted day dawned. Midsummer was now but a memory. By God, he was tired, though sleep had yet again eluded him to leave him pacing through the night like some cursed shade. Ever since Marianna had been taken, her loss weighed like a stone in his gut, and the carrying of it remained a burden he fought to keep from his men.

Through breaks in the clouds, distant stars lent their scattering of light. A half-century before, those stars had shone down upon pleasant childhood memories. Yet now they glimmered just as brightly over this blighted land and the tasks he would rather have never faced. The king's eyes sank to the tiny island a few hundred yards offshore, topped by its brooding fortress.

His army lay encamped at the head of the causeway jutting out across the shallows to the keep. Over the many weeks, they had seen enough of the tides to have an appreciation of the unique feature that must have drawn its original builders to this forgotten isle. When the waters rose with the tides, the causeway and its drawbridge became the only approach. But when the waters rushed out, expansive shoals of sand-washed rock allowed for easier access to the shore—though still too rough and shifty for tactical movement.

The castle itself was not overlarge by most standards. Even with the buildings, the curtain wall, and the gatehouse, it managed to enclose only about two acres. While solidly built, the keep showed its age. The fortifications rose directly from the cliff on the far side of the isle where the ground sheared straight down to the water as if sliced off by God himself. Not for the first time, Mattheus peered up the shore that reached away to both the right hand and the left, wondering whatever had become of Aldonzo's vessel. He had sent the Visigoth prince, Marianna's own betrothed, to recover her from this very place. The young noble had not been seen since. However, several of his men had been found some distance up the coast—or rather, what had remained of them. The smoke from their funeral pyre still clung to their king's own clothes.

From the site of that sobering discovery, Mattheus had led his troop to this place, fully expecting to find the band of cutthroats that held his daughter. Instead, when he had marched boldly to within earshot of the gate to demand audience with the lord of the place, Marianna herself had appeared atop the battlements. That moment had taken the wind from his sails, to borrow a droll turn of phrase from his long-dead father-in-law. So the army of the High King had settled in for a protracted siege, digging trenches and erecting mantlets, and each day he sent emissaries to the gate to demand an audience with her. Each day they returned, either ignored or outright rebuffed from the battlements.

That was until yesterday, when his plea for parley had been answered.

Reeves approached in the darkness and cleared his throat. "My lord," he began in a hushed voice.

Even here in the hinterlands, well removed from the fortress and surrounded by empty wilderness, Reeves remained ever the campaign soldier speaking in a disciplined tone. For the same reason, he required his men to extinguish their cookfires by sunset so as not to afford the enemy any unnecessary advantages in deducing their strengths or nighttime movements. The general had been taking good advantage of the darkness and the recent new moon.

"Sire, the latest scouts have returned," he reported.

"Good. Anything of note?" Mattheus asked.

"There are few enough people through this region," the general observed. "A few farmsteads, little more than huts. The locals are not inclined to interfere. Enough wild game about, but will not support additional troops without foraging further afield. Most of the trees are bent and twisted beyond use, but there is a stand of fairly straight oaks further east of here within reach. Stone for catapults will be easy enough to gather." Reeves gestured toward the rocky hills framing the beachhead.

Mattheus raked his hand through his beard. "Any other routes in or out besides the beach?"

"The valleys are choked with brush," Reeves replied. "The ridges are easier to march over. But that limits movements to narrow columns. Easier to spot and contain."

With his own keen eyes, the High King scanned the surrounding countryside. "We must remember that we are in unclaimed lands," he murmured. "Any of these local lords may decide to take offense to our presence."

"Already accounted for, my lord," Reeves said with a hint of steel in his voice.

"Of course it is," Mattheus agreed. "You are the sword of the king."

Reeves paused, then, "My lord?"

Mattheus guessed at what was on his general's mind. "None know yet where we stand. We shall see what the parley holds."

"Right you are, sire," Reeves replied with a smart bow, then spun on his heel and left.

Mattheus walked to one of the mantlets, a stout wooden shield the size of a large door supported by a pair of angled props. He dropped to his knees.

God in heaven, grant me peace, he prayed silently. *I do not know what to do with Marianna now.*

His mind flashed back to when she'd departed court for her pilgrimage. At the time he'd had no doubt that she remained ever his devoted daughter. But hindsight left him chilled to his bones. The queen, her mother, had arrived at his bed long ago in an arranged marriage. She had stood by him, ever stately and composed. How Mattheus missed her.

Allana, Allana, he pleaded. *Where did I go wrong? I was bereft without you. I fear I failed our little girl . . .*

⸙

On the uppermost level of the keep, Marianna, her pale face framed with raven hair, stood on a balcony looking out over the causeway and the troop of men clustered at its far end.

Donoch complains that he can't spy on them without campfires, she thought with some satisfaction, *but I do not need that.*

To her, the lifeblood of each individual soldier pulsed through living veins and arteries as clearly as a candle in a cave. She thrust her arms upward, stretching the loose robe that she'd taken to wearing while about the keep. She felt free within it—free of the constrictions of her previous life, both literally and metaphorically. The robe fell open, allowing the offshore breeze to embrace her cold skin with an intense touch on her heightened senses. With that caress, memories of Erik slipped into her mind, the stolen moments they had shared —and their last acrimonious encounter.

Fool, she mused to herself. *Leaving all this behind in the name of a silent god!*

Fear had gripped his heart when she had attempted to turn him. And that fear must have driven him away. She understood, to a point. When Blaine had forced himself on her with that cloying stench of death, she had choked in revulsion. The assault had nearly shattered her mind by the time his cold fangs plunged through her skin and into her breast to drain her until her heart stopped. Her fingers idly traced the scars.

But then her world had changed. The very act of rebirth had unshackled her from tradition and duty. No longer would she be required to share a bed with a torpid Goth just to bear him children. An entire world threw open possibilities to her, and with those, the princess realized all the time of Creation had been delivered to her.

Immortality offered her the power to create her own destiny, with a true god at her left hand to remove any obstacle to her pleasures.

And yet there stood her father, the High King, at the end of the causeway. And in that deep night, a lifetime had already passed since she had last seen him, the lion of Cymru—ever a pillar of strength throughout her life. His appearance before the castle threw her back into her previous life, for she had anticipated following her own journey while he remained in Caerleon on his lonely throne. Yet there he stood, an army at his back. And she must deal with him—for Arawn had commanded it.

She glanced about at the hoary crumbling stonework, wishing that he had not come while she was limited to this *hovel*.

"Mistress?"

Donoch's voice intruded upon her thoughts. Marianna cursed beneath her breath, snatching her robe closed.

"What is it?" she snarled.

"Time to prepare for the parley," he said with a formal bow.

"You know not to disturb me!" she barked, her voice cracking like a whip.

Donoch, a large, solid Scoti raider from Hibernia to the west, straightened and thumped a fist over his heart. This man led her garrison even though he was a mortal, bought for the price of a few coins. His simple motivations were what made him valuable to Marianna, but he was oft caught gawking at her when he believed she was not aware. Though she could snap his spine in half if she chose, she abhorred the way his gaze made her feel.

"My apologies, Mistress," he murmured, his tone not nearly deferential enough.

She swept her eyes from the causeway to her father's camp, dug into mounds of mud beyond the span.

"Damned parley," she said. "We have no need for them to surrender anything to us."

"We talk to them just enough to gauge their strength and resolve, Mistress," he replied.

"*I* know their strength. Three companies on the left, two on the right, about sixty men in each company."

Donoch cleared his throat, more like a lector than a common man-at-arms.

"I respect that, Mistress," he said. "But are you able to discern the siegeworks? The trenches, the escarpments, the—"

"If your patrols were more effective, Donoch, we would have all the information you need."

His answer was bland as dried wheat under a parched sun. "Of course, Mistress. But the counter-patrols of the High King—"

"*Do not call him that!*" she screeched. "Not in my presence."

"Of course, Mistress."

She returned to the rail, staring at the palpitating glow on the shore.

"I still do not understand Magwyn's insistence I participate in this damned parley," she fumed.

"All eyes will be upon you," the Scoti replied nervously. "Even men tasked with hiding will likely poke their heads out to see you in person. It will allow us to get close to their lines, to gauge their preparations, their forces—once and for all."

"And when dawn finally breaks?"

Donoch licked his lips. "We shall have returned you to the keep, my lady. Under cover of the night."

"And this is why I have to play at negotiating?" she snapped over her shoulder.

Of course, he would never recognize the source of her frustration. She was a royal, a *princess*. She had ordered Magwyn to hire men for handling such things—men who were expendable. But the reward for leaving these tasks in the hands of her underlings was that now *she* found *herself* paraded before the castle walls to allow Magwyn's scouts to gain a satisfactory look at the enemy.

Her eyes returned to Donoch. *The man will never be the stalwart Lord Reeves*, she ironically observed. Still, he carried himself well enough when he stood silently at attention. Perhaps she should send him on a fool's errand to test the limit of his coin-purchased loyalty.

But as calculating as he is, she thought, *he'd charge me extra.*

Unless, of course, she permitted him to help her don her armor and its layers of underlying garments. *That* would probably square the balance, even though he wasn't permitted to touch her. Besides, Mattheus was not the only one that needed to learn the pecking order.

"Donoch?" she finally murmured.

"Mistress?"

"Fetch my battle kit," she cooed.

She let the robe slip as if by accident, baring one pearly shoulder. "Alone, if you please." She allowed a faint smile.

He leered in return.

Nearly an hour later, flanked by a brace of guardsmen, a sullen Donoch trailed after Marianna as she swept into the courtyard, his face throbbing where she'd left an angry welt. Being taunted by a spoilt

129

royal did not sit well with the mercenary. Only the lack of any other witness on the balcony held his anger in check. He rubbed his jaw absently before catching himself—her flesh had been cold and hard, like a marble statue.

He forced himself to focus.

Two steps before him, Marianna strutted in supple leathern armor that cast an oily gleam in the torchlight. A slender longsword swung suggestively at her hip in a plain and functional scabbard. A common river stone, set atop the hilt, was the blade's only adornment. He recalled Magwyn mentioning that the stone had been a gift from the mysterious benefactor, the same who paid the mercenaries gold and issued their orders. The remainder of her equipment was far more ornate or, as outside observers might call it, even gaudy. Yet Donoch knew each piece had been finely crafted.

Every layer, right down to her skin—once again, he wrenched his attention back to the causeway visible beyond the portcullis.

She halted suddenly at the gatehouse, and he nearly walked into her.

"M'lady," he sputtered.

"Get me a veil," she demanded.

"A veil?"

"A veil. A veil, Donoch! Send one of your men back to get me one. Quickly, now!"

Donoch returned his attention to the escorts, catching them with jackal grins stretched over their faces. "What?" he growled, the tone of his voice transforming their expressions to something much more deferential. "You heard my lady! One of you go!"

The guards glanced at each other. One huffed, handed his spear to his comrade, and trotted back to the keep.

Marianna tapped her foot impatiently while Donoch, the escort, and the gate guards shifted uncomfortably from foot to foot. Finally, the errand-boy returned with a length of fine fabric coiled in his fingers. Marianna snatched it from his hand, then wrapped it around her face until only her eyes remained visible.

Assuming all was now in order, Donoch signaled to the gate man. The portcullis groaned, then rose. They stepped out onto the wooden planks of the drawbridge.

The great swirl of stars wheeled through the deep night sky as Mattheus made the final adjustments to his armor. While tugging at the last strap, he reflected with some irony on how he'd intended to meet his daughter as if she were the enemy. With a gravelly *harrumph* in this throat, he at last nodded to Reeves and together they strode out onto the causeway.

At the far end of that span, a cluster of figures crossed the drawbridge toward them. Mattheus marched to the midpoint, where he planted his feet with solid military precision. A few deliberate breaths whistled through his teeth, calming his racing heart. Sweat trickled down his back, despite the cool morning breeze.

Marianna led her retainers to within a few yards and clattered to a halt. He knew it was her by her build, by the way she carried herself, but he was surprised by the face covering. Only her eyes remained visible and deeply shadowed, so he couldn't even see more than the outline of her face. Surely not as he had imagined, but this was the reality.

"Are you well?" he inquired.

She waited for a few breaths before responding.

"I am."

He noted she didn't ask about him in return, and her voice held an edge that he could not identify. He, who had faced dozens of kinglets in battle, stood unmanned by the thought of asking his daughter just what had happened to her. That was it, really, he realized—he lacked the necessary information to even begin framing his questions. On his many campaigns, he deployed scouts to assess the lie of the land, the disposition of enemy forces. Here, he knew nothing, and that walking blindly could lead into a killing zone.

He unclenched his fists. "Marianna? What happened on the road to Princess Tudful's shrine? How did you come to be here?"

But she remained silent. With only her eyes visible, he could not read his child's face.

"Marianna!" Mattheus roared. "Answer me! Don't you remember what happened?"

"Of course I do," she stated flatly. "I was taken. We were ambushed."

Her eyes wandered, as if she were bored.

"Who did it? These Scoti?" Mattheus' voice was a sharp staccato. He chewed at the edge of his mustache, then, in a more conciliatory tone, asked, "Did you come here willingly?"

She shook her head and laughed, the sound emanating from deep in her throat. "No, Father. Not willingly. Not *here*."

"Please explain all this to me," he pled. "What of Aldonzo? He has been here? We found— we found evidence up the coast." He lowered his voice. "Has he betrayed us?"

"I would not know," she replied dryly.

"How could you not?" Mattheus growled. "He sailed to this very shore."

"Because he is no concern of mine."

Mattheus' fists clenched at his side. Then his knuckles cracked when he released them.

"Come home," he said, his voice cracking with a flinty urgency.

The High King disciplined his eyes to remain on her, even though he could see motion near beyond the fringes of the torchlight.

"I will *not*!" she spat back at him.

The High King sputtered, his beard blowing out as if his insides were deflating. "You are of royal blood . . . my family."

"My blood is divine . . ." she hissed.

He gave a deft wave of his fingers.

Nearby shadows swarmed from the darkness, a mass of men and weapons. Arrows flew, lashing Marianna's escort. The High King grabbed at his daughter. She moved with a speed that was blinding beneath the flickering light of the human torches.

"I will not . . ." she began. But Mattheus had planned his move well.

Men swarmed around them, yet Marianna fought with a viciousness that lashed flesh to bone, spattering blood across Mattheus' skin. The High King, however, remained undaunted.

"To me," he called. "To me!"

One of his scouts fell near his feet, his throat ripped out.

Men dragged ropes with them and entangled the princess, who now stood alone. Her master-at-arms now fought a rearguard action up the causeway, calling to the troops on the castle's crenelations above to raise the alarm of the ambush. Stiff cord scraped across Marianna's skin, then looped about her hands, her body, and her neck.

The princess lunged.

With her arms and legs tangled, men cursed, trying to regain control of the cords, and Marianna tripped into her father, bearing him to the ground. Long, terrible fangs gnashed and dripped saliva into his eyes.

"I am not your blood," she choked. "I am not anything of you . . ."

More ropes looped across her neck. She strained against them, those teeth—those wicked teeth snapping at her own father's flesh. Soldiers dragged her from the king, the rough camp cord lashed across her limbs. Mattheus lay gasping on the ground, his eyes wide, his daughter's saliva mingling with his tears.

"Betrayed the truce!" she shrieked.

But as directed by the king, the troopers dragged the trussed-up princess to the royal tent, leaving the bleeding wounded at the causeway, where their comrades gathered them up. And the whispers began. Whispers of the curse that had befallen a king and his get—that had befallen their kingdom.

The oil lamps flickered in inky smoke, illuminating the canvas walls. Mattheus swept into the tent and surveyed the bed where Marianna thrashed against her restraints. A cluster of troopers struggled to tie knots off when Marianna twisted, dragging one close to her jaws. He screamed, blood spurting across the bedcovers. His comrades cinched the ropes and hastily knotted them off on the bedframe.

"Get him out!" the king barked, plunging into the fray.

But the flesh tore, blood flowed, and a life was extinguished.

Mattheus straightened, flexing his fists open and closed. The creature that began laughing in a spew of blood was no longer his daughter.

The troopers gathered their fallen comrade, all the while collectively choking out apologies to their king. But he was not aloof. He grabbed a blanket off the ground and threw it across the still, warm body.

"Get him out," Mattheus whispered. "I will come to honor him."

"Honor him . . ." Marianna howled, blood bubbling out between her teeth and lips. "There is no honor here!"

The High King pulled the canvas flap open and his men scurried into the night. A   cleric stood outside—his camp chaplain, Father Aiden. The man wrung his hands, murmuring in a barely audible babble. With a bare gesture of the king's gore- covered fingers, the priest was urged into the tent. The man clutched the cross hanging about his neck.

"Quickly, Father," the monarch hissed.

Aiden lurched past the king, who then tugged the canvas closed behind them.

"Deus meus, deus meus miserere mei," the priest muttered, his face sagging.

My God have mercy; it lingered upon the king's ears with a profane mockery that the priest did not intend.

"You cannot save me, priest," she hissed. "Return me . . . I am no longer yours."

Mattheus strode to the bedside. "You are still my daughter. I will not leave you."

Her face appeared to soften beneath the recently applied rouge. "You left me years ago. Now you just need to let me go. Kill me."

"Sire!" Aiden exclaimed. "She is your blood."

The priest quickly traced the points of the cross across his breast.

"His blood no longer flows through my veins," she cackled, spattering his vestments and warrior's surcoat with flecks of red.

"*Pater et filius et spiritus sanctus nos defendat,*" the priest replied with a crack in his voice.

"Faith is more than words," the princess hissed.

Aiden thrust the crucifix toward her, the chain taunt on his neck. She squirmed against her bonds, her teeth chattering like a saw-toothed rodent. Mattheus' eyes narrowed, observing her movements, the crust forming on her skin, the sounds that escaped her lips. He struggled with his vision of this transformed creature—a creature he had once believed to be consigned to tales intended to frighten children or to impress travelers over a mug of strong ale.

"We must bring her home," the king said to the priest. "A cure . . . find some potion or tincture to free her from this."

"Free me?" she said with a distant laugh. "Why would I ever want freed?"

Aiden rubbed a hand across his bald head, wrinkles forming across his brow.

"This is not a malady I am familiar with, my liege," he murmured. "God help us all."

"Someone must know—if I must scour the world to find answers."

Marianna's body jerked, the bed rattling and bouncing beneath her. "It is time," she growled. "Let me go . . . let me return to the keep. You broke the peace!"

Mattheus knelt beside the bed. "I cannot lose you. I sent out the kingdom's best to find you."

"Let me go," she snarled.

"Many died while seeking you."

"Send your men back to Caerleon before you lose more, since they are so important to you," the princess shot back. "Just set me free!"

Father Aiden continued mumbling in Latin. Mattheus knew the words, but his heart overwhelmed his faculties. Words . . . just words that could not solve the situation before him—before his kingdom.

"I will not. We have scholars, men of medicine—sainted brothers who can pray . . ."

"Let me go!" she cried. "You will kill me. Let me go!"

She tore at the cords. Beyond the camp of the king's own troops, a wolf's howl echoed through the forlorn forests.

"I cannot!" he replied more firmly.

"Then I die," Marianna panted. "Let me go!"

She screamed.

Beyond the canvas walls, the darkest of the night finally broke. A sliver of diffused light clung to the far eastern horizon.

She tore at her bonds, writhing and convulsing.

"Father," the king urged. "A draught for sleep . . . anything!"

"Not natural," Aiden wailed. "I have nothing to combat this!"

Reeves tore open the canvas entry, rushing into the tent. "Sire . . ."

The princess lashed against her bonds, a cry of raw fury upon her lips.

"Prepare the men," Mattheus demanded of his general. "Surely they will not allow this to go unanswered."

"Yes, sire," Reeves snapped. But his eyes were riveted on the thrashing creature that was so familiar to them all, yet in this instance so horrifyingly strange.

"Reeves!" the High King barked. "Please. You cannot help me here."

The general offered his liege a stiff bow.

"You go with him as well," Mattheus added of a sudden to Aiden. "There is no more you can do. And the men need you."

Both men hurried from the royal canvas.

Turning to her father, Marianna's eyes gained a twisted hunter's focus.

"You cannot save me," she said with a painful modulation in her voice. "Father . . . king. Release me or I will die. There is nothing more to be done."

Mattheus' shoulders visibly sagged. "So many lost . . . dead. Let me take you home. Let us walk the gardens of the palace, where we can find ourselves. Please."

Marianna's harpy face softened beneath the rough crust of blood. "You know me, Father," she urged. "I am the one who comforted you when we lost Mother . . . I am your little girl. Let me go. I will come home with you . . . I will do whatever you wish me to do. I promise . . . I promise, Father . . ."

Mattheus took a faltering step forward, heart swelling from her words. Then his feet stopped.

"I cannot. There has been too much unanswered," he whispered with a choked sob. "There is more . . . something more that frightens me."

"Damn you, old man!" Marianna spat, her mouth filled once more with wild teeth. "I cannot remain here! Whether I wish to remain or not, you must let me go!"

"Tell me . . ." the king pleaded.

With the words leaving his lips, the darkest of the night passed, and a hint of morning crept over the horizon. Marianna writhed, straining against her bonds once more.

"I am your daughter!" Marianna sobbed. "Your little girl! Please, please . . . you must let me go!"

The glow grew, and with it the touch of a sunbeam began sizzling upon Marianna's skin.

"I will die with the sun!" she shrieked. "It is before you. I am not alive!"

Light flared, and she desperately threw herself against the cords, tearing her skin.

Mattheus cursed himself for a fool. Then he cut her free.

When her hand was loosed, she raked him cruelly, blood spattering the early morn. But she did not spare more time on her father and rushed for the tent's entrance. She snatched up her weird sword and threw back the canvas entrance flap, shielding her eyes against the barely perceptible dawn. A snarl upon her lips, she rushed past the horrified guards into the center of the High King's camp.

Sunlight flared.

Marianna threw her arms up to shield her eyes that burst of a sudden into agonizing flames. Her hair erupted as well. For a heartbeat she stood paralyzed, hunchbacked and arms spread, flaming like a phoenix. The soldiers around her scrambled away in terror. The pearly, perfect skin of her arms blackened, blistered, and sloughed off, exposing white bone beneath that quickly charred. Mattheus charged from his tent, waving for his men to stand back.

She curled into a smoldering ball, flames licking at her flesh.

The princess wrapped her clawed, blackened hands around the stone. Her ruined face twisted into what appeared to be a smile of sorts, her mouth crowded with wild canine teeth. The sword had been a favor from Arawn and a symbol of his endowment to her. The princess clutched at it, drawing the smooth river stone to her flesh.

That balm quickly spread up her fingers, into her arm, across her shoulders . . .

Though her master was far distant, across the Between and over the seas of Annwyn, the oathing-stone in the hilt of her blade acted as a lifeline to him. Shimmering heat blasted off her bones as if from a smelter's furnace. And yet her body respawned—skin, pure and white. Thick black locks reappeared on her blackened skull. She blinked her eyes and stood.

She held her sword close to her face.

The stone in the hilt glowed like ice in midwinter. Sheathed only in blue flame, she regarded her stumbling father, who showed the whites of his eyes. She snarled with the blazing orb thrusting up over the horizon.

Then—she was gone with a flutter, a shadow fleeing to the safety of the nearby keep.

Miles away, Tadhg the Scavenger ranged along the beach facing Monte Tombe, exposed by the receding tide. Empty Roman walls thrust up from the isle in imposing silhouettes into the skies. He liked this place, even though most local merchants knew to avoid the sudden tides. Occasionally, a foreign vessel plied the deceptively deep waters of the river mouth to become ensnared in the sand.

Then Tadhg would have his day.

And, as the fortunes would have it, today was such a day. Several cycles of surging flows had battered a craft nearly beyond recognition and thrown it up on the silt. Yet the ship's bones were no matter. All Tadhg cared about were the scattered casks and bundles. He eyed the scattered cargo shrewdly, finding a little of this, a little of that, mostly things of small space and large value—a raider's vessel. While this meant good pickings, there would be only a slight chance of finding a written cargo manifest to guide him to richer gleanings, unless these pirates had been literate like Tadhg. Nevertheless, he located what remained of the cabin in knee-deep water. He bent his back and sifted through the debris.

Charts—these are worth something, he thought, and into his pack they went. *This is shaping up to be a good day!*

Even though he pulled odd brooches, rings, and coins from the water, his disappointment grew. Any parchment was but sodden scraps. But Tadhg shrugged it off. He studied them gingerly, trying to interpret what scribbles represented wine, wool, or anything else. Apparently, the boat's quartermaster had had his own system of recording the goods carried in the ship's hold. He was not surprised. Most pirates that kept books encoded them to protect against others of their ilk.

A leather scroll case washed against his leg with the last of the tide. Tadhg scooped it up and pried the swollen cap off the end. A finger dropped into his hand, bearing an elegant ring. Without a second thought, he clenched the finger in his teeth to pull off the ring, then noticed a note, dry and protected, inside the case. He pulled it out and unrolled it with breathless anticipation.

A practiced hand had written the neat characters. *Hostage had to write his own note* flashed through his mind, for he knew not many

141

scoundrels who could even scribble their own name. But it was when he saw the name at the bottom that his breath caught in his throat.

Aldonzo de Languedoc, Septimania.

A name, along with several others, that had recently been noised about in the taverns as being of great worth to powerful and wealthy interests. Tadhg eyed the ring and note and smiled like a wolf on a new scent.

Yes. A very *good day indeed,* he reckoned.

Chapter Seven

RAVENNA

The paving stones of the Imperial Road felt reassuringly familiar under Cassandra's feet. She struggled to focus on them, one step after another, rather than reliving the previous frantic hours beneath Rome. In the darkness, she clutched the back of the knight's tunic, stumbling through a tangle of twists and turns.

Eventually they discovered a room lit by smoldering embers and glowing slag piles. From inside a blown-apart cage, the knight gathered the lifeless form of an old man and a torn, broken fox. With his charges in hand, Erik searched urgently until he located a leather sack with his armor and weapons. He fished around inside that kit and withdrew a dagger to press into her hands.

"Just in case," he said.

She pushed the weapon into her belt, then took the fox and wrapped it in a torn cloak. Once equipped, they hustled through the tunnels to the surface, where clean air awaited them beneath silvery light. After traversing the city, they climbed a broken wall and rushed along the highway to the darkened suburbs and the scattered farms beyond.

Watching the old man jouncing across Erik's shoulder like a half-empty sack stirred up an unwelcome memory of her father from many years ago . . .

Well before the races had begun, Flavius Timonius had arrived at the Hippodrome in Constantinople, the enormous stadium of the charioteers, with his daughter. But they were delayed in gaining their seats by feeding Cassandra's insatiable curiosity about how everything worked—the chariots, the harnesses, even the gates interspersed among the great columns. Despite, then, Timonius' standing as an imperial official and kinship with the emperor's own general, Belisarius, they had been relegated to perches high in the uppermost levels.

Thus, after a long day of races when the contests were over, they had been slowed in making for the exits—this time by a contentious crowd. The Blues had been victorious on the oval track, and disgruntled mobs supporting other teams flowed in all directions. The Greens especially stalked the streets as a salve to their bruised honor and fell upon those wearing the colors of the other factions with wild abandon. Through the evening and into the night, they pillaged their way through the city, staying a step ahead of the imperial guard. Cassandra's father was a simple man of an Illyrian family, from a small Thracian town, who had never allowed himself to succumb to the passion of the crowds. And he protectively guided his daughter through the back alleys and the side streets toward their home.

She could still see the faces of the thugs that had swarmed the alley and surrounded them. Some of them she knew from seeing them in the city day to day. But tonight, they were not merchants, stable hands, or carpenters—they were partisans, for they were Greens. Of course, Timonius and Cassandra yet wore their Blues colors, and the eyes of the oncoming Greens saw neither rank nor kinship.

She screamed when they smashed Timonius' head with a flagstone. She screamed yet again when frenzied hands tore away her offending azure chiton. Long, deadly minutes passed before the city guard beat their way through the mob with shields and batons.

In the aftermath, one trooper threw his cloak over Timonius' bloodied corpse, then hefted what remained of her father over his shoulder. The body jounced like a half-empty sack while making his last trip home.

The scene had been etched into her memory, much as the vision of Hilarion slaking his thirst from the throats of her friends and fellow pilgrims.

But on this night, she focused on the road ahead of her fellow escapees. Midnight approached. Then the quarter moon would soon set, bringing again the darkness to steal away her vision. Stumbling along after the knight, she hungered for what would be her first sight of dawn in many days. She studied her liberator in the fading moonlight. There was something different about him, an ill-defined quality so different from the cocksure soldiers at her family's estate just outside the imperial capital. He also carried himself with a soberness distinct from the drunken louts who accompanied Belisarius, those vain bravos who served only for title and recognition of the emperor. Without a word, the knight veered off the road toward an abandoned villa. Cassandra formed a question on her lips, but Erik had already pushed ahead through weed-choked gardens to a grove of scruffy trees.

Under the shabby, moon-silvered boughs, he probed dead brush with his boot, then gently laid Thelwyn on the ground.

"This place will do," he muttered.

He slid the cloak off his shoulder, then took the dagger from her. He knelt on the ground to use the short blade against the summer-hardened soil, tossing away roots and rocks until he gained a depth of a few feet. He took the lifeless fox from her, cradling it in the crook of his arm before laying it upon the cloak. Erik's fingers caressed the matted fur with unexpected gentleness. Then he wrapped the cloak over the creature one last time, lowered it into the hole, and piled in the dirt after.

Leaves stirred behind Cassandra, sending a chill up her spine.

"Something's here," she whispered.

But the knight had already straightened from the fresh grave, his eyes searching the deepening shadows.

A few yards away, the rippling underbrush parted. From the shadowed depths padded a creature, eyes reflected in the moonlight as it surveyed the humans before fully emerging into view. Another fox, but this one wore silver-black fur and stood taller than the creature laid to rest beneath the tree. Unfathomable eyes fixed on Erik. It crept with a hunter's grace to sniff at the knight, but Erik turned away.

"Just go away," he growled. "Better for you to just go away."

The knight held up his hand to ward the beast off, but it only pushed its head into his palm in a gesture unlike anything Cassandra had ever seen, even at the circuses in Constantinople. Again, a chill surged up her spine. She tugged her tunic tighter around her body, but that sensation still crept into her bones, compounding her confusion.

Erik withdrew his hand abruptly, but the silver fox did not flinch, and, with the moon finally settling, Erik turned his red-rimmed eyes on her.

"You should sleep."

Still in wonder about what she'd witnessed yet exhausted beyond measure, she had little mind to argue.

When she awoke, the sun was already high in the sky. Erik was nowhere to be found.

The fox lounged in the shade, tongue lolling out of its mouth as if laughing at her. Opposite the dead campfire, the old man lay where he had been deposited during the night. A cautious touch told her that he burned with fever, and her watchful eye noted the quick, shallow breaths. He might yet succumb to whatever afflicted him. Cassandra did not wish to think upon what Erik would do if he returned to find the old man dead.

The thought plagued her throughout the day while she kept hidden amid the trees, satisfying her hunger on the berry bushes within easy reach. However, that lingering fear kept her near the old man. In time the sun set, and the quarter moon assumed control of the night. Yet still Erik did not appear. While she was stretched beneath the undergrowth to watch the road, some of the plants stirred beside her. The fox crouched alongside, turning its oddly deep gaze on her. It sniffed the air.

Uncanny, she thought. Then again, the fae night could just be playing tricks with her. She blinked, then brushed a stray lock of dark hair back behind her ear. Yes, that must be it—her imagination. Still, she needed Erik to return, for she would never be able to drag the comatose old man along behind her all the way to Ravenna.

It wasn't until the moon neared the horizon that a footfall finally sounded—behind her. She brandished the dagger in reply, but it was Erik who regarded her under a raised brow.

He dropped a sack at her feet. "You must be hungry," he said matter-of-factly.

She tore into the sack, yanking out loaves of bread, skins of wine, and even cheese. After several swallows and swigs, she realized with a stab of guilt that he was not eating. She offered him some of the food, but with a gesture, he dismissed her effort.

Rather the knight knelt beside Thelwyn, who yet lay still as a stone.

After a moment, Erik's frown slowly gave way to a dawning hopefulness. Beneath the old man the very earth began to stir, leaves rustling, then tangling in the summer grass. From the blades rose flickers of light, specks even smaller than the faintest firefly that swirled around the old man's still form.

Erik's eyes rose to meet her curious stare. "The Earth, the sun, the moon . . ." he began, his voice hushed. "They are very important to his people. Threads of mystic energy—ley lines, he calls them. They connect all creation. But here, deep in Christendom, they have withered."

He reached out to the specks of light to run his fingers through them. They scattered in the wake of his hand like leaves on a pond, then flitted back to Thelwyn's motionless body.

"This will not be sufficient to restore what he lost when he blasted the dead," the knight observed.

Cassandra screwed her balled fists into her eyes. When she looked again, the lights were still there.

148

"It is unnatural. Demonic," she said, then asked, "Who *are* you?"

"I am a dead man," Erik stated flatly.

"You have a price on your head?"

"No," he rasped, snatching her hand to his chest. "Feel."

For long seconds nothing stirred beneath her touch. Then a single unmistakable thump moved her palm. She yanked her hand away to trace the cross over her own breast. "How . . .?"

"A pagan god's curse," he said blandly.

She gasped, then choked a few breaths until she regained her composure.

"Like that crazed priest . . . Why are you here?"

"I seek a weapon to kill him, the same who did this to me."

"To kill—to kill a *god*?" she asked in confusion. "What sort of weapon could do that?"

"A sword, forged by the fae and borne by Magnus Maximus himself."

"But the only killing of a god I recall was the Christ," she murmured. "Even then, He gave up His life of His own accord. How can a sword kill a god?"

"If I wield it. So Thelwyn believes."

By now, the lights had settled over the old man like glittering snow. "But this man. Thelwyn. Who is he?" she asked.

"A healer from Cymru—kept my curse at bay throughout our journey. I must sleep by day, so we travel through the night."

"How can I believe any of this?" she sputtered.

And then the damnable silver fox sidled closer, throwing itself at the knight's feet, rolling on its back like a puppy. Erik stepped away, but it scratched across the ground until it lay once more at his feet.

That, she had to admit . . . *that* defied rationalization.

149

In time the moon set, and Erik built a small fire in the shelter of the villa's walls. When the flames finally blossomed, he settled near her. To while away the last hours, he explained his time away, digging through the tunnels and warrens of old Roma in search for a trace, some record of this mythical sword.

"It is a dark weapon," he explained, "claimed to sing with fell fury in battle. Legends claim it drove the Magnus mad. The only remaining records are a moldering mess."

Cassandra spoke. "After the Vandals sacked the city—what remained was pillaged. Nothing left now but fragments. What did you expect to find?"

"When Magnus surrendered to Theodosius at Aquileia," the knight speculated, "his kit would have been taken to Rome as spoils. There would have been a record."

"If a record existed, young *eques*, it wouldn't be in Rome."

"Art thou an inscrutable oracle in need of my sacrifice?" Erik asked. "Where else could it be?"

"Why, Ravenna, of course," she replied with a grin that for the first time extended to her eyes. "Where the emperor fled in the days of the Goths."

At that moment, Thelwyn gasped.

Erik leapt to him, taking his twitching hands in his. Feeble fingers urgently grasped at the young knight. Thelwyn strained to pull himself up and whisper, "They will find us . . . from the skies they will find us . . ."

Then the mage fell back to the ground, his fever beginning to wane.

They continued their nocturnal travel, often skirting the road to remain in the shadows of empty fields, decrepit manor homes, and peasant hovels surrounded by crude fences and thin livestock. The last of civilization receded with the approach of the distant mountains, the range that split the peninsula and had bottled-up would-be invaders for over a millennium.

Despite bearing Thelwyn like a pack mule, Erik set the pace with a long stride and Cassandra hurried behind to keep up, his gear slung across her back. Along the way, the knight paused to pilfer additional supplies for the small band—a crust of hard bread here, a wrinkled apple there, a scrap of leather to bind a torn garment. But to Cassandra, anything that they could get their hands on was a welcome relief from many empty days of privation in Hilarion's subterranean prison.

On this day she lay deep in the Appian Forest on an outcrop of rock, watching the road below that was washed by the summer sun. Along that now rugged mountain path, a group of travelers traversed the way in a slow-moving clump. Simple garments betrayed them as pilgrims, for she had worn such garb on her own travels from the east. Men and women, noble or peasant, their garments made them indistinguishable. Even the few mounts of nags and donkeys would not divulge the identity or station of the individuals in the group.

A male voice rose from among the pilgrims—a haunting melody that had been heard on this road in a thousand forms since the very first sandal-clad feet had trodden these paving stones to sites of martyrdom.

We praise Thee, O God,
We see Thee as the Lord.
Yes, the Father eternal,
All the earth doth revere.

151

Unto Thee the angels,
To Thee the heavens and the powers,
To Thee, O Father,
The cherubim and seraphim do cry out without ceasing—
Holy, holy, holy, our Lord God.

The words dissipated with nary an echo, consumed by the vast surrounding forest.

The undergrowth rustled for a moment, then the fox emerged to crouch next to her, stretching on the warm ground, mimicking her own pose. It turned its too-intelligent eyes on her. She edged away to avoid its stare, scanning back across the road. Then something shook through the brush below. She shaded her eyes to squint for a better look.

Skulking figures shadowed the pilgrims from the covering verge.

Metal flashed.

Cassandra caught her breath, her heart pounding in her throat.

Her hand went to the hilt of the dagger tucked into her belt. Deep in her breast, she knew she could not see these innocents, who trusted in the hand of divinity, slaughtered by cutthroats. She glanced around for something to throw, something to draw the attention of the pilgrims, but she froze when she caught a flash of red in the fox's eyes. Her limbs felt a chill that belied the summer sun—those eyes were glowing like two flaring embers. There was no explanation for it, but there was something else behind those eyes, something that had not been there a moment before.

With a fluid motion the creature stretched its legs, launched into the undergrowth, and was gone.

The familiar dodged adroitly through the verge where it could and let brambles drag across its thick fur where it couldn't. Over a rotted timber, then around a twisted thicket, the familiar finally reached a place to peer further down the slope. Men—it could smell their stink. And these men crept along apace to the pilgrims below to take up position for an ambush. Some of the brigands clutched weapons that were more tools of butchers than of professional soldiers. An undisciplined lot, but for one thing—they moved with a practiced quiet.

The familiar crept forward until it had positioned itself beneath a low tree limb upon which one of the brigands crouched. With his free hand, the man eased a leafy bough out of his line of sight, and just then the familiar leapt. With unnatural precision born of its newfound union with the undead visitor from distant lands, it slashed its fangs across the man's throat. There was a gurgled cry. Hot blood spurted into the familiar's mouth, but before the body even convulsed to the ground, it darted further on into the shadows.

Pandemonium broke out on the hillside. The brigands rushed to aid the fallen man thrashing in the broken bramble. Below them on the road, startled pilgrims clambered to hurry their pace.

From beneath another patch of scrub, the familiar spied its next target. The back of a man's leg flashed white skin. The beast pounced. Enhanced by the supernatural melding, it tore deeply into flesh and gristle, nearly severing the limb. Blood once more filled the creature's mouth.

Its eyes flared with that wicked crimson.

Screams echoed along the ridge. Tramping feet scraped the loose soil, and the brigands beat the foliage with their weapons. The familiar crawled on its belly until clear of flailing arms and stomping feet.

"Here, here!" the man with a torn ankle groaned, grabbing the dangling joint in both hands. "I see it!"

The pilgrims fled on the road below, while above, the familiar finally leapt from cover, howling at the marauders with a supernatural timbre.

"There, there—there it is!" the man shrieked. "Sweet Mary, that is the beast!"

The familiar darted farther away through the underbrush, then leaped atop a stump, head cocked to the side, tongue dangling. The bandits slowed to a halt, frustration on their whiskered faces. When the leader caught sight of the animal, he shook his fist at it, then turned away cursing. The familiar barked, loud and throaty, and shook out its fur. Though its exceptional height nearly reached the knee of the tallest of the cutthroats, it was the flash of red eyes that appeared to regain their attention.

Another yowl from the familiar taunted them before it crashed back into the forest, angling lower along the ridge away from Cassandra and Thelwyn. When their footfalls wandered to other paths, the familiar reappeared to lure them farther down the ridge. Branches and leaves snapped and whipped by. The men fumbled behind with a stream of foul words. When the chase finished, more than one of them threatened to wear the familiar's pelt.

The familiar leaped across a ditch to scramble up the opposite embankment but lost its footing in the loose soil and tumbled back toward the excited bandits. One of them, a lanky sort with rot-brown teeth and a tangle of dark hair, deftly avoided the sudden scrum of arms

154

and legs trying to snag the beast. He grabbed it firmly by the scruff of the neck, then grunted when he hefted it into the air.

"Got you!" he bellowed triumphantly.

"Make a good hat and mitts, you will," roared another.

"You will do no such thing," said the first. "It killed Renwald— tore his throat out, it did! The beast is mine!"

He narrowed his eyes, examining the familiar more closely, then murmured, "But I never saw such a thing. Might make some coin bringing it to Lord Theobald. You know how he likes such things."

They clenched the squirming familiar's feet in rough fists, then bore their prize down the slope to the edge of the road.

Once there, they halted in dumbfounded silence. Even the familiar squirmed around for a better look with its tail curled between its legs.

"Put him down!" Cassandra demanded, suddenly behind one of the ruffians, her dagger's edge creasing the skin of his throat.

"Now, now," the brigand leader clucked. "No need to be so hostile . . ."

He gestured to his band of thieves and grinned at the prospect of female quarry. But the leader's glee quickly turned to bewilderment when one after another of the pilgrims stepped from the trees.

"Why, you brought them back for us, mädchen!" he guffawed.

The familiar stopped struggling. With its tongue lolling out of the side of its mouth, the beast looked for all the world to be wearing a smile.

One of the pilgrims pulled back his robe, drawing a long, curved sword. This was not a repurposed kitchen utensil or a cheap iron blade but a quality weapon sourced from imperial suppliers. He shrugged back his hood, revealing a grizzled, gray-bearded face. With a casual flourish of the weapon, he smiled. Behind him, the other pilgrims

155

tugged off their homespun as well, revealing chain coats and even more swords.

The cutthroats had selected the wrong targets.

"You see," Cassandra whispered into the brigand's ear, "you need to be more observant. Most *pilgrims* don't wear soldiers' boots."

The nearest imperial soldier gave her a smart bow. "Our orders were to not create an incident among our allied *hosts* who serve the boy king," he said with a wry grin. "And return you, who was feared lost."

Not long after, the brigands stumbled up the road, barefoot and sans their outer garments.

Many nights later, above the city of Ravenna, Erik crept across tiled roofs dimly lit by scattered oil lamps that marked the walls of the old imperial palace. Below him lay the tangled streets, surrounded by the city's curtain wall. Torches punctuated the crenelations. Beyond that wall stretched the lowland swamps separating the city from the Italian peninsula proper, a natural barrier the long-gone emperor Honorius had depended on over a century before, when he had holed up here to evade marauding Germans.

In those long-forgotten days, the son of Theodosius the Victor had waited here behind these same walls with bated breath for an attack that never came. While his troops paced the catwalks, the wily tribes of Gar-Men had settled the peninsula with a hungry determination to become more Roman than the Romans. They left the city be until the German general Odoacer finally put down the Roman Eagle in the west once and for all.

Now the Germans' own child-king, Athalaric, ruled from Ravenna with his mother serving as regent. His grasp on the throne relied on these very bogs to keep him above the machinations of his own nobles.

And somewhere in the warren that lay beneath those walls, Erik of Birkenshire sought the residence of the Byzantine ambassador. With any luck, a clue to the disposition of the spoils of Theodosius' campaigns had been tucked away in a dusty corner. Earlier, during the day, Cassandra had attempted to gain an appointment on the diplomatic calendar, but the ambassador's social scheduler had stubbornly confounded her efforts. Thus the knight now played the thief amid the shadows.

After hours of frustrating exploration, the young knight finally came upon the place—a traditionally styled manor separated from the surrounding alleys by a stout wall. The ambassador, Erik was unsurprised to see, kept a fine house with neatly trimmed garden paths lit by oil lamps reflecting wealth and means that had fled Rome a century before. Erik scanned trellises green with rose vines tangling up the side of the house's elaborate portico.

"Damn . . ." he grumbled.

Since his experience on the aqueduct, climbing held little excitement for him. He dropped into the alley, hugged the plentiful shadows to the porch, and leapt at the wall. Unnatural strength gave his legs extra lift, launching him toward weathered masonry halfway to the crest. From there, he clawed higher, taking toe- and finger-holds where he could find them. Finally, he reached the top of the breastwork and rolled down into the garden.

Laughter fluttered about the garden grounds. Erik crouched behind a row of oleanders when a group of guests strolled past, leaving a perfumed aroma in their wake. He wrinkled his nose, crossed the path, and ducked behind an oak by the house proper. A glitter in the nearby lamplight caught his eye—a man in robes of jeweled silk leaned close to another in deep conversation.

"And you truly believe the queen will be able to retain the scepter?" said the first.

The other, a German by his accent, laid a reassuring hand on the man's shoulder. "Petras, my friend. Amalasuntha is Theoderic's own daughter. A friend to the empire. Strong-willed, I grant you. But she acknowledges imperial authority."

"Yes, yes," answered the man identified as Petras. "But the nobles fight her on the education of her son, he who is the rightful king. If she cannot rule her own house and raise her son to be a cultured Roman, then we must prepare for the eventuality of conflict with the empire."

Erik left the two men to fret over machinations of the kingdom while he searched for a route into the house that did not involve scrambling up thorny rose vines—in full view of a party, no less, that spilled into the garden. But all he found were bars on lower windows and small vents in the foundation.

"Damn my eyes," he growled again under his breath.

Each passing moment cost precious time to search for clues. His elaborate plan was coming to naught. He scanned the genteel party once more, then caught his breath—

She stepped from the doorway.

The light from the mansion's interior illuminated Cassandra's deceptively delicate form in a way he had not expected. She must have convinced Thelwyn to alter the plan while he'd slept during the day, and now generated the very attention that he had sought to avoid.

Yet there she stood, adorned in sky-blue silk trimmed with gold, glinting in the light of a hundred lamps. When she stepped from the doorway's glare, her head was held high. Her cheekbones sported not the thick make-up caking those of many other participants but rather bore, like a soldier's scars, the marks of a survivor.

Immediately the patricians ceased their chatter, and the swarm began to move. At first it was only those in her immediate path, but word spread quickly and many more—curious to see this cousin of wily General Belisarius returned to them from a horrific pilgrimage— gravitated toward her. Mystery glided in her wake. Her responses to their anxious queries were low-toned, intended to draw them after her.

Her skill with the crowd was apparent. Within a few breaths, only Petras and his German friend remained outside her orbit. Petras' eyes followed after her, and he chuffed in consternation.

"Back from Rome with tales to tell, I hear. She will stir up the worst in the Goths," he said. "They will certainly try to stem the attacks on the faithful."

His companion nodded, taking a moment to genuflect most piously.

"A worthy goal, on the face of it," the German whispered in reply.

"But in so doing," Petras bemoaned, "that will challenge negotiations on more pressing priorities."

"But she has family in high places and the interest of the emperor."

"Yes, I suppose," Petras grumbled, chewing at the fringe of his oiled mustache before throwing up his hands. "Ah, we Illyrians must stick together. Our blood is thicker than the imperial purple. There will be a use for all things."

He clapped his companion on the back. He then strode across the garden on the trail of the crowd, donning the gracious smile of a host anxious to inquire after the well-being of his countrywoman.

Eric watched them for a moment, chagrined at the unexpected. But he had to admit the timely providence her intervention had provided. He darted back to the trellis, tangled the vines within his fingers, and pulled himself up to the second-floor windows. These wore no bars, for those high openings were assumed to be safe from thieving intruders.

Tucked away within the uppermost floor of the old storehouse, Thelwyn gauged the mystical currents throbbing beneath him through the bones of the earth. He bent to the floor and touched his forehead to the old floor planking. These mystical flows were so vibrant, so different from the shriveled courses around Rome. Ravenna lay along an artery of ley lines that drew energy from across the seas that channeled it through northern Italy into the wilds of Europe. These lines pulsed with power generated by potent strivings from distant regions that knew little of *civilization*. He wove his hands in an intricate series of wards over a wineskin, and soon energy distilled from the air, condensing at his fingertips. Drop by drop, it fell into the brew of herbs sloshing within.

The fox watched intently from the corner with that unnerving stare that was far more intelligent than it should have been.

"Don't you have something else to do?" the mage grumbled. "*I* do. I've too much to do . . . too much to do."

He shoved the stopper into the wineskin with a twist, then slapped it with his palm just to be sure. His knuckles cracked with the effort. His reserves were replenishing, but with the return of his strength and wits came also the memories of the catacombs.

His skin chilled when those memories were loosed upon his waking thoughts. Once again in his mind's eye, the shambling dead growled and groaned, pressing cold flesh against the bars of his cell, goaded on by hunger and the raving of mad Hilarion. His resolve for the secrets of their quest had eroded with the weakening of his body from the poisonous iron that had enveloped his cell. What he may have told the creature, he did not know. And what power had seduced Hilarion into capturing him and given him the means to do so effectively, he also did not know.

And that worried him. Thelwyn tugged his fingers through his beard. Of course, he realized that taking Erik from the isle to the continent had been a risk, but a calculated one if they could gain the sword. Even after centuries of separation, that damnable weapon appeared to be entangled once more with his own wyrd. If Keenan the smith had stood near him at this moment, he would likely have clucked his tongue and reminded Thelwyn that he'd allowed the sword to slip from his grasp in the first place. How it had come to be in the possession of the Magnus, the mage knew not. But one thing was certain, his hands were steeped in the blood of thousands for not fulfilling his master's command to hide it deep in the fae lands.

But what is past cannot be changed—this also he knew. And with Excalibur hidden up by the Norns, this sword of darkness, this Bane of Demons, was all that remained to stop the Grey God and protect the young nations struggling to spring from the ruins of fallen Rome.

He shook his hands, flexing his fingers once more while he hobbled to the window. Across the tiled rooftops he could see the Basilica of Christ the Redeemer dominating the palace grounds, built as the royal chapel by the late king Theodoric. As in Britain under Arthur, those that the legions had left behind clung to the trappings of

161

ancient imperium to legitimize their own rule and provide the masses with a modicum of stability—even in the face of brutal invasion and chaos.

No matter how long Thelwyn dwelt among men, he would likely never fully understand them and their desire for eternal lineage. Maybe that was because his own people, the Tuatha dé Danann, had lived under the rule of Oberon for a thousand years.

And who am I in this world of Men? he thought. *Nothing more than a broken old relic.*

A relic that sent out his companions to seek the trail of the sword that the very marrow of his bones knew was no longer here. As a youth, the blade had branded those very bones when his hand had slipped back the canvas cover to brush the cursed furniture of the hilt.

His eyes narrowed to focus in the darkness. Something had moved along the upper roof of the basilica, above the windows in the upper clerestory. Then his heart chilled. He caught a glimpse of rippling magical power flowing across the tiles obscuring whatever was moving beyond.

Someone was here.

Through every sympathy offered for her ordeal and every inquiry into her well-being, Cassandra merely smiled. Her responses remained polite, framed with encouraging niceties that made others feel better for asking. Since her arrival in Constantinople as a young girl, such banalities had become second nature—but it remained a circular, exhausting practice.

A corpulent German noblewoman snatched her hand, gushing about the dangers of the old city overrun with common plebes and cutthroat thieves. Cassandra reassured her that the Lord was aware of her long-suffering perseverance and had blessed her with a beautiful refuge in Ravenna. But her eyes darted about for an escape route.

Surely Erik must have gained entry by now? she reassured herself.

A firm hand took Cassandra's arm and, to her surprise, Petras, the emissary of the Roman emperor, offered her a toothy smile.

"I thought you would rather rest this evening?" he said with the smooth tone of a career diplomat. "Surely our little *perturbatio* did not interrupt your sleep?"

"Oh, no," Cassandra replied, feigning chagrin. "How might I thank my deliverer if not with—you know, a bit of conversation and a glass of wine?"

"Ah, yes. But you are welcome," Petras murmured, disengaging the noblewoman with a quick apology. He tucked Cassandra's hand into the crook of his arm to lead her away from scrutinizing eyes. "My men surely enjoyed the march and thwarting yet another robbery on that road. And here you are—finally. Freed by . . . what were they? Oh, yes—pilgrims from far-off Britannia. How exciting. A testament to the Roman commonwealth, for certain."

"Yes, we are all family, from Stanbul to Ravenna to far-off Londinium," she agreed, flashing her most disarming smile.

"Now the world seems to truly observe our common Roman heritage," he said, nodding toward an approaching couple. Then his tone turned grim. "Your cousin has returned to the capital."

"Belisarius?"

"Yes, yes. He had a bit of a challenge with the Persians at Callinicum, I'm afraid. Forced to flee with his men after a savage

163

pitched battle. I hear the emperor threatened to take all the tribute due to the Persians from the general's family in Illyria alone."

She brought her hand to her mouth. "That's just horrible!"

But Petras could not maintain his somber display and chuckled at her discomfort.

"Ah . . . I cannot—rest assured, my dear. Belisarius and his valiant guard mauled them so brutally that the Persians will likely not be able to field a force in the region for years. They've even opened talks of an *eternal peace* with the empire. So from the jaws of defeat that damnable cousin of yours snatched a thundering victory. I hear that his wife is lobbying the royal family to have him serve as consul next year. But that must be just gossip, no?"

"You scoundrel," Cassandra hissed back. "What have I done to deserve such use?"

"Why, my lady, surely you will indulge an old man his fun? It was an epic jest, intended for an even more legendary maiden. Look around you." His voice dropped to a partisan's whisper. "See how they follow your every movement! For the rest of the night they will be a flittering flock, a-twitter on your every word."

"So your jest is my price for admittance this evening, is that it?" she asked.

A bored smile touched Petras' lips. "I am sent hither and yon by the emperor to negotiate in the courts of barbarians and rogue kings. Humor is one of the few things I truly control. But tell me, why did you come tonight? After such an ordeal . . ." He waved his hand across the garden. "This is but a dinner party, and not a very good one, I must admit," he confided.

"Oh, you're too harsh on yourself," Cassandra cooed. "I've been literally locked among the damned for God only knows how long. Being here is a diversion from— well, it wasn't pleasant."

Petras nodded. For even in the lamplight he could see the dark bruises on her skin.

"Well, the timing of your rescue is fortuitous. I sail on the morrow for Stanbul." He steered her further from the partygoers. "It has become . . . a bit unstable here since Theoderic died. The emperor has interests in continued uncertainty."

"You have no idea—even within the walls of Rome . . ." she said.

"I do not doubt you. Between dangers for the pilgrims and a squabbling royal family, there may be a day when Justinian's firm hand is required in the peninsula."

"You know I have no interest in things political," Cassandra replied.

"Keeps that pretty head on your shoulders. Look, I leave on the tide. And your cousin would much rather you sail home with me, rather than leaving you to venture overland."

She laughed and squeezed his arm. "Ever the gentleman—"

The words had barely escaped her lips when light flashed from above. Someone screamed from inside Petras' villa.

Papers and ledgers filled the room from top to bottom, just like the dozen other rooms Erik had searched. Beneath the layers of dust, these appeared not to have been moved in the century and more since Ravenna had eclipsed the city of Rome. Stiff vellum and delicate papyrus yielded long-hidden tales to his undead sight, stories of myth and history. But those records would have to wait.

Erik continued moving through the stacks with a supernatural efficiency. Something rustled behind him, but he barely noticed it.

At last, on a shelf above his head lay a clutch of volumes from the reign of Anastasius. He coaxed the first carefully off its high shelf and leafed through its pages with growing excitement. There, amid the yellowed pages, lay only the barest mention of the Magnus' defeat at the hands of Theodosius the Great and the looting of his baggage train. Erik's pains had at last bore fruit. He grabbed another volume, then another, then another, and there, within the verses in the fourth volume, it stated how the Goths who'd assumed control after the collapse of Latin rule had, as a sign of good faith, shipped much of the remaining monies and artifacts to imperial Constantinople. Erik's finger thumped the page a couple of times while he thought about this ledger notation.

The familiar whistle of a cleaving blade sliced the air where the knight had just been. A willowy figure wrapped in loose clothing arrested the stroke, then turned the blade, leaf-shaped and pulsing with azure runes, toward the undead warrior.

"Abomination!" his attacker hissed.

Erik growled. He drew his father's sword just in time to deflect another cut from that weapon. The intruder crashed into him. The cross guards of their weapons ground together. Shelves gave way, dumping their contents across the floor to be quickly trampled. Two more attackers surged into the narrow space, checking Erik's momentum and pinning him against the stone. The first regained his footing, then advanced with that wicked leaf-bladed sword.

"I will take your head!" he cried, driving the sword into Erik's belly.

The blade's runes flashed red, then black. Fire flared through the Albion knight's guts, but he kept a stoic grip on the pain. The assassin twisted his blade, his deep forest-green eyes never leaving Erik's. His attacker produced a thick wooden stake from his belt, the slender piece of wood carved with intricate details that drew Erik's eyes.

"A sliver of heartwood from an apple tree," the assassin hissed. "From a distant and ancient orchard, blessed with power beyond your—"

"Shut up, Trisan, and use it now!" the other huffed, still struggling against Erik, who worked to free himself from their grip.

Dark elves. Thus did Erik mark them—they who had not followed Oberon to the west but had remained behind on the fringes of humanity's kingdoms, hidden in deep forests and tall mountains.

Erik threw his body against them again, but the fae creature with the applewood stake drew it back with graceful precision, then lunged.

"Release . . . release from this world . . ." his attacker said.

Erik wrenched his body to the side, throwing one of his captors into the path of the stake. The man howled when the wood pierced his back. His grip loosened enough for Erik to wrench his sword arm free. He inverted his spatha, then drove it into the other's neck. Wrestling free at last, Erik grabbed at the gore-covered stake, but the wood burned his skin, causing him to recoil.

"What the hell?" he gasped, parrying the leaf blade almost as an afterthought.

Trisan wrenched the stake free of the fallen man to attack once more, stake in one hand and fae sword in the other. Erik parried with the flat of his spatha, shouldering the other attacker out into the passageway. The maneuver gave Erik the opening he needed. He propelled his blade deep under Trisan's ribs with a flowering of dark blood. The fae warrior struck the knight across the face with the stake, scorching Erik's skin. He swatted after it, even while the dark elf recited words that caused the very air within the library to crackle with power.

Blue energy ignited around them.

"St. Michael's bones!" Erik cursed. For he had witnessed such a use of power but once before upon the waters of the Middle Seas.

He leapt for a nearby window as incalculable power coalesced around the mortally wounded dark elf. Brilliant energy exploded with a concussion of thunder, blowing furniture, books, and Erik out of the window.

The oil lamplight from the embassy reception provided a slight glow over the high walls surrounding the homes of Ravenna's wealthy. Many years had passed since Thelwyn had spent time in a city of this size. The place reeked of iron in everything, from the walls to the gardens to the citizens' very clothing. Nowhere within the cramped spaces of the warehouse could he escape it. At least the iron was scattered enough that it sapped his strength much more slowly than had the bars in Hilarion's catacombs.

Kneeling over his concoction of herbs and magicks, Thelwyn held up the last flask, nodding with satisfaction. His handiwork would do for some time now to keep the knight's hunger contained. He tucked it into his pack alongside the others. In the shadows of the room, a rodent scurried across the floor. Thelwyn pulled back his hand, a tremble in his fingers. Since escaping Rome, Hilarion's shambling creatures drooled black gore, and their chattering teeth filled his waking hours.

Suspicion preyed on his mind that that undead creature had somehow managed to *orchestrate their capture.*

That meant word had reached Rome in advance of their arrival.

Thelwyn glanced out of the narrow casement overlooking the warren of streets below. A cerulean flash caught his attention and, three heartbeats later, the concussion followed. The mage leaned out the window for a clearer view. Overhead, a distinct rustling caught his attention, drawing his eyes upward. Shadows plummeted from the rooftop. He threw himself back into the room, his hands gesturing to activate protective wards.

Red and blue bursts of energy illumined the room. The first attacker sidestepped the mage's rising defenses to land adroitly onto the floor. Thelwyn countered by generating spikes of energy drawn directly from the pulsing ley lines beneath the building. The attacker fell back into another intruder who'd already crowded the casement. The second pushed the first aside, with two more springing into the room.

These strangers wore magic about themselves like fine-spun cloth, woven on metaphysical looms with skill and knowledge. Thelwyn gasped for air while the motions of his hands raised additional magicks to counter them. In doing so, he discovered these fae bore power like his own. However much it had been colored by different climes and traditions, their countermeasures stymied his ability to effectively repel their assault.

Then, just as he threw up another spell, the door behind him exploded off its hinges. This time, magic would be of no use—rather, the mage employed the effective use of arms and fists.

A wooden club skimmed his scalp, splintering the wall framing behind him.

Thelwyn thrust the edge of his hand into the soft cloth beneath the club-wielding lout's chin, felling him backwards. It was no use, though, for with conjury on one side and brawling on the other they swiftly overwhelmed him. The dark elves drove their magical assault straight into his chest like a spear of light, rending open his insides. With Thelwyn's energies siphoning off, they dragged him to the floor.

But the healer from the backwater of Albion refused to surrender. He focused his magical attack on the closest body. The man shrieked, flailing his limbs with his blood boiling in his very veins. Thelwyn twisted his wrists free from their clutching fingers, then released what remained of his mystical energies. The discharge crackled upward through the rafters, forcing the attackers to cover their eyes. Tiles shattered and shards rained down, then the bolt of energy exploded, causing the roof timbers to ignite in orange and red.

They beat him.

And his world went black.

Erik was flung from the window, breaking through layers of tree branches before impaling himself on a broken limb halfway down the tree. He wrapped his arms around the trunk to keep from falling further. Sluggish gore oozed around the branch, a groan escaping his lips when he eased himself off the jagged sliver to grab for another purchase.

But more foliage crashed above him. One of his attackers, clothes smoldering from the mystical discharge, dropped amid a rush of debris to strike Erik, hurling both downward. Erik twisted, snatching another limb with one hand while pushing off the dark elf's flailing hands with the other. The elf clawed at another branch. But he was not so fortunate as it tore from the tree, peeling bark, and the elf hit the earth head-first. Chaos erupted when guests stampeded through the gate to the streets beyond.

Erik lowered himself to the ground.

Cassandra released herself from Petras' grasp, pushing through the retreating guests to Erik's side.

"You bleed!" she gasped.

She touched the stain spreading across the knight's midsection, but he pushed her hands away, more roughly than intended. He rolled up onto his feet and stalked over to the elf's body.

"Who is this?" Petras demanded, equally indignant and incredulous. "And what were you doing in the embassy?"

Erik ignored him and stooped over the supine form. He tugged back the folds of the elf's garments to reveal what once must have been delicately pale skin, now blasted and torn. He had a slender face, with hair the color of weathered thatch pulled back over pointed ears.

Erik looked up at Cassandra. "Thelwyn—"

The word had barely escaped his lips when a hand shot from the fallen elf's cloak, seizing his throat. Icy fingers crushed his windpipe. The elf's eyes, almond-shaped and deep as the sea, flashed open.

"Abomination!"

Blue steel flashed, and a dagger buried itself in Erik's shoulder. The knight's grip faltered. The dark elf rolled aside, tumbling Erik to the ground.

The elf leaned in close. "Creature conceived in corruption and decay! You will not survive!"

He twisted the knife, flaring the burn in Erik's undead flesh.

"Who are you?" Erik howled. "I have no fight with your people!"

171

"The dead war with all the living! Corruption begets corruption!"
He jerked the knife free, then pushed it against Erik's neck.

A goodly length of steel sprouted from the elf's own chest—
straight and true Roman steel. With a sluggish twitch, the elf turned to
see Cassandra holding Erik's spatha in her clenched hands, then lunged
against the steel, jerking the sword from her grasp. His breath rattled
when he crumpled into a heap.

Erik rolled back atop the creature, wrenching his face toward him.
"Who are you? Who sent you? Arawn? Did he—"

The creature cackled. "You . . . simple obscenity . . ." it choked,
blood oozing from its mouth.

Another explosion rocked the upper levels of the embassy. Dark
shadows sloughing embers took wing like crows above the flames and
vanished over the walls, where voices churned in the streets at the threat
of fire in a very old city.

"Who sent you?" Erik demanded again.

With his own blood oozing, he lifted the dying elf's head,
capturing his eyes with his own.

"I'm trying to do the honorable thing," Erik pleaded. "To stop
Arawn—send him back to the eternities."

"Abomination!" the elf croaked. "How arrogant to think . . . to
think . . . you can kill a god!"

The creature sagged out of Erik's grip.

The knight lifted himself to his feet. Cassandra hovered close by,
her hands clenched and shaking.

"Thelwyn?" he asked once more.

Her eyes rose to meet his. "In the room where you left us—the one
arranged by my family's agent."

And in that moment, the red-fringed vision of his familiar flooded his mind with the combat in the upper storehouse room—a vision of Thelwyn being dragged down into bonds. Erik staggered when the vision faded, but he recovered, wrenching his sword from the fallen elf's gut. He waved it toward the ambassador.

"Are you Petras, who will get us to Constantinople?" he growled hoarsely.

"On his ship, yes," Cassandra confirmed. "It flies Justinian's own standard. Our safe passage will be assured."

"Who *are* you?" Petras stammered, waving madly at the chaos that had been his dinner function and the diplomats, merchants, and nobility escaping to the street. "We must—"

"Take her to safety. *That* is what you must do. But when you get to the docks—wait for us."

With his body protesting, Erik sprinted across the garden, then vaulted over the wall.

Frightened guests bottlenecked the street, fleeing into a press of nervous citizens who attempted to enter through the gate with buckets, ladders, hammers, and saws—anything that could be put to use against the blaze that could spread embers and destruction swiftly through neighboring buildings.

Ignoring the panicked crowds, Erik scrambled and scratched his way to the rooftops once more. With the return of his strength, he skipped and bounded like a cat over the city's alleys. When he reached the warehouse district, the streets widened, compelling him once more to earth, where he navigated afoot through the city's frenzied citizens.

When at last he reached the storage house, he shouldered his way to the doors. He had barely laid his hands upon the wooden portals when the sky overhead erupted with another massive concussion. High above, silhouetted against a moonlit cloud, a long slender vessel rose into the sky, turning slowly while what appeared to be a handful of crows flew from the storehouse, a bundle trussed between them.

From his many weeks at sea, Erik recognized the sound of sails being sheeted. Delicate sailcloth blossomed from the ship's masts, tautening against a scant breeze. The ship heeled over then, picking up speed with its prow pointed north—the vessel riding the sky from the wreckage of the warehouse.

"Saint Michael's bones be damned!"

He threw open the warehouse door. "Thelwyn!" he called. "Thelwyn!"

The knight ran up the long flights, clattering and shouting, until he reached the landing and the splintered doorway. Beyond the broken plaster and timber, sky gaped where the wall had once been. There the fox stood, shaking from what must have been a staggering fight. Erik searched the wreckage with a desperate urgency, but while Thelwyn's gear was strewn throughout, there was no sign of the old druid.

Suddenly, Erik was very much alone in a strange land.

Chapter Eight

THE ISCARIOT

Marianna stalked the castle halls like a sea-borne gale. The weather had taken a turn for the worse, and heavy clouds roiled overhead from an unexpectedly cold seaward zephyr that carried with it the first fall leaves. At least the clime matched her mood. Her senses detected the luminescent trails of her father's troops bustling about the head of the causeway, and her fury grew by the hour. But her anger extended further beyond her father and his swarming troops.

Magwyn had crafted her armor to replace the equipment incinerated during the parley. Most of the gear fit well enough, almost, but the breeches rode loose about the hips. She cinched her thick leather belt tighter. All she had wanted to do was drop them back into the steward's hands so he could get it fixed.

But he hadn't been in his rooms.

Or the audience chamber.

Or the hall, or the armory, or even at the seaward postern gate.

She was now on her way to the courtyard with those offending leather breeches still clutched in her white-knuckled fists. If he was not to be found there, then he would no longer be in the castle. Which meant he traversed through the Rift to report to Arawn.

And he had not told her.

The thought incensed her—*she* who ruled the castle. *Not Magwyn.*

By Arawn's own decree, the castellan was commanded to her support. That he would steal off without her approval amounted to insubordination. Just because she left the men to work out the details of their tasks did not mean she wanted them thinking and acting for themselves. The near disaster at the parley had provided ample evidence of that. She should never have been across the causeway in the first place, far from the castle and nearly in the arms of her father's men.

Growing up in a king's court, she had picked up enough siege-craft to know what they were about digging up earthworks to ensure she remained bottled up in this god-forsaken enclave.

They won't be leaving now, she concluded bitterly, for her father had always been stubborn to a fault. Sweet words alone would never penetrate Mattheus' thick-headed skull to encourage his return to Caerleon.

Closer to hand, she focused her attentions and supernatural senses to search for Magwyn's unique signature—not alive, certainly not dead, but somehow . . . *different from anything else she had known*. But that creature was nowhere to be found.

Damn him for an ambitious bastard, she cursed, reaching for the door to the courtyard and flinging it open.

Through the portal, Donoch lorded over a ragtag formation of the sluggards he optimistically called his "troop." She crossed the open yard toward them to where the master-at-arms was delivering what appeared to be an important briefing.

"... they won't be able to respond to any but the simplest commands. Do not expect them to be capable of carrying out any direction beyond a single step. Does everyone understand?"

The mumble of affirmation quickly died when Marianna appeared behind him with fire in her eyes.

"Donoch!"

Her master-at-arms hesitated only the barest moment before facing her. As expected, his face remained a mask of obedience.

"Mistress?" he growled.

"Where is Magwyn?"

"Haven't seen him, Mistress," he snorted with a gruff annoyance.

"But did he tell you where he was going, perchance?" she persisted.

"I'm afraid not, Mistress."

By now he had assumed the posture that had been stock in trade for command-rank professional soldiers when facing a civilian leader ever since the first centurion long ago had caught trouble from his tribune while standing before his men—face bland, with a neutral tone of voice. But the tension etched into his face reminded the rank-and-file behind him, as clear as words, that any effluvium rolling his way he would surely slop onto them.

Marianna chewed her lip. Magwyn was gone, and now she surmised where. And why.

Then she realized Donoch was still standing by, regarding her with a carefully disinterested cast. She was perversely irritated that he did not show more concern for her dilemma.

"What?" she demanded.

177

"Nothing, Mistress," he hissed, but his eyes glanced reflexively at the leather breeches she held in her hands.

She curled her lip into a sneer, then shook the garment under his nose. "Yes. Nothing fits right. Your ineptitude nearly got me killed, but your armorer believes me a dwarf."

He clenched his jaw and said the only thing a man in his position could, if he possessed any wisdom. "I'm . . . sorry, Mistress."

"And you!" She faced the man at the end of the forward line of troops, who suddenly turned a shade of pale to rival her own. "Why are you all just standing around?"

The poor wretch cast about a panicked glance, like a drowning man waving to shore.

"As a matter of fact, Mistress . . ." Donoch began.

But Marianna had stopped listening, for she sensed something stirring at the edge of her perception. Not a living soul—this thing moved with purpose and direction.

By now Donoch had embarked on a disjointed narrative involving moving bodies through the postern gate, modified low-level command structures, and reduced equipage. His voice disrupted her focus.

"So, I have been explaining to these men who will be handling them directly . . ."

Could it be Blaine? she thought. *No, he was swept away by Arawn's power.*

Donoch continued to plow ahead, masking his discomfort with the words spilling from his mouth until Marianna held up her hand to his face. "Enough! Why aren't these men shoring up the defenses with the others?"

"But Mistress—" he stammered.

"Don't you realize what's happening?" she barked, her voice rising. "Mattheus styles himself High King. And he has good reason! He squats on our beach, preparing to force his way in here. He won't stop until he is either victorious *or dead.*" She jabbed a finger at the assembled men. "You need to have every last man jack out on the walls, digging the trenches, and filling the pitch pots!"

"But Mistress—" Donoch began.

"Have I not given you an order?" she shrieked.

And at that moment, she saw it in his eyes.

In all their eyes.

They care about the coin, but they do not care whence it came. These are not citizens tied to the land who have sworn oaths of loyalty to their princess. They are mercenaries, and mercenaries follow the coin.

"Mistress . . ."

"No. No more, Donoch!" she cried.

The turmoil had gone out of her voice, but the edge remained, clean and bright as a headsman's axe. She squared her shoulders, her anger cooling into resolve.

Donoch appeared genuinely confused. "Mis— um . . ." he sputtered.

"You will address me as *Highness.*"

Marianna had determined that the time had come to be *queen.*

Kraken hunkered down in the curragh as best he could while bending his back to the oars. He grumbled for the hundredth time just so he could get through all the things that needed grumbling about.

Traveling alone.

Dodging a rabble that squatted across the road.

Crossing the water.

Rowing his own boat. *On the water.*

Nursing a stiffening neck wound from an out-of-control undead rival.

Leaving his brood behind to nurse that wound.

All his hardships had become the motivation to continue into these unknown regions beyond the cosmopolitan Londinium and the Council of the Dead. He glanced back over his shoulder. The distance between the bobbing boat and the castle had closed considerably. The Higher Dead creature believed he might reach the isle before dawn.

With a determined effort on those oars, at last he maneuvered the clumsy craft into the postern gate while a guard bearing a torch above his head watched from within the sheltered wharf.

His gut gave a predatory growl. But there was only the one, and he needed a guide. The man reached out with a boathook and dragged the craft close to the stonework. Kraken awkwardly stepped onto the wharf, taking a moment to straighten his robes and collect his dignity.

"Take me to your master," he said.

Marianna set a tiara on her head to hold back her raven locks from her face. She buckled her sword about her waist, then stepped out of the dressing room to the passage leading to the audience chamber. She could sense below the new presence, much stronger now by its proximity. She motioned to the guards at the chamber door to follow her inside.

The audience chamber was the largest of the rooms within the fortress, though not nearly as impressive as the main hall in her father's manor. She ascended the steps to the worn carved stonework of the throne, where she settled into a dramatic pose among the cushions. In time, someone rapped at the door, followed by a whispered conversation between her guards and whoever stood without. The guard gestured for the unseen visitor to remain outside while he pushed the door shut, seemingly with some difficulty. He approached the throne, stopped six paces before the steps, and, with his spear, executed a half-turn to rap on the floor three times.

"Master Kraken Long-Blade, of the Council of the Dead!"

Through the door swept what had apparently once been a man— once. Red eyes darted from side to side under ragged black locks, taking in the chamber, its furnishings, and its occupants with the practiced eye of a predator. His hands were deathly pale, like Marianna's but more talon-like. Raw dark streaks like claw-marks ran across his throat.

Kraken stopped at the foot of the steps to examine who sat atop the throne. The creature's brow furrowed. Marianna leaned forward, took a calculated breath to press her breasts against her robe, then rested her elbows upon her knees. She intended to encourage him to do most of the speaking.

After some moments of locked gazes, Kraken rasped, "I seek Lord Blaine."

"Blaine is not here," Marianna purred in reply. "*I* am master. And you are . . .?"

He straightened further, standing taller, his dark eyes narrowing.

"Was I not announced? I am Kraken," he said in a haughty tone. "An honored member of the Council of the Dead."

181

"I see," she murmured, making a mental note to query Magwyn on this Council. "And your business here?"

He snorted. "That is for Blaine alone. I shall wait for him."

"That could be a long wait, indeed," Marianna said, shaking her head and leaning back against the cold stone. "You came by sea, Master Kraken. Yet you are one of the undead. Not an easy thing, I should think."

"Tis no concern of yours," he snapped.

"Since *you* appeared on *my* doorstep, I should rather think it is," Marianna replied. "You have seen the soldiers arrayed against me—else you would not have taken to the seas. Your power must be great indeed to take the journey."

"A small troop," Kraken observed. "They would have been no match for me."

"And yet you avoided them. You have secrets, I think. Things you cannot afford to let be known." She leaned forward again, this time placing her chin atop her clenched fist.

"As I said, I am one of the Council of the—" Kraken started.

"And you are here to betray them," she said matter-of-factly.

He shifted impatiently. "I need to see Blaine. I have news for him alone."

She rose from the chair and looked sternly down on him, hands on her hips. "Is this news destined for the Grey God? Or does it stop at the ears of his lackey?"

Kraken screwed up his face in discomfort. "For Arawn."

"Then I will bear that news to him."

"I only speak to Blaine," Kraken insisted.

"*I* am here," she hissed, descending the treads to step closer to him. "Lady Marianna, the *Voice of Arawn*."

She half-drew her blade, brandishing the smooth white pommel-stone under his nose.

"Know this, Master Kraken, that by this oathing-stone, I am Arawn's delegated agent here," she said with a steely timbre to her voice. She slammed the sword home into the scabbard. "Now then, I will have that information you went to such great lengths to deliver."

When he stood silently, she spun on her heel and ascended to the throne again, gesturing to one of her guardsmen. "Send for Donoch," she said. "He can rid us of this—"

"I have seen Erik of Birkenshire," Kraken murmured.

Marianna could not control the reflexive jerk of her head.

Kraken continued: "Then you know of whom I speak."

"We know of him," she admitted dryly, settling gracefully once more onto the throne. "Let us dispense with the games, Master Kraken. I presume you desire some reward for your revelation?"

"I have no need of gold, lady," he said stiffly. "I have enough of my own."

"What precisely would you expect in exchange?" she asked, her voice low and firm.

He studied her with those predator's eyes.

"We want immunity."

"We as in who?" she asked. "This Council of yours?"

"Yes."

"I thought you were here to betray them?" she purred once more.

His face fell into a scowl.

"So, you want what *you* think is best for them," she continued. "Act out of your deep and abiding love for your brethren."

"A tremendous motivator, my lady."

His red-rimmed eyes darted away.

"And I am sure anyone who fails to appreciate that will be removed. And out of your overriding sense of duty, you will take your rightful place at the Council's head. From what do you desire immunity?"

"Arawn moves within Albion," he confided. "He reaches forth to reestablish his rule. The Blood of the Christ fell into his hands. Soon the entire isle could be his."

"So you turn over the quarry in exchange for being left free?"

Kraken offered a small bow. "Essentially, my lady."

Marianna leaned back. "No."

"I— I beg your pardon, lady?" Kraken started.

"We have other spies to find this knight. What makes your effort so invaluable?"

"We are the most powerful coven of undead in the southern kingdoms!" he sputtered. "We have reach—"

"All the more reason to bring you to heel."

"We would be a powerful ally," he pressed.

"Would you?" she countered. "You are not even true to your own Council."

He snarled, revealing yellowed fangs. She bared her own teeth at him in response. The guards stepped up, arms at the ready until Kraken relented, sulking.

"I cannot go to Arawn with this proposal, Master Kraken," she finally said in a flat tone of waning interest. "Do you have anything else to offer?"

He stood for a long moment.

"I do," he seethed at last.

"Then out with it."

"Oh, no, my lady. I need guarantees."

184

"You get no guarantees from me without speaking," she retorted.

He nodded at her blade. "Your sword. You mentioned the oathing-stone," he said, his hungry gaze meeting hers. "I want one."

"This?" Marianna replied with a laugh. "This is the symbol of my sacred covenant with Arawn—it joins us in a bond closer than matrimony. It is not a boon given lightly." She stroked the hilt suggestively.

"I want one, nonetheless," he said.

"I do not have the power to offer such to you."

"Then find someone who does."

"Sheep-headed creature!" Marianna spat, leaping to her feet. "What do you have that could entitle you to such a gift?"

A crafty smile crept across Kraken's cruel mouth.

"A very long time ago, your master lost something of great value, something of great power," Kraken said, drawing himself up. "He has searched for the lifetime of a man since, without success. He thought to replace it by theft from another deity."

The hairs on Marianna's nape prickled as Kraken spoke.

"I have learned who has the great Cauldron".

Chapter Nine

IMPERIAL CITY BY THE SEA

Ravenna's port lay along the western edge of the city, its perimeter softened by encroaching marshland that kept many hands busy during summer months dragging muck and growth from shipping lanes.

Erik strode along the docks under cover of darkness, ignoring the pungent smells of rot and waste. He carried over his shoulder the soldier's kit that had served him since departing far off Caerleon—as well as the satchel of Thelwyn's mystic brew. At his heel trotted the gray Italian fox, tongue flopping out of the side of its mouth while its wary eyes roamed the surrounding buildings and alleys.

Erik scanned the moonlit harbor for Petras' ensign, but of course his ill-fated luck still held, for the ship no longer lay among the vessels crowding the wharf. More ships tugged their anchors in the channel, but the ambassador's warship was not among them either. Nearer the water's edge, a watchman leaned against the wooden railing above the slap of a receding tide.

"Hello!" the knight called out in common Latin, hand raised in greeting. "The ship of the Roman legate—where might I find it?"

The guard squinted beyond the lantern light to get a better look at the newcomer.

"Who are you?" he grumbled.

"A traveler meant to sail with members of the legate's delegation," Erik offered. "When did they sail?"

"Well," the watchman said, watching the gray fox suspiciously, "right about when the alarm bells across the way stopped." He pointed toward the center of the city. "But the imperials have a building just over there," he continued, thrusting his arm out across the waterfront. "Their steward may be able to help you."

Erik mumbled a grudging thanks. Then he brushed past the man, trotting down the wharf toward a building lit by several lamps and flanked by guards equipped with fine-ringed hauberks and well-wrought conical helmets. These were no common German locals.

The first of these guards that Erik met was a younger man with a thin wisp of a beard.

"Hold," he commanded in Latin that was crisply articulated. "Right about there—close enough. Now, keep your hand off your weapon. State your business."

The second guard, an older man, snorted in Greek. "Nothing but thieves about this time of night," he said to his comrade. "Slit his throat, I say, and be done with it." He turned to Erik and, in Latin, demanded, "You heard him. Spill it. Why are you here?"

"The harbormaster thought you would know where I could find Legate Petras' ship."

The younger guard studied Erik in the dim lamplight. "And just who might you be? Just move along!"

Erik remained rooted in place.

"I am traveling with members of the ambassador's retinue," he said diplomatically, though his ire began to rise. "His ship was to be here for me to meet it."

The older man leaned close to the younger and in Greek again urged, "He's a barbarian. Slit his throat and be done with it!"

"I assure you," Erik said, this time in Greek, "I am no more a barbarian than you. My mission is critical to the empire—so my demise will not please the legate. Or so I would venture."

The older guard sputtered, "Liar. The legate made no mention of you."

Erik eyed the lightening east, sensing the imminent arrival of the sun.

"Get Marcus," the younger man suggested. "He will know what needs done."

The older guard shuffled toward the warehouse door and whispered against the wooden surface. Latches clattered, then rattled. He slipped inside. A few moments later the door opened once more, and the soldier beckoned for Erik to follow.

Once inside, their footfalls echoed off stacks of crates and bales from the exotic kingdoms beyond the eastern empire's distant borders. Heady aromas of spices tickled Erik's nose when passing toward the end of the row, where a small door punctuated the wall.

The guard rapped his knuckles on it, then gestured for Erik to enter. The man named Marcus hunched over a simple trestle table littered with ledgers and loose pages of vellum. His bald pate glimmered in the oil lamps lighting the windowless room. When the guard banged the door shut, he looked up with a watery-eyed squint.

"Eh? So you are the man who was to accompany the ambassador to Stanbul?"

He rose from his chair to step closer and sniffed at the knight, then rubbed at his temples thoughtfully.

"Well. Not much more than a boy."

"Sir, I am on an errand from a distant—"

"A distant land. Yes. Yes, of course you are."

Marcus shuffled back to his table, then slid a sealed packet across the planks.

"Do take it," Marcus urged when Erik hesitated.

Erik snatched it up. A seal of crimson wax embossed with the imperial eagle had been pressed into the folded sheet. He cracked it to find two leaves. The first was a writ of passage with assurance of government payment upon Erik's delivery at Constantinople. The other was a scribbled note from Cassandra, expressing regrets for the ambassador's hurried departure and assuring him aid when he reached the Imperial City. Erik tucked the note into his tunic and handed the writ of passage to Marcus.

"What do I do with this?" he asked.

Marcus scrutinized the document.

"Well now," he murmured once more. "It appears someone wants you to arrive in Stanbul with, shall we say, efficiency." He squinted up at Erik again.

"My travel companion," Erik said. "The woman, Cassandra."

"Her cousin the general holds considerable sway, you know," the man observed. "Well, for now, anyway. We have much more pass these walls than even the bureaucrats realize . . . Don't look so surprised. You should probably know there are other interests at court beside the emperor and his favorite. And some of those interests are not . . . natural."

"I don't understand," Erik began.

"Really?"

He rattled about on his desk for a moment. Then he stopped, a look of concern on his wizened face.

"Petras was disconcerted, no?" Marcus asked. "He scurried off with his entire entourage before the ash even settled, didn't he? Granted, he holds little trust for the Goths and their games—but something else frightened him. And I have never seen an imperial afraid like that before."

"Well, whatever it was, the whole affair left me stranded."

"And yet he left you well cared for, no?" Marcus pointed at the writ.

"I suppose," Erik said. "Look, you should know, I cannot just take any passage."

"Oh, don't fret yourself," the steward interjected. "We've transported your ilk before."

"My ilk?" Erik asked with a hitch in his throat.

Marcus sniffed again, deeply, and curled the corner of his mouth down. "Surely just the sort—arriving in the night, covered in . . . well, is that all your own blood on your clothes?"

He squinted once more, and Erik felt those weak eyes drill into his very core.

"You only breathe to speak," Marcus pointed out. "Seldom blink. And if I were to place an ear to your chest, I doubt there would be a heartbeat, would there? And that beast at your heel—that is a creature of rare occurrence."

"You have the advantage of me, sir," Erik admitted.

"Well," Marcus said, his face becoming animated, "don't mistake poor eyesight with an inability to be observant. Make use of those gifts the Lord God blessed you with—no matter how limited. But you are not as the others who have been conveyed through this port. And yet, in some ways, you most certainly are."

He rubbed his bare scalp and waved the writ in the air.

"But be that as it may," he declared, "we must find you transport to Stanbul."

The clouds had piled up over the Italian countryside by the time Petras' dromond exited the swampy channel leading to the sea. The pilot boat a few yards in front of the warship's bow cast off her tow lines. Rowers shipped their long oars. The crew scurried about the decks to haul the single lateen sail up the mast. With a heave on the tiller, her bow plowed into the deep waters of the *Mare Adriaticum*. A gray dawn greeted them with drops of rain before a stiffening wind stretched the canvas, which slapped at the rigging.

Inside the shelter of her cabin, tucked below the main deck, Cassandra heard the groan of the ship's bones. Only a lumpy horsehair cushion softened her perch atop a sea chest, where she tried vainly to keep her feet from the seawater sloshing up through the deck planking. She knew from experience she had a three-and-a-half-week voyage ahead, even for a fast ship like Petras'. She wondered if she were better off here, with the late summer storms blowing in. Not that she was given much choice. Petras had spirited her away with the force of embassy guards immediately following the chaos in the city, and all her protests were met with the simple invocation of *"Cousin to the emperor's own general."*

Only upon her insistence of providence for Erik and Thelwyn did he grudgingly leave the writ with Marcus. This, at least, had finally been done, but she remained angry with the ambassador for not allowing her to remain.

So here she sat, cold, wet, and very seasick.

If these dark elves of Thelwyn's did not chase them down and kill Petras, then she just might end him herself before this voyage was done.

Someone rapped on the makeshift cabin door, a hasty fabrication of sailcloth and crate slats.

"What?" she replied without getting up, for she refused to get her feet soaked in the swirling brine. "Whatever do you want?"

The crude latch lifted, the flimsy door swinging open. Petras stood with his hair and clothes plastered to his skin, soaking wet.

"I . . . well, I thought to check on your comfort," he said almost apologetically. He quickly scanned the tiny cabin. "Oh, this will not do at all. After the storm blows over, I shall instruct the *kentarchos* to install a proper hammock and bring dry bedding. I'm afraid the ship is under orders with the weather, so a brazier is not permitted. Are you angry with me?"

"What did you expect?" Cassandra snapped. "We were to sail tomorrow at the earliest. You told me this yourself!"

Petras grabbed the door jamb when the ship lurched beneath them.

"I apologize, but the necessities of state, you know. An attack on me is an attack on the person of the emperor."

"And I told you," she shouted, jumping off the chest into the salty puddles, throwing herself toward him with a dangerous force of passion, "it was not an attack on you or even the embassy!"

"How can you possibly know that?" he asked, standing his ground. "How could I know that?"

"Well, if you had let me go after Erik, we would know for sure!"

"And then what?" Petras retorted. "You disappear once more? I would have been crucified at the palace gates! And what was that— that apparition? A ship from some mad dream? We could not stay."

Cassandra clenched her fists, straining to quell her passion. She did not want to admit it, but she could see that Petras truly thought he had saved them from forces beyond explanation.

"I told you," she said in a much more restrained tone, "I fear they sought out the Briton and his companion. They had fled their homeland under some duress."

"So they were wanted men," he said, words dripping with accusation. "All the more reason—"

"But I cannot even begin that tale," Cassandra said. "Petras, Erik saved me."

"*And* he returned you to us. I do not understand why you could not just ask me to pay him for his efforts and send him on his way. What binds you to him?"

Cassandra bristled at the critical tone in his voice. "My virtue is intact, if that is what you suggest."

The ship rolled and Petras' fingers clenched the jamb again, but his face remained a mask.

"Even with all the knowledge of the ancients, Archimedes never conceived a ship that could sail the skies," he retorted. "It must have been a trick, an illusion of pulleys and mirrors—nothing more. Sweet

Jesu, nothing more. Flying ships and blue fire be damned. I still have my duties to attend. With all the chaos within the Goth nation, there is opportunity for Justinian to reclaim lost imperial prerogative in the very heart of the Roman homeland. *My* job is to keep sorcery and magic out of it!"

Cassandra folded her arms and frowned.

"Mary, Mother of God," she said more evenly, knowing full well the weight Justinian placed on his shoulders. "I wish no fight with you, dear Petras. But something did happen—something fantastic. My fellow pilgrims were slaughtered. Literally slaughtered. I was held by a mad creature. Not a man, at least not by any definition of the word. And in the very tunnels where martyrs sought protection from Rome hundreds of years ago. Forces are bubbling up from the cracks of the old order—dangerous forces. We cannot simply cover our eyes and hope all will be well for the empire."

"Don't think for a minute that I am blind," the ambassador snorted back. "But some things are not for public consumption. Here."

He handed her a folded note sealed by a beeswax puddle pressed with the familiar imprint of her cousin Belisarius. After Petras had closed the door, she broke the seal, unfolded the missive, and read:

Dearest cousin,

Greetings. While I write this, you are on pilgrimage. I want you to know that I have sent Marcus to Ravenna to ensure you and your companions return safely to us. Marcus will, as he must, fulfill my request and bring you home.

Yours,

B

He knew.

Her cousin had known that something brewed in the west, and he had taken steps to have his people in place to pick up the pieces.

That son-of-a-bitch, she thought.

She quickly touched the points of the cross on her breast and breathlessly begged forgiveness from the Virgin Mother for offending her sweet aunt.

The next weeks passed more slowly for Erik, much as had time aboard the *Pagan Dancer*, with days spent hiding in the hold and nights amid the stars stalking the docks of Ravenna. Missing Petras' ship had been inconvenient enough, but now the knight endured delays with Marcus arranging alternate passage that was able, willing, and trusted enough to handle such a unique consignment.

Then there was the paperwork—oh, sweet Jesu, the imperial paperwork!

Erik marveled that this great machinery of the kingdom accomplished anything of note. No, even once they had finally gotten underway, the ship was required to stop at every third port along the route to take on provisions and to exchange one cargo for another, all of which required more paperwork. Day after day, the knight secluded himself below decks and found himself obsessively counting the sips he took from the precious flasks of Thelwyn's brew. Only when they passed the Hellespont and finally began the last run through the Sea of Marmara to the great city of Constantinople did he begin to regain some hope for his endeavor.

Hills and rolling farmland twisted and turned amid beaches and broken coastline littered with rugged stone. Each new shoreline brought them closer to the heavenward glow as only *Nova Roma* could. The knight stretched over the rail of the wallowing tub, fighting his revulsion of the water, to catch a glimpse of the place where he believed many of the secrets to his quest would be revealed. This stretch of coast had seen from earliest times the rise and fall of empires, from Priam of Troy to Alexander and the Caesars. As when he first saw the Portus at Ostia and the immense lighthouse built to illuminate the harbor, he was sure the city of Constantine would be nothing short of a revelation to the pilgrim from far-off Britain.

He was not disappointed.

When the last high ground fell away, the sight of the impenetrable walls rising on the horizon would have been enough to take his breath away, had he any. The waters ahead were filled with vessels he guessed were laden with goods from lands within the empire as well as regions beyond—furs from the distant north, spices from the Indus in the east, and silks from even more distant China.

Above the piers, the suburbs stretched miles beyond the Marble Tower on his left that marked the juncture of the massive Theodosian wall with the seaward fortifications. Ignoring the bite of the chill autumn air, Erik leaned further across the rail to better examine those massive fortifications that were both imposing and well maintained. How different from what he had seen in Rome, where a century of neglect had allowed their escape through the tumbled remains.

He searched the seaward walls, lower than the soaring bastions built to repulse overland invasion. But the unbroken fortifications stretched as far as he could see, and those stout bulwarks were punctuated with towers at regular intervals.

Any unplanned exit from the city would be much more challenging, should he find himself on the run.

"Sir!" a young sailor called, skidding to a halt from across the deck.

Erik started when he turned, for the inevitable need to escape remained on his mind.

"Master Arias has prepared your transport into the city," the youth gushed.

Erik followed the boy to the ship's stern, where a handful of men, bundled in jackets against the cool air, surrounded a wooden crate. Overseeing them was Arias, the ship's captain, a skeletal figure that could have been mistaken for one of Hilarion's shambling dead. He directed the gaggle in the final assembly of the large box. Erik saw it was lined on the inside with sailcloth and tar to keep out the sun.

"The days are becoming short," Arias quipped, "but not short enough."

Erik shrugged, reaching to scrawl with a crude quill pen on a document offered by the ship's steward.

"They will take you to an imperial warehouse, I am sure," the captain continued. "Once there, you will be left on your own. My apologies, sir, but I have transported many of your kind to and from the city. This is all I can do."

"Yes, of course," Erik murmured, tossing his travel kit into the crate. The gray fox trotted in after, its predator's eyes warily watching the movements of the crew.

"If you have need, we'll be in port for the next month," Arias said.

"Of course," Erik repeated.

But he could not read the captain's eyes to gauge his sincerity. Arias had spent much of his time during the nights when Erik had been on deck locked away in his own cabin.

Crouching for the lack of headroom, Erik crept in to sit atop his gear. The fox turned circles for what seemed a dozen revolutions until finally settling by his side. The crew nailed the final panel into place. Thick cords slithered over the outside, and with a *thump* the imperial seal was affixed to the side.

Shortly after, a voice hailed the ship. The arrival of nosy officials set off a round of clomping when they boarded to inspect the boat. Erik could hear Arias haggling over their assigned berth, the value of various loads of furs and the length of the ship's stay at the docks. But the crate with the imperial seal appeared above inquiry, at least within earshot of its occupant.

From within that crate, Erik settled into his gear when the sun broke over Anatolia. The ever-present hunger lunged from the depths of his belly—a ravening want that could very easily be sated in a back alley or beneath the shadow of a domed church.

He searched his travel kit for one of the flasks of Thelwyn's potion, then sipped it gingerly. However, he was ever fearful of consuming too much and running out of the elixir before he could be either cured of the malady or reunited with the magicker. The liquid burned down his throat—something to which he likely would never become accustomed, for ultimately his body craved fresh, warm blood.

He stoppered the flask, staring at the canvas lining of the crate. The predator sun lurked on the other side. Closing his eyes during the day brought the slumber of the damned, accompanied by rampant dreams. And he wanted no part of those. In ancient days, God had used dreams to communicate with his prophets, to inspire and uplift the dreamer. But Erik's experiences with the sleeping visions had not been as Daniel's, nor even like the prophesies of comfort brought to pagan Greeks by Morpheus. Rather, his had been terrifying and confusing—

such as visions of Hadrian, his war horse and companion since his days as a squire, charging mounds of corpses as a harbinger of the apocalypse. Or apparitions of his home at Caer Baen, where friends and family had gone down fighting the horn-helmeted Huntsman, and the foul magic that had spewed the reanimated dead against the village in massed phalanxes.

His eyes cracked open from his reverie when the box lurched. Voices called out. The crate heaved, swung, then thumped firmly on solid ground. The noises of the busy port assaulted his supernatural senses—shouts, laughter, squeaking pulleys, ox-drawn wagons, and crying birds. Somewhere nearby, a voice carried to the crowds like an Old Testament seer calling the dock crews and sailors to repent of their sins and cleanse themselves, for the day of the Lord's coming must surely be at hand.

Suddenly the crate lurched, then slid. Once again, ropes slithered above and tightened with a creak. After a moment someone clucked, a draft ox bellowed, and the crate jolted into motion.

Erik had assumed the trip from the wharf to be a short one, but the wagon took several leisurely turns through the streets. Around the wagon milled people—and the stampede of their hearts was more intense than he had ever thought possible. He tried to focus on where this route took him, since his daylight eyes lay curled near his leg. Constantinople teemed with activity, so different from Rome, which rotted amid ruins of grandeur and echoed with deteriorating memories. He quickly lost track of their path. He lay back, looking at the crate's ceiling and tracing with his fingertip the ascent of the sun through the sky.

A smattering of bells clattered and clanged in the distance. Then others joined the chorus, echoing across the midday.

He pulled his hand back.

The wagon continued its trek through the city until the sun split the sky between that midday and evening, when the progress slowed even further. Here the noise of civilization became muffled, which accentuated the cloppetty-clop-clop of hooves and the creaking of wagon wheels.

The caisson stopped, voices spoke, then the vehicle lurched forward again. Erik pressed his palm against the wooden planking once more, but the sun no longer shone directly on the crate.

"No," he hissed.

The shadow of a very long building, the echoing, isolated sounds of the wagon, and the absence of the sun meant something else—either the wagon had entered a tunnel or traversed a gate.

Then he felt the sun's rays assaulting the crate once more, and the driver picked up the pace.

They had departed the city.

"Where is he?" Cassandra's voice echoed through the hallway.

She scattered the villa's servants like a falcon among hares when sweeping up to the doors to the chambers of the great *generalissimus*, Flavius Belisarius. After all the disorder at Ravenna, the ship bearing her Briton companion had finally arrived, weeks behind her, when the city was swamped with ships and travelers anticipating the feast days. Thus it was that when she arrived on the dock to take possession of his crate, she found he had already been sent off under imperial escort.

And had been lost.

"My lady! My lady!"

She nearly collided with Procopius, the exuberant scholar and historian that attended to her cousin. His wide brown eyes lowered with respect. But his cheeks were flushed, sprinkled with dark wisps of whiskers to match his curly black locks, reinforcing the appearance of a schoolboy academic.

Yet behind that harmless mask lurked a shrewd wit and a steely devotion to her cousin. Veterans of the wars in the east reported that this sliver of a man had scribbled madly on scraps of vellum while at the walls of Dara, where he stood among the front ranks of Belisarius veterans. He recorded the entire engagement even as blood and mayhem raged about his very ears.

But for all his storied bravery, he winced when she stabbed a finger at his nose.

"Where is my cousin?" she demanded.

"Why, Lady Cassandra," he huffed in reply, "he attends the emperor. The chariot races, you know—"

"Games?" she snorted. "Enough games! Angels could stand at the gates to trump the Second Coming and they would not halt the games!"

She thrust Arius' manifest at him.

"The ship Petras contracted in Ravenna—it arrived, but I was not notified, and my companion is missing!" she stormed, her eyes fiery.

Procopius offered a feeble smile. "I'm sure it was just a minor mix-up with the manifests. I am not involved in all the general's affairs, you know."

"He does not change his boots without you!" she cried. "My servant Sergio watched the docks for days for his arrival. Yet my friends were whisked away before dawn—before anyone else disembarked. Do you know what the harbormaster did when Sergio demanded an

201

explanation? Shrugged his shoulders. Just shrugged his shoulders! Said we could *file a claim*!"

"My lady," Procopius stammered, "what could I know? I am but a chronicler, not the general's confidant!"

""You know every detail of his life," she hissed with exasperation. "From his official duties to his meals to who he sees after the theater closes for decent folk."

"My lady!" Procopius exclaimed, a scandalized expression on his face. She felt a pang of guilt for hinting at her cousin's trysts, but needed answers.

"Look," she said, dropping her hand. "They are here. Somewhere. And if your master will not help me, I'm certain the empress will be happy to seek what my own cousin has hidden from me. You know how she is so . . . *helpful*."

Procopius' face visibly paled.

"Dearest Cassandra, you would not . . ." he sputtered, swallowing the remaining words best left unsaid with a cautionary glance for those who might be a bit too close to the conversation.

Cassandra touched his shoulder almost affectionately. "We stand in my cousin's house," she offered more gently, changing tack. "Come now, loyal of heart. Friend to my cousin . . ."

"My lady, surely there are things afoot which I do not understand," Procopius admitted.

Cassandra leaned in conspiratorially and whispered, "We do not need to understand all things. We just need to know where to find those I am concerned for—those your master assured would be delivered to me."

"But they—well . . ." His voice faltered. "They touch upon things I know nothing of. Things beyond even my—"

Cassandra pressed onward. Her cousin had taught her not to retreat when victory was within one's grasp.

"Dear sir, I bear no concern for those other things," she cooed. "But this *kataphraktos*, this eques from Albion, he aided me when no other even knew where I lay hidden. I owe him a great debt—a debt that cannot be abused. He will not be a pawn of the court."

The scholar spoke quickly in a very low voice. "The broken columns—his coming was foretold in a dream. Find him in the ruins. Not even the patriarch or the emperor himself would deny *him*."

Procopius lowered his eyes and, without another word, scuttled off.

The columns? She mulled over his words. *Find him in the ruins.*

She ran back down the corridor toward her own chambers. She would need warmer garments against the cold of the coming night.

Erik traced his finger over the carvings adorning the applewood spike he had liberated from the dark elves. The letters, such as they were, were alien to him, though he was certain Thelwyn could have deciphered them without a second thought. Something emanated from the wood, something that in the dark elf's hands had caused his skin to crawl, raising an irrational fear within his undead breast.

From a distant and ancient orchard, blessed with power, the elf had said. The significance of that remark was lost on him. And then the elf had uttered the command *"release"* in perfect Latin. Erik could only assume his attacker had meant to send him to some fae netherworld with this elaborately carved stake.

203

The wagon stopped with a creaking jolt and Erik slid the dé Danann handiwork into his belt. A flurry of fading hooves marked the escort returning to the city before dark, then all seemed silent beyond his pine enclosure. He pressed his hand again to the sailcloth lining to gauge the sun's descent. When the orb had sufficiently descended over the horizon, he leaned back and kicked his way out of the crate. He swore his slowed heart missed a few beats—he already knew he wasn't in the city any longer.

The landscape that greeted his eyes was bathed in the bloody throes of the dying corona falling over the western hills. Greek columns rose from the ruins of what was once a city, weathered and broken by the passing of the centuries. Distant lights to the south outlined Constantinople's impenetrable walls. Even at this distance, Erik could sense the heart of an empire pulsing with life. The city represented an order that now relied less on the hobnailed boots of soldiers and more on the convoluted ministrations of wily bureaucrats interpreting laws and chasing coin. All this so that the empire could send bare-heeled monks to far-off corners of the world, where they scratched letters to preserve some knowledge against the barbarian darkness threatening to envelop civilization. His own father had lived, struggled, and fought so that such devotees could educate his children.

When Erik's eyes turned once more to the ribs of broken columns, a biting rush of cool air whistled through the landscape, bearing a warning to his stilling heart that this was holy ground—somewhere he no longer belonged.

Then came the sound of whispers haunting that same wind.

Erik stepped away from the wagon to examine the ruins. His nose wrinkled. The air carried not just the hint of voices but also the stench of human waste. He could sense men and women, likely pilgrims,

204

huddled against the oncoming night while the first cherry-colored firelight blossomed to cast their distorted shadows against the fallen walls.

"What place is this?" Erik growled.

But the voice that answered spoke so subtly, so reverently that it distilled upon Erik's cold flesh like the appearance of the first morning dew.

"You are welcome here."

He searched through the shadows for the source.

"Knight of Albion, you are welcome here."

At his feet, the fox took a few tentative steps forward, then looked over its shoulder at him.

Erik reached for his gear, buckled on his blade, and nodded to the beast. "Show me," he muttered.

The fox trotted into the ruins, its nose high in the air. Into the deepening night, Erik followed with the surety of the Higher Dead, past the pilgrim encampments to a gently rising hill marked by a track well worn from the passage of many, many feet. Atop the slope stood a single thick column—a fluted pedestal twice as wide as a man's height and rising twenty feet into the sky. Amid the stench of humanity, rats scuttled between ice-frosted relics and offerings left all around the base.

A single flimsy ladder leaned against the column, inviting him up.

Erik's skin prickled, a warning against the unfamiliar. He scanned the top of the column for movement, but the heights were obscured by a ragged canvas sheet teased by the drafts.

"You are welcome here." The words repeated yet again on the wind.

"Keep an eye out," he growled at the fox. "Saint Michael's bloody bones, I have no desire to be ambushed while I'm up there."

The fox plopped onto its haunches, its tongue lolling ever out of the side of its mouth.

Erik tested the ladder, then started to climb.

Far above the broken column, stars filled the clear sky. Rung by rung, Erik ascended, staring up into the dizzying expanse of that nocturnal bowl until he could place a hand on the upper lip. He peered over the edge to see the canvas tarpaulin stretched over a simple frame to form a tent. Someone waited for him within.

"Not much room for a visitor," Erik observed aloud.

"Most of those who visit," the reedy voice replied, "do so in the daylight and speak to me from the ladder. But . . . *you are welcome here.*"

That voice was the same, in his ears now rather than his head. The knight took another step up, then slid onto the rough surface.

"Well, well . . ." the voice observed. "Britain yet survives, yes?"

The figure emerged from the shadows. His face was covered with years of silvery white strands that blended with the threads of the homespun garments covering his emaciated body. Bushy eyebrows perched over narrowed eyes. This was a *stylite*, one of the holy men spoken of by his childhood tutors. Such monks dwelt atop broken columns, where they sought to become closer to God. They were driven in that effort not just by finding proximity to the heavens but through the rejection of all things dross or worldly.

The hermit grinned, exposing his few remaining teeth. He reached out to touch the hem of Erik's shirt with skeletal fingers.

"Oh, I can see you're wondering why a man would suffer in the cold to remain here," he said. "It is a long story."

Then, of a sudden, his language changed from Latin to Cymric, catching Erik off guard.

"Albion's shores are so far away. You could say memories of that land are the anchor to this world that keeps me from shedding my flesh to rise with the saints. But what keeps *you* here, walker in shadows?"

"You know?" Erik asked, also in his native tongue.

The stylite looked past Erik's shoulder. "The passage of one consigned to limbo—this dead purgatory—is something that travels before you, like a dream or a vision."

"How did you get the imperials to bring me here?" Erik asked.

The mystic touched the side of his nose. "Favors owed . . . favors paid. Tis the way of this land," he said with a laugh, a dry cackle that still carried a touch of humor. "Not all who seek guidance beneath the hand of a crazed old monk are the unwashed."

"But why?"

The stylite's eyes narrowed. He reached out, placing his hand flat against Erik's chest.

Something powerful exploded within the young knight's chest— something he'd not felt since his father had lifted the crucifix before him to keep him, his own son, at bay so long ago at Caer Baen. The energy of faith burned through muscle and bone to Erik's very core. His head snapped back—

A horn echoed across the waters surrounding Constantine's city, a series of notes that broke from the plains of Thrace with urgency.

The sea churned, wild and thick with crimson foam. Again, the notes sounded, this time along the low-slung hills of the coastline— familiar tones that recalled forests and fens of distant isles. Baying hounds followed, racing along the ridge, accompanied by shrieks and screams from homesteads in their path. Horsemen chased after the hounds under exotic banners trimmed in gold. Their lances dipped, and the screams fell silent.

In the distance, a great army camped beyond arrow shot of the city's imposing walls. A series of staccato flashes marked shots of rock and iron thrown against those walls.

Within the shuddering bastions, shadows moved through the alleys. They jabbed, then darted into corners and crawled from sewer grates. They raced across the great plazas and around the stolid basilicas with their thick foundations and religious embellishments—flowing webs of darkness that twisted under doorways and through the meanest taverns as well as the great halls of the wealthy and powerful.

The horn sounded yet again. Hounds responded throughout the city in tens, then fifties, then hundreds. The cries of the Hunt echoed across the waters of the Golden Horn.

Erik stood at the water's edge, which was awash with broken timber, torn canvas, and bloated corpses.

"Where are you?" he shouted into the tumult. "Surely you'd not have me believe this is another's work?"

From deep black pools, that figure emerged, gray, tall, and straight against the chaotic sky.

"You believe this my handiwork?" the apparition replied with a hint of amusement in his voice. "Oh, my son, I am not a being of war. I am the harbinger of peace. I am but the guide to the life beyond—the steward of the dead for a short time. But now, after months of searching, you are found."

"For what purpose? You cannot torment me further. My fear of you died in Caer Baen."

"Oh, yes . . ." the Grey One replied. "The remains of that muddy burgh have nearly disappeared already. But your family . . . a father and

208

a sister, if I recall. They wander the fens of Annwyn. Don't fret for them. An eternity is plenty of time to search for the loved one lost to them that night."

Erik clenched his fists. "I will free them—by Saint Michael's flaming sword, I will take your head!"

A smile touched the Grey God's cruel lips.

"Tch . . . never fear. I shall not be overly eager to help them ascend. Oh, and do thank your friends in Londinium for consigning them to this vagabond fate—for they chose to steal you away rather than allow you to defend them."

He waved an arm across the battle that played out in the distance.

"Would you bring such a doom to this place?" Arawn continued. "For the tides of wyrd are rising, and I have need of sons of Albion in my own kingdom. We can protect the isle from this."

He took a step toward Erik, and that step jarred the earth and echoed in the knight's bones.

"Even at this great distance, you shall not slip through my fingers again," rumbled the god of the dead.

A light flashed near Erik, white and hot, driving back the writhing shadows. Arawn's eyes darted to the presence.

"Who are you?

The crippled figure of the stylite appeared next to the knight, his form bathed in the pure white light.

"You . . ." the Grey One murmured. "You!"

The stylite waved a hand.

The vision erupted in a storm of brilliant colors, and the Grey One was gone.

Erik staggered and skeletal hands clamped his arm with an iron-banded strength, keeping him from toppling over the edge of the column.

Erik sank to his knees.

"I had to be sure," the stylite whispered in his ear. "They seek after me as well. Here I am called by the name of my predecessor on the column, who was Daniel. But I am of Albion's shores. My name, given by indifferent parents, is Dylan."

The crisp night air bit Cassandra's cheeks but could not deter her from rushing through the Blanchernae Gate into the streets beyond of Constantinople's Kosmidion suburb. Empty churches and shuttered manor homes fell away while she cantered in the trail of her family's steward, flanked by two of her cousin's soldiers who rode along to ensure her safe return. If she hadn't been so cold, she would have snickered at the guard captain's face when she rode up with orders for passage and Belisarius' own men at her back. She just hoped the old officer would be equally compliant upon her return.

She tucked her chin further into the edge of her cloak, but the gesture was futile against the chill wind. Ahead lay the edge of cultivated gardens, where the road darted deep into the northern environs. This was a place the ancient Megarian colonists had once called home but was now a pilgrimage destination for many who flocked to consult the ascetics who dwelt in the ruins.

The mare pounded along the deserted track, plumes of steam racing past Cassandra's face from the steed's nostrils. To distract herself from her own discomfort, she took a moment to ponder the lives of these column-dwellers, isolated and exposed. Even with her penchant for traveling the pilgrims' trail, she never desired such an existence—even in the hope of losing enough of her flesh to lighten her soul. Then again, *her* travels had led her to the pits of a dead city, where dangers dwelt that were far more horrifying than she could have ever imagined.

Something rushed through the air above them.

Then another. And another.

The horses spooked and bucked, causing the riders to struggle for control. Three figures whirled before them, their forms obscure in the darkness but for their faces. Parchment skin, which even in the dark bore a starkly visible pallor tinged with frigid blue, was stretched tightly over their skulls. Their eye sockets were empty wells of deepest black.

One apparition rushed Cassandra in a fury that blotted out stars and sky. Her horse skittered sideways, then bolted.

She tumbled to the hard, frozen ground, gasped for breath that fled upon impact.

The creature pounced, thrusting its face close. Hair like wild frosted grass lashed Cassandra's skin. She turned dazed eyes to those bottomless voids sunk in the horror's visage. Then it shrieked, expelling breath that brushed her eyelashes with ice.

Chaos erupted. Horses screamed. Soldiers cursed. Steel weapons clashed with the supernatural. Cassandra forced out a supplication to Saint Helena, but the creature thrust an ethereal hand through her flesh into her chest, clenching its fingers around her heart.

Cassandra screamed.

Wiry fingers remained about his arms even as he regained his balance.

211

"I had to be sure," Daniel pleaded, "that you were the one from my dreams!"

Erik struggled to cast off the cobwebs spun about his mind, to escape the voice of the Grey God echoing in his head.

"There is much you need to know," the stylite continued. "So much! But now you must go."

Erik fought to focus his eyes on the monk. "I do not understand," he said.

"There is no time. Go!"

Daniel released him. Erik staggered until he snatched the top of the ladder rail. Somewhere in the hillocks a woman screamed. The knight scanned the ruins, but with the echoes through the stones, he could not place the origin of the cry. However, the familiar already darted ahead, showing him the way like a Northman's sunstone. Erik swung onto the ladder, gripped the rails with his boots, and slid to the ground.

By the time he arrived at the scene, the silvered glow of the quarter moon showed there was no longer a skirmish. Before him lay broken bodies. Fine Roman armor had proved of little worth against the lingering ethereal attackers clothed only in shreds of swirling black. Those creatures hovered over a fallen form lying apart from the others. One of them rose above the others, its face twisted in a predator's snarl.

"The cup!" that harpy hissed in Greek.

The others joined in to form a shrill chorus. "The cup! The cup! The cup!"

Erik drew his spatha, striding forward with a will.

"I've no knowledge of a cup," he growled, swinging the blade at the apparition that drifted over Cassandra. "Move aside. I will not ask again."

212

Still chanting their screeching litany, the creatures rushed the knight. They shot past with bone-chilling screams, raking claws outstretched like furies that tore his flesh and burned to the bone. But when Erik swung his spatha, its edge bit nothing.

"The cup! The cup! The cup!" The words jumbled through his head, over and over again.

"I've no cup for you!" he shouted. "But I *will* have her *back*!"

He charged toward Cassandra, who struggled weakly beneath the last phantasm. But the two other creatures returned with a ferocity that bore him down, grinding his flesh into the earth. One thrust a clawed hand into his back, reaching for his heart, its probing of supernatural substance causing excruciating pain even to Erik's own undead flesh.

Then it screamed.

Black wings beat the air furiously when it lifted, pulling away from Erik with baleful cries that echoed into the ruins. Eager for prey and undaunted by the failure of its companion, the second pounced and Erik thrust the spatha's blade, but the semi-substance of the creature changed, and it hit him with the full weight of a living body. It drove him down into hard gravel once more, fracturing stone, and what felt like a branch thrust against his ribs—the dé Danann stake.

Erik threw himself against the fury with all his strength, then flung himself onto his back. The creature floundered for only a heartbeat before lunging again. When it struck, its ebony orbs revealed a desperate hunger like that of the Higher Dead yet different or farther lost from the path of the living. He threw an arm against the creature's chest, a futile move against its remarkable power, but one that gave him an opportunity to thrust the applewood spike into its breast.

The runes erupted in blue flame. The phantasm beat at the air with its wings, but its substance tore apart into effervescent cinders like a log in a fire. The other creature hovered just out of reach. Erik staggered to his feet, shaking off the icy cold that lingered around his stagnant heart.

"You want the cup?" he snarled, thrusting the stake at the phantasm.

Cassandra gurgled. Erik lunged toward the third fury that held her in its claws. The creature recoiled, releasing its talons from her body, but Erik caught it before it took wing. Runes flared and those wings boiled into ash.

The surviving fury loosed a wail that reverberated through the very stones beneath Erik's feet. It winged upward until it was only a shadowed blot against the sky.

Erik fell to his knees next to Cassandra, pressing his fingers to her neck for signs of her heart. There was nothing but cold stillness.

The cup . . . the cup . . . echoed in his mind. Yet the meaning of the refrain was beyond him.

Erik scooped up Cassandra's still form, scrambling back the way he came through the ruins toward the broken column.

"Help me . . ." Erik choked when he found the ladder.

Nothing replied from atop the stone.

"Please," he implored. "Help me."

Still there was no reply from above. Yet within his head continued the spectral refrain of *the cup . . . the cup . . . the cup . . .*

He hefted Cassandra across his shoulder, then reached for the ladder. Through his familiar's vision, he became aware of curious pilgrims gathering, marveling at what they had witnessed. But he remained focused upward on the height of the column. Pain shot from his wounded back to numb fingers when he started to climb.

"Michael, Champion of Heaven, please . . . please . . ." he prayed.

214

He strained upward with each step, but each increment appeared to bring the stylite's hovel no closer.

The cup . . . the cup . . . the cup . . . continued to echo in his mind.

Somewhere between ground and summit, he slumped against the ladder. Clearly, he was not a true *vrykolakas*—he had seen those cursed creatures demonstrate horrifyingly amazing feats. But the fury's talons had wounded him deeply, those open gashes sapping the strength from his body with each oozing step.

Then someone creaked the ladder behind him. A hand gently pushed him.

"Keep on," a quiet voice said.

Keep on.

Erik took another rung, then another, then another. His hand trembled each time it clenched around the next, threatening to falter. But the hand below steadied him, urging him further. The mantra of *the cup* was soon drowned out by a steady choir of voices from the ground urging him onward.

At last, he gained the top, where Daniel's own skeletal hands pulled Cassandra onto the broken column. Erik looked down to discover this Samaritan's identity. But the ladder sagged under only his own weight. No one else stood beneath him.

The stylite placed a hand over Cassandra's mouth, checking for her breath. Then he pulled back her cloak to expose the frostbitten, mottled flesh that marked the fury's attack.

"Dear God on High," he murmured, tracing the points of the cross over her body.

He grabbed a nearby wooden bucket that sloshed and crackled with ice. He reached inside his homespun habit and, after a moment of fishing around, produced a simple cup, which he dipped into the bucket. Cradling Cassandra's head, he gently pressed the vessel to her lips.

A blinding concussion threw Erik backwards toward the ladder. Daniel pressed his fingers to Cassandra's throat in long strokes until the muscles in her neck moved and she swallowed the fluid. Then he tipped the cup once more to her mouth. This time she drank of her own accord, breath flaring from her nostrils. She gasped, a desperate sort of noise. Her eyes fluttered.

"You are here, daughter," the stylite said, setting down the cup to examine her face.

Cassandra's eyes remained unfocused.

Erik picked himself up from the heap in which he had landed, regarding the stylite in wonder.

"The cup," he said pointedly. "Those creatures wanted a cup—that cup."

He reached for the simple vessel, hammered of copper or bronze, but pulled back his fingers before laying his hand upon it.

"Yes, yes." Daniel grimaced. "They came for the cup. Relics are bearers of power that act as honey to the bee, drawing those that consume light and life."

"It is but a cup."

Daniel's eyes met Erik's.

"It is *the* cup," he whispered. "Many have sought it, and, I suppose, mainly the unfortunate ever have found it. Joseph of Arimathea, the same who tended to the body of our Lord, carried it to Albion."

"That can be but a legend," Erik said.

"Then we exist in myth and legend, young knight . . . and it is time to return items of power to those same realms."

"I still do not understand," Erik said.

216

The stylite lifted the cup reverently. "Two very young men once upset the balance between light and darkness, and only misery has followed."

Then he returned his eyes to the knight, and Erik saw the glint of tears, warm and steaming, rolling down the holy man's ruddy cheeks.

"The cup no longer belongs with me."

Philosophers have oft spoken of understanding one's place in the world as the key to enlightenment. Yet even as Erik settled Cassandra into the saddle of a trooper's horse, that understanding appeared more and more elusive. He glanced at the ruinous scene that remained among the broken stones even with the pilgrims helping to lay out the bodies of the guardsmen for collection by the authorities.

Eastward across the waters of the Bosporus, the coming of *Sol Invictus* once more was heralded by the knight's own undead senses. Since the beginning of time, the ancients had revered the power of the *Victorious Sun* that drove back the minions of the darkness. And yet he knew it for a temporary illusion. Darkness remained always beyond the reach of its light. Those that hunted in the shadows had to await its regular course.

Erik looked to the west and wondered at the chaos that would be unleashed in this city should the mustered forces of the underworld find the power to spew beyond Albion. The world already faced an age of men and iron—such an eruption of the netherworld would consume those who remained.

Of this he was certain.

Cassandra pushed his hand aside from her saddle.

"I am fine," she murmured. "Truly, worry more about the sunrise."

He could not argue that point, but he found his priorities shifting. He had meant only to defeat the resurgent Arawn and to stop the doom that god had promised. Yet other powers threatened him with distraction from that seemingly straightforward task. He attempted to order his mission into some form of priority but finally had to admit that for the moment all was beyond his understanding.

He grabbed the saddlebow of another horse and swung himself onto the beast.

Cassandra reassured him with a weak smile, and with that they rode through the remaining moonlight to seek shelter from the coming day.

Chapter Ten

To Succor The Weak

Aldonzo leaned against the tree, stretching his back with a creak. He scanned across the hillside to the horizon. The prince enjoyed these brief respites from the jarring wagon, where he could regain his bearings and search their surroundings. The stalwart Kien had taught him an old scout method, taking in details bit by bit with successive quick glances to build up the picture in his mind. The southern prince missed that old soldier. Of a certainty, he had deserved better death than expiring in the dirt of that accursed castle with his body trampled beneath a pirate's boot.

Retaining the details, however, troubled Aldonzo, even with repeated practice. His mind had always been a bit scattered, easily distracted by trivial things. Focused effort required committing things to memory, then recalling them later. Still, his social diary held no entries for feasts and poetry recitals. Days had run into weeks, and the brilliant foliage of autumn was already a muddy memory blanketing the ground during their interminable journey to Brest. And, worst of all for the prince of rags, boredom began to overtake fear.

Not far off, the wagon leaned against the roadside like a drunkard where the wheel had spun off the axle. *That* had been a rough moment for all the passengers, not least because of the immediate return of Whip's temper after dragging himself from the mud. Axe had borne a share of Whip's wrath for breaking out into a guffaw. He now perched atop the wagon, alternately watching his charges, who huddled in chains against a tree, and the road.

Whip rode out with the wheel to the nearest village in search of a craftsman to repair it. After the slaver had been gone for a time, apprehension spread across Axe's face when he spied up the road.

They were not alone on the old Roman road.

The day before, the wagon had trundled along with Aldonzo folded into his usual corner near the front. He had watched Elaetha and Fainche since dawn, patiently reminding himself not to push their budding trust. The younger girl had come to sit by him with her straw doll. He felt the suspicious eyes of the older women. Yet this child and her sister were probably the only souls on the wagon that knew the Arree Mountains rising on their left hand. To return to his mission to recover Marianna, he needed their knowledge. However, making a new ally was not enough, for knowledge meant nothing without the opportunity to apply it.

For weeks the bedraggled prince had watched his captors in their routines. One day, while fashioning Fainche's plaything, a dirty straw companion, he had decided to focus on the wagon's carriage, since that lay within reach.

Their conveyance was an old Roman *plaustra*, likely obtained by the slavers from their eastern travels and more solidly built than the cumbersome oxcarts of the locals. The wheels were reinforced with iron bushings, pinned into place by wrought collars locked in place with a retaining pin.

Forests lay south of the road, stretching to the horizon. Beyond the edge of the road to the north ran the stream they had crossed that morning, lined with thousands of flat rocks. During their midday break, Aldonzo palmed a smallish stone and slipped it inside the shackle on his left arm. He ignored the pinch against his skin for the remainder of the day. Hours later, when the wagon finally stopped for the night, he strained for the wheel just at the limit of his reach. Thankfully, the rig was old, and the shaft was rusted thin. Once he had the pin straight, he waited until the slavers were looking the other way and, with a few discreet raps, dropped it into the weeds. Then he gently worked the collar back and forth until it barely rested on the hub. He left it hanging there. Aldonzo curled up and dozed till morning.

While the rest of the group made ready to clamber aboard once more, the prince gave the collar just enough of a twist to ensure it was loose. A few agonizing miles passed before the road jostled the collar off. It fell into the stones with no more of a clatter than any of the other loose pebbles beneath the wagon's wheels.

They rolled on for several hundred more feet before the hub splintered and the rig slammed precipitously to a halt. Arms windmilling, Whip flew into the river. This was when Axe committed the grievous sin of laughing at his comrade's misfortune. The slaves tangled in a painful heap on the side of the wagon. Aldonzo, afraid he would suffocate amid the press of bodies, struggled to loose himself.

Whip staggered to his feet, wiping the silty water from his eyes. Then those same wicked eyes fell upon his heckler. He sloshed to the shore, cursing loudly. Whip grabbed his namesake weapon to lay all his outrage into Axe, who quickly recovered to brandish the tool of his own trade with equal fervor. Facing the prospect of more than a lash, Whip sulked off, blowing foam and spittle from his lips. He flung the cage door open, hauling the slaves from the broken cart. Most held up hands in supplication. When Whip raised his arm against them, Axe admonished him with a single word that left him frozen.

One must not damage the merchandise, Aldonzo thought when he could breathe again.

Nevertheless, a few of the captives snickered behind their pleading hands. But the vengeful Whip tripped them onto their backs, lashing the bottoms of their feet with pent-up rage. Axe appeared oblivious to this torment, and Whip took it to heart. When the rawhide fell on Aldonzo's soles, the prince cried out unexpectedly from the pain. However, in short order he found himself hobbled in chains to a nearby tree with the rest of his companions.

Satisfied the slaves were under his control, Whip set about determining the extent of the damage, curses still frothing from his lips. He gathered up the shattered wheel and set out to find assistance. From that point on, Axe stood guard, his eyes shifting first to the slaves, then to Whip's empty route, then to the way they had come—before returning to the slaves.

It was late in the day when a pillar of dust appeared in the distance along the road.

<hr />

Near evening, the source of the dust revealed itself as a long train of slow-moving carts, wagons, lorries, and stooped human chattel. The rival slavers had crossed their path once again.

"What was it you were all fighting about?" Aldonzo asked in his scholarly Celtic, mouthing each syllable carefully.

The curt dialect spoken by his jailers was hardly recognizable, but he believed they knew enough of the region's native tongues to get by. Aldonzo's carefully correct enunciation reinforced the outward image of a soft and simple house servant that knew little of the world beyond a comfortable manor.

When a faint stirring among the indistinct shapes on the horizon hinted they had been spotted, Axe took up the chain, dragging his charges deeper into the wood. Amid the bramble, he found a soft mossy patch and gestured to the slaves to sit on the ground. They complied. Aldonzo did the same, though irritated to be farther away from Elaetha and Fainche. Two dour matrons squatted between him and them, stodgy women who had likely spent years in middens slaughtering boars and beating down bread dough. They each had thick muscled hands that would put many warriors to shame. Axe wrapped the chain round a tree, then secured it with a barrel-shaped lock.

Before long, the train of slavers reached the abandoned wagon. Axe watched intently through the screen of trees while those other brutes poked around for anything of value, grumbling when they found nothing. A few cutthroats carefully examined the trampled dirt and grass around the wagon. From his vantage point, Axe nervously twisted the weapon in his hand.

An outbreak of laughter startled him when one of the slavers found a straw doll trampled in the mud by the water.

Aldonzo's stomach began knotting. He needed a confrontation, anything to cause confusion.

So he belched, and loudly.

Axe shot him a furious look and hugged close to the tree. Shouts carried from the road as his competitors plunged into the trees. Axe growled an abrupt curse and sprung the lock. As he fumbled for a heartbeat with the chain, Aldonzo snatched the links from his captor's grip and heaved with desperation, snaking it out of the rings on each captive's ankle cuffs.

The rival slavers crashed through the trees, shouting when they caught sight of the escapees.

With a murderous snarl, Axe hefted his weapon toward their unruly pursuers. Aldonzo took that moment to launch himself toward the slaver, planting his foot firmly on Axe's arch and driving the heel of his hand up under the man's chin. Blood spurted from Axe's mouth over the matrons. The women screamed, then the other slavers pounced upon them.

Aldonzo ducked under one of Axe's meaty fists, not stopping to see if it was meant for him or their attackers. The prince snatched up Fainche and grabbed Elaetha's hand.

"Run!"

Elaetha stumbled but caught herself, then quickly fell in alongside. They dashed through the underbrush and trees, legs pumping to put distance between them and the chaos.

"Those slavers . . . they will come for us . . ." Elaetha huffed.

"That's why I left Axe standing!" Aldonzo replied. As the prince predicted, the rival slavers clustered around the easterner and his deadly blade, too intent for the moment on relieving him of all his prizes rather than paying attention to a few bolters.

Aldonzo dragged the sisters along for hours, weaving between the trees in the scant moonlight while intently listening for noises of pursuit over the rustle of leaves in the night breeze.

They pushed on despite their exhaustion to make as much distance as possible before the moonlight was completely gone. With little Fainche clinging to his back, progress remained slow through the wood. Elaetha kept up handily, more than once catching Aldonzo by the arm when he tripped on a hidden obstacle.

After a time, he spoke: "You have not asked me . . ."

He realized, too late, that he wasn't sure how to finish the question.

Elaetha padded silently around a sapling and let the query hang.

"Um, I escaped?" he continued awkwardly. "Took both of you with me? You must wonder why? You *must* wonder why."

"Do I?"

"Do you not?"

She did not reply.

He attempted to puzzle out her expression, but the light was already fading, leaving her but a shadow in the deepening dark. When her veiled eyes met his, he felt an unnerving sensation of her seeing right through him, though in reality her vision must have been just as obscured by the encroaching night. He took a few more steps, nearly sprawling over a tree root. Elaetha caught his elbow.

"Maybe we should stop for a while," she said finally.

He laid the dozing Fainche against a tree. "I guess that would be best," he murmured.

Thankfully the weather had been sunny and dry for the past few days, so Fainche's nest was mossy and soft. He searched for another place to settle into but changed his mind. He shook out his tired limbs.

"I have first watch," he declared.

"Nonsense," Elaetha replied. "You must be exhausted."

"The situation demanded a forced march," Aldonzo said, leaning against a tree.

"I have not been carrying a little girl."

And with that, he could not argue.

"Get some sleep," she said reassuringly. "I will take the watch."

She picked out a spot nearby to also settle against a tree. "When Cetus rises, I will wake you," she murmured.

Cetus? he thought. *The Greek name for the Whale . . .*

Part of him debated remaining awake, but of course she was right. Exhaustion was catching up with him. Besides, they were all on the run together now. He settled next to Fainche, figuring if she moved, he would awaken.

And so he slept.

"Aldonzo . . ."

He stirred, momentarily groggy, then suddenly snapped awake. Elaetha leaned in close to his ear, whispering his name.

"What's happening?" he sputtered.

"I am exhausted." She yawned.

He rubbed his eyes, then scrambled to his feet. When his arms tangled in twigs and dry leaves, he realized that Elaetha had not been idle during her watch. Scrub brush had been piled around and over him and Fainche, shielding them from the chill breeze and trapping body heat.

"Might rain again," she explained. "Or worse."

"Has there been any trouble?"

"None," she said simply.

She crawled into the boughs that still retained warmth from his body, curling up against her sister. After a few moments of stirring, Elaetha snored quietly.

Aldonzo stamped his feet to stir the blood in his legs and ward off the cold. The wood was silent, such as woods are. Birds still flitted through branches and squirrels stirred in the underbrush. Somewhere overhead was the leathery flap of a passing bat.

So not the deathly silence that suggests men nearby, he thought with relief.

High overhead rain pattered onto high leaves. A few moments later, those leaves shed large drops in irregular rhythms, in direct contrast to the soft sprinkling above. Aldonzo dodged the raindrops to the relatively dry shelter of a nearby ancient pine, carefully maintaining a line of sight to Elaetha's shelter.

He sniffed the air, then himself. He wished he had not taken that final whiff, so he stepped back out into the rain. Surely they had left traces of their flight that could be tracked in the light of day. The prince determined to rise before dawn to once more begin their journey. But he had no idea where to lead them.

To the south rose the slopes of the Arree Mountains, by Fainche's own admission the girls' old home. His entire plan hinged on keeping ahead of their captors long enough to reach the safety of guarded walls—somewhere out there. But gaps in his knowledge of these two Breton girls could throw his whole scheme off track. They were educated, they were locals, but they were also slaves. And despite all his efforts, he could be leading them all back to a former owner and renewed bondage. He wondered if the girls would help him if they realized the possibility. They'd remained cooperative enough thus far, but he had shared little of himself.

Still, nothing could be done until the girls awoke and they began moving again. Escape from the immediate problem was imperative.

And then, in typical fashion, the prince of rags and chains began to question dragging them into the wilds on his mad quest. Surely Fainche with her child's legs could never keep pace, and she would accomplish the coming journey on his back. Yet Elaetha was necessary, but she would not accompany him without the child.

Thoughts such as these kept his mind active and awake. He was surprised how energized he felt. Freedom, once more regained, was a heady thing for the young Visigoth. For the first time in months, he no longer suffered the lash or feared for his life. As well, for the first time in years, he realized with a start, he was not living a routine proscribed by courtly obligations. The coming day was all his, to do with what he may.

At that moment he realized the wood *had* become truly silent.

Hardly daring to breathe, he scanned the wood, watching, listening, smelling—and caught the unmistakable stink of wet dog. But dogs typically create noise, and he heard none. The only time he'd encountered such silence, without men around, was at that blasted fort on the Cymric shore months ago. But this time nothing happened.

After a very long time, the canine odor faded. The returning sounds of woodland animals were a welcome familiarity, though for hours after, his senses were on edge. In time, birds filled the branches with sweet songs, heralding a day that looked as though it would dawn bright and clear, if a bit cold.

As soon as there was enough light to guide them through the bramble, he bent down to shake the girls gently awake. By the time they continued their hike, he had determined to push for the mountains. While it was the most straightforward plan, the prospect of giving Elaetha an explanation kept gnawing at him. But he set it all aside when he hefted Fainche onto his back. He placed his feet on a southward path and began to walk.

Elaetha wordlessly followed, though when he glanced back for signs of pursuit, he caught glimpses of her watching him with those piercing eyes.

He only lasted a few minutes before the tension rose to an unbearable level. "You are from this area originally, aren't you?"

"Yes," she replied after several paces. "But you are not."

"Septimania," Fainche chimed in, proud of her new word.

"Yes," Aldonzo confirmed. "I did say so before, didn't I?"

He tried not to sound petulant, but she was as skilled as a Roman orator in turning the conversation back on him.

"So how did a Goth noble come to be a Breton slave?" she asked.

His mood darkened. "Is it that obvious?" he asked.

"Pardon my saying, but you appear too soft to have been long a slave."

"Yeah, too soft!" Fainche slapped him on the top of his head.

"You handled yourself well back there," Elaetha observed. "Skilled, and you fight with finesse. Not the clumsy flinging fists of a common slave."

"Yeah, you showed that Scowl-Britches!" Fainche agreed with gusto.

229

While her compliment was satisfying, he determined to navigate the conversation back on course.

"Elaetha," Aldonzo ventured, "do you have family nearby?"

She stared at the ground for several more paces before replying in a neutral tone, "I do not know."

Fainche yelled loud enough to make him wince. "Elaetha! You said they were!"

"Shush, Fainche," Elaetha whispered, her finger pressed to her own lips. "Someone might hear."

Suddenly the child became frightfully vigilant, her wide eyes darting to the nearby trees and undergrowth. "You think Scowl-Britches followed us?" Fainche asked breathlessly.

"Let us avoid that," Alonzo whispered, then asked the older sister, "So. *Do* you have family nearby?"

"They were," Elaetha replied.

Several more fragments of their past fell into place, and a stone weight dropped into the prince's belly. The picture of what awaited them in the mountains had become overgrown and abandoned.

"Can we take refuge there?" he queried, trying to keep some hope alive for all his effort.

Elaetha looked straight ahead, jaw set.

"Maybe."

They hurried on through the day, lapping water at streams to slake their thirst and plucking at berries to take the edge from their hunger. Aldonzo's growling stomach betrayed all their thoughts—say what you would about the cruel and murderous Axe, the man could *bake*.

With the urgency of their pace through the wood, they could not set snares to catch game or approach the occasional farmhouse to beg or steal. Once beyond Whip's reach and further removed from traveled roads, Aldonzo thought they might risk such contact. But for now, the prince led them through the tangle of trees and brush, for he had a sense of the direction they must take.

The nearby mountains stretched for miles to the east and west, so he reassured himself with the likelihood that she did not yet recognize the route and could not contribute any direction to their flight.

Fainche, however, took up a new mission to scout the surrounding wood, craning her neck back and forth, starting at any small noise. The twisting and writhing weakened Aldonzo's grip on her. Soon after midday, Fainche's grip began to slip, forcing Aldonzo to slow his pace. After what felt like a painful eternity, they finally stumbled upon a stream that led them to a stand of wild apple trees. There they sprawled for a rest, picking puckered apples from the ground.

Aldonzo screwed up his face and chewed on one cold, soft globe.

"Why *did* you bring us along?" Elaetha asked, a reserved expression on her face.

"Um . . ." He fumbled, caught off guard by her sudden return to the conversation of the day. "I needed a guide."

"Is that all?"

"It is," he replied, focusing on uncovering another apple among the leaves.

"Then why bring her?" she asked, nodding at her sister, who dangled her feet toward the icy water at the stream's edge.

"You wouldn't have come without her," Aldonzo said matter-of-factly.

"I am a slave. My desires aren't part of the picture."

231

"Would it have been better if she remained in a cage?" he riposted.
"Would it?"

"Why do you do that?" he snapped.

"Do what?"

"Never mind!" he said, sinking his teeth into another bruised, sour apple.

Then he stood and threw it into the stream, scattering a flock of ducks. Fainche squealed when they burst into the air. Aldonzo cursed himself under his breath. *What if Axe and Whip see that, idiot?* he thought, gritting his teeth and forcing himself to breathe slowly until the frustration passed.

Elaetha's face remained maddeningly calm.

He retook his seat.

"I was a guest of Mattheus, High King of Cymru across the sea to the north," Aldonzo said. "I was serving him on a mission when pirates captured me. Eventually, I escaped. But slavers found me when I came ashore."

"So you want to return to Cymru?" she asked.

"I do," he said simply.

"And our family might help you do that?"

"Would that be a bad plan?" Aldonzo asked.

Her shoulders sagged for a moment.

"I just thought you were a bit more than a mercenary. Although it still doesn't explain why you brought Fainche."

Aldonzo lurched to his feet, suddenly tired of the question-and-answer game. Fainche flinched when his shadow fell over her.

"Climb on up," he barked. "Time to get moving again."

She scrambled up onto his back, and they forded the shallow water. Elaetha splashed after them.

While plodding through the trees on the other side, his thoughts wandered through memories of his father tossing aside his story books and sneering at those tales of noble heroes and selfless deeds. *You need to think less about the unfortunates,* he would say, *and take actions for the more powerful.*

Elaetha had unwittingly struck close to the mark.

Fainche leaned her bony chin on his head. "Aldonzo!"

He jerked his eyes back across the wood, scanning for trouble. "What? What is it?"

"What did you do with that funny-looking puppy last night?" Fainche asked.

"Puppy?" he asked, the back of his neck prickling. "What puppy?"

"The big black one with the red ears," she said, tugging at his ears to make the point. "I saw it last night, standing right behind you! Didn't you smell it? It stunk! Did you scare it away?"

"Scare what away, Fainche?" Elaetha gasped, out of breath from hurrying to catch up with them.

"The big black puppy. Last night."

Elaetha's eyes narrowed. "Black puppy?" she recited suspiciously.

Fainche regarded her sister like she too was a child, then continued slowly, "With the big red ears and big red eyes?"

"Tell me you were dreaming, Fainche," Elaetha said, fear in her voice. "Please tell me you didn't really see a red-eyed dog."

233

Chapter Eleven

IMPERIAL COURTESIES

A knock rattled the door. Cassandra gingerly rolled over, groaning with each movement. Breathing pained her ribs where the fury had reached to grab her very heart. Days she had been like this, the soreness proving stubborn even through the court physicians' best remedies.

She gingerly tugged a robe about her shoulders, then squinted at the window illumined by the sun. A brilliant, cold day waited beyond the rough-cast panes. She pushed herself off the bed, shuffled to the door, and cracked it open.

Procopius waited on the other side, looking concerned.

"Yes?" she rasped.

"My lady, I've the information you requested," he said. He held up a bit of parchment.

"And my cousin?" she asked.

"Aware of your intent, lady. It would be obvious to advise caution."

Yes . . . yes it would, she supposed. A member of a general's family does not often reach out to the surviving kin of a former emperor that has been *superseded* by the current emperor and his family. But these were not normal times, and she found herself becoming more and more involved in very dangerous affairs.

"He will see you later this eve," Procopius continued.

Trembling slightly, he passed the parchment through the door. Beads of sweat ran down the scholar's brow. Cassandra offered him a subtle nod, acknowledging the risk he took on her behalf.

"I will tread with care. Thank you for your kindness."

When the scholar had scuttled down the corridor, she closed the door, then opened the bit of crinkled paper. Scrawled across the inside was the name *Flavius Hypatius*, along with directions to a home near the Julian Port that lay just a stone's throw from the emperor's own palace. She folded the paper and hurried to gather warm garments for the night. This was a visit with political imports that she had come to appreciate more fully in recent years.

Before Justin's elevation to the throne, she had been a stranger to imperial authority. But as Belisarius had risen through the ranks of the new emperor's palace guard, his family had been caught up in the wake of his success. Exposure to the machinations of the court had taught her much. And now the man who might direct them to the object of Erik's quest in the east was, as luck would have it, the nephew of Flavius Anastasias Augustus.

Many at court yet recalled the fateful night over fifteen years ago when Anastasias had wrestled with the matter of succession to the throne. As Cassandra had heard from loose-lipped courtiers, the emperor sought out God to decide the matter.

During his meditations and fervent supplications, it had been impressed on Anastasias that the first person, regardless of rank or station, who entered through his bedchamber doors would become his successor. Upon the first light of the rising sun, that person was none other than the captain of the palace guard, Justin, a common man. Now Justin's nephew Justinian held the throne, but members of Anastasias' family yet remained in the city.

She would need to be careful.

Quitting her chambers some hours later in garb more appropriate for an autumn evening, she hurried down the hallway to a door leading to the street outside. She gave the porter there the barest acknowledgment and slipped out of her family's apartments.

Across the garden square rose the Hippodrome, the enormous stadium erected centuries before to house the sport of nobles, merchants, and peasants alike—the chariot races. Grand columns rose above the streets in an oval perimeter that dominated the skyline. The imperial residence lay close enough behind it that the emperor could stroll across an enclosed causeway to take in the spectacle before attending his scheduled prayers at the Hagia Sophia.

Despite the late hour and the proximity to imperial authority, the Hippodrome stood besieged by an agitated rabble who contended against the cold, straining for word from within on the winners of the last race. This was, after all, the House of the People in an empire ruled by divine edict from the lips of the emperor, where their cheers for their favorite racers thundered through the adjacent palace. Citizens from all corners of the empire were wont to descend on the temple of Nike, the goddess of the races and victory, to fight for seats from which to cheer their beloved charioteers.

After the adoration, covered with dust from the track, the crowds lurched drunkenly into the streets to argue over which team should have won. Cassandra's family had always patronized the Blues, as did the emperor. But this attention by Justinian was oft perceived as a slight by the Greens. In the dusty passion of the chariot races, their heroes revealed themselves to the masses. And in fear of those same crowds, the very emperors themselves had been known to tremble.

At the porter's whistle, the family *bastazo*, a sedan chair borne by two mules, appeared from around the corner. Constantinople's streets were narrow and crowded, and, as per ancient Roman custom, wheeled vehicles were rarely permitted among the throngs during daylight hours. She would have preferred a *cisium*, a carriage of larger size that would keep the crowds at arm's length. The bastazo allowed the masses to crowd in close in with noise, waves of gaudy colors, and flesh. And she dared not simply shut her eyes, for when she did, Hilarion's horrifying face full of tangled teeth, or that of the soulless fury, appeared unbidden.

Cheering ruptured the evening sky in raucous waves from the Hippodrome. Cassandra pulled her cloak up against the cold night that threatened to claim her fragile warmth. She skipped down the steps to the street. At the lead mule, she whispered instructions to the driver who sat astride the beast. Then she settled into the blanket waiting on the nearby seat. With a jerk, the bastazo lurched into the clotted masses.

Once beyond the palace quarter, the driver quickened the pace. Manors and buildings rose above the street, shuttered for the night against the cool damp air. Beyond the obscured warmth of human habitation and into the deepening night, the stars began to emerge.

Even though she pulled the blanket up to her chin, a shiver raced unbidden the length of her spine. The stars had not been the same since her pilgrimage to Rome. The lights in the night sky were now far less benign.

Cassandra recalled unblemished days in her sleepy Illyrian hometown northwest of Constantinople. There, she had run through the streets with other children, unaware of anything other than candlelit stories told by her nursemaid to scare her off to bed. Her heart longed to return to those days.

In time, the driver pulled the conveyance to a stop before her family's dimly lit warehouse. Cassandra kept the blanket wrapped about her when she stepped down to the street.

"Thank you," she said to the driver. "I will return shortly."

She hurried to the side door, giving it a series of short knocks. It opened, then she slipped inside. A steward eased the door closed behind her.

"This way," he directed, holding an oil lamp high to navigate the rows of cartons, containers, and shelves.

At the far end of the warehouse, the steward opened a small office door with a heavy key. He motioned her urgently through, then quickly followed, pulling the door shut behind him. Once he'd shuffled across the room, he opened a second door that led to a dark downward staircase.

"The cellars," he whispered, touching the points of the cross on his breast.

He stepped into the darkness that threatened to swallow the flickering light. Cassandra followed him. The steps were close and steep. When the steward offered his hand, she gladly took it.

238

At the bottom, Erik paced before a rack of wine kegs. His eyes flashed when he looked up at the flickering light. The steward gestured toward him, then handed Cassandra the oil lamp.

"I shall wait at the top of the stair," he said.

But before a reply could be spoken, he retreated up the stairs.

"Here," Cassandra said, handing Erik the crumpled parchment before the door banged shut behind the steward. "The nephew of the former emperor. He lives near the palace. A bit of a scholar. He holes up in his study while his wife dotes on him. I think that's why Justinian continues to let him live. My cousin thinks he may be able to help you."

Erik scanned the scrap, then folded it up into his gear. He immediately draped his harness over his shoulders and cinched it about his waist. Then he paused for a moment, holding the applewood stake.

"What is this?" Cassandra asked.

He held it out to her. "Those who stole Thelwyn, they sought to end me with it. I used it to free you from the creatures that stalk the stylite."

She took it, then held the stake close to the light, rotating it slowly to watch the flames reflect across the runes. They appeared to squirm along the grain like octopus tentacles. The hardened wood tingled against her skin.

"It's— it's almost alive," she whispered nervously.

"Fae magic, I suppose," Erik replied, accepting it back to tuck it into his belt. "Meant to free me from the curse."

"You mean kill you."

"Or something akin to that," he hissed. "Ready?"

"You need to go on your own," she said. "Empress Theodora is a bit paranoid of those closest to the emperor. I can't be seen there."

239

He smiled, but she couldn't read the expression. That shouldn't have surprised her either. Throughout the painful months she had known him, she had only ever glimpsed the young knight's mind as if from a distant shore.

"I shall return here after," he declared.

"And I will see you on the morrow," she said, reaching out to touch his arm—but she quickly withdrew her fingers. "Please do not break anything. I would hate to hear that you have been found in pieces."

"That would not do," he said, then gestured toward the door and followed her up the stairs.

Noise echoed through the streets. For even in the night, the residents continued to pursue their nocturnal passions. By this hour the chariot races had all but ended, yet the crowds lingered, milling excitedly about the grounds. Erik crouched in the shadows of an alley near the Hagia Sophia, the city's great cathedral. Like the churches he had seen in Albion built after Constantine's time, it was a plain-looking basilica more like a government structure than a house of worship. Only the higher stained-glass clerestory windows hinted at its function and at the wonders within—sights he was no longer entitled to view. He turned his attention back to the parchment in his hand, committed the directions to memory, then struck out with the gray fox at his heels.

The Julian Port neighborhood lay close by, and he could see the homes through the flood of people. Keeping to the shadows, the knight used his familiar's vision to augment his own in an almost panoramic survey of the crevices and corners. He doubted not that the city's undead surrounded and watched him. They were native fauna of this urban terrain as much as Flavia's brood had been in Londinium. There, her efforts had propped up Magnus in his mad run to Rome to snatch the purple for himself.

People flowed through the streets in a shouting surge to the square. Greens and Blues jostled and shoved, each side taunting the other while imperial guardsmen sought to separate them with clubs and sharp warnings. Through the edges of that spreading chaos, Erik moved steadily onward, straining to keep his landmarks fixed while avoiding the worst of the congestion.

One denizen of the city, knocked off balance by a rival's elbow, ran into Erik while holding his mouth with splayed blood-dripping fingers. He babbled something in drunken anger, but Erik shoved him back toward his assailant and continued onward.

Voices rose and so did tensions, fueled by passion, loyalty, and wine—lots of wine.

Flames flickered in the fireplace above the cherry glow of winking embers. Outside, the noise from the Hippodrome remained a constant drone, even with the shutters closed against the night. Flavius Hypatius set down his pen, rubbing his blotched fingertips against a cloth. The noise always made him uncomfortable. He disliked the rabble, preferring the quiet library to the spectacle of drinking and racing.

He scratched the tip of his nose, leaving a dark smudge of ink. Hypatius was more at home with his books than with people, though he often told himself his wife was the one exception—even as she would likely have argued differently. Despite being the nephew of the former emperor, Hypatius kept to his studies and gave controversy at court a wide berth. Not only that, but the house of Justinian was not known for its tolerance of *monophysites*, those who believed in the single divine nature of Christ. Hypatius found certain orthodox beliefs more confusing, such as Christ being both divine and mortal in the single Personage. For those beliefs also he was a pariah to the royal family. Such was court life—a roiling series of family scheming as well as doctrinal controversies between the orthodox and the heretical, each alternatively championed by the emperor or the empress.

He double-checked the ink on the pages prior to stacking them together in a corner of his cluttered desk. He would have to organize the mess one day, he thought, but it pained him to lose track of even a single slip or scrap. He pursed his lips, causing his bearded jowls to roll, and glanced back at the window, where he thought he heard a scraping sound. The gardener would need to trim those trees before spring.

He stretched to cup his hand around the flickering flame of his oil lamp. Tonight, he would not fall asleep in his chair with a book open on his bulging stomach. He pushed himself up, opened the door to his study, and stepped into the hallway, where he was immediately greeted with a cold blast of air.

"Damn . . ." he muttered, seeing a window cracked open. "Damn, damn . . ."

He shuffled to the window. He leaned out over his garden, lit by the revelries in the square. "Heathens," he groused, reaching out to grab the shutter.

Fingers, iron strong and bitterly cold, grabbed his hand. Hypatius tried to wrench his arm free but could not break the grip. What appeared to be a young man clad in a woolen cloak topped with a deep hood dropped from the sill and clamped another icy hand over his mouth.

"Shhhh . . ." hissed the intruder. "I've no wish to harm you, sir, but we must talk, and the hour is late." His Greek, like his garb, carried a foreign accent.

Hypatius nearly dropped the lamp.

"The general sent me to you," the intruder explained.

Hypatius tried to reply, but the grip over his mouth stoppered his tongue. The newcomer's eyes pierced deep into his being, and Hypatius gave a twitching nod. With a pop, the fingers loosened from Hypatius' jaw. He gasped for breath and used that moment to study the man.

There was outdated cavalry armor under the intruder's cloak, and though the hood shadowed most of his face, his eyes somehow reflected the lamplight.

Hypatius rubbed his jaw and considered that if Belisarius were the source of this intrusion, at least he stood little danger of bodily harm— at least not at this moment. "Come with me," he whispered, with a gesture toward his study.

Once within the comforting stacks of documents, Hypatius eased the door closed. With his heart pounding in his chest, he turned on the young man. "What is this about, then?"

The warrior remained silent.

Hypatius grabbed the iron poker from the hearth, jabbing at the fire. Then he threw splintered logs onto the embers. When they lit up in bright flame, he turned back to study the interloper. Now well lit, the young man came more fully into view. His tattered cloak was blotched with dark stains, yet the fringes were outlined with a gold stitch that was unfamiliar to the scholar. Under the cloak, he wore an antique armor not seen since before the fall of the western empire. His visage was pale and light haired, with a prominent chin and . . . odd eyes.

The scholar rubbed his wrist to warm it up.

"You know, we have tales of night walkers. The *strigoï*. The Higher Dead. *Drinkers of blood*," he finished, with a pause for breath. "I suppose I must have invited you into my home at some point, didn't I? Did you come to drink my blood?"

"No, sir," the youth said. "The general sent me. He believes you might be of assistance."

Hypatius mopped at his brow with his sleeve. Even though the room had not yet recovered the warmth lost from the opened door, beads of perspiration blossomed across his brow. The scholar had spent most of his life avoiding imperial attention, and now a request stood before him from Justinian's most powerful warlord.

"Yes, well . . . at your service," Hypatius stammered.

"Thank you. And my name is Erik."

"Yes, yes. Then what can I do for you, Erik?" the scholar said, waving a hand toward two chairs near the fire.

The young man remained standing. Hypatius, however, did slump into one of those chairs.

"I am not sure where to begin," Erik said. "But I seek something— something of great significance for my homeland."

Hypatius leaned forward in his chair, eyes puffy from the lateness of the hour. "And what might that something be?" the scholar ventured, masking the dread in his voice.

"I hail from Albion—Britannia, you may call it. Many years ago, an adopted son of the isle, Magnus the Spaniard, enticed the legions stationed there to march on Rome."

"The tale is well known, lad."

"Tradition holds that he carried with him not just enormous ambitions but also a relic," Erik said. "An ancient sword crafted by Albion's first peoples."

"This is the weapon you seek?" Hypatius asked with strained courtesy.

"After his defeat, the victors carried it off, and it became lost in the Roman bureaucracy."

"We do love our governmental efficiency, don't we?" the scholar quipped.

"I left Albion to search for it," Erik continued, taking a few steps in one direction before turning and returning. "I started in Rome, but the trail led to Ravenna. Documents revealed that the sword had come east, either with imperial shipments or personnel, but it was confusing."

"Well, yes." Hypatius tapped his finger on his temple. "So much of our last hundred years is clouded in confusion—wars, pestilence, and loss of the Roman body . . . our lands. You have these documents with you, no? I did not think so. So let us start here. Flavius Magnus Maximus Augustus, he usurped the Emperor Gratian, no? And was finally defeated by Theodosius at the Battle of Poetovio, his head carried before the victorious armies on a pike to the Eternal City."

"The spoils of that battle, was the sword among them?" Erik asked.

Hypatius only frowned.

Erik stopped pacing.

"I do not seek what the Magnus craved!" Erik hissed with an intensity that surprised the old scholar. "There is unrest in my homeland. If unchecked, it may engulf all, even to the shores of the east."

"It must be quite a threat to require such a weapon," Hypatius acknowledged, tapping his chin with a finger. "One would have to be careful into whose hands it was committed. Young man . . . I do not involve myself in the designs of the court. The only way I am permitted to keep my head. You will have to tell the general I am not the man to help—"

Erik pounced quickly, lifting him out of the chair by the collar of his robe. Hypatius' breath stopped up in his chest when their eyes met. The nephew of an emperor knew, more than at any previous time in his life, a fear that clutched his very bones.

Erik said nothing for a very long moment.

"Yes," Hypatius finally squeaked. "I will help you . . . please."

Erik released him, and he slumped back into the chair.

"I am sorry," the strange young man whispered. "But it would have been a trophy of great significance if there is a record."

Hypatius cleared his throat uncomfortably. "Of course I shall search the records. But so many things slipped through. And, well, he was not in good standing with the Church when they took his head, so no clergy would have . . . but his men, his own men might have—"

In that moment, Erik remembered clearly an almost forgotten dream.

"Where would his own men have taken it?"

In the early hours, Erik crawled out the window of Hypatius' home with no clearer direction than when he had arrived. However, the academic had agreed to assist in the search, and that, at least, was something.

The knight jumped down into the garden, trotted over the square of lawn, then leapt into the boles of the tree near the outer wall. The alley without was quiet, though the imperial square beyond still ebbed with revelers clustering around bonfires, waiting to secure seats for the coming day's events. He dropped to the ground. The fox stirred itself from the shadows to fall in at his heels.

At the alley's mouth, Erik pulled his hood over his eyes and wrapped his cloak tightly about him, seeking to give the appearance of nothing more than another overly chilled Roman hurrying home. He hastened across the open plaza, sidestepping a gaggle of ruffians festooned with blue and green swatches of cloth, slurring oaths to the heavens against each other. Erik maneuvered politely aside when one man in green tripped into him.

Crispus laughed until he collided with the stranger's hard shoulder, his smile leaving as fast as his breath. Of course, the collision was not *his* fault, for he had been pushed into the man. One member of his group had done it. He thought of them as *his* group, though he had only fallen in with them during the night. Men who caroused and chased fellow revelers with balled-up fists. Blue or Green, they hadn't cared much for team affiliation by that early hour, choosing rather to laugh and terrorize their way through the city before the midmorning races.

"Hey . . . hey now . . ." he slurred at the stranger, while those who had shoved him hooted and laughed at his stumbling steps. "I'll wipe the smile from yer . . . face!"

He threw a wild fist at the stranger, but the man moved so quickly, he seemed to blur across Crispus' muddled senses. Then he was gone.

"Where . . . where did he go?" Crispus grumbled, tugging at the beard of the fellow nearest him.

His comrades laughed and he puffed out his bony chest. "I'd have . . . you know . . . cut, yes, cut his throat for disrespecting me! You know I would have!"

The men around him, none of whom he knew beyond this night, shoved him off into a ditch and laughed when he sprawled in the muck.

"I would have . . ." Crispus muttered as he dragged himself to his feet. "You watch . . . next time I will . . ."

The men around Crispus shoved him toward another gang waving torches against the night sky. Sailors, vagabonds, and migrants whooped and taunted until someone threw a punch. Everything quickly descended into bloody chaos. Knuckles smashed into Crispus' temple, followed by the blunt end of a torch into the back of his skull. He fell like a brick, scraping his face on the paving stones. Booted and sandaled feet kicked at him. He pushed himself upward with his arms, but someone stumbled over him with a grunt. In the light of a sputtering torch, he saw blood spurting in a gurgling fount. Someone screamed. Steel glinted, accompanied by the gruff voices of palace guards.

The tangled knot of bacchants, most of whom would not remember the fight in the morning, broke apart, scurrying for anonymity in nearby alleys.

Crispus stumbled to his feet, staggering to regain his equilibrium.

Someone grabbed his collar, tearing the poorly stitched toggles that held his well-worn coat closed against the cold. Crispus flailed his arms, but a fist struck him in the gut. He doubled over, choking for breath, then someone got between him and his attacker. Something warm covered the back of Crispus' head.

"Run. Run!" rang in his ear.

Crispus sucked air between his teeth and pounded his feet against the paving stones. He stumbled into an alley, turned a corner, then another, and gradually straightened while the noise faded into a distant echo.

But the words *Run! Run!* looped through his mind. So he did.

He ran until he found a grotto in the city wall far from the ruckus. There he curled up painfully and fought for warmth until the coming morning.

Chapter Twelve

To Champion The Right

The old tenant farmer called after them with a nervous wave of his hand toward the wood not far distant. "If you are to travel tonight . . . be mindful of the Hounds."

Elaetha's breath caught in her throat.

"Hounds?" Aldonzo blurted.

"The Hounds of Annwyn. Been about these last many nights. Searchin', they seem to be," the old man said with a shudder. "I wish they would find whatever it is they seek already. Leave us be. Their bayin' keeps the animals up all night, and the cow's milk is dryin' up."

"Hounds of Annwyn," Aldonzo murmured, turning the unfamiliar words over in his mouth. "Annwyn is . . . wait a moment, the Underworld that Mattheus' old pagans speak of."

"Are they big?" Fainche chimed in eagerly. "And smell bad?"

"I know naught of this Mattheus, but you be right, my young friend," the farmer continued. "Hell-Hounds, the Christianers call 'em.

Din't reckon them as evil before. But I might believe it now, what with the trouble they cause."

Elaetha busied herself with packing the loaves given them by the old man. While they initially had been nervous approaching him in the fields, Aldonzo had solved this by chasing down the field to take the plow from the old man's hands and finish turning the rows over for the winter. Elaetha allowed herself a satisfied smirk at his lack of skill with the ox. Yet, in the end, Aldonzo's willingness appeared to bless the farmer with a sense of empathy. Not only had he provided the food, but he'd even given them a few lengths of coarse homespun sorely needed for the cold nights. All had turned out much better than expected.

Until his parting words.

Despite the old man's generosity, Elaetha was suddenly eager to put some distance between him and his tales. She now fought to quell the old fears that threatened to break into the daylight from the depths where she had locked them away.

"Here, Aldonzo, I'll take her," she said. "I'm used to it."

Elaetha lifted Fainche from Aldonzo's back when they set off from their too-short break. Though Aldonzo said nothing during this respite, the flexing of his shoulders showed his relief. Elaetha settled her little sister into place in a piggyback position and followed along a few steps behind him.

He is a clever one, she thought, *more so than those louts we got away from, by realizing we used to live here.* He likely hoped returning her and her sister to her family would earn him a great boon of passage back

251

to Albion. But she knew that such thinking would bring disappointment—and anger.

A dark time had descended upon the two sisters, now fleeing from the mob. Then, as now, she and Fainche had trekked with only the clothes on their backs. They ate whatever odd fruits and plants they could scrounge along the way. Eventually, with hungry bellies and tattered clothes, they were forced to offer themselves to servitude with the first decently noble house Elaetha could find. Such a position was a significant fall from their former station. Yet her humiliation had at least provided food and had hidden them from the rapacious gang pursuing them.

Now they hiked back *up* the mountain to an uncertain reception. And yet despite the sinking feeling in her belly, she found she really wanted to return home—to find out what remained.

"Something is there," Fainche said for the tenth time in the past hour, her chirpy voice breaking Eleatha's nervous thoughts.

"Shhh . . . just some rabbits," Elaetha whispered.

"No!" the younger girl protested, drumming her hands on her sister's head. "It's bigger than that. I think it's a dog—one of those hounds!"

"You are being silly. Look at the daylight." Elaetha frowned, squinting up at the sun, which lent so little of its warmth.

"Do they only come out at night?" the child asked in a much-hushed tone.

"I hope so," Elaetha replied in earnest. "I do hope so."

But just at that moment, a great beast of a horse erupted from over a rise on their right to bear down upon them.

Whip clung to its withers, swinging his long leather lash.

"Aldonzo!" the girls yelled together.

The Visigoth froze for a brief instant, enough time for Whip to close the gap and be upon him. Aldonzo dove away from those pounding hooves a moment too late. Whip lashed at the prince. Aldonzo tumbled to the side, blood weeping from his arm.

Elaetha dropped Fainche to the ground. "Hide!" she shouted.

The younger girl eagerly obliged, scampering off into the wood. Elaetha faced the slaver, that whip raised for another blow, its length of attached metal glistening with blood. Aldonzo clutched at his right arm, now soaking through his grimy sleeve, and floundered to escape the whip's next kiss.

Elaetha cast about for a weapon. The ground was soft and loamy, and there were few rocks at hand. She snatched up a heavy branch, then hurled it at the horse's head, catching it squarely in the eye. The beast squealed in pain, rearing wildly. Whip, precariously overbalanced with his lash cocked, dropped to the ground with a crunch and a thud. The beast bolted back over the hill.

Aldonzo got to his feet first. He kicked firmly into Whip's temple. The slaver sprawled, his eyes lost and unfocused. Aldonzo lurched against him and slipped the man's knife from his belt. Whip rolled over, planting a foot to lift himself from the ground. Aldonzo kicked it from under him, dropping him with a grunt. Then the prince grabbed him by the hair with his bloody right hand.

A cold knot formed in Elaetha's chest, knowing what was coming next.

"Fainche. To me!" she called.

Aldonzo planted a knee into Whip's back, holding the action just long enough for Elaetha to turn her little sister away before he sawed the knife across Whip's throat.

Blood spattered across the ground. With an unceremonious tug, the prince of rags removed the man's boots. "Pity the horse got away," he grumbled.

The exhausted trio stumbled down the twisted pathway that, at times, blended into the grass covering roots and rocks. Aldonzo continued to lead, but his gait dragged a bit, while he kept his head up to continuously survey the area.

He stumbled on a twisted root.

"Is something wrong with Aldonzo?" Fainche whispered, with a slight whistle through her teeth.

"We do not know if Axe is behind us," Elaetha huffed.

"Oh," Fainche murmured, before blurting out, "There's too many bugs out here . . . Ouch!"

"What now?" the older sister snapped.

"Why are you yelling at me?" the girl wailed.

"Can you just be quiet for a while?"

Fainche pouted, her lower lip rolling expertly, but only for a moment.

"So, what is wrong with Aldonzo?"

Fainche did not enjoy walking on her own. But the encounter with Whip had taken a toll on them all. After Aldonzo had raided the body for useful gear, Elaetha stripped off some precious homespun for a makeshift bandage. But the wounds on Aldonzo's arm were deep and had bled too much. Now with his skin pale, he stumbled more frequently. Elaetha found her attention more focused on keeping him upright than on directing Fainche.

"I said what's wrong with—" the girl pressed again.

"He's injured," Elaetha replied curtly. "Now please be quiet!"

The air stirred with the swish of their feet through the waist-high grass, and soon insects buzzed merrily about them. While they stumbled onward, Elaetha continuously searched her memories to identify familiar landmarks within the countryside around them. At the sound of a low whisper, she nearly rebuked Fainche again until she realized the noise had arisen from her other hand.

"We will take the ship and recover the princess . . ." Aldonzo slurred. "We will find her, my lord, I swear."

She reached out, and where her hand touched his arm the skin was hot. With no remedies in hand, she guided him along in the hope of finding monkshood among the brambles. In the meantime, his mumbling Latin was understandable, even if occasionally less coherent.

"Weylin . . . oh, he knows a little too much . . . Has he betrayed us?"

They reached the trees on the other side of the clearing, where the undergrowth thinned out and, most importantly, the forest's features appeared more familiar.

"Come on . . . we might find some shelter before dark if we hurry," Elaetha urged.

"Are we almost there?" Fainche asked hopefully.

"I think we are."

"We are here . . ." Aldonzo hissed. "The castle stands on that island . . ."

"What is he talking about?" Fainche glanced at Aldonzo, looking puzzled.

"Just keep moving," Elaetha said.

"Caerleon . . . a great castle of the Romans," Aldonzo murmured. "Well, at least life will not be all bad here."

Elaetha goaded them onward through the remainder of the afternoon. And as the day unfolded, she began to recognize elements of the wood, like the brook where she'd once watered her dappled mare after a long ride. There was also a hillock with an old tangled oak she'd once climbed to survey the great valley down toward Brest. These landmarks awakened memories of a merry time, memories she had cried over and buried long ago. She determined not to shed a tear over them now.

Her lips folded into a resigned frown. Prodding Aldonzo forward grew more difficult with each step, for the prince leaned more heavily upon her. He muttered low and barely understandably about events only visible to him, reliving them through delirium.

"Few of the scouts have returned," he frothed. "What do you mean, they still haven't found her?"

By now Fainche stumbled as well, but she didn't complain. Elaetha was grateful for that small blessing, as much weighed on her besides their current situation. The closer they drew to their goal, the greater her foreboding. Fainche had been very young when they had left their home, so Elaetha doubted she remembered much of their life there. Elaetha, however, had wondered many times over the last three years about it. But lacking any real knowledge, she simply assumed the worst. What she had gleaned from travelers and merchants passing through the master's household had offered little hope that anything remained of their familial enclave.

"*When* do we leave, sire?" Aldonzo grimaced, waving his free hand. "My blade demands action . . ."

And yet she pressed ahead, each weary step carrying an irrational hope that when the last corner was turned, everything would be revealed as restored—the villa, the pastures . . . *her family*. So she dragged the others along on this borrowed mission thrust upon her by an unlikely foreigner, a man come to their rescue by only God knew what path.

"Oh, Marianna . . ." babbled Aldonzo. "She is comely, I give her that . . . keep your head down . . . far down . . . she wields vases with a vengeance . . ."

When they finally reached the old path, everything was overgrown. Her own legs grew leaden. She stumbled, fear rising in her throat despite a fierce effort to swallow it back down.

Then the last bend in the trail lay before them. The only sounds in the air were the chirping of birds and the chattering of squirrels. There were no voices, no neighing horses, no clang of the smith's hammer. The place was devoid of human sounds.

She slung Aldonzo's arm over her shoulder, tightened her grip on Fainche's hand, and rounded the turn.

Before them rose charred, weed-covered rafters thrust into the evening sky, grasping for the last rays of the sun as if they could be lifted by that light out of the thick brush and roots that entangled them. In their shadows, fragmented stone walls gaped over courtyards dusted with dead leaves. A wind stirred, whispering through window casements and still mourning the long-forgotten lives snuffed out like so many candles within their very sight.

"I dealt with the traitor . . ." Aldonzo spat the words. "Kien! Kien?"

The images of that terrible night flooded back into Elaetha's mind. A sob escaped her lips. She dropped to her knees, sending Aldonzo sprawling. She swallowed hard to keep her emotions in check, but it was no use—her head rocked back, and a hoarse wail escaped from deep within her throat.

Aldonzo rolled to his feet, turning fevered eyes on Elaetha.

He raised his fists. "Damn you, Axe! Damn you! Leave us alone!"

He lunged.

Elaetha scrambled away to keep from Aldonzo's fevered hands, tangling her own feet. In the confusion, she had become separated from Fainche, but there was no time for seeking her out. Aldonzo's eyes had become wild, saliva spilling from his mouth onto his quivering chin. He chattered about the sea washing, crashing over him, but Elaetha ran toward the bones of the manor.

Inside, she skittered through the collapsing hallway, onward to a juncture of corridors that she knew led to the kitchen and great hall. Crawling around that corner, she stilled her heavy breath, then carefully glanced around the corner. Aldonzo shuffled, the fever clearly clawing at both his mind and body. He appeared lost in whatever visions clouded his mind—the madman on the hunt. But she did not know if she was even his quarry. Her ribs hurt, and her breath burned from the chase.

She risked another glance around the corner.

"Got you!" she heard from behind.

258

She ducked, twisting to avoid being trapped against the stonework. Aldonzo's eyes flamed from fever, his arm raised with the borrowed blade poised to cleave her.

But he hesitated. Something scrabbled in the rubble somewhere behind her, and Elaetha gasped in horror at the thought it could be Fainche. But Aldonzo craned his neck in that direction, for he likely heard it as well.

"Aldonzo!" Elaetha shouted.

His expression suddenly softened.

"Nana?" he muttered hopefully. "Nana, is that you? Where have you been?"

"I . . . have been out," Elaetha answered vaguely, her mind racing to keep time with his fevered reality.

"Shall we have a story?" he asked breathlessly.

"Yes," she replied instantly. "What story would you like to hear?"

"The one about the *Briton King*. You know, the *Briton King*."

"An excellent choice, Master Aldonzo," she said, relieved that she knew those tales. "Shall I tell you of his quest for the graal? Or about how he wrested the Great Cauldron from Arawn, Lord of the Dead himself?"

Aldonzo's knife drooped. In his fevered state, he appeared to be burning energy faster than ever.

"The one . . . the one . . . I . . . I guess it doesn't matter . . ."

"Why doesn't it matter?" Elaetha asked, pressing him to focus on something that could distract him from attacking again.

Aldonzo's shoulders rolled with a shrug. His face sagged.

"Father doesn't approve anyway," he huffed, his breathing labored.

259

"Why not?" Elaetha probed, all the while praying silently that Fainche would remain silent.

"Those stories . . . the world is not like those myths," he said in a high, mocking tone. *"You act like that prancing buffoon, thinking to be better than everyone, and you shall end up with a dirk in your ribs."*

Elaetha knew where this tale started. Noble stories were fine for entertainment, but court life and duty were not always tolerant of such high-mindedness.

"Surely he enjoys a little storytelling?" she ventured.

Aldonzo dropped to one knee, panting, sweat running down his face.

"Father will not understand . . . All he wants me to do is use everyone. *That is the only way it's done,* he always says . . ."

His grip tightened on his blade. He pushed himself to his feet.

"You never understood. You never did!" he shouted, looking blankly at some phantom above him and brandishing the knife. "Faithful knights! Noble kings! *I* loved them! But *you* always found fault! Never let *me* be a *noble* man. Well, *Father*," he added with a sneer, *"I have had it!"*

Aldonzo spun the blade so it pointed beneath his own sternum. He dropped to his knees once more.

"If I must live as a scoundrel . . . then I shall *die* as one!"

"Aldonzo, no!" Elaetha screamed.

He hesitated, brows knit, eyes clenched shut.

"Why?" he demanded, body quivering with rage and infection. "Why, Nana?"

In truth, she could not know how to respond.

"You are not a scoundrel. You *have* lived nobly," she said earnestly.

The prince of rags gulped down a few breaths.

"You know nothing," he spat. "You are nothing . . . just a wet nurse confined to a sheltered castle. I endure schemes every single day, every single hour . . ."

"What of the Breton girls?" Elaetha asked.

Aldonzo cocked his head, a wild look in his glazed eyes. She pressed on, hoping to penetrate the fog of his delirium. "You helped them when they were hungry. Saved them from the slavers. You took on warriors, armed with nothing."

"I needed . . . to escape too."

"But you didn't go alone," she said.

"Easier with others . . . couldn't survive . . . alone."

"A woman? And a child? There were other men around. Someone useful in a fight. You could have taken them."

"Bad . . . judgment . . ." he choked through cracked lips.

"Bad judgment?" She forced a laugh. "*You* cheated pirates out of their own ship. *You* tricked slavers into fighting among themselves so we could escape. Your judgment has been sound, Aldonzo . . . as a noble man, holding on to noble ideals."

The prince of rags squinted at her, for a moment appearing to recognize her through his fevered consciousness.

"You, a self-described opportunist," she continued, "took in two useless wretches to rescue them from a horrible fate—and did it cleverly, using whatever you had at hand. Why? Even now. You've chased me through this house—had me in your power at least a half dozen times. You could have killed me. An *opportunist* would, you know—but you held your attack each time."

And suddenly she knew why she had stopped him.

"Only a noble man would do that," she continued matter-of-factly. "Only *you*, Aldonzo of Septimania."

261

His shoulders slumped, his body still poised to sag against the knife.

"You are not what you have been told you are," she proclaimed. "You are a *good man.*"

She inched toward him until she could reach a reassuring hand to his shoulder. Aldonzo cried out, eyes fearful of some apparition only he could see. He snatched at her neck and wrested her torc free, tearing skin and throwing her off balance. Her gasp appeared to startle him. He whipped the blade around, slashing recklessly across her calf, parting both skin and sinew with ease.

Elaetha shrieked, falling to the ground.

Aldonzo fled into the night.

Rain sluiced from the leaden sky in torrents, icing on the ground. Aldonzo plunged down the hillside, heedless of the slick grass and stones, away from the remains of Elaetha's family estate.

What have I done? raged in his fevered mind. *I struck a woman. How can I be honorable?*

But then a shade of his father tugged at the fabric of reality.

She tried to deceive you, the presence chided him. *She lured you from what you knew so she could take your weapon.*

Aldonzo scrambled through overgrown hedges that tore at his clothes and sharp stones that snagged his feet. All the while, he fought to escape the confused war breaking out within his head.

Elaetha's words had pierced the fever, penetrating to the remote, rational part of his mind. There they had lodged, refusing to leave.

A good man.

Like it or not, memories of Longinus still held the power to reduce Aldonzo's self-worth to bitter ash. But from his mind's slowly dispersing fog came a still, small, but ever-so-persistent voice.

To succor the weak.

His father's image demanded his full attention, but these thoughts refused to budge.

To champion the right.

To defend the defenseless.

He fell against a rocky shelf, panting and dizzy from the wild run. The lowlands spread before him to the sea, where a town lay with a large central castle. *That would be Brest*, came the thought. He desperately channeled his remaining energy into that one clear notion, holding on to it like a mariner with an eye fixed on a lighthouse. He collapsed then, bracing his hands against his knees.

The next several long minutes he remained with his face upturned, letting the rain drown out the chaotic thoughts warring for his attention.

Below him he heard a nicker and a shaggy draft horse ambled into view. Trying to focus, he turned to the sight before him.

Here he sat, alone but for this horse and the animal's presumed-sleeping master somewhere in a nearby farmhouse. Within view lay a port city from whence he could sign on to a ship. Surely his ordeal with the pirates had at least given him experience that someone would find of value. And he had lost any semblance of discrimination. Any ship would do. Any ship, going anywhere.

He realized, just then, that he was still clutching Elaetha's torc. Tarnished curves gleamed in the lightning flashes, its cold reality taunting him anew because of his actions. But the memory of the fight came also with the memory of the struggles leading up to it—the escape, their pursuit, the defeat of the slavers. And before that, the pirates, the fight at the marauders' castle, his reluctance to risk his own neck on the quest to find Marianna.

With shame, he realized that, for all his reverence for the old tales, he had lived his life exactly as his father had taught him. Along that path, his actions had nearly killed him, leaving him only with the wound he'd inflicted on his . . . *friend.*

He could just as easily die here. Just a misstep on an ice-rimed rock. No one would mourn him. At the same time, no one stood over him, taunting him to correct his thinking or telling him which path to choose. Of course, he could carry on and find his way back to his old life. Or he could run, leaving all his mistakes behind, and risk making them again.

Or . . .

Or the prince of rags could look forward to living the life that *he* thought he should—to stand with his scars and neither flee from nor return to the patronage that stood too ready to judge him.

Below him the horse nickered again, calling him to a different path.

The freezing rain lashed at the barn's door, rattling the oddly out-of-place bronze torc knotted to the latch string. A note had been inscribed in the door's planks in roughly scratched but cultured Latin.

Ego reddam ei. I will return him.

The horse cantered back up the slope toward the wreckage of an abandoned villa with a ragged Septimanian youth clinging to its mane. Aldonzo wiped sleet from his face that resembled tears.

Somewhere in the distance, a dog howled.

Chapter Thirteen

CHOKE POINT

The island fortress blazed with starlight under the surprise dusting of early snow. At least that's how it seemed to the brothers and scouts, Haervu and Seisyll.

Haervu paused silently in the shadow of a large tree. Off in the distance, the campfires of Mattheus' troops at the head of the causeway lent just enough glow to force him to take each step with care. Ahead, less diligent movements betrayed the patrol from the castle that he and his brother had been tracking for the past few hours. He uttered the soft purr of a storm petrel, the signal that alerted Seisyll of trouble ahead. Ten paces to his left, another shadow halted, then voiced a similar sound in return.

A bowstring *twanged*.

Haervu froze when a shaft whistled past his left ear. Hoping it was a blind shot, he refused to flinch. He spotted the faint glint when the dueling archer nocked another shaft. Another *twang* followed. This time the missile passed wide on the right side.

Haervu smiled grimly, tensed his muscles.

Only the merest rustle betrayed Seisyll's movement toward the bowman, the barest twitch of underbrush that could easily have been the wind. But several long moments later, when the man drew back another arrow, his body crumpled to the rocky soil.

Haervu slipped forward to Seisyll's side, a sharpened wooden stake held at the ready. Though a primitive weapon, the stake was as deadly as a dagger and had a finish as dull as a scholar's memoirs—perfect for subtle work. Haervu squinted to see Seisyll, little more than a silhouette, leaning over the dead archer. In the starlight filtering through the branches, Haervu could barely make out his brother's face—except for his grinning, gleaming teeth. He smacked Seisyll on the forehead with the stake to bring him to his senses, then gestured down the slope.

Seisyll raised three fingers, then pointed to his right with one. Haervu peered into the darkness, then marked the muted sheen of armor before him. He snatched the bow from their late adversary's fingers. He nocked an arrow, then drew the bowstring slowly to his cheek, sighting along the shaft to below the glint. He paused his breath and held his mark. A bow creaked when the other man pulled back too quickly. Haervu counted *one, two*, then let fly as the other did as well.

There was a *thud*.

Seisyll elbowed Haervu in congratulations, then crept forward.

Mattheus had many good men in his army, and a fair number of them he had personally chosen for this expedition westward. But Haervu and Seisyll, brothers from the far side of the Beacons, held a special place even among his Home Guard—stoic as Greek philosophers, stealthy as dire wolves, hardy and clever as Cataibh ponies, and blessed with the eyesight of gyrfalcons. Tasked with scouting out the hills surrounding the castle, they were largely forbidden to engage enemy soldiers due to the risk of dying with their precious information.

If you so much as engage the enemy, they had oft been told in no uncertain terms, *they will know you are watching, and you will have failed your mission.*

But this scouting assignment was different. They had discovered the patrol on the far curve of the beach when pebbles had accidentally tumbled from under Seisyll's foot. Now the two guardsmen were obliged to prevent these skirmishers from returning to their own commanders with news of Mattheus' activities.

They slipped down the slope toward the bluffs above the beach, where the remaining men now clustered behind a small rise. Following their standard practice, Seisyll peeled off to the left, while Haervu circled around in the opposite direction.

The brothers whispered to each other to track their movements, which in the right air carried farther than if they had been speaking. Haervu moved quickly, taking great care to tread such that his footfalls made no sound. His trusty stake suited the tasks at hand, but the length of sharpened wood was no match for a sword.

Like good scouts, the brothers had taken careful note of their opponent's equipment, their dispositions, and even their mood, which appeared somber. As far as Haervu was concerned, though, their dragging feet were welcome information. Many times the tide of battle had turned because the other side had only *thought* they were losing.

He hunted patiently, for he knew the three had likely spread out and, at worst, two were together and the third alone. Haervu took a

267

ready position five long paces from the other two and waited in the dark undergrowth.

A muffled grunt made just enough noise to catch the attention of Haervu's quarry. One muttered to the other, then stalked away into the darkness, unsecured armor and gear clinking. Stake outstretched, Haervu crept closer to the remaining soldier, circling around the downside of the slope.

When his intended victim turned his attention back uphill, Haervu stepped up behind his man and quickly reached over his shoulder to clamp his jaw shut. The scout drove the stake up through the back of the soldier's skull. The man crumpled without a sound.

Just then the wind gusted, dust stinging Haervu's eyes. He sucked in a breath and immediately cursed himself. The last man stopped short, calling out loudly for his comrades. Haervu froze, but it was too late.

The man broke into a run. Haervu slung his bow and launched into pursuit. Ahead, Seisyll's dark mass leapt from a clump of bushes and the man reacted by lowering his head to duck under Seisyll's vicious stroke and headbutt him in the ribs. The pointed crown of his helm smashed the air out of Seisyll's lungs, sending the scout tumbling to the ground. The enemy soldier hurled himself headlong down the bluffs to the beach.

Haervu ran up to his brother, Seisyll, all pretense of stealth cast away. "Hurt?" Seisyll clutched his side but shook his head.

Haervu tore off in pursuit at full speed. He skidded down the steep bluffs to the beach. The other man, with only a small head start, ran headlong with a fleetness that belied his armor and gear. Unencumbered by a weighty kit, Haervu sprinted after him and caught his quarry in less than a furlong, shoving him hard between his shoulders. The man sprawled onto the sand but regained his feet, swinging a mailed fist with surprising speed. Haervu ducked, but the blow clipped his temple with an explosion of lights in the night sky. The scout shook it off, lunging after the man, who turned once more to flee. Haervu snatched a heel, toppling him yet again. The soldier rolled onto his back, but Haervu had him. He snatched the man's hand before it reached his blade, wrenching his fingers back until they cracked.

The man screamed in pain.

"Who are you?" Haervu demanded. "Where have you come from?"

He gave those fingers another twist. The man writhed in pain. Haervu stomped the soldier's left arm under his boot and twisted the hand. Bones crunched beneath his grip. The man's eyes shot toward the castle, brooding over the waters that lapped at the shore. And that was all Haervu needed. With his free hand, he drew the stake from his belt.

The soldier choked a ragged breath, then kicked his legs, catching Haervu across the knees and simultaneously jerking away his shattered hand. Haervu fell atop his adversary but used his momentum to thrust the stake under the man's ribs into his lungs. The man choked, spitting red into Haervu's face. The scout rolled off, withdrawing the stake with a flourish. He watched the man drown in his own blood.

Seisyll tramped to where his brother lay. Haervu still held his side, while the soldier sputtered a last rattling breath.

"Good work," Seisyll huffed. "You look a mess."

"But mine washes off," Haervu replied with a wicked grin. "So, my brother. Where do you think he was off to in such a hurry?"

A clutch of rocks lay twenty yards beyond them, the only break in the bare sand. "I'd wager there," Seisyll said with a gesture.

On the far side of the outcrop, they found the boat.

They searched through the vessel but uncovered nothing of use. Then, while they examined the waters before the distant castle, Seisyll pointed to the eastern sky, where the last traces of the waning moon competed with the dawn.

"Tide will go out soon," he murmured.

"It has already begun," Haervu countered, his eyes focusing on a faint current that flowed at an odd angle from the seaward side, just visible in the low angle of moonlight. "There. See?"

He gestured, placing his finger over the ripple. Seisyll sighted along his brother's arm.

"Must be a hole in the wall," Seisyll murmured.

The brothers grinned wickedly at each other.

"A way into the keep, you say?" Mattheus said between gulps of a small bowl of the mare's milk that sufficed for his breakfast.

He regarded the two scouts before him, each filthy and bloodied from their expedition. Their bedraggled appearance had been by design, of course, allowing them to blend in with the terrain and not be seen—a tradition dating back to the *speculatorii* of the old legions, and thus bestowing a sense of heritage on his reconnaissance elements. For that he tolerated it.

Seisyll nodded excitedly.

"Yes, sire," he said. "We did not see the gate itself, of course, facing the sea as it must. But judging by the size of the outflow, it could not have been large."

270

"What if your man was just a Scoti raider?" the king harrumphed. "Or an outrider from some local prince with adventure brewing in his veins?"

Seisyll's face drooped, crestfallen by the challenge from his monarch.

His brother, Haervu, on the other hand, graced the king with his finest—but still unpracticed and awkward—bow.

"We did verify with the last man before we finished him off," he said smartly.

Mattheus took another gulp from his cup. "Good work. As always."

"A small gate," Reeves mused. "Not an entry for attack, then."

"But we could probably get a man inside," Mattheus said looking up at Seisyll and Haervu. "Or two men, if the situation warranted."

The brothers grinned like feral wolves, teeth shining in their muck-covered faces.

"Our adversary"—Mattheus' voice caught, but he pressed through—"has managed to examine our position. We must not leave them an advantage."

"Of course, sire," Reeves agreed. "Haervu? Seisyll?"

Seisyll thumped his chest. "We are your men, my lord," he crowed. "We can get in."

"I have no doubt," Mattheus agreed. "But can you get out again?"

"This will challenge even your skills," Reeves cautioned. "You will be spying on them from within."

"*Exploratorii!*" Haervu mouthed, clearly relishing the prospect.

"Exactly. But they are likely not a large band, so you will not have many faces to hide among. Find out what you can. And—and you know this is important, but I must repeat it—at least *one* of you must return with what you learn."

"Yes, my lord," Seisyll affirmed.

The brothers exchanged grim glances, but the fire in their eyes burned unabated.

"Death will surely shadow our path," Haervu growled with a bow. "But we will find what we can. You have our word."

He nudged Seisyll, who mirrored the gesture.

Mattheus eyed them closely.

"I will take that word," he growled. "How soon can you be ready?"

"We can leave tonight," Seisyll said without hesitation. "Um . . . if we have a boat, that is."

"These men you found—didn't you say they had one?" the king asked.

"Too large, my lord," Haervu explained. "Too easily noticed."

Reeves blew out his breath in annoyance. "I'll see to it," he grumbled. "I'm sure there's a former fishmonger among the men that will whip up a curragh for us."

"Good," Mattheus said, gauging the sun that crept over the horizon and the brooding clouds hanging over it. "Have it ready by nightfall."

Within that keep overlooking the sea, Marianna sat on her throne with her lower lip thrust out. Her fingers *thrumped* on the solid wood arm.

Magwyn stood at the bottom of the steps, maddeningly serene.

"It's the creature again, my lady," he intoned. "The one calling himself Kraken."

"Where do you think he's been hiding these last weeks?" she mused aloud. She had no patience for this self-styled ambassador of some raffish "Council" brooding in the dregs of Roman lands.

"One could only guess, my lady. He did leave previously in some frustration."

"He offered little useful information when he realized Blaine no longer existed," Marianna snapped. "He betrays his own. How can we trust anything he tells us?"

"A risky ploy. If Arawn finds out we lost an opportunity, right in our hands, to find the very thing—"

"Negotiations, Magwyn!" Marianna threw her hands up in exasperation. "I want to find the Cauldron as much as any who serve the dread lord. But did you never haggle for anything? Do not forget *this Kraken* came to *us*. I had no reason to doubt he would do so again."

Magwyn inclined his head in the barest of deference. "You appear to be right, my lady."

"Of course," she snapped.

She settled into a more commanding pose on her seat and lazily raised a hand. "You may show him in, Magwyn. Then leave. I will call if I need you."

The brothers paddled the hide-covered yew frame out a good distance. Then they circled back to approach with the incoming tide. Fortune swam with them, for a fair bit of flotsam also rode the waves, and cloud cover obscured the moonlight.

Soon enough, their curragh scraped against the cliff and, with their leaf-shaped paddles digging furiously in the churn, they clawed along

273

the craggy face. Beneath the shadow of the keep, they found a battered root thrusting out of the rock. They lashed their craft to its shoots and upended the craft to sink it undetected beneath the waves but ready for instant retrieval.

They swam then crawled through the cold foam until they reached the entry, a hole little more than man-sized that remained open to the world. Scattered hammers, chisels, timbers, and rock fragments suggested that someone had attempted to build a more elaborate entry.

Beyond the watery threshold stood a jetty with a small boat bobbing at the end of a rope. Barely discernible in dim candlelight, a sleepy warden manned the door—until his body fell into a spreading pool of blood.

Once inside, the brothers found dank passages that traversed unlit storerooms. They holed up in one square-cut cellar room for a time, listening for sounds of movement along the floorboards above. The night wore on, and activity diminished. From the corridor nearby, a relief guard stumbled past the room to replace the original. A knife awaited him, opening his throat.

Now the bodies in the storeroom matched the number of living souls. When Haervu judged the time to be right, he signaled his brother to follow him into the corridors beneath the keep.

When departing, they left their victims as they'd happened upon them, for their garb had no discernible uniformity on the half-dozen men they had encountered over the last few days. The two spies relied on anonymity and camouflage. Dark-toned, homespun linen and their trusty stakes would be sufficient for this task.

They slipped through the corridors, then climbed stairs to higher levels. They crept through chambers, armories, empty barracks until they found a room that looked like a temple, freshly chiseled out of the bedrock. In the center of that room lay a large pool with a dark gaping doorway at one end. Haervu shivered, though he couldn't say why.

The brothers stole higher into the keep, scouting through clusters of rooms while counting stockpiles of iron billets for smithing, wood for burning, and sacks of flour for baking bread for troops. They took the opportunity to raid several small amphorae of lye from one of the middens to lace barrels of apples and salted meat.

In time, they entered furnished areas that could only be living quarters. The scouts stopped just short of a doorway opening into a large corridor. Voices became audible in the distance—at this late hour, someone remained awake. And judging by the tone, tension between the parties rose with barely recognizable words.

Seisyll laid a hand on Haervu's shoulder, nodding toward their previously trod pathway before leading him ten paces back to a small door. Beyond the portal, stairs beckoned upwards. Moonlight shone through the cloud cover, illuminating the upper reaches.

They padded up the steps, then crouched along the railing overlooking the chamber below. After scanning the opposite gallery, they risked a peek over the edge. Below them, a raven-haired young woman, whom they recognized as Mattheus' daughter Marianna, stood before a throne. She was garbed in a flowing dark gown with a sword hung at her hip. Before her, framed by blazing torches, stood a most curious creature, hunched over, withered, who almost appeared winged. He argued in a voice like iron nails on stone.

"I said," the creature repeated as if to a child, "I must speak to Arawn directly!"

"Yes, I heard what you said," Marianna snapped. "I heard it the first time you visited. But the answer is the same—I am his emissary. I am his Voice."

"I bear information vital to His Divine Shade," the odd one pleaded. "The very thing he has sought for a generation! You are apostate to continue to refuse me an audience with him."

"Master Kraken!" she barked with a steely timbre that brooked no more argument. "What you have to say will be said to me!"

"How do I know you will not betray me?" the wretch demanded. Marianna hissed in response.

"Yet I have seen nothing yet to incline me to trust you, my lady."

"How dare you!" she said, bounding to the edge of the steps and gripping her sword threateningly with her right hand. "*You* came to *me*, Master Kraken, do not forget that!"

Haervu unrolled a lambskin scroll from within his tunic, deftly catching the charcoal stick rolled into its center. Furiously he began jotting down figures, supply counts, and what fragments of the argument below made sense to him.

Seisyll watched the stairs and the gallery opposite.

A shadow moved unnoticed on the stairs behind them.

"Now, then . . ." Marianna continued in acidic tones that rang off the upper ceiling. "Where is the Cauldron?"

"What reason have I to tell *you*?" the creature seethed.

Haervu scrawled *Cauldron* on his scroll. Then something made him underline it, though he did not understand the reference.

A scuffle broke out to his right. Haervu jerked his eyes up to see Seisyll headlocked by a guardsman, a large bear of a man.

Haervu attacked like a graceful great cat, silent as death. But the man responded with a quick counter, swinging Seisyll around so his legs cut under Haervu's. The older brother sprawled, biting back a grunt, then gathered himself for another lunge. Seisyll's eyes bulged, his muscles straining as he pulled his assailant's head into his shoulder to keep him from crying out.

Haervu reached around the soldier's back to pry his arms off Seisyll, but the stubborn trooper refused to let go. Haervu shifted his grip, wrapping one arm over the man's mouth before driving his other thumb into the notch behind his ear. Many a boastful warrior had gone down under the intense pain of such a maneuver, but this seemed no ordinary man. He grunted, huffing against Haervu's sleeve, tenaciously keeping his grip on the younger brother.

The silent battle in the upper balustrade was lost in the spit and bile flung in the exchange below.

"Do you really even know?" Marianna's voice shrilled from the rafters. "For if you don't, why should I keep you here?"

Kraken shifted his weight from foot to foot.

"Very well, then," he conceded. "Ganelon has it."

"Ganelon?" Marianna's frustration bubbled just beneath the surface of her composure. "Am I supposed to know him?"

"No, lady, but he knows of you," Kraken replied. "He is the presiding hunter in the Council of the Dead."

"Very well, then," she murmured. "*Ganelon* has it. Where does he keep it?"

"I do not know that yet, lady. But I will."

"And you came to me for parley without that information?"

"There is more, lady," Kraken assured Marianna.

"Please enlighten me," she purred dangerously.

The barest of grins cracked Kraken's face, exposing his yellowed teeth. He raised his hands before him, pressing them together in a sign of fealty.

"Ganelon plans to close the Rift between the realms," he hissed.

"He plans to do what?" she asked.

"The Rift, lady . . . the Rift. The tear in the Veil that allows you to move between here and Annwyn."

"And how would he go about that?"

"I do not know." Kraken released his hands when she did not respond to his gesture.

"Does he even have the means to do it?" Marianna asked.

"I know not that either, lady."

"Then what exactly do you know?" she snarled, her voice rising once more. "You know who has the Cauldron, but you know not where. You know of our desire to find the knight of Birkenshire, and you have seen him, but you know not whence he has fled. You know of a plan to seal our gate between worlds, but you know not how or when."

She slid her blade from its scabbard and advanced down the steps. Kraken drew himself up to a surprising full height.

"I came to you in good faith, lady. I need assurances . . ."

"You know only that the Cauldron is out there somewhere, and so is Erik. Such things I had surmised *myself*."

She lunged at him with the blade.

Kraken's attempt at intimidation was his undoing, for his greater stature ensured that her impassioned thrust landed at such a height to pass just beneath his rib cage.

There was a gush of blood. He fell, a startled look on his face.

In the sudden silence, there was a gasp above.

———— ⊗⊗⊗ ————

Haervu and Seisyll gulped ragged breaths, the body of their attacker finally stilled between them. Haervu rolled over to collect his scroll, then glanced down through the railing. Below him, Marianna searched upward into the higher levels, but her eyes had not yet found them.

A shudder crept through his spine as she gestured to her guards, who ran for the great door at the end of the hall.

Haervu thrust the scroll at Seisyll. "Get back to the king!" he urged his brother.

Seisyll's eyes met his for the barest instant, then he took it without a word. Not far away, the lumbering creak of the hall doors sounded as Seisyll disappeared into the darkness. Haervu struck off down other passages, creating just enough noise and clatter to ensure the guards would follow him.

Only one needed to escape.

———— ⊗⊗⊗ ————

The sun went down early. Mattheus grumbled under his breath.

We should be home preparing for Yule, he thought. *Not stuck out here hacking trenches and building ramparts on a hardscrabble beach under snow clouds.*

But the day's work was done, so at last the king allowed himself to join the tail of the chow line. He waited, patiently tapping his empty bowl against his thigh.

A handful of the new recruits appeared startled at the presence of their liege among them. One stepped aside, but his more seasoned comrade snatched him unceremoniously by the scruff of his neck and shoved him back into place. Any of Mattheus' troops who had previously campaigned with him knew that court was a world unto itself, but in the field, he was the *commander*. That meant he always made sure his men were fed, and he himself would not eat until they had been served.

But when his turn finally came to fill his bowl with porridge from a dripping ladle, rather than following his custom of seating himself in their midst, he steered toward the shore. Today he desired—no, rather he needed—solitude. He found himself an isolated tree root, then sat staring out over the sea.

"Sea" may have been too generous. The water was the mouth of the Môr Hafren, the river separating Mattheus' Cymric brethren from the degenerate Romans to the east and the stubborn Kernowyon to the south. The bards sang that, according to legend, the body of water was named after the water nymph Sabrina and, through convoluted theological arguments, symbolized rejuvenation. He wondered if this represented a corruption of baptism, which itself symbolized death and rebirth, or if it was some parallel reasoning. Legitimate or not, though, it brought his daughter to mind, who now took that road a step too far—a journey from being dead to being wondrously alive, to, somehow, being lost again.

Marianna brooded, lower lip extending to the full, while Magwyn examined the warrior's body on the stone slab before her.

"Do you know him?" the steward of Annwyn asked.

"Haervu. His name was Haervu." She seemed to spit the words.

"One of your father's men?" he asked.

"This man was a lout."

"His personality makes no difference now." Magwyn sniffed dryly, holding up a warding hand at the retort forming on Marianna's lips. "In any case, a far more important question is *was he alone?*"

She crossed her arms. "He never went anywhere without his brutish brother, Seisyll."

"We found no other?" Magwyn confirmed. "Then we have to assume . . ."

"Yes, Magwyn. We must assume that his brother returned to my father."

Magwyn started. "Arawn—"

"He must not know!" Marianna hissed. "If he learns of this, he will . . ."

Her voice trailed off while she almost played with that particular thought. But she was unwilling to venture further down that particular path while she harbored thoughts that Magwyn was now actively betraying her to the Grey God.

She stroked the oathing-stone on her sword. The smooth coolness yet again confirmed the permanence of her bond with the god of the dead and shored up her confidence.

"If you even think of telling him, I will rip your—" she snarled.

"No need, my lady," he said, looking up from the body to meet her eyes. "No reason to apprise him of this development. It would be unfortunate for anything untoward to color your relationship with Arawn."

"Then we are agreed," she stated quickly, binding him to the unspoken conspirator's oath. "Dispose of him, Magwyn. And see to those who discovered him."

Magwyn's face fell into a frown. Nevertheless, only a simple nod and "Of course" answered her order. "But one last item."

"What is it?"

"His brother returned to Mattheus. One can only guess at what he discovered during their time here—our preparations, our defenses, anything and everything."

Marianna did not like the sound of that at all.

"Our response will have to be quick," she said.

Mattheus leapt from his pallet, tearing open the canvas flaps of his tent. His bare feet skittered over the icy gravel outside. He already wore his mail shirt—too many seasons on campaign had taught him against sleeping otherwise. But he cursed the need to dry his feet at night.

The peal from the carnyx that had awakened him sounded again from the rampart facing the castle. Beyond the causeway, massed helmets and spearheads glinted pale silver in loose formation. The king bounded onto the catwalk abutting the wooden palisade and clapped the nearest sergeant on the shoulder.

"Looks like we got ourselves a fight!" he roared.

"Infantry up the causeway," the sergeant said, then pointed beyond to the castle walls. "Archers on the battlements."

"We should be out of range here. Stay off the causeway. Pass the word. Whatever happens, we will not pursue them beyond our defenses. We need only contain them, nothing more."

"Right you are, sir."

The sergeant barked at his subordinate to take charge of his section. He gestured to a well-equipped veteran some distance down the wall even while he jogged to meet him.

Reeves appeared at Mattheus' elbow. "So, it begins," he said dryly.

"Not a well-thought plan, I would say," Mattheus observed.

"I assumed they would move troops seaward and mass them up the coast," the general observed. "But a frontal assault on a narrow approach? They crowd into a killing field. Something provoked action before they were ready."

"Haervu's sacrifice won't go to waste," Mattheus said. "Prepare the archers. We start with volleys of flaming arrows."

"We will put the fear of God into them, sire."

By now the castle's vanguard had filed close enough that he could see the two siege ladders they carried. *Marianna—ever impulsive and no tactician*, he thought. This could be dangerous in unexpected ways. Veterans were predictable. Amateurs attempted desperate moves that could catch one off guard.

"Reeves?" Mattheus called out.

"My king?" the commander replied.

"Ready the pitch pots. Just in case. And strengthen the flank patrols."

From atop the highest tower, Marianna watched her forces advance up the causeway.

A trumpeter stood nearby to relay commands, but Magwyn doubted his services would be required. The plan was simple enough. There had been no time for subtlety.

"We are here, and they are there," Magwyn rehearsed.

"What?" Marianna asked, distracted by the scene.

"Should a breach be made, well... then things would get interesting." He wore a mirthless smirk.

Marianna's hand shot forward to lean on the battlement as a volley of fiery points raced from the siege wall onto the causeway. Then the ladders went up, and her troops ascended to face her father's men.

The ladders *thunked* against the palisade rising above the mudwork walls. Young men eager to face their foe suddenly choked the narrow catwalks. Older warriors berated their impatient charges for the lapse in discipline. A battle-tested squad shoved the restless recruits out of the way to block the catwalks, taking the first blows, and as they engaged the attackers, forcing themselves over the walls, others brought up long poles on the inner side of the wall to push the ladders off the parapet.

Mattheus strode to a flanking bastion above the immediate conflict.

"They've thrown their best-equipped men to the fore," Mattheus called to Reeves when the first of the fort's defenders, lumbering Norsemen by the look of them, landed on the parapet and engaged the High King's Celts, who mostly stood a head shorter.

"Then we've agility and speed," Reeves answered.

As fortune would have it, he appeared to be correct. Mattheus' men avoided the Norsemen's blows to counter under their guards. Nevertheless, their adversaries' scale armor held up, and Mattheus' men

284

made no headway driving them back over the wall. More reinforcements spilled over the walls, pushing Mattheus' troops back.

Then the first real casualty occurred. A man from one of Mattheus' western villages took his foe's blade in the chest, then pitched slackly over the far side of the palisade. His body was quickly followed by a second, then a third.

"Maces and cudgels!" Reeves called over the din. "Bring up the falcatas!"

Mattheus' unoccupied men swapped straight swords for bludgeons and lunged to relieve the now hard-pressed front rank. From a dozen yards away, a different unit marched smartly up to the catwalk, bearing the heavy curved swords that had been so devastating to Caesar's legionaries five hundred years before.

In a matter of moments, the High King's troops contained the threat, leaving the two dozen or so of the castle's complement struggling to maintain their ground.

A *boom* shook the walls.

Mattheus leaned out over the parapet. Their adversary had brought up a massive log on the shoulders of their biggest brutes. Even now, they battered the gate at the causeway's end.

"Buttresses!" the High King urged the men stationed nearby in the arming yard.

But it was too late. The gate had been built quickly and, after only a handful of blows, splintered with a great *crack*. The portal gave way. The castle troops let up a war cry, surging forward in a clot.

Mattheus snorted. He had built too many field fortifications in his time to ignore the obvious limitations of his own siege-craft. Beyond the gate, the passageway through the earthen walls snaked tortuously under the ready bows of a dozen archers.

"Give them hell!" he shouted above the din.

Iron-tipped shafts flew, and men fell. The invaders scrambled undeterred over the bodies of their comrades.

Then Mattheus saw something he had not anticipated.

One figure scrambled rat-like over the corpses, arrows sticking out of its back like hackles. The creature was Mattheus' own man—the first that had been killed off the wall. In the time the king took to digest this abomination, a mist swept over the entryway. Fallen bodies lurched to their feet with unnatural movements to resume their advance on the fortifications. And the bright tunics of his own men shambled among them—dead only moments before, now reanimated to fight for the enemy.

Mattheus looked aghast at Reeves, who said only one thing.

"Caer Baen!"

The reports had reached them, and many at court discounted them as wild rumors of the ungodly host that had leveled that small village.

"Fire the pitch pots!" Mattheus shouted defiantly. "Fall back! Clear the field!"

His men responded smartly, and not just from discipline and trust in his leadership. Those men on the line could see better than he the transformation of their comrades. The Welshmen pulled back, creating a gap between them and the castle troops, the living of which slowed their advance to keep pace with their horrid undead reinforcements.

Flaming clay pots arced overhead, bursting among the assaulting troops and splattering sticky tar over living and dead alike. The victims screamed, swatting vainly at the hungry flames. If one man thought to help his comrade, the flames took him as well.

Then panic set in, and the rout began.

At least, among the living.

The undead continued to amble onward, oblivious to the flames until they fell in smoldering ashes before disintegrating into the sandy ground.

Mattheus' men also flung more pots onto the causeway's ranks. The stench of burning oil mingled with that of charred meat. The climbing glow showed the backs of the castle troops fleeing in a terror all their own.

Marianna's limbs trembled, while her dispirited forces staggered back up the causeway for shelter behind the castle walls. Her fists clenched the stone of the merlon until bits cracked off under her fingers.

"Arawn must not know of this," she said, straining with anger and fear.

"He is a Lord of the Afterlife, my lady," Magwyn said dispassionately, looking beyond to the siege wall and the ashen piles clustered by the splintered gate.

The remains of Marianna's dead were already being shoveled aside by men repairing the portal.

She turned wary eyes on her steward, lips pressed thin, brows drawn tightly.

"Believe me," Magwyn continued, nonplussed, "he already knows."

Across the smoldering field, Mattheus stood on his own earthworks.

God help us all, if it be His will, he prayed. The High King recalled the town that had lain in the land of Birkenshire Erik had hailed from. As far as anyone knew, the youth had visited this very shore and had laid eyes upon this keep before them. Then—if the king could believe the reports—the knight had reappeared at St. Bride's with Marianna.

A passing merchant recalled someone of his description, much the worse for wear, at Caer Baen just before the attack. But no one remained at the hamlet now to report the knight's whereabouts. Aldonzo was likewise gone without a trace. The answers remained locked behind the gates of this keep, beyond the causeway in the heart and mind of his own daughter.

Mattheus' aching heart sent a prayer heavenward for Allana. *Please forgive me, my love, for what I must do now.*

"Reeves!" he barked.

The man appeared at his elbow. "My king?" he said.

"Send a rider to Caerleon. But make it a fast one. I want the steward to send every siege engine he can muster. I don't want to spend *all* winter here."

"The sappers will start extending the earthworks immediately, my lord," Reeves said.

"It can wait until morning. They've earned that much. But we spare no more time than that."

"As you will, my king." Reeves bowed, then was gone.

Mattheus returned his gaze to the keep and offered another prayer.

Dear God in Heaven, spare her if you can, he mouthed. *And grant me peace if you cannot.*

Chapter Fourteen

⸻⟨⟩⸻

THE SECRET HISTORY

Voices grumbled from somewhere nearby. Urgent voices. Dangerous voices.

Crispus' eyes fluttered open. Even they hurt from the cold and from too much ale the previous night. The back of his neck ached, and bruises covered his body. He went to push tangled hair from his face, but dried blood had matted it to his skull.

The morning sun blinded him for a moment. He threw up splayed fingers. Nearby, the uniform *tromp, tromp, tromp* of marching boots echoed down the alley. He tried to move, but he managed to gather his feet beneath him and scramble up against the stone wall.

The smell of piss and ale clung to him.

"He slept down there . . . right against that wall." A female voice trembled. "I saw him . . . when carrying in the wash. Look at him—his clothes are covered in blood!"

Crispus caught his breath, eyes darting about for a place to hide. He had to get home. Amelia would be worried if he failed to appear for breakfast, and Severus, his own father-in-law, expected a full day of cleaning horse shite from stalls. There was a cellar door further down the alley. He scraped toward it but slid to a stop when soldiers, wearing surcoats of imperial purple, appeared at the alley's mouth just beyond. Behind him, more guards rushed into the alley from the other end.

Crispus stutter-stepped, then stutter-stepped again.

"Please . . ." he stammered. "I must get to work . . . please . . . my wife—she will worry over me . . . please. Please!"

But the guards rushed him, wrestling him to the ground. He squirmed and squealed, but they beat him with wooden clubs, then trussed him up.

Hypatius hunched over a yellowed and stained ledger, eyes asquint to make sense of the entries. Ink blackened his fingers from hours of scratching notes with a sharpened quill. Books and scrolls lay scattered and heaped over his desk, the floor, the shelves, some piles threatening to tip into the lamps still burning after the long night. But he did not trouble his mind with the risk of imminent conflagration. Rather, he searched with zeal to ensure the promise made to him that his service would be honored.

For years since the ascension of Justin's house, he and his wife had skirted the fringes of the imperial court. For in the eyes of many partisans, Hypatius remained a threat to be monitored by prying eyes—many of whom also had wagging tongues. So he made it a habit to never give them cause, living a bland life in the shadow of the palace.

He blinked, then rubbed carefully at his eye, leaving a dark smudge. Outside his window, the day blossomed.

Belisarius could be toying with you, he thought all of a sudden, and that thought sent a numbing chill up his spine.

Cat-and-mouse with Justinian's own general would be a dangerous game indeed. He shook his head, praying that he knew better. Of all the intimates in the emperor's circle, the general remained the least likely to engage in deceit or subterfuge. But why would he send an undead creature with parchment written in his cousin's own hand? Trust remained his most valued possession and was not easily given. He had met Cassandra at court functions on several occasions, this young woman from the frontier regions of Illyria, the general's own homeland.

Not someone to play me, he thought. *I should think.*

Unless, of course, she had become Empress Theodora's creature, whose vindictive, ruthless, and ingenious hand was legendary. In which case, he had been caught up in a supernatural net that would ruin him and endanger his wife.

He set down the pen and stretched his tired back.

Amid the endless documents, he began seeing the pieces slowly fall together. The Romans had always been fastidious record keepers, if one could sort out where the documents had been stored. He made inquiries, then waited. The wrong documents arrived and had to be sent back, and he read everything that came into his hands. Some of the old tallies had even been bought up by collectors, eager to enhance their appearance of academia by stuffing their shelves with century-old harvests of Palestinian olives and levies of Alexandrian wheat. Then there would be an appeal to the general, always with circumspection, for funds to convince these antiquarians to part with their specimens.

As devoted a scholar as he was, even he began to tire of the search. Then appeared the transfers of imperial property, beginning in the reign of Theodosius the Great and accelerating under his son Honorius, emperor of the Western Empire.

Now, as the Yuletide revelers filled the city, the pages before him began detailing those transfers of imperial property out of besieged Rome.

His fingers thrummed along his desktop.

In the same way as the civil service, the army recorded everything they confiscated, including weapons, armor, and other equipment taken from the defeated Magnus. Much of the mundane had been transported to armories scattered throughout the provinces, while the imperial household absorbed the usurper's personal effects. Records from the Praetorian Guard were meticulously complete in this regard but mentioned no sword, no dire myth unleashed.

Damn you, Belisarius, he protested in his own brain. *Why put me in the middle of this?*

He glanced at a map and thought about the movements of men and goods. Soldiers moved on orders. Supplies were collected, scavenged, or even destroyed on orders. Defeated troops were incarcerated or executed on orders. But the youth had shared his memories of a dream, a strange and horrifying vision at the gaping maw of a cave: a cave with pillars, steps, and ironworks about the entrance, with troopers giving their lives to enter the pit to deliver the sword. A place plagued with vapors and death. He had found no orders for anything like this. If there were none, and the lad's vision carried any weight, they must have journeyed somewhere without, or even against, orders.

Somewhere beyond imperial authority.

His finger tapped absently at a point on the map in a far-off region of myth and legend. Suddenly his eyes came alive and he rushed from the room, tumbling scrolls and codices in his wake.

"Anna!" he yelled. "Anna, I need my boots and cloak!"

The insipid sun failed to chase off the cold that rushed in when the imperial guards opened the jailhouse doors. They hauled the five prisoners into the daylight. Though these men had passed the days in confinement, they still sported the remains of the blue and green finery they had worn the same night they had roamed the streets—the night they had found themselves swept up in an altercation that had left a palace guard dead.

Crispus stumbled along in the middle of the gaggle, dragging his chained feet across the jail's yard and into the imperial square, where the crowds yet surged into the Hippodrome. Before him, behind him, all around him, the throng jeered and rumbled with passion. Each faceless visage was a speck of flotsam in a changing cross-current of Constantinople's humanity that drew out the rabble and good folk alike. The soldiers pushed with elbows and prodded with spear butts to carve their way through the crowd.

The great arena loomed above the square, tall arches and pillars enticing the eyes to drift upwards. But Crispus could not lift his eyes. They were shot with red, and his head ached from the beatings that had occurred after he was taken into custody. They had accused him—and the others shackled to him—of the death of a soldier. But Crispus knew he had not killed anyone, even though he was covered in dried blood not his own.

293

At the gates of the arena, more soldiers pushed back the crowds, forcing the rabble into the *cunei*, or the common seating area, rising above the dusty sand of the chariot track. Blues and Greens, along with other chariot team patrons, already filled the rows of stone benches.

Though the day was frigid, the heat of thousands of massed bodies mitigated the temperature inside the enclosure. The Yuletide games were just getting under way, stoking the crowd's excitement. They packed in for the spectacle, for the Hippodrome's sand oft dripped with blood and gore in the wreckage of broken chariots. Today, however, promised a different spectacle.

The troops marched the prisoners across the sand, lining them up at the foot of a platform built of fresh timber. From the platform rose a single gallows. A knotted rope hung down from the crossarm. The magistrate, dressed in black robes, stepped forward in the emperor's box overlooking the track and the crowd. The noise rose to a crescendo, then fell silent when he raised his hand.

"Citizens of Rome!" he bellowed. "You are here to celebrate the birth of our Lord Jesus Christ and the passing of the old year. The emperor, even our Justinian, has granted you his peace and protection that you might partake of the races and sacraments in safety."

Another roar issued from the masses. The magistrate again raised his hand for silence. When he spoke again, his booming voice carried a more somber tone.

"But these"—he waved his hand at the men cowering at the base of the gallows—"these have violated the word of the imperator and broken the peace of this city! Killed a palace guard, and assaulted the Night Watch."

He held up a scroll, broke the seal and shook it out.

"By decree of Augustus Caesar, these men, under Roman law, forfeit their lives. Following the execution of this order, the races will be closed for two days."

Shocked catcalls broke out around the circumference of the track.

The magistrate gestured to the troopers. They shook the first prisoner loose from his chains and hauled him toward the platform, up steps slick with frozen dew. They stood him on a tall wooden bench. The executioner settled the rope about his neck and, without any further ceremony, kicked the bench out from under him.

The man dropped with a firm jerk of his neck. His feet kicked in vain for the edge of the floor, his eyes bulging and face turning purple. Long minutes passed until his struggles ceased. He was hauled down, and another prisoner was marched up the steps.

Crispus felt warmth run unbidden down his leg.

One after another, they were dragged up the steps. The raucous factions in the crowd cheered, shaking their fists in approval if a rival-garbed prisoner danced from the noose, or praying and screaming in outrage when one of their own was led up.

One after another.

After another.

And then it was Crispus' turn.

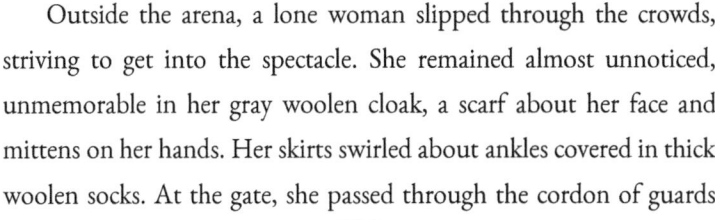

Outside the arena, a lone woman slipped through the crowds, striving to get into the spectacle. She remained almost unnoticed, unmemorable in her gray woolen cloak, a scarf about her face and mittens on her hands. Her skirts swirled about ankles covered in thick woolen socks. At the gate, she passed through the cordon of guards while they were distracted by a man dressed in blue causing a disturbance.

With the crowds jammed against the stairs to the seating, she veered off toward the track and unlatched a small door leading down into the corridors beneath the Hippodrome itself. The dark passages smelled of horses, urine, and sweat, but the noise of the masses was much less down here. She kept her hood over her face and moved into the shadows, a prayer upon her lips that she was not too late.

At the center of the arena, she ran up the ramp connecting the stables to the track above. When her feet hit the track's sand, she paused to gain her bearings. A roar erupted like a wave when the crowd spotted her, the stomping of feet beating through the Hippodrome's structural bones.

She waved her hands for attention, running headlong toward the gallows.

The magistrate loomed high above this scene amid the grandeur of the imperial platform, his face set and stern. He raised his hands to quell the noise, but the people would not be stilled at the sight of the woman boldly dodging a soldier's grasp and rushing to the thin man being marched up the gallows steps.

"Stop!" she screamed. "For the love of God, please *stop!*"

But her words were lost in the clamor.

A soldier finally managed to grab her arm, but she wriggled loose and skirted around him. She fell to her knees before the magistrate, with clasped hands outstretched.

"Silence!" he shouted, trying to get the crowd's attention. "Silence!"

This time the crowd complied. All eyes remained fixed on the unlikely pair. The one representing the law, accustomed to dispensing

296

justice with impunity, stood perplexed by this effrontery. The other was a homely woman of modest means but passionate bearing. She clearly understood the gravity of her actions. The voices throughout the Hippodrome quieted in an unruly ripple of intrigue. Soldiers dragged her to her feet, though jeers from the stands caused the magistrate to gesture them away. She stood straight and free, squarely facing the official.

"What is this?" he demanded in a voice trained to carry to the highest seats. "You interfere with the emperor's own justice. These are convicted killers. Guilty of disturbing the emperor's peace and killing one of the Night Watch!"

The young woman lifted her face with a nobility that quieted the crowd. They listened with bated breath.

"Great lord of the empire," she mustered, her voice quivering despite her brave face, "my name is Amelia. I am a daughter of Cornelius Severus, a charioteer of renown to all—to all colors!"

A ragged cheer rose from the stands, but the unimpressed magistrate wagged a finger at her.

"You have disrupted the carrying out of imperial decree!" he bellowed. "Your lineage has no bearing here!"

But clearly it did, for calls of "Hear her!" and chants of "Severus! Severus!" began sweeping through the crowds.

"My husband stands at the step of your justice," she countered, clenching her shaking hands and emboldened by the crowd's encouragement. "Crispus Galus is the steward of my father's stables. He is my husband!"

"And what would you have of us?" the magistrate demanded. "Do you intend to establish the innocence of a man covered in the blood of a soldier of the empire?"

Her eyes fell on Crispus, who remained on the step, hands shackled, hair matted, and clothes blackened from blood spilt on the imperial square.

"He did not kill anyone!" she asserted, though her voice faltered at the sight of her husband in the crusted gore. "He was on his way home from the races!"

She raised her eyes once more to the magistrate. "He is to be a father. I bear his child! He would not risk his family with reckless brawling!"

The crowd stomped their feet against the stonework in a deep thunderous rumble.

"*Severus! Severus! Amelia! Amelia!*" echoed above the Hippodrome and out over the city.

"Enough!" the magistrate demanded, pacing the length of the box. "These men have been sentenced under Roman law for the murder of Arius Valla, a good man taken while doing his duty. The emperor's peace is not to be violated!"

"He would not have!" Amelia shouted. "He doesn't even carry a blade! He is a peaceful man . . . a Christian man!"

Despite the magistrate's stern gaze across the sea of citizens, the rumble of stomping feet increased, along with a threatening growl that rose and raced the length of the arena.

He waved a hand toward Crispus. "He fled the scene, to be found in the dawn's first light covered in the blood of the slain!"

She thrust her chin out in defiance.

"I know him. You— you have slaughtered men here this day, truly. But you do not know of their guilt! You pulled them off the ground. You could just as easily have pulled any one of these from their seats—" She swept her hand across the crowds and they cheered in waves to

298

match. "Greens or Blues, it would not have mattered! Crispus doesn't own a weapon. He would never have killed anyone. Free him to his wife and child!"

The magistrate crossed his arms until the noise abated enough for him to proclaim, "His guilt is visible yet to all!"

The clamor in the Hippodrome lifted, defiant and angry, refusing to be stilled by the magistrate's renewed gestures for silence. Red-faced and realizing he'd lost control of the crowd, he thrust a commanding finger at the soldiers on the scaffold. "Finish your work! Do your duty!"

Troops snatched Amelia and finally managed to hold her. The officer in charge, no longer wasting time with the rope, drew his spatha and struck Crispus down. His blood splattered the wood and ran through the floorboards to pool in the sand below.

And then it began.

By nightfall thousands of torches still lit the Hippodrome, the crowd refusing to disperse. Indeed, thousands more people choked the streets, attempting to push their way into the vast arena. Many more thousands swarmed through the surrounding streets, choking the entries. At the edge of this spectacle, troopers escorted senators and citizens under the gazes of the hordes into the Daphne wing of the imperial palace. Erik and Cassandra slid through the gates behind them just as the ironwork barriers clanged shut on the surging rabble being driven back with the blunt ends of guardsmen's spears.

"This way," Cassandra directed, pulling Erik behind her through the palace corridors.

Even in the palace, the sounds coming from the nearby Hippodrome had taken an ugly turn. They threaded through the anxious elites to a side door, where Procopius greeted them.

"The emperor assembles his council," the scribe said. "Belisarius is with him. You are to see the general this night."

"And Hypatius?" Erik asked.

"He arrived earlier with his wife, Anna. The Senate, government officials, and prominent citizens—everyone is here in the main hall."

The scribe hurried them through hallways lit by dyed glass oil lamps hanging on bronze chains. They dodged courtiers scurrying with parchment scrolls toward the back of an imperial audience chamber. There, nobles and their families crowded into the room for protection from the mobs spreading through the city. The tension in the air was palpable.

"Come along, come along," he urged, shepherding them through to an adjoining antechamber.

Tapestries and silks covered walls that were brilliantly lit by dozens more lamps. At the far end of the chamber, an expansive window opened to the adjoining gardens and the shadowed outline of the Hagia Sophia. Around the basilica, the unrest had taken hold with determination, for the cathedral's foundation stones were already awash in the rabble now fighting against the city guard with sticks and broken tiles.

A tall man paced near the window, dressed in a brocade trimmed in purple and gold. Justinian, emperor of the Romans, was a handsome man with a face framed by dark locks punctuated with bold eyebrows and a hooked nose that lent a predatory shape to his lean features. Despite his position as imperator, his hands fidgeted while he paced. His eyes darted from the crowds below to the faces of his counselors.

He looked like a man hunted by the rabble that had exploded into the streets of his city.

And then the twittering cluster of courtiers parted like a bireme's bow wave. Breasting the gap, a man in military kit strode toward Erik and his companions, his coat of chain mail overlaid with a surcoat emblazoned with the imperial eagle. A simple soldier's spatha hung at his hip. His boots were scuffed from campaigns in the east where he'd dueled with the satraps of Persia and brought home to war-weary Romans many victories not seen in a hundred years. This Illyrian officer strode with the confidence imbued by those victories.

He offered Procopius and his guests only the thin smile required by good manners.

"Belisarius!" Procopius gushed.

The general nodded politely, but his attention was immediately with Cassandra.

"Cousin," he murmured, exchanging kisses on the cheek. "Good to see you, though the timing is unfortunate. And your guest. Erik, isn't it?"

He clapped the knight on the shoulder and met his eyes.

"We've much to discuss, yet there will be little time, I fear," the general continued. "But I may have need of you—and your talents, shall we say."

"What is to become of the city?" Cassandra whispered, her own attention drawn to the frost-trimmed window.

It was then the emperor cleared his throat. A hush fell across the room, and Belisarius smartly faced his master.

"They protest the mandate of their emperor—their *emperor!*" Justinian's voice rose with passion. "Roman law cannot be disputed!"

301

"Yes, sire," Belisarius said soothingly. "We have men deployed through the city to contain the mobs."

"Contain? We must do more than contain. But . . ." Justinian's eyes returned to the window while his voice wavered. "Shall we spill Roman blood? Christian blood? And the Hippodrome, we can secure that, can we not?"

A tall, handsome woman, clearly older than the young emperor, stepped to his side. Exotic powders colored her features, and her face was framed by ringlet curls. She pursed ruby-shaded lips, then turned cold eyes to the chaos outside the palace window.

"They take liberty with your indulgence, husband," she murmured.

"Theodora—my love."

He took her hand and appeared to lean upon it. This empress, daughter of a circus-bear baiter, had been elevated to the purple seven years before and now stood second only to Justinian's own authority.

"We staged races for them . . . summoned the greatest competitors from all regions—" the emperor huffed.

"And then hung a group of paupers gathered in a round-up off the streets," she interjected with brittle irony.

The emperor wrung his hands, then jabbed a finger at the antechamber door, beyond which clung senators with their families and wealthy merchants.

"Too noisy!" Justinian exclaimed. "I cannot think with all the wailing in my own home. Good God . . . is my house so full of them?"

"Many of your court sought refuge from roving bands that infiltrate the neighborhoods, sire," Belisarius explained.

Color rose to Justinian's face. He strode to the doors and threw them wide.

The crowd of nobles quickly fell silent in the face of their emperor. Some of them met his sweeping gaze, but others could not.

"So much for the bravest of my citizens," he observed wryly. "Would you stand before them, any of you? I thought not. Christ only knows, the emperor is the sole light of the empire!"

Theodora glided to her husband's side, then leaned close to his ear.

In the sudden hush, Erik's curse-enhanced hearing caught her whispered admonition. *"Unleash Belisarius and his armies. End this now, or, God as my witness, we will be driven from the imperium!"*

But instead, with a haughty twist of his lips, Justinian turned away from the nervous courtiers to once more survey the unrest beyond the palace walls.

"I am their *pater!*" he exclaimed with force. "Father to all Romans! I will speak with my children!"

The courtiers erupted into chaos.

The Hippodrome was packed with an agitated mob spread up to the seats around the imperial dais. The noise struck Justinian like a wall. He put on a stern face and hurried to keep up with the brightly armored men who battered the crowd aside with indignant iron fists. Imperial robes, more appropriate for presiding over the Senate than facing the rabble, fluttered about his body, and upon his brow rested a circle of gold that glinted with the torchlight.

The mood in the arena shifted as instantly as wind travels over a wheat field.

Caesar had descended to the masses.

303

Erik jogged along behind the guardsmen, appearing very ragged in his journey-worn kit of chain mail and helm among all their martial splendor. Belisarius, who marched at the emperor's right hand, had insisted he accompany them to the Hippodrome. Though the general let little slip from his lips, Erik believed he knew much about the Briton's circumstances and mission in Constantinople.

Noise broke over them like roiling surf when they passed through the imperial portal to the great arena. From there they climbed a few steps into the emperor's box. Word spread in a seething instant. This appearance of God's anointed on earth fanned the frenzy, and the Hippodrome's very foundations shook from thousands of raucous feet pounding the structure ever harder. Erik remained at the doorway, blended with the shadows to watch the whole scene with an outsider's eyes.

With the imperial box secured, the guards smartly stepped aside. The emperor strode to the railing above the surging rabble. He raised his hands, holding them high, higher, until the crowd realized they were not to hear his words until they quieted. Finally, the noise subsided. Justinian swept his eyes over his people, this mob that simmered barely a breath away from a riot. He shouted—

"Citizens of Rome!"

With the common people pressed so close, he would not be able to count on the usual upper-class faithful to relate his words to those who could not hear.

"For you are all citizens of the Roman state!" he cried, his voice ragged with passion. "I come to you as your emperor . . . your father . . . the office to which God himself has appointed me and all Caesars from the time of Constantine the Great. These games, these very games are for you—given to you by my own hand in gratitude for the year that has passed and in anticipation of the year before us."

A smattering of cheers greeted him. He raised his hand once more as if to silence the whole, rather than only the few. "On the morrow, if it please you, I will reopen the games that we might celebrate this time together. This season of renewal that begins with our celebration of Christ and his birth!"

This time more of the crowd cheered. But below the emperor, on the steps to the broken gallows, a hooded figure rose from the rabble to the platform. This time the crowd came to a hush without a gesture from Justinian.

"This cannot stand!" the broken voice called over the noise.

Flustered, Justinian leaned forward against the rail, scrutinizing the figure in tattered rags. "Pray tell, what cannot stand? The emperor wills it—therefore it will stand!"

The cowl fell. Amelia raised her bruised face, framed defiantly with tangled hair.

"The emperor is God's anointed on earth, we have been told," she replied. "So when an injustice is done in your name, it is an injustice to God Himself!"

The crowd let loose a primal roar until the rail beneath Justinian's hand swayed with the shuddering vibrations. From behind the imperial party, Erik searched the crowd with a hunter's eyes, finally resting once more on the emperor. Fear of that man's imperial office melted in the face of the crowd's feral hunger. His head pounded with the passion of their collective emotions, the racing of hearts, and the pulsing of blood through agitated veins.

"There *was* justice—righteous justice!" Justinian shouted, but his voice was consumed by the mob's raucous response.

Once again, he raised his hands to gesture for silence, but only catcalls shrilled in reply.

"My friends . . . please . . . *please* . . ." he called.

Eventually the mob subsided, but only to a small degree.

"Those men were caught with blood on their hands!" the emperor cried. "They were judged before the praetorian prefect!"

"The prefect?" another voice called from near the gallows. "The same John of Cappadocia who taxes us until we cannot even kindle our hearths?"

"We are all Romans here!" Justinian asserted, though now his voice held a nervous edge. "I guaranteed peace in the city. Those men broke that peace and honorable men died!"

Amelia cried out above the percolating din, "You speak of blood, but my man did not shed that blood. He would have sooner pissed in the streets than harm another. Your *imperial* justice . . . your justice is— is *false*!"

She leaned into her rising passion, shaking her fist at Justinian.

"You are a false emperor!"

A hush fell upon the crowd. Justinian's face reddened.

"I have given you games and our guarantee of safety," he countered, his voice wavering. "That is far more than you'll get in barbarian lands! Roman law guides us. It provides us with a steady hand. These laws have governed our republic from the earliest days!"

"Those laws condemned an innocent man," she spat in reply. "So they cannot be given by God. If you rule by anything other than God's laws, you are a false emperor!"

Once again, profanity-laced heckling filled the arena. The agitated rabble raised their fists. Amelia stood on the gallows, a smug smile touching her swollen lips. The seething masses pressed against the emperor's box. Wooden panels creaked and rails cracked until guards beat back the mob with the blunt ends of their spears, yet still they surged against the barrier.

Erik pressed his thumbs into his temples, burdened by the roar of all the hot blood coursing through the arteries of the living. An unholy heat surged through his own veins—the hunger in his gut unleashed in a fury. Red tinged his vision.

Bleed them. Feed on them all, my love. Bleed them . . . Marianna's voice crept into his mind, the words playing over and over while the rabble's noise fed the hunger threatening to consume him.

Return to me—be one with me.

Cobwebs blew from his thoughts, his vision clearing when a flung clay bowl clipped his brow, drawing him back from the suffocating allure of her voice.

The crowd pelted the emperor and his entourage with food, wooden spoons, cups, and crocks of pungent fish sauce. Belisarius cast his cloak over Justinian, gesturing for the men to form a square about him. Erik fell in with the troopers, but Belisarius caught his arm. "Make sure we are not consumed by this crowd as we pass," he hissed low and purposefully.

Erik dropped to the rear of the formation. A large balding man in blue jumped the rail, followed by another in green, then another and another. The guards' spears warded them off. Not a breath later, however, the rails cracked before giving way and spilling the riot unabated into the box. Erik dragged his spatha from its scabbard, this weapon that had in decades past ridden into battle for Rome. But he had no time to linger on that, for the chaotic crowd pressed against the emperor's retinue, testing the resolve of the spears of the steel-clad guardsmen.

The fight erupted, frenzied and brutal. But discipline and loyalty prevailed. Justinian was quickly whisked way to the inner passage while Erik remained with the rearguard, beating rioters with sword pommel and fist until his knuckles dripped blood.

After several exhausting minutes, the last soldiers followed their emperor, slamming the great palace doors closed and sealing the tempest on the other side.

Along the length of the passage to the imperial chambers, Erik could hear the feral roar of the crowd. The pounding of their feet began to sound like war-drums echoing over the city.

"They made demands of me—of *me*!" Justinian fumed, pacing before the palace windows. "I am *emperor*, by right of *God*, not one of the rabble!"

From within the crowd that had followed the sovereign from the antechamber, a senator called out, "And what of those demands? We must think of the city!"

"Think of the city?" Justinian's voice was incredulous. "I am *pater* to all!"

His hand swept across the scene beyond the windows, where the human mass surged from the palace gates to the Hagia Sophia, punctuated by fires set to keep the rabble from freezing. Then he turned back to the senators, eyes narrowed. From where he stood amid the imperial guard, Erik followed the emperor's gaze. Justinian cursed under his breath when his eyes landed on Hypatius. The scholar's face paled.

Justinian's voice suddenly boomed above the chatter.

"I will grant them their wish. As a mercy from their emperor, our Praetorian Prefect John of Cappadocia, Tribonian Quaestor of the Sacred Palace, and Eudaemon Urban, Prefect of the city, shall hereby be removed from their positions."

Then he tugged at his beard, giving Theodora a sidelong glance. But his empress averted her eyes, a look of disgust visible on her face. Undeterred, he gestured Belisarius to his side.

"Send word to the people," Justinian said. "Their emperor has heard them and in his own wisdom has determined to make changes to his court. Demand that they now look to their families. Return to their own hearths."

"And the races?" Belisarius asked.

"Will resume when they have complied," Justinian said flatly.

Belisarius bowed, backed away, then gestured to his men standing by in burnished steel, trimmed in gold and brocade. His eyes met Erik's.

"My friend from Britain," he said, hooking his arm around Erik's shoulders and leading him a few steps from the soldiers. "Someone must carry the message to the people. This is a perilous mission, one that may necessitate a certain viciousness. I will send of my men, but I want you to accompany them."

"Sir, my mission rests in Hypatius' hands. He must remain safe."

The general thoughtfully considered for a moment.

"Of course. We shall keep him and his wife here. They will be safe within the walls of the palace, I assure you. Return quickly, before sunrise. There are places beneath the palace where you can wait out tomorrow."

Belisarius selected four additional soldiers to accompany Erik to the Hippodrome—a bare handful to follow the undead warrior from a distant land into the maw . . . and back again.

The crowd parted for them when they stepped onto the firelit sands of the Hippodrome's track. Anger hung heavy on the night, growing stronger the closer the imperial authority drew to the gallows. There yet stood Amelia, now surrounded by a cluster of men clad in knee-length winter coats, fur-lined boots, and gloves—garb that would require years of labor for those surrounding them to purchase. They were in fact senators who now stood before the platform as if it were the dais of the emperor's own throne room. But the appearance of the guard caused them to lose the resolve that had inspired them to negotiate with the mob without Justinian's sanction.

A gap-toothed man, covered in rags, shuffled before the soldiers. "And you are? All here at the emperor's command?" he cackled, his eyes shifting between the gallows and the soldiers.

None of the rabble had ever made demands of the government before.

One of Erik's escorts, a young officer but a few years older than he, stepped forward. He sized up the self-appointed *papias* responsible for the security of his fellow conspirators, then spoke past him to Amelia herself.

"I am *Kentarch* Cornelius. I bear the words of the emperor. Why do you consort with these?" He tilted his head toward the senators.

One of those noblemen shouted back, "The emperor executed innocent men! These are the results of wanton injustice. Not Roman law!"

His response appeared to steel the spines of his colleagues, for they stood the straighter, clutching their lapels and staring down their noses.

Cornelius squared his shoulders. "Your emperor has done as you asked," he said. "John of Cappadocia and Eudaemon, and others as well, have been stripped of office and title. They will be escorted from the city in the morning."

A smattering of applause rose from those within range of his voice.

"But these men," Amelia said, sweeping her hand toward the senators. "They have shown us that we do not need to bow to a false emperor!"

The crowd erupted in agreement, emboldened by the fact that the empire's mightiest had come before them for approval—first their emperor, then these senators, and now the imperial envoy with caps in hand. Nevertheless, the senators themselves squirmed as if the crowd might devour them at any moment.

"And these," she shouted, casting her other hand at the troop of soldiers. "They arrive with weapons! They treat with fine words—yet carry the tools of our subjugation!"

Amelia stalked across the gallows toward them, her eyes alight with a fire born of her pain—pain that, in a few scant hours, had transformed her from a broken widow to the master of the Hippodrome.

"Tell your master that we reject his rule!" she cried out.

The crowd roared, unbridled and filled with a dangerous hunger that grew deafening. Erik's hand dropped to the hilt of his weapon, where beneath his touch he could feel the crusty blood from his previous encounter with the mob. This time the surge of the howling masses reached the uppermost tiers. Suddenly the last of the knee-walls surrounding the track collapsed, and the rush of humanity, mindless with collective passion, swarmed past the cowering politicians to close

311

on Erik and his comrades. Shoulder to shoulder, the soldiers withdrew, again using pommels and fists to keep the rioters at bay.

Erik smashed his way to Cornelius' side. A ruffian thrust at him with a wicked length of steel. Erik grabbed the man by the throat and threw him into the arms of his fellow rioters. Then something flared on the periphery of Erik's vision. Plumes of smoke and glowing ash exploded beyond the arena's perimeter.

The Hagia Sophia, that holy edifice built by Constantine, went up in flames.

⁓

"And that was their response?" Justinian whined, wringing his hands.

Beyond the great window, flames spread from the centuries-old basilica to the buildings across the gardens from the palace. The conflagration filled the sky with billowing smoke and glowing flickers of ash.

"Sire," Cornelius recounted, his face still covered in crusted blood. "Members of the Senate . . . they stood with the mob. Encouraged them to revolt."

Justinian sputtered, facing the packed nobles. "You," he stammered. "You stand here while your own colleagues are in rebellion!"

"My emperor," one senator ventured, "we are your loyal—"

"Get them out of here!" Justinian roared, his features hardening, the muscles around his eyes twitching. "All of them. All these vipers. By God Almighty, I'll not have their daggers in my back while the city burns!"

312

"My emperor," a fat balding man pleaded. "The mobs, they will tear us apart—we are *your* Senate, *your* subjects!"

"Then treat with *your* cronies," Justinian spat. "Convince them not to plot against me!"

Belisarius bowed, then gestured to the guards, who drove the senators and their families toward the great hall. The terror-stricken crowd resisted, and spears and shields were employed with forceful effect. Wails rose when the guards folded the flock to the door, leaving dark stains on the tiles. Amid the chaos, Hypatius and his wife, Anna, were swept along with the rest. The scholar pleaded to remain, his sobbing wife in his protective arms, but the guard was undeterred. Erik lunged toward them, but Cornelius held him in place.

"Not now, brother," he cautioned. "The emperor watches and we must obey. You do none of them good if you die here."

Erik shrugged him off, but he could feel the emperor's eyes on him even before he turned to see Justinian presiding over his edict with a righteous indignation. Within only a few moments the courtiers were gone, and the great doors clanged shut.

Theodora stroked Justinian's cheek, cooing in his ear. He pushed her away.

"The city is lost," he moaned. "I have been given this precious jewel of empire, only to have it snatched from me by this unwashed rabble—and my own Senate!"

His eyes darted around the room, catching the eyes of those remaining. Erik stood boldly and took his turn in a furious dare for the man to question his loyalty, even while he stood in garments now twice blood-stained to defend his dignity.

"Belisarius, prepare my barge. We will cross the waters to safety, and when the city burns itself out—"

313

"What?" Theodora challenged with a steely voice, dark eyes flashing. "You would flee? How can you do this? They will raise up another, and we will lose not only the city but the throne!"

"We must away before they overrun the palace," Justinian stammered, clearly taken aback by his wife's defiance. "Come, they will tear down the gates and we will die here!"

Theodora straightened to her full, considerable height, her eyes passing purposefully over the room to meet all who dared hold her gaze. Erik did not flinch when those deep pools met his, but he could clearly see the steel in her that refused to accept flight. She glided to the window, surveying the horrific fires that grew continuously in the ancient city.

"I will stand here, right here in this palace," the empress said, "and die in the purple—I will not flee for my life to end in disgrace. You may go if you wish, but I will not."

Belisarius stepped forward, placing his hand over his heart.

"Sire. Please allow me to remain with the empress. Our troops cross from Nicaea within hours. I will put down this rebellion."

Justinian exhaled. Then he took his wife's hand in his.

"You are my strength, beloved," he said breathlessly, awkwardly matching Theodora's lofty posture. "We will remain in the palace. We will defend and die in the purple!"

His keen eyes again swept the few remaining courtiers, soldiers, and clerics.

"With God as my witness, I am emperor of Rome, and I will exercise my rights under the law!"

He turned to the burning city beyond his window and raised his supplicant hands.

"Great Father in Heaven, have mercy on us all . . ."

Procopius led Erik down a dim hallway toward doorways isolated and dark, well away from the frantic, prying eyes in the audience chamber. He fumbled with rusted keys on a heavy ring.

"Which one . . . it is here, Belisarius said it was here."

He tried one, then another, then another. Finally, the door opened to show oil lamps lighting a staircase leading downward. A chilly, stale odor wafted up. Procopius tucked his hands into his tunic sleeves and shuddered. He gestured for Erik to follow.

"The general will send for you when night falls," he explained when they took to the stair. "He even now mobilizes troops to retake the city."

"But Hypatius . . . I must find him."

Procopius nodded. "Of course. His residence is near the palace. I shall send after him. We will find him, I am sure."

But Erik knew it would be near impossible to find a single man in a large and cosmopolitan city during a revolt full of raging fires and chaos—more likely he would be overlooked as a nameless pile of charred bones and ash.

At the bottom of the stairs, torchlight illuminated elaborate stonework that had been finished by the finest craftsmen. The rooms beyond were covered in fine silks and carpets with costly wooden furnishings. The richness of this dark basement would have put the royal quarters of High King Mattheus to shame. Only the lingering scent of mold marred the initial impression.

"You should be comfortable," Procopius said, a hesitant hitch in his voice. He sketched Erik a bow, then scuttled back toward the stairs and the world above.

From the shadows further down the corridor, motion stirred in the darkness. The knight laid his hand on his sword, then took a step forward. A tall, lean man emerged from the void before him, shadowed eyes framed by dark locks. His clothes were of finely spun materials and trimmed in threads of gold that added a glimmer to his movements in the oily light. A twisted smile crept onto his lips, laced more with danger than any humor. He raised his hands, fingers splayed, palms forward.

Erik's hackles tingled. This was no courtier or member of the imperial household. This one was of the Higher Dead. Light blurred around him. Erik raised his hands to fend off the creature, but reality seemed to somehow *shift*, and the newcomer's long-nailed fingers quickly encircled Erik's throat.

The creature's stretched-parchment face leaned close to examine him. "So you are the stylite's pet," he hissed.

"I'm no one's—" Erik started.

But the creature released him to glide away, its form hovering off the floor and robes flowing fluidly as if immersed in the sea.

"So, tell me of the cup. Of course, the old man keeps it with him, does he not? My belated master offered to take it off his hands, you know. But he refused, and . . . well, the swarming of the Furies attested to his stupidity."

"Who are you?" Erik demanded.

A wry twist of the lips appeared, but the smile did not extend to his eyes.

316

"Why, I am Lucian, or so I am called of late. My rule extends from dusk to dawn throughout the city."

He appeared bemused by the young knight's confused expression and leaned closer with a conspiratorial grin.

"And it appears that, as of this day, we are both soldiers of the empire."

Chapter Fifteen

To Defend The Defenseless

Elaetha leaned forward from her perch atop the horse to bury her nose in its mane. She thought it wonderful to smell something, even a musty old draft animal, that did not bear their own unwashed stink.

Aldonzo led the animal with a rope, concern writ across his face. But he said nothing. Elaetha didn't really expect him to. He had not uttered a single word since returning to take them off the mountain—and that had been weeks ago. Even now, avoiding more populated paths until the last of the season's caravans passed had continued to slow their progress. All the while, autumn grew colder, trees shedding their leaves until they had been compelled to take even more time to hunt game for raw pelts.

Yet during this entire time, Aldonzo had not spoken. He wrestled with demons that remained all his own, this she knew.

What happened to you, Aldonzo, that night in the storm? she wondered time and again as the days unfolded and the seasons turned.

He had snapped out of his delirium that night, and for this she was thankful. While priding herself on looking after Fainche for the last three years, it now appeared their lives as slaves were finally behind them. And she had no desire to tackle that challenge again. Once again, she had a traveling companion, this time someone skilled in steel and bloodletting. In violent Gaul, the added protection was a necessity.

Finally, they were bound for the coast, away from the ruin that had been their home. She leaned against the horse and rubbed her ankle where the slavers' shackles had scraped the skin raw. Something to be grateful for, finding tools in the old estate to be rid of those. Now she rode in relative comfort, swaying back and forth with each *clop* of the horse's hooves. And in that extended reverie, she feared Aldonzo's purpose to return to Cymru and to take up again his mission to rescue this woman named Marianna.

Brest lay before them, where he could take up ship—any ship. In the pit of her stomach, she feared that he would cut them loose, allowing them to fall back into forced servitude. Fortunately, their previous master had been aged and unable to pursue his lusts. Likely they would find themselves in worse circumstances next time. When their old master died, this young man had crossed their paths in the slave caravan—this southern Christian who should never have been in such circumstances.

A Christian.

Perhaps my grandparents were onto something. If given a choice, she preferred continued travel with Aldonzo. He appeared a decent sort.

As the miles wore on, she tired. Contented for the moment, she again breathed in the horse's smell and dozed.

The next morning, sleet pierced the cold air. Though chill and gloomy, the precipitation washed away the scent of old fallen leaves with the crisp bite of new winter. Elaetha limped out from under the heavy boughs where they had rested, leaning on the crutch Aldonzo had made for her. The prince had left during the night to forage, again without a word, and his reticence concerned her. She decided her challenge would be to pull him from the darkened vale of his mind before he did anything rash. Talking with him would be her weapon— talking about anything.

When they reached the bottom of the hills and set foot on the stolid Roman road, she began in earnest.

"Our grandparents were Christians," Elaetha reminisced.

Nearby, a delicate wooden crucifix thrust up from the ground near the paving stones. The weather-worn memorial, bedecked with the withered remains of last fall's blossoms, marked some poor traveler's demise. Such was not an unusual sight in Gaul, where loved ones often returned to pray for their family dead.

"On my father's side," she continued. "Not that they were born into it. They were sea-traders, you see."

Aldonzo said nothing, but Elaetha marked the subtle shift of his head.

"They sailed often to Albion," she continued. "It was there they met a pair of very eloquent missionaries near Gall Arus. In any case, they left home living the Old Ways and came home talking of *blessing*

320

them that curse you and *turning the other cheek*. They refused to take part in the festivals. It caused an awful row among our neighbors."

She paused there, gauging her companion, but he trudged steadily onward. So she continued her tale.

"After a while, everyone just thought of them as the crazy old couple that had lost their wits. But that wasn't the case. After a while, they were not content worshiping in their own private chapel at the back of the family lands. I suppose they kept running into other Christians while trading their crops. Finally, they concluded that it would be a grand idea to become missionaries themselves.

"At first, they held secret meetings with their friends. They met every seven-day. Every single one! But then the group started to grow. And their rejection of the traditions became more disagreeable. Arguments started, first with family, then with friends. Eventually the discussions got louder—more bitter. One day, the ruckus attracted the elders in the city."

She wondered if Aldonzo realized where this tale was leading. But the story needed telling, for, like it or not, they needed a healer. And the only place to find one skilled enough was in the very city that had destroyed her family. But Aldonzo gave no sign, so she took a deep breath, pressing on as resolutely as Aldonzo's own relentless traveling pace.

"There came a time when the elders decided to act. One night, they arrived with a mob. They had . . . they worked them into a frenzy at our gate." She drew a another deep, more trembling breath, then forced the rest of the words out in a rush before she could stop. "They wanted to drive out the heretics in one fell stroke. When my parents opened the gate, the townsmen were beyond, sorting out who was loyal to the Old Gods and who was not . . ."

321

She fell silent, her throat constricting. But one memory led to another . . . and another . . . and yet another, until a rushing flood surged uncontrollably through her mind. The recollections themselves were like those townsmen, pounding at a gate that only needed to be opened a crack before a torrent burst through. They had trampled everything underfoot. She cursed herself for showing pain that she had come to terms with long ago, or so she had thought. But the memories of that night were too much—the blood and mayhem, the fire and the screams. Under the hazy moon, the image of her parents being struck down by unheeding men mad with fear and rage was seared into her eyes.

And behind *those* memories came the worst part . . . the long reach of the Old Gods themselves. Deep in her very bones, she believed that the fell Hounds had been summoned by the priests. The yowling pack had swept in behind, between, and above the crazed mob. These finished the task with relish, zeal, and dripping, mauled flesh. Yet for some reason, those canines spared a pair of insignificant children too terrified to flee.

She stifled the sob in her throat, tightening her grip on the horse's mane and pulling it up to a halt in mid-stride. Exhausted, Elaetha slid off its back and crumpled on the ground. Before she could raise a warding hand, she found herself wrapped in the arms of both Fainche and Aldonzo, who bowed his head with hers and cried the tears she could not.

After a time, Aldonzo lifted Elaetha back atop the horse, seating Fainche behind her. Patting the beast's neck, he turned once more toward Brest. With the telling of Elaetha's tale, he now knew the city could be the proverbial lion's den. Caution would be the watchword for this leg of the journey.

Elaetha had shown trust in him, and that oddly flattered him. She could have simply warned him of the bad blood between her family and the city's elders. But in the telling, she had laid bare a very painful past. And yet for all her reasons to never trust again, she had put herself and her sister into his care, to be this intimate with him. If she expected him to be their champion, he hoped to be worthy of the title.

Night fell. The sleet became a full sweeping snowstorm.

Elaetha shielded a squealing Fainche with her arms from the icy pellets. "We need to find shelter!" she called to Aldonzo.

Aldonzo swept his arm back the way they had come. "There's an abandoned villa about a quarter of a mile back," he replied.

He dragged the horse around and broke into a run.

Elaetha was almost too busy holding on to the horse's bare back and keeping her sister steady to notice that Aldonzo had finally spoken.

Almost.

They clattered up to the old *urbana* that appeared to have once been the hub of a farming estate in the long-ago days, when legions had regularly trod the road passing before it. Lush fields would have produced abundant crops while the estate's master reclined in his dining hall, enjoying fresh meat and wine as travelers from distant lands regaled him with exotic tales. Life would have been good in those days.

But dark times had fallen on the land when Frankish and Alamanni raiders struck from beyond the frontier, igniting feuds among the nobility as they jockeyed for power. A succession of minor emperors, fueled by ambition for the title, had proved too weak or self-absorbed to stem the tide. So the raiders plundered, the economy collapsed, and this once-grand *villa rustica*, like so many around it, crumbled with neglect when the owners either fled, were carried off, or died defending their holdings.

The rising wind lashed overgrown trees, while the three fugitives stumbled over fallen roof timbers to find a place in a deep corner out of the elements. The girls slid off the animal's back and let it wander for forage. Clearly the snow did not bother the horse.

Aldonzo opened the linen bundle that secured the few remaining crusts of bread, doling them out. Fainche wolfed down her scraps, then immediately fell asleep bent over her now empty hands. Aldonzo arranged some broken boughs for a more comfortable bed and laid her in it.

"Aldonzo," Elaetha said, watching the prince with her sister.

He looked up, almost reluctantly, his face neutral.

"I forgive you," she blurted out.

His jaw sagged like she had cut the strings holding his face intact. "You . . . you what?" he stammered.

"I forgive you. What's the matter? You act like no one has said that to you before."

From what she had learned during his fevered delirium, she realized, as the words spilled from her mouth, that they probably had not.

"You forgive me?" he asked.

"For this," she said, waving her hand at her scarred leg.

Now he appeared even more confused when he replied, "But how? I hurt you."

324

"It wasn't you," she answered.

"Elaetha," he began, speaking as one would to an errant student, "it was my blade and my hand."

"You were mad with fever," she reminded him.

He buried his face in his bread again. "It was me."

"*You* have done nothing but fuss over Fainche and me since we escaped," she said, gesturing toward the makeshift bed where her sister gently snored. "This is the real you. You've cared for us like we were your own family. And don't—don't say your family wouldn't do these things. Maybe your father wouldn't. But if you had your own wife and child, I think *you* would treat them so."

Aldonzo fell silent for a long moment, his brow furrowed.

Then his face changed. His nostrils flared, his lips pulled into a tight frown, and he stared fiercely straight ahead.

"Aldonzo?" she asked.

She reached for his shoulder. He winced at her touch and turned away in embarrassment. Yet she kept her hand on him. After a few moments, he breathed deeply, mouth still twisted tight like he was clamping down on something, but his eyes were brighter.

"Forgiveness . . ." he managed.

"Forgiveness," she replied.

Suddenly Fainche sat up, wide awake. "Why does it smell like wet dog again?" she asked.

Aldonzo motioned Fainche to be silent, took her by the hand, and beckoned Elaetha to follow him out of their shelter.

When they had entered the villa, their first thought had been simply getting out of the weather. But now, after all the strange happenings surrounding them, Aldonzo's hackles rose upon his neck. He led them through the rubble, hopeful that the driving snow would

325

mask both scent and sound. They crept through boggy mud, over broken pylons of a once-prized hypocaust, and under rotted arches into decayed sleeping quarters.

There was a thrashing noise in the nearby overgrowth, punctuated by stamping hooves and angry, bellowing barks. Elaetha snatched Fainche close and pulled her behind a broken foundation wall. Aldonzo remained ready with his blade to cover their retreat. The hooves sounded too small for the old draft animal they had commandeered.

I hope you are going home, Aldonzo thought gratefully of the horse. *I meant to send you, faithful steed. I pray whatever beasts are out there do not find you.*

After several minutes of dodging around the unseen threat in the dark, he found a space to his liking—an elevated room that lay high enough to see most of the ruin. At the far end was an egress down a slope of fallen masonry that had once been an angle in the wall. Aldonzo tucked Fainche into a dark corner, placing his finger to his lips. She bit her lip to stifle a whimper. He gestured for Elaetha to watch the collapsed breach while he gently pulled branches into place to better conceal her and to shore up a defensive position facing the way they had come.

Suddenly, dogs yowled and branches snapped. Elaetha tugged frantically at the prince's sleeve. He looked down into what had once been the kitchens. A heavy-antlered hart burst from the underbrush ahead of the pack. Three great hounds with glossy black coats exploded from behind him—each one at least twenty stone apiece, red eyes and lolling tongues flinging spittle. The closest one lunged, swiping the buck's back legs and sending him sprawling into the wall he had prepared to hurdle.

In a flash, all three tore into their prey. Elaetha's breathing grew quick and heavy. She crouched down, eyes clenched, mouth open. After another moment, she gulped air, visibly gaining control of her fear.

The hounds sniffed around their kill, snapping at each other. Then, one by one, they stopped, smelled the wind, and bayed that ringing howl that had echoed for so long in the wake of the slavers' caravan.

Two identical but very ethereal beasts appeared out of the white gloom and trotted up to the first trio, gaining substance as they approached.

The wind shifted, but Aldonzo could not mistake the unique scent that he had noticed the night of their escape from the slave wagon. He and Elaetha watched in fearful rapture while the unearthly canines pawed at each other like long-lost friends. In time, the first three stretched out, panting heartily, while the two newcomers sniffed at the ground.

"Are these the hounds that attacked your home?" he whispered to Elaetha.

She nodded stiffly, wide-eyed. Aldonzo watched the dogs prowl, their noses to the ground in ever-larger circles.

"Who is their master?" he asked.

"They are the Hounds of Annwyn," Elaetha hissed breathlessly. "Arawn is their master."

Questions poured into Aldonzo's mind, but there was no time to voice them. He pulled a branch back to risk another look at the scene. The searching hounds sniffed uncomfortably close.

Elaetha abruptly snatched his arm. "Swear to me, Aldonzo of Septimania," she whispered so low that he could barely hear her.

327

Aldonzo released the branch. It flung forward, slinging icy slush toward the dogs. The closest one approached to investigate. He ducked back out of sight.

"I'm sorry?" he croaked.

"Protect Fainche with your life. Whatever happens."

"I— I so swear it."

Elaetha threw her arms around his neck. Then she skittered away on her bottom before surging to her feet at the very second the hound pushed its great head over the branches.

They stood for a moment, staring at each other, until the dog stretched to smell her.

For Aldonzo, the blowing flakes seemed to hang motionless in the air. Then he regained his wits to lunge into the corner, snatching up Fainche and sliding out of the back of the room and down the rubble slope.

"Elaetha!" Fainche called, sobbing.

Aldonzo roughly clapped a hand over her mouth. "Not now," he hissed.

At the bottom of the slope, he stumbled to his feet and dashed into the encroaching forest. The dogs howled. He focused only on the trees ahead, shutting out the bloody imaginings of what must surely be happening behind him.

"Elaetha?" Fainche whined through his fingers.

He stole into the woods as deeply as he dared, heart pounding every step with the conflicting needs to stay quiet and to just *move*. It wasn't nearly long enough before he could go no further. After a brief search around them, he set Fainche on a low bole. A frightful baying erupted, accompanied by more of the sickening whipping of the underbrush. Aldonzo slumped down at the base of the tree, blade out, not even sure if his defense would do Fainche any good.

After long minutes the howling finally stopped, and the villa fell silent.

———⚬❈❈⚬———

The moon rose, and the night once more filled with the skittering of ordinary creatures. Fainche had cried herself to sleep on the tree when she realized Elaetha was not following them. Aldonzo supposed she would be safe enough while he took care of the unpleasant duty that lay before him. He placed a few branches around the child, as much to block her view as hide her.

In the moonlight, he retraced his steps to the villa and up the scree to the room that had been their last stand. Shadows now littered the place, and it took a moment for his eyes to adjust. She appeared from the shadows, kneeling in the darkness as if praying. Finding suitable stones to start building a cairn would be his next task.

"Aldonzo?"

He nearly jumped out of his skin.

"Aldonzo . . ." Elaetha murmured again, then stood. Her face was pale, even in the moonlight reflected off the snow. "They left me alone."

"Why didn't you follow us?" he asked.

"I—" Her voice broke. "I didn't know where you went!"

Aldonzo clasped Elaetha's hand in his. With a newfound rhythm in his step, he led her down the scrabble to the woods. The prince of rags laughed from deep within his chest. On reaching the tree, he raised his arms to catch Fainche, who had flung herself down at the sight of

329

her sister. He wrapped his arms around them both and held tight, still laughing. Fainche giggled, and after a moment even Elaetha joined in with the tired, surprised laugh of one who had cheated death.

"I thought they were coming after us to finish what they had started," Elaetha said finally. "They are the hounds of an angry god. If they search for you, there is no escape. Ever."

But Aldonzo thought not about the hounds. Rather, he saw the two girls in a new light—for something had changed, and it took him a moment to put his finger on it. *Protect Fainche with your life*, she had pled in desperation. And to these two he had now pledged *his* sacred honor. They were now bound together. That thought brought an unexpected emotion he could not identify, but he realized with a start that, despite everything, he was like unto those heroes of old.

Suddenly Elaetha stopped laughing.

"But if they left me alone," she whispered, "then they were not sent after us . . . Then what exactly *are* they after?"

Chapter Sixteen

NIGHT OF REVOLT

B linding smoke hung thick in the air. Screams and trampling feet punctuated the night across a hellish cityscape. Hypatius and Anna fled, hands entwined, dashing across open boulevards and ducking through alleys toward their home hard by the Julian Port. Fires leapt across the buildings that flanked the palace grounds. Crowds shouted in unholy cadences, fanning out through the adjoining neighborhoods, carrying fear and flame in their wake.

The city that stood as a beacon to the world of ancient learning and law now lit the night sky like a common torch.

Once they had fled through the gate into his courtyard, Hypatius flew about, barking orders to the servants to lock the windows and fortify the doors with the heaviest furniture.

Anna hurried into the home, where she gathered the household staff to comfort them with gentle words. But her eyes kept darting to the windows lit by rising flames and shadowed by blood-riled mobs. As if the raging throngs were not enough, the fires they had set consumed the city with an infernal thirst that would require water and blood to slake. Likely in equal amounts. The fire brigade's alarm bells clattered along the street nearby through the rabid masses.

"My lady!" her handmaid gasped, reaching out to check her mistress's blood-soaked garments. "Please, sit and allow me to—"

But Anna waved her off, staggering to help a steward who was pulling in bags of cheese and salted pork. Hypatius, appearing at the door, lunged to steady her.

"What happened?" he queried, seeing the dark stain on her garments. "Is that your blood? Oh, dear God—"

He gathered her in his arms, carrying her to a nearby sofa. The handmaid quickly tore open Anna's blouse to expose a ragged gash below her ribs. While the woman worked to staunch the flow, Hypatius brushed his fingers along her brow.

Her skin was warm to the touch.

The handmaid's voice came as if from a distance. "My lord, we need a surgeon."

Hypatius shook his head.

"But she will die," she said with a finality that forced Hypatius to reconsider.

He gently tucked a strand of hair behind Anna's ear. His eyes narrowed in thought as anger kindled in his heart. His dear Anna, who had pledged her life to his, who had always kept away from the prying eyes and gossip of the court, now leaked her life into the cushions.

He took clean towels from the handmaid, then used her hand to press them against the wound. "Keep on with the pressure," he urged, leaning down to kiss Anna's forehead. It tasted of salt and smoke.

A trembling smile touched her lips.

"It really is nothing . . ." Anna started, but her tone changed and her voice grew thin. "Come back to me. Come back to me soon."

"Of course." His voice cracked, but he too put on a brave face.

Hypatius motioned to a pair of servants to reopen a side door. After the barriers were cleared, he fixed each of them in his gaze.

"Do not let her die," he said with a steely timbre in his voice. "I will not be long. Seal the door behind me. No one may enter."

They whispered their commitment to his command.

When the door had closed, Hypatius could hear furniture being dragged once more against the stout door. He raised his eyes to the sky. No bright filling of cold sunshine here, only a dark smudge hanging over the city. Always a pious man, he genuflected but then swore under his breath—not at his misfortune, but rather at the curse of serving an emperor who'd abandoned those loyal to him in their hour of desperation.

Cold breath chilled his heart. He genuflected again, more resolutely touching each point of the cross on his chest, barely daring to give voice to a prayer.

"Keep her . . . God, please . . . she does not deserve your wrath."

With that, he ducked through the garden, unlocked the gate, and darted into the streets to find a surgeon.

The thoroughfares about the palace were choked with crowds chanting a single word over and over—*Nika! Nika! Nika! Victory to our righteous cause!* While they looted shops and tore into homes, word spread from the Hippodrome that the Senate had convened in the sand of the great chariot track, the soil more sacred to the rioters than the anointed grounds of the Hagia Sophia that still spouted flames into the sky.

333

Through an apocalyptic haze of ash and smoke, they now undertook to rebuild the state in their own image. Ruffians scoured the streets for nobles. But not just any nobles—they sought those bearing the blood of the beloved former emperor Anastasias and had little mercy to spare for those of the "new court." They flooded into the Julian Port district with a revolutionary madness that drove them from house to house, leaving torched ruins in their wake. Screams marked their relentless advance, and rough voices cackled in delight when those screams went silent.

Hypatius dashed along a side street to avoid being caught up in the surging mob. He had already come three times upon the homes of various surgeons, only to find the structures already stripped and smoldering.

One more, just one more, he thought. He reached a wrought-iron gate that dangled from twisted hinges. The scholar squirmed through the opening. He knew Hippolytus from court. The old man was well respected throughout the capital for his kindness and medicinal arts.

But the gardens were empty, the doors and windows torn open. Hypatius crossed the entry threshold, catching his breath. The foyer had been ransacked. Trinkets and treasures were crushed amid the wreckage of the mob's passion during the night.

"Hippolytus!" he called. "Master! Are you here? Are you here?"

When no voice answered, Hypatius sank to the floor, tears stinging his cheeks.

Then he heard it: a tapping sound. He lowered his ear to the frigid floor tiles.

Tap-a-tap-tap. It took him a moment to realize that water pipes ran beneath the floor. Gathering the hem of his robe, he picked his way through the debris, searching room to room for a panel that would lead into a basement.

But there was none to be found. Defeated, he stumbled back out to the haze of glowing ash falling from the sky.

"Hippolytus!" he wheezed.

He scrambled around the stucco walls, kicking up debris and pushing back what once had been carefully tended shrubs. A scraping noise above caused him to look up just as a heavy tile narrowly missed braining him right there. He scanned the sagging roof. Smoke plumed from the attic rafters. The house would come down soon with no one to beat back the fire.

"Hippolytus!" he called again, more desperately this time.

He flailed about the base of the wall until he stepped on something that gave under his weight. Then he thumped his boot on wood. He bent double, shoveling bare-handed at the charred brush to expose a cellar door. His fingers curled around the latch and hauled it open.

Fumy winter light reached into the darkness. Hypatius squinted into the shadows, then descended the stone steps. Something rustled in the shadows. Hypatius took another cautious step.

"Hippolytus, it's me. Hypatius. You know me . . ."

The voice that replied was low and drained. "Hypatius? Is that you? Oh, God in heaven, please let it be you!"

"It is—it most certainly is me," Hypatius said, rubbing at stinging ash in his eyes. "Anna—she's been wounded. She needs you!"

Hippolytus shuffled into the thick light. He was an old man, with a snowy beard and eyebrows. He was followed by a bent over, balding crow of a man and a young boy.

"I cannot leave," Hippolytus said, stepping forward to take Hypatius' extended hand. "They broke through my gates . . . stormed my gardens. I don't even have what I need to be helpful."

"Please, Hippolytus. They haven't breached the Julian Port. We can be safe behind my walls."

Hippolytus shook his head. "I cannot," he said, releasing Hypatius' hand, then wringing his own together. "I've not seen a wound in many years . . . very many years."

"She is bleeding out while we speak. Please!"

The ancient one stepped close, taking Hippolytus' hands in his own. "Go, my son," he croaked. "You must. Take Manuel with you. He understands the healing arts and can assist you."

"Father—" Hippolytus started.

It was then that Hypatius realized the wizened old man was Fulgentius, once physician to Anastasius himself. His encouragement appeared to straighten Hippolytus' spine.

"I will go with you," the physician said. "Then I will return, Papa. Please, stay out of sight."

He gestured to the youth, then kissed his father's forehead.

"Tch, now—I'll be fine here, my son," the ancient man urged. "Do something good on this dire day."

The old man offered his son a reassuring smile and patted his hand. Without another word, Hippolytus led the way up the steps to the city beset by calamities.

Lucian held Erik's eyes with his own: two deep dark wells, fathomless, denying the knight the ability to see in them his own reflection.

Then he chuffed scornfully. "So, you're the creature that Belisarius imported to deal with his master's dynastic troubles? The killer of Rome's horror and protector of pilgrim families?"

"I am no one's creature!" Erik hissed. "My own reasons brought me here, not the bidding of a general, or even of an empire."

The creature sniffed at the air. "Do you seriously believe that?" he asked with a wry smile. "There are always forces at work with their own agendas. Take the one who made you, for example. Oh, yes—you stink of the inexperienced one who thought to cross you over from death back into life. But no matter. Think on this—Belisarius is not just Justinian's servant, though he makes a masterful show of it. The Church has him entangled in their own works. I'd kill to understand those cords. Yes, he is caught in a web that even includes your stylite squatting on his perch."

"Lies. Are you not born of the Father of All Lies?" Erik spat, even though the back of his neck crawled at the creature's speech.

"Oh, *that* Daniel is much more than a naked monk living atop a ruined column. He brought powers to this city—powers such that have not been unleashed here since Constantine's mother Helene returned from pilgrimage with fragments of the True Cross. *That* was a day when the underworld fought to gain that power. You should have seen it—the horrors of the old pagan order arrayed against the dead heretics of the new, while above us the depredations of the living poured their own fuels on the flames."

He licked his lips. A tight smile creased the edges of his mouth, revealing wild canines yellowed with age and stained by gore.

"Now imagine the thirst created by the arrival of the graal. When it landed on these shores . . . why, the cup that held the lifeblood of God drew things from fissure and crag of darkest legend, like moths to the

337

flame—supernatural flotsam in the wake of a frightened novice fleeing his homeland."

"This has naught to do with me," Erik murmured.

"It has enough to do with you," Lucian declared, his words precise as a predator toying with its prey. "Everything and all things are entwined. Oh, I am certain you were schooled in much more than you let on, warrior from Albion. For you are his, as is the dear general. So, tell me, have you seen it? Oh. You have seen it!"

"I did not journey all this way for a cup and stories," Erik said without flinching.

Lucian laughed, his breath washing over Erik with the stink of death. His hands shot up for Erik's throat, then dropped back to his sides, clenched into bone-white fists.

"What you came for matters not. *All we do is predetermined.* And the stylite is as complicit in manipulating our wills as is the state or the Fates. Belisarius believes he can satisfy two masters: the emperor and the priest. But that is not reality."

Erik digested Lucian's words while staring defiantly into his veined, red eyes.

"I cannot know such things. All I can rely on is faith. But I've no faith in words from—"

"Such as me?" Lucian finished for him. "Do you not know? I am the king of the undead in this cesspool of a city! Lord of the night shadows, by dispensation of the crown, and protector of the lost . . . well, most of the lambs that grovel on pilgrimage by writ of the Church. Who else might you believe?"

"I keep my own company," Erik observed, stepping around Lucian.

The creature moved to block him. "And where are they—these comrades of which you speak? Have they left you in this gilded hole to be used, chewed up, and spat out for the Roman good?"

"I am not here for Rome," Erik retorted. "My journey results from your kind opening dark doors—doors leading beyond Hell itself. I've not lost sight of who I am—or even who I was." Erik's hand dropped to his sword hilt.

"And yet you are not who you were—some goat herder or muddied peasant swirling around the filthy Roman pond," Lucian sneered. "Why, I venture that when you leave Constantinople, you will no longer be the same as when you arrived. You saw the cup, *did you not?*"

A chill crawled up Erik's spine.

"Experienced its works," Lucian declared. "Then you also saw what lurks in the darkness—the ancient creatures from the pit. Furies that skulk like ravenous ravens about the holy ground. Mindless. Vicious. Creatures unable to break the siren call of Christ's cup. While for all its paradoxical glory, it resides on a broken column in the hands of a madman. It is he who controls you, the general, the city, and even me. Remember this: power is never free of entanglement."

Erik shrugged, unbuckling his sword to toss it onto an opulent sofa. "I hear you," he replied. "But your words are twisted by the blood of the innocents you have murdered. I am from Albion, far removed from here, where a different bloodline and sorcery creates us."

"You are not so very different from me," Lucian hissed. "Children of Lilitu, the stoic *strigoï*, even the *vetalas* from the east beyond the Persian frontier . . . oh, I have seen these and more. You may be none of these, but you are more like my own folk, the *vrykolakas*, than your own kin. Beware! Your own hands are stained. Beware your self-righteous pride, *knight* of Albion."

Whatever Lucian is, it is something that clearly admires the sound of its own voice, Erik thought. The knight stretched out on the sofa beside his spatha, closing his eyes.

"And yet still different from your bloody brood," he murmured before he let the sleep of the damned bury him.

For the hundredth time, Hypatius wiped his teary eyes. The smoke hovering about the Julian Port had thickened while he had been gone. Now the haze blanketed everything in gray. He searched for a landmark before motioning for Hippolytus to follow along a thoroughfare made alien by smoke and charred walls.

All the while, he reassured himself that he had done the right thing by convincing the man to come with him. His walls were higher, thicker, and secured with stouter gates—surely able to hold any at bay who would try to enter until the emperor could restore order to the city.

The emperor . . . damn him and his cowardice, Hypatius thought.

He hurried his steps. Any delay could escalate the risk of making that an eventuality.

Crashes and clatters arose behind the villa walls lining the empty street, interlaced with sinister laughter and reckless shouts. Smoke rose from more homes to join the toxic swirl overhead. The looters made steady progress outward from the inner city.

"Uncle? I am scared," the child whispered to the physician. "Can we just go home? I won't cry anymore. I promise."

Hippolytus ruffled the child's hair. "Tch . . . now, now," he cooed kindly. "We will be there soon. Then we must care for the lady. Now dry those tears. Keep close."

Hypatius swallowed hard, realizing what he was requiring of this man and his kin. *For Anna*, he reminded himself. Everything from this point forward would be for Anna and her alone. Yet even that thought caused his chest to constrict.

At an intersection of streets awash with the twittering caws of seagulls, he pulled his companions down an alley when a gang of ruffians emerged from the haze. Hypatius wiped again at his watering eyes and saw a richly clad man in their lead, his face obscured by an embroidered kerchief. Hypatius pressed himself into the shadows, reflexively counting heartbeats until the thugs and their leader reached the center of the intersection. When the man briefly lowered his cloth to take a deeper breath, Hypatius recognized him—Theophiles Flaccus, one of the senators that had decided to look after his own neck rather than stand with the emperor.

Flaccus gestured down the street. "I believe it lies there," he hacked. "If he is anywhere, it will be in his family townhouse."

After all the upheaval, the rebellious senator was not his usual elegant self. His finely combed beard and styled muddy brown locks were streaked with soot that highlighted the creases across his forehead and the bags around his eyes. His expensive clothes were torn, with dark stains laced over the folds of the coat pulled up tightly about his neck.

"This way," he directed with a shrill voice. "To the port."

The ruffians laughed, pushing him along. He stumbled. They shoved him again. Once they had turned the street corner, Hypatius gestured for his comrades to follow, hurrying them off in a tangential direction.

And hurry they did, down back alleys and through gaps in garden walls, watching ahead, to the side, and over their shoulders for the dregs of the mob. At last, Hypatius' own wall came into view. He quickened his step to the back gate, where he inserted an iron key, turned the lock, and stepped through into a gray brume swirling through the fruit trees. The other two rushed through behind him. Hypatius closed the gate, forcing himself to lock it carefully.

"This way," he whispered.

He trotted across the garden to the back door, then pushed it open.

Inside, voices barked back and forth. Hypatius scurried through the kitchens but slowed in the hallway, motioning for his companions to stop as well. He pressed a finger to his lips.

"Not here, sir," rattled the steward to someone at the front entrance. "Lady Anna . . . sir, she has been injured. She may not survive the day."

"He must be here!" cried Flaccus' halting voice. "You must give him to us!"

"Please, the lady needs a physician. He went to fetch someone to take care of her."

"Where is he?" a deeper, rougher voice cut in. "We need to find him. He must do his duty to the state!"

"I don't understand—"

There was a fleshy *thump*.

"You don't need to understand," sputtered another gruff voice with impatience.

"Rufinus," Flaccus pleaded.

Hypatius peeked around the corner into the room beyond. A scrawny brute pressed a notched meat cleaver against his steward's throat.

"Where is the true heir to the throne? His subjects await him!"

A chill ran down Hypatius' spine. He retreated from the doorway, motioning the physician and his nephew back into the shadows. But that simple attempt to regroup was their undoing—for the youth stumbled upon on a hallway table, rattling an oil lamp. Hypatius snatched at it, but to no avail.

Rufinus shoved the steward into Flaccus' arms. Then the ruffian stomped into the hallway.

There was no one there.

His eyes narrowed, sweeping the length of the corridor. A staircase to the next floor rose to the left. The ruffian almost turned away when a shadow flitted across the wall from above. He hefted the cleaver. Smirking, Rufinus climbed the steps, then paused at the top of the staircase. A rustling, scratching noise sounded from the room on the left. He padded to the door, then pressed an ear against the varnished panel. Hushed whispers were audible beyond. He braced a shoulder against the door and shoved.

Light spilled from the inside.

Hypatius, one of the last living blood kin to Anastasias, stood at the foot of the bed, fireplace poker in hand.

"Come no further!" the scholar warned, shaking the wrought-iron hook. "We've no quarrel."

Behind Hypatius, another man stooped over a woman stretched out on a divan, face pale as death. Blood stained the bed covers around her. The ruffian bounced the cleaver in his hand, a wicked grin printed on lips still blue from the cold outside.

343

"We searched high and low for you, sire," Rufinus challenged. "You are needed at the Hippodrome."

"No. My wife . . . one of your thugs hurt her!" the scholar hissed, raising the poker higher. "Tell your masters I am not here. Flaccus can find someone else for your ambitions!"

"No, sire," Rufinus snorted. "There is no one else whom the Senate and the people both can trust to enact the Divine will. You carry the blood, and I will make sure you fulfill your duty!"

He lunged at the scholar.

Hypatius awkwardly swung the poker, but the ruffian deflected the blow, wrapping Hypatius in a bear hug and dragging him to the floor.

"Keep still and these might live," Rufinus snarled. "Come on, boys—I've found our prey!"

Feet pounded up the stairs. Before long, more of the rioters crowded into the room. They trussed up the scholar, lifting him from the floor to their shoulders.

"Anna!" Hypatius cried. "Anna!"

Manuel hurled his fists at the taller men, but they just laughed. One of them cracked the youth across the face, sending him sprawling to the floor. Hippolytus dropped to his knees at his nephew's side, reaching a hand toward Hypatius. "I'll watch after them!" he promised.

But they'd already carried Hypatius out the door.

Whatever else Hippolytus had to say was drowned in an echoing cheer from the outer gardens when Hypatius' captors emerged with their quarry.

The mob now filled the street before Hypatius' home. Raucous laughter and insolent cries of *"God save the imperator!"* filled the night. Hypatius twisted desperately against the cords to gain one last look at his home and instantly wished he had not. His final vision was of flames rising from the lower levels and smoke darkening the courtyard.

His desperate cries for Anna were lost in the death throes of the Julian Port being consumed by fire.

"You will let me see him." Cassandra's voice echoed into the basement quarters from the stairwell. "By God, you will stand aside, or I will bring you an order from the emperor himself!"

Erik stirred. The sleep of the dead had released him from nightmare-filled slumber. He rolled up from the sofa to grab his gear. Lucian was nowhere to be seen. A flurry of feet on the stairs heralded not only Cassandra but also Procopius, who waved the guard back up the stairway.

"They've done it!" Cassandra said breathlessly. "They've crowned a rival in defiance of Justinian!"

"Crowned?" Erik repeated with a rasping voice.

"Yes, yes!" Procopius blurted out. "The army mobilizes to put down the insurrection!"

Erik's eyes darted to Cassandra's face for confirmation, for this was worse than he had feared.

"I must find Hypatius," Erik said, shrugging into his mail shirt before tugging on a simple linen surcoat.

"But the port district is in flames," Procopius protested. "And you have been summoned to the general's quarters—with the other creature."

"The other creature?" The words hissed from a dark corner. "Oh, I should be wounded that you would not recall my name. I do believe I have fed from your own family, dear Procopius."

The ancient vampire appeared at the historian's shoulder with a thin-lipped smile barely concealing his stained canines. "Surely that makes us more than just colleagues at court?" he asked, cruel humor adding a crispness to the creature's voice.

The scholar shrank back a step. "P-p-please, sir. The general has need of you both."

Cassandra tugged at Erik's sleeve. "You should know that Belisarius received word from the Julian Port. Hypatius . . . his home is burned to the ground."

Her words caused a tightening around Erik's slow-beating heart. Everything hung on finding the lost sword, the artifact from the shores of the fae that he could only hope would kill a god. He clutched at the door jamb, holding himself there for a moment.

"It appears your cousin is entangled in this more than we thought," he said. "The emperor calls. Then we must not keep him waiting."

The burning city offered a brilliant glow that outshone the sun. Beyond the great window in the emperor's chamber, the Hagia Sophia smoldered now, a heap of stone and ash piled against the fires raging through the heart of the city. The noise rising from the Hippodrome was no longer that of an embittered mob, but rather that of a cocksure rebellion seeking the demise of an emperor.

From that grand window, Belisarius observed squads of soldiers reinforcing the garden gates that flexed from the mob pressing against them. Messengers came and went, bearing updates on the expanding mayhem and the troops crossing the Golden Horn to respond to the chaos. When Erik stepped into the room, the general noticed the knight immediately and gestured him to the side.

Erik offered a curt bow. Lucian, on the other hand, merely appeared at Belisarius' elbow, stepping from shadowy nothingness into substance.

"I have no right to ask this of you," Belisarius began.

Lucian did not miss a beat in the conversation's opening salvo. "And yet you will, dear Belisarius."

The general's eyes narrowed, a slight hint of humor tugging his lips upward. "And you, dear creature." Belisarius acknowledged him with a nod. "You wore a very long leash for some time. It may be time to reexamine the arrangement. Should we bring the patriarch into those discussions, do you think? After all, it is God's house that lies smoldering at the feet of the rabble."

Lucian dismissed the suggestion with a wave of his hand.

The general pressed on.

"There is talk from the Hippodrome that senators have convened a rump session to elevate a new emperor. Troops assemble in Galata, but shuttling them across the Golden Horn in barges is slow. And I have not enough men in the city to enter the Hippodrome."

Lucian laughed, a reedy, rushing sound. "You wish for us to take the horde—to drive them back from the very gates of Rome? Madness. We thrive in the shadows. Not in restoring your authority or controlling your mobs."

"The city is in flames," Belisarius pressed firmly. "What has not yet burned will in the coming hours. Insurrection must be crushed before

347

the city guards melt away, to be followed by rank-and-file troops that may not stand in the face of the mob."

Belisarius stepped close to Lucian, lowering his voice. "You thrive by his majesty's grace. Do not forget that. My vows are to him alone. So help me, I will turn my legions loose on your warrens until we eradicate all your kind. Not just within the city, but throughout all the empire's provinces. And I can promise you—I will not stop until the task is finished. *Completely.*"

"I fear the edge of your steel more than your words, General," the demon replied. "But to commit the dead, there must be, shall we say, concessions."

Belisarius' face tightened. "Do not push me, Lucian."

The creature's face suddenly lit up at the general's seriousness. "For such as this?" he asked. "My people could be lost in violence or fire, or who knows what other dangers would face us?"

"In far less numbers than at the hands of my legions," Belisarius countered.

The general's gaze crossed the room to the emperor, nervously consulting advisers under the stately shadow of Theodora. Erik suspected it was only her presence that kept the emperor steady and focused, combating the fire while the general formulated his plan.

Another disturbance broke out at the doors. A squad of palace guards escorted a shabbily dressed man into the emperor's chambers. The rags hanging off his scarecrow frame clashed with the court's opulent environs. Though his face remained hidden by a tattered woolen hood, the guards escorted him with smart deference to stand face-to-face with God's anointed on earth, where he stood with a poise that belied his trappings.

Theodora examined him with a haughty, critical eye.

Belisarius crossed the room quickly to the ragged man, who leaned toward the general's ear. Then the scarecrow bowed to the emperor.

Justinian waved a hand. "You may speak."

"And what news? Tell us, what news have you?" Theodora demanded with a bitter edge to her voice.

The hood turned ever so slightly to the general, who nodded again.

"My emperor." The newcomer's voice, even though subdued, carried uncannily well. "The rebels have crowned a pretender to the throne on the sands of the Hippodrome."

"A beggar, no doubt," Theodora hissed with thinly veiled amusement.

Justinian nodded. "We know that. Where did they find this usurper?"

"Sire," the man acknowledged, "they scoured the city for anyone of royal blood. In the Julian Port... well... they found Flavius Hypatius."

"What?" Justinian's face paled. "Hypatius was here with us! He has no such ambitions. He never has. How can this be?"

"Sire, he was bound in cords," the spy replied. "It appeared they held him against his will. A priest from the basilica blessed him, then Senator Flaccus... sire, he crowned the prisoner 'Imperator of the Romans' to the acclaim of the mob."

Justinian cried out in agony, tearing at his robes with clawed hands. "How? How can this be? I showed Hypatius favor. I gave him solitude. Just as he wanted!"

He wrung his hands while pacing across the dais. His eyes cast about, seeking an explanation for the betrayal in the blank faces and cold architecture surrounding him. Then his gaze fell on the men once again securing the chamber's great entry doors. The emperor remembered how Hypatius and the members of the Senate had cowered in his chambers—until he had driven them out in a fit of rage.

"Husband," Theodora cooed, "you have been most kind—even generous to a fault with the family of the sainted Anastasias. But this is treason. You must treat it as the betrayal that it is."

Justinian thrust up a hand to her, trembling fingers belying his true feelings. "It is I who did this thing," he said simply. Then to Belisarius he declared, "You must end this. Tonight!"

The general smartly stood bolt upright. "Sire, troops assemble in Galata. I have double their number loading in Nicaea for transport on the morrow. Those ships will allow us to strengthen our position for an assault."

"But they've crowned a rival—with Senate approval! When word spreads into the provinces, there will be rebellion in every corner of the realm. Our cities will burn from Egypt to the Black Sea. Then we will not just fight for a city. We will be fighting for the empire! You must finish it tonight!"

Ever the wily strategist, Belisarius ran his fingers through his dark beard, eyes narrowed on the two undead creatures.

Erik's stomach dropped. His journey had brought him across the world only to be stymied by an insurrection worsened by every imperial attempt to quell it. Now his escape to seek the sword of the Magnus felt as ephemeral as a child's dream. Erik's world would be crushed beneath the heel of an angry god. Everything, including this very nation, was doomed to feel the weight of that malevolent boot. Anger rose within his breast—a vicious, hungry anger.

A skeletal hand buried claws into his shoulder.

"Use that," Lucian whispered. "Find your strength in the curse. Give up this war you make against it!"

The creature's breath frosted the back of Erik's neck.

Belisarius spoke once more. "You are right, sire, as always. The Hippodrome must fall tonight. We will cordon the building to separate it from the crowds in the streets."

Justinian surveyed the ruin beyond the window, the distant fires burning in his eyes. He clenched his fists at his side. When he spoke again, his voice was flat.

"You will crush this rebellion. You will bring the Senate to heel. But you will spare the life of the pretender Hypatius. Bring him to me—he is a friend to this court and from an honored family."

Color rose in Theodora's pale cheeks. "You cannot leave a rival alive. Not after this—our home lies in ashes all around us. Hypatius must die as a traitor, or it will embolden usurpers for years to come! We will fight one after another, with a living rival right here to inspire them." She clutched his arm, holding him in place so that he could not escape the passion of her plea. "Set aside emotion, my husband, no matter how noble. Hypatius must die!"

Justinian wavered, then his resolve melted away. "I see the wisdom of your words, my love."

"Then make it so!" she urged. "You have generals and soldiers. End this rebellion with swift and complete justice to those who would overthrow God's anointed. If you do not, it would have been better if we had fled the city this very night. Kill him. And kill all who have sought your life!"

Justinian raised his arms towards the heavens, and his words brooked no challenge.

"Take the Hippodrome," he said. "All traitors will be put to the sword."

351

⊶⊷

"This must not happen," Erik snarled to Belisarius.

Lucian and Erik followed the general into the hallway. Belisarius paused, gesturing for his officers to continue without him.

"You both are here for a reason. And while neither of you believe this is your fight, the outcome will impact you both."

Cassandra and Procopius scurried to catch up. The historian opened his mouth to speak, but the general cut him short with a gesture. "And you," he said to the scholar. "You will not write this— none of it. I have indulged you in the past to record beyond the scope of official history, but none of *this* will be written."

Procopius clamped his mouth shut, offering the general a stiff bow. "Of course. I would not know where to begin, and no one would believe me anyway."

"Good man," Belisarius murmured, then turned to Cassandra. "For your safety, remain at the palace." He thrust up a hand to stifle her retort. "I will have no argument, cousin. Once we've finished this business, you and I will discuss your penchant for pilgrimages."

"What? You will not order me. I am not one of your soldiers!" she snapped back. "I have dealings with this knight."

"Yes. He is your savior," the general snapped. "But I am your family and your elder. Procopius, both of you will remain in my chambers until this entire affair is done. Or we are dead."

Procopius quickly nodded, tugging Cassandra along with him. Belisarius led his eldritch irregulars on to the war council. Lucian narrowed his dark eyes and opened his mouth to speak. Belisarius cut him off. "Save it. You have no place to hide. The inferno will drive even your people from their warrens. You will need a respite when this is over, not a war with me."

Lucian snarled, his incisors gleaming, but Belisarius refused to flinch.

"Very well," Lucian conceded. "But we must be fed while the city is rebuilt. Surely you cannot deny us that?"

"Plague, famine, and war are ever your friends," the general observed wryly. "They keep your bellies full while the rest of us starve. I am certain you will find your way."

The vampire clamped his teeth together with a perceptible *snick*, but Belisarius had already moved on.

"And what of you, knight from Albion? I would have you lead this rabble of undead in defense of Rome."

"What?" Lucian erupted, scandalized. *"Him?"*

Erik ignored the creature.

"With all due respect, General, I care not for your empire. Hypatius—he is the one I must save. He holds the key to victory for all of us."

Belisarius' dark eyebrows knitted together, then he observed, "And yet he is a dead man, by order of the emperor. Rest assured Theodora will have his head."

"I will go to the Hippodrome on my own," Erik snarled. "Give me this one thing. Find a way. I am sure you can. Do this and I will do your bidding in everything else."

"I cannot," Belisarius whispered, stepping close to Erik. "Do you not understand imperial authority? Hypatius must die." His eyes burned toward Lucian. "And not with his throat ripped out and his shambling corpse haunting the palace halls!"

The vampire raised a dramatic hand to his mouth but threw himself into a proper bow.

"Of course. It shall ever be as you say, my general."

Belisarius offered Erik a regretful expression. "You will only have a few hours before my troops are in place. You can take the tunnels beneath the palace to the Hippodrome now. Have your conversation concluded with Hypatius by midnight. Once the fighting begins, I cannot guarantee his survival." Questions must have lingered on Erik's face, for the general leaned in close to whisper into the younger man's ear, "There is much I would share with you yet, if I could. Your passing through the empire was not without cause. But it must wait for another day."

With that, Belisarius strode down the corridor to his chambers.

Cassandra grabbed the door latch, then pulled her hand from the frosty bite of the iron handle, leaving skin behind. She shook her fingers. But there was no time to wonder, for Procopius and his escort clattered down the hallway after her. She tested the latch with her sleeve and pushed the door open.

Dark basement apartments lay below. From a nearby hook, she lifted a flickering lamp and began her descent in an oily trail of smoke.

Soon, darkness consumed the lamplight. Cassandra quickened her pace when she heard Procopius at the door above, though he would be held up for at least a short time while they secured another lamp. She skipped steps, lamp held high, until she approached the bottom.

"My lady . . . please . . ." Procopius' voice trailed above her. "The general requires that you remain in his chambers! Please . . ."

Frigid air settled into Cassandra's lungs, even with her heart pounding against her ribs. Moving shadows populated the chamber beyond the stairs.

Eyes flashed.

Undead motion swept in and out of the shadows. A bone-white face flashed before her eyes, wild fangs extending from a gaping mouth and dripping with hunger and lust. Death-stench stung her nostrils, nauseating. The armored rattle of Procopius' guards above came to her as if through a fog. More faces appeared, and with them the memories of her ordeals in the catacombs.

"Erik!"

But her own voice sounded far distant in her ears as the cold bodies plunged and danced about her.

A growl rumbled across the chamber. The dead encircling Cassandra parted for Erik, now donning the armor of an East Roman knight—mail coat under lamellar scales, topped by a surcoat bearing the imperial eagle in scarlet and gold. In one hand he clutched the precious skin carrying the remaining dregs of Thelwyn's brew, and across his opposite shoulder lay the leather satchel he had borne from the distant shores of Albion. At his elbow hovered the same gaunt, sharp-faced creature she had seen in the palace earlier in the evening.

"Enough!" Erik snarled at the creatures. "Release her! All of you!"

Cassandra staggered against the cold wall. Above her, Procopius finally appeared, swinging a lantern. Steel flashed from the shadows right on his heels.

"You should not have come, Cassandra," Erik said sharply. "We have no time to spare."

"Yes," she replied breathlessly, "but I bring you word. Belisarius has paid off the Blues with gold and promises of renewed favor from the emperor."

"Yes, yes, my lady," Procopius chuffed. "But the general ordered you to—"

"The Blues even now leave the Hippodrome!" Cassandra said.

"The soldiers would have brought this information," Procopius pressed. "Please, my lady. This is no place for you!"

Then the cadaverous man laughed, a strange sound like the cracking of ice. With a flurry of shadows, he stepped onto the stair next to the scholar, his eyes lit with a wicked red glow. He laid a gaunt hand on Procopius' shoulder.

"And where in this city would be safer, dear historian? Do tell me that?"

Procopius shrank back. The guards behind him brandished their weapons.

"Enough, Lucian!"

Erik's voice took on a dangerous edge that Cassandra had never heard before. She knew he was dangerous—a predator that had been infused into the body of a youth. Yet she also knew she could trust him, for his soul had been forged of an honor running far deeper than the fires of hell that threatened to consume him.

"I'm coming with you!" Cassandra blurted. "You'll not leave me here!"

Erik tossed his satchel to one of the guards, who almost dropped it, then adjusted his imperial kit uncomfortably.

"I will not put you into harm's way, my lady."

She leaned close. "No more than just coming into this hole has put me into harm's way," she whispered. "I fear I'll spend the remainder of my days on holy ground, having been discovered by this lot."

"Why, should I take offense at that barb, lady?" Lucian chortled from the stairs. "We can be a very acquired taste, you know."

"All right," Erik conceded, "But this must be done quickly." Then he directed his words to Procopius. "You will take her to the docks and get her on a ship to Galata. My lady, at dawn you must ride to the stylite and wait for me there."

"But sir . . ." Procopius stammered, "the general will have all our heads!"

"Not for this night's work!" Erik snapped. "And if you do not ensure her safety, I will hunt you down. You and all your kin—and I swear I will ensure many long nights before they expire!"

Procopius swallowed hard. "I will do my best, sir."

"You will do it regardless," Erik countered, then coaxed the gray fox from the shadows with a gesture. "Take my gear and my companion. He will travel with you."

The creature leaped at Procopius' boots, causing the scholar to jump and stumble into the guards.

"I will be there," Cassandra answered. "I swear."

She thought a smile touched his lips in the light of the feeble lamps. But before she could tell for certain, he swept back into the shadows, the city's undead roiling in his wake.

The tunnel to the Hippodrome led directly to a staircase that reached up to the emperor's box. The passageway had been sealed at the

357

outbreak of the riots, with iron gates, chains, locks, and soldiers forming a layers-deep barrier to keep the rabble from the palace. When the squad of undead approached, the guard detail opened the way. The Hippodrome's stone structure trembled with the pounding of the mob's feet. And through that cacophony, the undead knight became attuned to the raging of the rabble's hearts.

After allowing them passage, the guards slammed the gates shut once more.

Erik rushed up the stairs, the undead snaking behind him. On reaching the outer door at the emperor's box, Lucian's claws gripped his arm. "Remember Hypatius must die," he hissed. "If you fail this, the general will never rest until we are all hunted down. Make sure you complete the task!"

Erik shrugged off the demon. "I know my duty."

The lock sprang open. Erik pressed a shoulder to the portal, but it resisted.

"Get your bodies up here," he demanded.

Lucian's undead conscripts pressed forward, lending their strength to his. The door groaned, the ancient oak bending, then issuing a flinty crack. Splinters exploded into the outer corridor with the sound of thunder.

Erik leaped through the wreckage, the very rogues of hell pouring through behind him.

Down the dark corridor they charged. The heart of the mob occupied the emperor's box where, according to Belisarius' own spies, they had crowned the frightened Hypatius with a crude circlet of tin.

Erik and his accursed company erupted into their midst, carving into them with a fury never seen in the ancient arena. The vampires of Constantinople shredded flesh, reveled in the splashing gore, and shrieked with unholy delight. Hapless mortals not killed outright began to panic, struggling to flee over the sides into the press below. Their terrified screams bewildered, then angered the thousands who could not see the immediate attack.

Erik fought through the din, scanning for his quarry, but Hypatius was not among the crowd swarming around him with knives, clubs, and broken tiles. Almost apologetically, Erik's trained sword-arm wove a web of death through falling bodies and dying faces. On reaching the front of the box overlooking the track itself, he saw the gallows, which now served as a throne. The scholar was slumped miserably in a chair among his mob of followers, his hands and feet tied to the wooden arms and legs.

The noise of the undead assault washed over the crowds, who finally realized something was amiss. They turned their collective faces upward to the imperial box to see a figure rising from the chaos, a Byzantine knight standing on the rail. He raised his sword above his head and, at that signal, the entrance gates at the far end of the track screamed under an outer assault. Defiance and despair alike rose from the tens of thousands.

The knight leaped like a bloodied eagle from the rail into a knot of rioters, who quickly fell before his long spatha. From there, he dropped to the next tier with an urgency made all the more terrifying by the dark swarm surging behind him like great four-limbed crows. Desperate screams broke out when the undead erupted from the emperor's box.

The noise at the main gate swelled, massive timbers bowing inward. Hinges whined, metal bent, and stone burst in, flinging shards with the collapsing gates. Soldiers dragged the wreckage away at the ends of thick ropes lashed to heavy warhorses. Roman troopers rushed into the gap, shields locked together, swords thrusting into rags and flesh. Step after heaving step they advanced until resistance crumbled. Panicked rioters bolted to escape. But those who fled the soldiers found themselves instead facing the flow of darkness erupting from the imperial box and racing down the tiers of the Hippodrome's seats, leaving the fallen twitching and bleeding in their wake.

For Erik, Belisarius' assault meant a foot race to the reluctant rival. The knight barreled over a man reckless enough to stand in his path, pulling his sword from the man's throat to leave him clutching desperately at fountaining blood. Onward, downward he sprinted, leaping over men, women, and children, shoving aside those he could and cutting down those he couldn't. Hot tears stained his cold cheeks. He clutched at that remorse like a drowning man would a raft, assured some part of him was still human.

Panic burst all around him. The battle against the riotous rebellion became a stampede and a slaughter.

Erik vaulted the rail that bound the track, landing heavily in the sand. Those nearest him stumbled away, only to be torn apart by Lucian and his minions. Nearby, elegantly robed senators trembled on the gallows platform, crying out in horror at the advance of the undead and the troops behind.

A handful of men halfheartedly shuffled toward him, clutching an array of impromptu weapons. Amelia, the daughter of the former chariot-racing champion and widow to a hanged man, urged them forward.

"You!" the disheveled woman shrieked over the clamor.

Insatiable hunger rose in Erik, a lust for blood and souls that threatened to tear him from any saving grace. Dark stains covered his hands, seeping through his leather gloves. His canines grew, framing wild teeth and shredding the inside of his mouth.

360

Take the covenant! chanted a voice in his head. Cayl's diminutive, grotesque shape danced before him on the gallows' stage: Arawn's unfortunate messenger, who had tormented him time and again through the shadows of Albion. Back and forth the demon swayed to its own musical cadence, arms weaving a strange pattern against the torchlit shadows.

A hand clutched Erik's shoulder.

"There is but one pathway forward," Lucian cooed.

The words wormed through his brain—*Take the covenant . . . take the covenant . . .*

Erik thrust his sword over his head. "Take them!" he roared. "But Hypatius is mine. Do you understand? He is mine!"

Without another gesture, the vampires swarmed ahead to the gallows platform. Torn flesh and pools of crimson froze on the icy planking. Cayl continued his grotesque contortions between the vampires, crowding the terrified senators, arms gyrating and face cut with an obscene grin.

Erik rushed to Hypatius' side, rending the scholar's bonds. But the dark stains on the knight's armor and the feral teeth filling his mouth did nothing to calm Hypatius' terror or to stem the steaming of the scholar's own piss down the legs of the chair.

Lucian, on the other hand, ignored everyone on those gallows—cowering senators, exultant vampires, even Erik and Hypatius. He held that woman, Amelia, in a predatory gaze. Wild hair tumbled about her face, covered in dust and crimson spatter, yet she did not shrink from the demon's crazed interest. Flakes of ash drifted like snow from the pitch sky. Though Lucian's hunger had since been sated, his intensity could have brought an emperor to his knees.

"You are glorious!" Lucian hissed, his tongue darting out to lick the gore from his lips.

Though his words elicited no response from her, the gaggle of senators took the advantage of his distraction to plead for their own lives. Lucian laughed, flicking a finger, and, as quick as that, his minions silenced them. But she remained defiant before the beast, daring him with her eyes—this disheveled daughter of a former champion.

Erik pulled Hypatius to his feet. "You're coming with me." His words slurred around his fangs.

"He will hunt you down and end you if you flee," Lucian said, his eyes locked on Amelia. "You must complete your obligation, or your head will top a pike!"

Erik snarled while struggling to reassert control over his faculties.

"And you would assist me?" Erik asked, a plan forming behind the crimson haze of his vision. "What is the price of your aid?"

"I would have her."

"As you will," Erik conceded. "And Hypatius. You will keep him safe until I conclude my affairs with the general."

"Of course," Lucian agreed. "I could not offer otherwise."

Erik began stripping the corpses of nearby dead senators. He tossed them at Hypatius.

"Quickly, if you would save your skin!" the knight demanded.

The scholar's face drained of color when he realized what was afoot.

Belisarius led his troops, all of them heaving with exhaustion and covered in sweat and blood, at double time onto the blood-soaked track. Those of the rioters who yet breathed fled before them. Soldiers peeled off in squads to round up survivors, many of whom yammered about evil spirits unleashed from the pits.

In the center of it all, torchlight glowed across the gallows, where Erik stood alone. The knight raised a bundle overhead in salute. Belisarius grimly mounted the stairs, his keen eyes surveying the slaughtered senators garbed in slashed and bloody robes.

"Hypatius?" he rasped, the words steaming in the chill air.

Erik tossed that bundle at the general's feet. The stained cloth fell open, disgorging a face whose features had been violently obliterated. But a crude tin crown tore loose from its brow, rolling to rest near a headless body clad in Hypatius' blood-soaked robes.

"Hypatius is no more," Erik snarled.

Belisarius rolled the head around with the toe of his boot, frowning at its condition. "And you gained the information you desired?"

"Of course," Erik replied, thrusting out his hand.

Belisarius gave the head one last, long look, then met Erik's eyes.

"Yes, of course." Belisarius hefted a short ivory staff topped by the imperial eagle spreading gold wings. "He was a good man and an even better scholar."

He pressed the totem into Erik's hand. "This will provide you passage through the empire," he continued. "None will question you. From Justinian in gratitude for your service—your assault saved the lives of many troopers this night."

Erik snatched it with a stiff bow. "I will leave the city now," he said through his teeth.

Without further ceremony, the knight turned his back on the general and left.

Belisarius' eyes returned to the battered head. The first knight of the empire frowned.

The dawn's earliest rays broke over the ruined city. Imperial troops disembarked their ships to march the short distance to the palace grounds. Amid the ashes of the Hagia Sophia, they deployed to restore order by pressing the surviving citizens into service gathering the masses of carcasses, limbs, and entrails that would have to be disposed of before disease could spread. The work progressed slowly beneath the flinty sky. Soon enough, a steady flow of oxcarts flanked by sweaty laborers and the occasional mourner plodded out of the city's landward gates. Beyond the edges of the suburbs, thick columns of inky smoke marked the fires that consumed the bodies.

By mid-morning, Tetrarch Ionnes had become thoroughly bored with his shift at the Regia Gate. At least he'd finally become accustomed to the stench, and he thanked Heaven above he had not been assigned to the unloading detail. He waved the next wagon through without looking until it turned onto a street heading northwest through a residential area.

When he commanded it to stop, the scrawny driver produced an imperial token worked in ivory and gold. The soldier grunted, but he well knew his place within the city's fabric, and so waved the caisson onward. Idly, he watched it rattle slowly away until it rounded a bend. Then the moment's distraction ended. He turned to his work without sparing it another thought.

—∞∞∞—

Chapter Seventeen

DIVINE MANDATE

Marianna swept her hand across the table, scattering the carved markers off the map. "I do not care. Can you not see that?"

"Please, my lady," Donoch pled. "Listen to Lord Magwyn. He has a workable plan."

"Do you understand what we're facing?" she growled, turning her fury on Donoch. "Arawn knows we failed to break out."

"In truth he has said nothing," the ever-stoic Magwyn offered. "And it has been many weeks since our first attempt."

"And four attacks more since. All have failed. And yes—we have heard nothing."

Marianna leaned hard on the map table. Her shoulders quaked with nearly more rage than she could handle, and deep in her soul smoldered more embers of fear than she wished to admit.

"Why has he not said anything? *We have failed him.*"

"Have we?" Magwyn purred with a galling calm. "Or should I say have we yet?"

Marianna's brow furrowed. "Make your meaning clear, castellan," she snapped.

"What exactly does our master need from us?" he asked. "What, truly, is our purpose here?"

A puzzled look crossed her finely shaped features before she turned her gaze to the map on the table.

"We are to defend the Rift?" Donoch offered.

"Which we have done," Magwyn confirmed, his tone one of condescending boredom. "I am sure Arawn will approve."

Marianna groaned and threw her head back. "It's in removing the threat that we have failed, gentlemen. I know our purpose. Soon reinforcements will arrive to bolster my father's forces. Or even allies to finish us off. More enemies to discover what is here. I am not ignorant of the strategic situation!"

Donoch fidgeted, while Magwyn's face continued to reveal little of the steward's thoughts.

"My point, Magwyn, is this," she continued with a snarl. "We must get my father off our doorstep. But if we only drove him away, he would find the means to return. We must annihilate him, and every man in his company."

"We have inflicted many casualties on them already, my lady—" Donoch replied.

"You dullard!" she snapped. "Shut your mouth!"

Donoch visibly bristled at the rebuke, but Magwyn laid a restraining hand on his shoulder. Marianna continued, choosing to ignore the gesture.

"We cannot deal with him as we must with the forces remaining us. I doubt we could even break the siege at this point. And I want to know why"—she clenched her fists—"why Arawn has not communicated with us. Not to guide us, not to reassure us . . . not even to rebuke us."

Magwyn took a step toward the door, clearly wanting to end the conversation. "Arawn is yet weak," he murmured. "He must prioritize his strength. I would postulate that he has been very busy with the young knight."

Marianna bowed her head, shaking it from side to side so that her hair fell across her features. Then she folded her fists into her armpits.

"Even gone from us, the errant dictates my actions," she seethed.

At length she lifted her chin, squaring her shoulders to reframe her orientation to the two men.

"Magwyn, a moment ago you were certain Arawn would approve of our efforts."

"Yes, my lady."

"Yet it is I, not you, that will rely for my very existence on that," she said pointedly.

"Well, my lady, you are correct," Magwyn admitted.

"Then your words are but empty assurances."

Magwyn chewed his lip. "That is always possible, my lady."

"Then make it up to me," she said. "Tell me of this plan of yours."

The corridor was still shrouded, illumined with smoking lamps. Beyond the windows, panes frosted with iced lace, the sun would soon test the night with the first light of dawn. Night. Day.

Regardless of the time, the two men traversing those halls had tasks to fulfill, which would not wait for another cycle of time. Her sharp words still fresh in his mind, Donoch stomped down the middle of the corridor, slamming his fist into his palm.

"Why does she not understand?" Donoch muttered.

Magwyn gathered his cloak to keep the hem from dragging on the floor. Winter storms swirled outside the closed windows, and the inner stone walls wept with condensation.

"She is proud," Magwyn mused. "She believes all our efforts originate with her, but there is not time to bring her around to this action."

"She is a royal brat," Donoch spat. "She kept going on about obliterating her own father. I think she liked that idea a little too much."

"She will come around to what we need," Magwyn said. "Then we can allow Mattheus to overpower the last defenders and invest the castle."

They arrived at a hallway juncture, where Donoch mockingly bowed to Magwyn. "Then I will leave you to your duties," the soldier grumbled. "And I will scour the countryside to collect some poor raven-haired, heavy-chested maiden. And I swear I will throttle her myself."

Magwyn regarded him with bemusement.

"We must make do when we can," Donoch said, a crooked leer across his lips.

Many hours passed before Magwyn's errands allowed him to return to the map room. However, the castellan was surprised to find that Marianna, with remarkable precision, had replaced the markers on the vellum.

He paused on the threshold, then knocked against the door frame.

"I heard you coming," she said.

"My lady," he replied coolly. "As perceptive as ever."

"You have completed your task? I assume the lower levels are sealed."

"Mattheus will find no evidence of the Rift when he enters," he assured her. "It will be safe until our return."

"My father is stubborn. And aggravatingly thorough."

"When he sees nothing, he will pack up and leave," the steward said. "And this agglomeration of stone and mold will be empty as the day I first installed Blaine in the days of Arthur."

"And Donoch?" she asked.

"Gone to find you a suitable stand-in, my lady."

"I see. So you are moving forward already. For what it's worth, I hope he nabs one of the Donno family," she continued. "I never liked them."

Magwyn felt a chill run up his neck, not only at her perceptiveness but her spite.

"I doubt my father will fall for the ruse, though," she continued. "He saw me. He spoke with me."

"His heart will convince his mind that the woman with whom he spoke was not you but another whose body will be found here instead. He will conclude this was an unfortunate, wasteful goose chase. He will leave."

"We are in a precarious position. Our options *are* limited," Marianna said, noticing a quizzical look on his face. "What?"

"My lady. Just a question, if I may. Why did you do it? Why did you accept the Blood?"

"Why?" She hissed at his boldness. "You of all the undying should understand the answer to the question."

Magwyn's face regained his cool detachment. "Mere curiosity."

She scrutinized him with those dangerous dark eyes, then lifted her hands to his face. "Look at me, Magwyn," she cooed, flashing her beguiling eyes and pushing her breasts against him. "Am I not beautiful? If I were to cast off my clothes and stretch upon this table, would you not desire to take me?"

Magwyn's face remained stony. "You belong to our master. There is no need to speak of such things."

Marianna laughed, a scathing, mocking cackle. "Belong?" she asked. "Do the morals of God hold any sway here? Can I not straddle my legs over any man I choose? Even that fool Donoch? Arawn has been centuries without a body. Does he feel desire, lust, or an animal hunger for anything but raw power? What is skin as pale and smooth as the cliffs of Dwfr to the rush of a wind blowing across vast domains? Nothing! Not to him! But to me . . ."

She leaned over the table, arching her back suggestively, feet apart and swaying her hips from side to side. Magwyn averted his eyes.

"For me," she continued, resting her hand upon her chin, "I need to feel a touch. A caress."

She faced him, stretching her arms over her head to lift her breasts nearly out of her bodice.

"I saw my grandmothers advance in age," she said. "I cared for them when their bodies withered and their minds faded. I cleaned the filth from those decaying bodies—and I listened when they said things better left in the past. Things that could have torn our kingdom apart if anyone else had known."

She lowered her arms, readjusted her dress, then slid her hands over her ribs and down her belly.

"Oh, the stories they told. I wanted to experience those things myself!" She clutched her sash in knotted fists and took a deep breath. "But to accomplish so much, and discreetly? That takes time. Too much time. And I have no desire to become them—aged, senile, lying in my own waste. There was no other choice."

Magwyn swallowed hard, clearing his throat. She stood before him trapped forever in the flower of youth, eternally perfect in form and face. His eyes traced the sweep of her gown, the curve of her hip, the arch of her back. When his gaze reached her shoulder, he instantly saw tension in her neck muscles. He swept along with her eyes to a corner of the room.

A small form huddled in the shadows, hooded, squat, misshapen, and breathing heavily. The creature giggled, a raspy, demented sound.

"Cayl!" Marianne breathed. "How long have you been there?"

"A-a-as long as . . . cliffs of Dwfr!" the creature sputtered, swaying its hips in a freakish burlesque.

"And you appear to have grown a sense of irony," Magwyn observed dryly.

Marianna slammed her fist on the table, toppling the markers again. "What do you want? Speak, imp!"

"You," Cayl shot back, slamming its clenched fist on a chair in mock anger. "Master wants you!"

The imp giggled uncontrollably, then rubbed its hands over its crotch. Then it collapsed to the floor, spittle flinging in thick strings.

With one swift, agile motion Marianna drew her sword, lopping off Cayl's head. Before the fountaining ichor could strike the flagstones, the creature had crumbled to dust.

371

She swung the blade through wide arcs, inspected it to ensure the steel was clean, and sheathed it.

"It appears," she said with a throaty voice, "you must break those wards below."

Magwyn roughly clutched her arm before she could slide past him. "Say nothing to the emissary of the Council."

"Would I admit another failure?" she said, regarding him as if he had lost his mind before jerking her arm free and striding away.

He watched her go for a long moment, then glanced back to the pile of dust in the corner. "Such a waste. It was learning to be funny."

Under the lowest storeroom in the castle was an expansive, rough-hewn chamber lit only by luminescent fungi that clung to its walls. In the center, a stone fount, three rods across, fed a pool filled with water so dark it ate all surrounding light. On the far side, a crack in the living bedrock issued wisps of fog that curled out like beckoning arms.

Marianna inspected the chamber carefully, from the fresh chisel marks on the walls to the fine dust that had not yet been swept up by the hands that had opened this room.

Standing near, Magwyn said, "I have not been here for quite some time."

"Not quite the dusty storeroom it once was, is it?" Marianna observed, not believing a single word that came out of his mouth.

"The pool is a nice touch," the castellan noted. "For the return of our forces—"

"Once we have the Cauldron in our possession again," she finished with certainty.

Marianna stepped gracefully toward the gap in the far wall. The mist folded, swirled, then reached out to her once more. This was the Rift, torn decades ago into the rock wall. She closed her cloak about her shoulders.

"You may seal the lower floors once I depart."

Magwyn smirked, asking with a flinty voice, "You are not expecting to return?"

"When I need you, you will know," she said.

Without another word, she stepped into the mist.

In time, the stony walls of the gap fell away until only the fog surrounded her. Her soft-heeled boots made nary a sound on the floor. The dark was absolute, but she had no need of light, for she relied on the supernatural guidance of her species. She found comfort in this, her true element.

Yet she had not made this journey before. In her previous travels through the planes of reality, Magwyn had brought her back by ship, entering Annwyn through one of Arawn's gates. But that voyage expended much glorified energy—energy that the Grey God could ill afford to squander. Her unfamiliarity with the pathway mattered little, for her master awaited at the end of her trek. She walked steadily through the Between toward him, quickening her pace.

Thinking of Magwyn brought to her mind his last comment in the map room. Why shouldn't she tell Arawn of the vile Kraken and the creature's connection to the Cauldron? Clearly the castellan worked his own scheme, and for this Marianna remained wary of him. The hypocrite had the nerve to accuse her of not furthering the master's command, all the while testing the waters to enlist her as a confederate for his unknown machinations. However, only oblivion lay at the end of *that* path.

Her musing ended abruptly when the swirling mists parted and she found herself before an ornate door.

She rapped once.

The door's latch clacked, the door creaked open, and she heard a quietly commanding voice.

"Enter."

Head bowed reverently and hands clasped over her heart, she did as she was commanded: She entered a room of dark stone and approached the great black throne planted on the dais on the far end. At the foot of the steps, she sank to her knees. Heavy silence stretched on for several heartbeats. No, not quite total silence. A sound emanated from beyond the throne, past the great basalt pillars that soared up to the vaulted roof, past the expansive balcony overlooking Arawn's city. A sound like waves pounding a shore, which was odd, as the seas that surrounded Annwyn were calm as glass.

"Arise, *a thaisce.* Come closer."

She rose, then stepped gracefully up the few stairs to the arm of Arawn, Prince of the Otherworld and Master of Albion's Dead. She demurely laid a hesitant hand on his shoulder to be absorbed into his steely orbs that drew her very spirit into him. She swayed with a sensation like blood rushing from her head when she was a mortal. Except that now she was quite dead.

He laid a hand over hers. Her undead heart leapt in her chest.

"How fares our redoubt in the lower plane?"

From the timbre of his voice, she realized there would be no further pleasantries.

"We hold our own, my master."

"We do. That is well," the god intoned.

He stood, beckoning her to follow him to the balcony. He glided across the smooth flagstones past the pillars. She hurried to match his steps.

"I have seen the dead traverse into Annwyn from your skirmishes," he said. "This has not been without cost."

"No, Master, it has not."

They reached the stone rail at the edge of the platform, and there Arawn swept a hand expansively across the city below. Though the talus of the castle's foundation walls was lost in darkness, the buildings below were illuminated by brightly lit torches and lamps.

"Behold the honored dead," he said. "Here they lack for nothing."

"You care for them, Master. Your divine Shadow shelters them like babes."

"Indeed," he said, as taciturn and unreadable as ever. "Remove your clothes, princess."

"I— I'm sorry, my master?" she replied with a confused scan of their surroundings.

They were alone, but the entire city lay just over the balcony.

Bewildered, she complied. In turn, she removed her sword and belt, bodice and dress and handed them over. She was grateful she no longer felt the cold.

"The chemise as well. And the mamillare."

With growing excitement, she slid out of her undertunic and unbound her breasts. Clad now only in her boots, wind swirling over her exposed skin, she boldly handed him her last coverings.

He encircled an arm about her waist, easing her to the battlements. She panted, her skin tingling with the divine sensation that washed over her. A stronger wind from the city slid between the railing stiles to climb up her body from her ankles to her throat. She felt his hand move down to her hip, arrive at the small of her back, her shoulder, and finally her neck, triggering bursts of energy like lightning up her spine.

He pressed against her from behind, pinning her against the rough stonework. With his hand on her neck, he pushed her head out over the empty air, and she nearly shrieked. Far below she could see the milling populace, intent on diversions that occupied their eternities, oblivious to the spectacle above. The smooth stone rail dug into her hip, and she snatched back reflexively to grab it. Then her crumpled clothing flew over the rail, fluttering down, down, down. Arawn snatched her hair and wrenched her head back, arching her back painfully.

"See you the restless dead!" he growled.

No longer aroused, she was suddenly afraid. Dead though she may be, a fall from this height could still be ruinous. The dead far below were not milling about aimlessly as she had thought, but were agitated. Fires burned in the streets, licking at the eaves of buildings as mobs raced the thoroughfares.

"I give them everything, and they want more," he mused. "They want the Blessed Isles."

"Surely— surely—" she gasped, dismay in her voice, "the wicked understand they must do their penance, do they not, my lord?"

"It is not the wicked that resist. They know their lot. It is the just, the valiant. And even they are willing to tolerate setbacks. But the children . . . the innocent children do not move up to the Isles, and for this the base and the noble join against me!"

He dragged her from the rail until her ear was at his lips. Sudden pain shot up her spine. She heaved a much different gasp when his words spilled over her like an oily glissade.

"I took the Ebon Throne by rebellion. Think you not but it can happen again. I need my Cauldron, and the Rift must stay open to find it!"

He reached his other hand over her shoulder, her sword clutched blade downward, his thumb on the pommel. With a swift and sure movement, he snapped the oathing-stone clean off the hilt. It bounced on a crenelation at her feet, then disappeared into the gloom above the city.

"I have had my fill of failure," he whispered. "So, Princess . . . do I send you back or destroy you here and now?"

Chapter Eighteen

---⊗⊗⊗---

I Pledge My Sacred Honor

The air was thick and earthy, even on a cold day. Wiping a foul-smelling hand across his brow, the prince of rags leaned on the shovel. With midday approaching, Aldonzo scanned the nearby paddocks. His breathing stopped, but the mist of his breath rose before his eyes.

The baying of the hounds had stopped.

He leaned the shovel against the barn, then trudged wearily back to the old inn. On his right, the still waters of a small lake sparkled, an icy crust around the edges. To his left, a tall, silent, and venerable forest stood between the inn and the city of Brest.

Brest. Entering the city had been simple enough, though Elaetha had been visibly uncomfortable passing through the arched gate. But the young woman had insisted they find lodgings in the city. She even led the way to a stall in an out-of-the-way market where they exchanged

378

Fainche's torc for needed coin. But rooms within the walls were expensive.

After three days and satisfactory advice from a healer, Aldonzo packed up his little band, moving them out through the north gate to this inn. They had chanced upon the aged, squint-eyed proprietor, Judoc, during their first hours in the city. Over a mug of warm ale, he lamented his lack of trusted labor for his establishment. Desperate for shelter, Aldonzo presented an offer to him—a cook, a stable hand, and a miniature scullery maid for the price of room and board. That had been a few weeks ago, just as winter began setting in. In recent days, those few flakes of snow had continued to melt, making Yuletide a sloppy mess. During that entire time, the Hounds could be heard baying through the night, sometimes close, sometimes distant, but always there.

He rounded a corner of the inn. Movement in the great room cast shadows against the covered windows. The prince continued to the back of the building. Aldonzo had become accustomed to coming and going from the rear entrance, for he was the *married* man with no need for nocturnal attentions in the great room among the patrons.

When they had arrived at the inn, Judoc had assumed they were married. Elaetha and the prince simply let it go uncorrected. Aldonzo recalled the story of Abraham in Pharaoh's court passing Sarai off as his sister to save his life. Aldonzo felt much the same way here, though there was no fear of death—they simply could only negotiate for one room, and this was a necessary untruth to avoid uncomfortable questions.

Aldonzo opened the back door and stepped inside to hang his cloak on the peg. He mounted the back stair, avoiding the kitchen's sweltering oven. This hostel had been active since the days of Roman

Gaul. It boasted very sophisticated imperial-style architecture, with an upper floor and even an attic, to which he now ascended.

At the small door at the top, he smelled the pleasant aroma of fresh-baked bread. *Even better than Axe's,* he thought, *and that animal could cook.*

He opened the door.

Fainche was sprawled on the bed, mangling a small bun of her very own and feeding crumbs to her doll. Elaetha sat cross-legged next to their fireplace with two more golden loaves. She looked up, wrinkled her nose at him, and pointed to the wash basin.

"Just like a Celt," Aldonzo joked. "Always obsessed with bathing."

"Well, you should smell yourself. I am not having that stink suffocate us tonight."

She teased him, of course, for he slept on the small pallet across the room. They may have been masquerading as a family, but that ruse only went so far.

"As you wish, my queen," he said with a bit of a laugh before plunging his hands into the water and scrubbing.

When he looked up, a towel struck him in the face. Elaetha snorted with a smile that extended to her eyes.

"Have you noticed the Hounds?" he asked.

She limped across the room, taking the towel from his hands. "Let me do that," she replied, snatching the towel from him. "What about the Hounds?"

She wiped the water away with more authority than Aldonzo thought was necessary. The casual intimacy carried with it a sensation he could only describe as *comfortable.* He savored the experience for that moment.

"What about the Hounds, Aldonzo?"

380

"Oh. They made no noise tonight—" His words blubbered when Elaetha rubbed the towel across his lips.

Fainche laughed. "Blub, blub, blub," she mimicked.

Elaetha cocked an ear. "I did not hear them," she said.

"I cannot smell them, either!" Fainche chimed in.

Elaetha's brow furrowed. "I thought they were part of me for so long," she murmured. "Well, I for one am glad to finally be rid of them."

"Though there must be a reason," Aldonzo said. "Such a blessing cannot be without consequence."

The evening had long since become night. Amid squawks and fidgets, and under the light of a single lamp, Elaetha gently tugged up Fainche's hair. Aldonzo stretched on the pallet, rubbing his calves. The inn had quieted already, so the creak of a foot on the step drew their instant attention.

Someone rapped on the door. They scrambled to their feet and Aldonzo opened it.

Judoc wheezed, clutching at the door frame. "Aldonzo, me boy," he sputtered, his tone amiable even as his eyes shifted back and forth, unfocused. "There's a man a-down below asking for ya."

What sort of man?" Elaetha asked.

"An old traveler. Bent. He walks with a stick," the innkeeper said. "Damned if I ken where 'e hails from. Got a strange tilt to his lingo."

Aldonzo thought that observation odd, for Judoc had been a seafarer in a former life. After one too many stormy voyages, the old man had taken up running this successful stopover outside a busy port town. Nearly every language in the world must have fallen upon his ears, and he probably spoke many of them.

"Have a care, my boy, sure enough," the innkeeper advised. "Seems dodgy."

"How so?" Aldonzo asked.

"No name. Shifty, very cautious. Kept looking at the door like a man hidin'. Not afeared, mind. Just wary. Do not think ya could dodge 'im. Though I could cover for ya."

"It'll be fine," Aldonzo muttered. "Feed him. Fill his belly with wine."

"Yah, I got that handled. Take yarself a moment or three. I will keep 'im occupied till you get down."

He let go the door jamb, then headed back down the stairs.

"What do you think?" Elaetha asked.

"Sneaking around looking for me," he said with a wry grin. "So not one of Mattheus.' Must be on good enough terms with the Bretons. He moves openly."

Fainche spoke up from the bed, clenching her bread until it crumbled. "Scowl-Britches? Get him, Aldonzo! We can all fight back!"

"I doubt *he* would go to that much trouble to track us," he replied thoughtfully. "Our trail is long gone. No. That just leaves my family."

Elaetha shrugged, folding her arms. "Only one way to find out," she said. "Besides, your mission to save Marianna cannot be accomplished from here. If you remain much longer, you will either wind up a brigand or a slave, unless Judoc takes you on for good."

"I would make a fine innkeeper," Aldonzo posited. Elaetha snorted, but Fainche fairly guffawed.

Aldonzo exhaled through pursed lips. "Fine, then." He snatched his boots and tugged them onto his feet. "I need you to come with me. Both of you."

"What for?" Elaetha asked, a bit off guard.

Aldonzo tucked the bread knife into his boot. "In case we need to run," he said. "If he tries to take me back."

The man sat on a bench in a corner of the common room, far from the glow of the fire. A dusty, shapeless cloak hung over what appeared to be monk's robes. The cowl shadowing his face remained still, facing his table, as they creaked down the stairs. The man sat well-postured on his stool, hardly wearied the way you'd expect of a man who'd traveled a long way. Aldonzo took the bench across from him and gestured to an adjoining table for Elaetha and Fainche.

"You sent for me, sir?" he asked.

The newcomer reeked of fine scented oils that twitched Aldonzo's nose. But the traveler did not appear to notice. Rather, he shifted in his seat enough to see the girls when they clambered into their seats, then shrugged and reached into his robes. Aldonzo's hand dropped cautiously to the knife handle in his boot, but the stranger only pulled out a small golden object and rolled it across the table to him.

It was a ring.

It was *his* ring, the same taken by the pirate Fenyas months ago. Aldonzo's left hand clenched reflexively over the stump of his missing finger.

The old man grunted and said, "You are Aldonzo de Languedoc of Septimania."

383

"So you say," Aldonzo replied.

"I could kill you now and dispense with the dance," he hissed with palpable disdain. He angled his hood fully toward Aldonzo.

"Then do it," the prince said flatly.

Elaetha audibly caught her breath.

"Oh, surely not in light of your feelings towards them," the man replied, gesturing toward the girls. "Young one, I have made a very, *very* long study of men. You were revealed the instant your eyes caught the ring. I know about your journey from Albion. Come, now—there is no reason for us to be at odds. You have information that I desire. In return, I can be an ally."

Elaetha interjected herself into the conversation and said, "What is it you want, sir?"

"Tell me of this expedition you participated in—the one for Mattheus, King of Gwent."

"How do you know of that?" Aldonzo asked, feeling like he stood on sand with water lapping at his feet.

"Cymru is an interesting region of late. A very interesting region."

The air took on a thick quality. And while Elaetha had tried to keep Fainche occupied, the hour was late. The child grew fussy. She threw her doll on the floor, folded her arms with a huff, and kicked her legs against the wooden bench. Elaetha reached for the toy, but her hand froze before touching it.

"They have returned," she breathed.

Far in the distance, the hills beyond the oiled skin windows echoed with the baying of the Hounds. The traveler stole a glance at the door, a move well marked by Aldonzo.

When the man spoke, urgency laced his words. "Tell me of that expedition!"

A cranky squeal from Fainche snagged Aldonzo's attention. The prince realized a tantrum could unnecessarily burden an already very dangerous moment, so he dropped his pretenses.

"You know my name, stranger. What of yours?"

The man drew back his cowl, revealing a handsome face that wasn't much more aged than Aldonzo.

"You may call me Ganelon," he said.

The baying drew closer to the inn.

"Whatever is to be said can be said to all of us," Aldonzo prompted.

The traveler leaned in close, urgency in his voice. "You were trying to recover Mattheus' daughter Marianna. You are betrothed to her?"

"I . . . was," the prince replied.

"Did you find her?"

"No."

"Did you at least find where she was held? Tell me where that is."

There was a loud *bang* on the door, accompanied by a canine panting noise. Shapes moved outside, silhouetted against the window's oiled skins. Judoc shuffled to stand sentinel near the front door, massive cleaver in hand, while stealing nervous glances at the exchange.

Ganelon squirmed in his seat. "I must know. Name a price for your assistance."

A whip cracked outside. Shouts and calls closed on the inn. Ganelon slammed a hand on the table to push himself to his feet.

"You will take us there," Aldonzo blurted. "To that place."

"Us?"

"Me and them." He nodded toward the girls. "We all go. Or none."

Elaetha's jaw dropped, parting her lips until Fainche reached up to push on her chin. Ganelon cocked a brow but waved a dismissive hand.

"Easy enough," he agreed. "Now to get you out. Innkeeper!"

Judoc flinched, nearly staggering into a nearby table.

"My good sir," Ganelon said, asserting an authority that deepened the timbre of his voice. "Back door?"

"Just there." The innkeeper waved the cleaver before lowering it sheepishly.

"Why do we need to flee?" Elaetha started. "The Hounds aren't after us."

"No time for questions," Ganelon replied with a haunted ripple in his voice. "They've summoned the Hunt!"

Elaetha scooped up Fainche, then Ganelon ushered them all out of the back door. When they stepped into the cool of the night, an ethereal light beamed through the trees on the far side of the inn. Shadows moved within that light—large ones that stirred a primal fright.

Ganelon whistled out over the water.

"What is he doing?" Elaetha panted to Aldonzo.

"Quiet!" Ganelon cut her off. "I'm getting you out of here."

He whistled again, the shouting behind them growing louder. An eerie light emerged from the darkness. He whistled a third time, almost desperately. A gray mist rose from the water, drifting to the shore, where it formed a silvery, ethereal war horse, its mane flowing endlessly back into mist.

"Ceffyl Dour!" Elaetha gasped.

Ganelon hustled the three onto the horse's broad back. He then whispered instructions into its ear before pulling a ring from his finger. The traveler handed that to the prince.

"My friend will take you to the docks in Aletum," Ganelon said. "There you will find my ship, the *Pagan Dancer*. Give this to her master. He will take you across the Saxiconum."

The horse danced when a *crack* echoed behind them, as if from a falling tree. Ganelon raised his hand over the animal's flank.

"Whatever you do, do not ride over water!"

Before Aldonzo could vocalize a question, Ganelon slapped the horse. Great misty wings erupted from its withers. The beast flung itself into the air, carrying the three terrified refugees into the wind-whipped sky.

Eyes watering from the cold wind, Aldonzo dared a look down. A tall shade in an antlered helm rode a chariot drawn by stags, surrounded by the Hounds, nine of them now. They rushed from the wood toward Ganelon, who yet stood by the lake. But the traveler was visible for only an instant before bursting into a dark cloud that swirled away. The beasts and men that followed the Huntsman spread out like a great dark fan. Aldonzo was relieved to see the pack ignore the inn itself as they surged toward the lake.

At the water's edge the Huntsman stopped. He sniffed at the air, then looked skyward, shaking a fist at the trio before Ceffyl Dour swooped down low over Brest, then struck out to the northeast.

Two hours later, the spectral steed winged over a Roman fortress city, which Aldonzo could only assume to be Aletum, in great sweeping circles. Throughout the flight, he had followed their progress across the countryside to keep his mind occupied and distracted from the numbing cold. Nevertheless, while he had seen many maps of the continent in his day, under the moonlight every river, every lake, every mountain looked like every other from the mythical steed's back.

Aldonzo grabbed Ceffyl Dour's mane at the roots beneath the strange mist-like filaments that trailed off into the wind. The prince coaxed the beast further inland, mindful of Ganelon's admonition about flying over water. After a spectacular approach, Ceffyl Dour alighted on the docks with a whoosh of mystical wings and a clatter of hooves.

A single ship lay tied to the rail. Aldonzo slid onto the planking, then assisted the girls, who groaned, stretched, and limped around in circles to regain circulation in their frozen limbs. Once they were clear, Ceffyl Dour burst into the air once more, surging over the waters of the bay, where he promptly dissipated into fog.

Don't ride over water, indeed! Aldonzo thought.

The boat creaked and stirred against its moorings. Aldonzo wrapped his arms around the two girls, urging them to the ship, where the gangplank invited them to board. A single lantern burned at the stern.

"The *Pagan Dancer*, I presume?" Elaetha said, arching an eyebrow.

"I hope so. The only tub available, it appears," Aldonzo huffed.

"Why, do you suppose, did he not kill you?" Elaetha asked, watching Aldonzo out of the corner of her eye. "Although he made the right decision, mind you."

"Comforting indeed," Aldonzo replied.

Elaetha moved close, nudging him with her shoulder. "Do not be like that. I am much happier with you alive."

"Are you?" he said, trying to make it playful. But her eyes in the moonlight became suddenly serious, and her voice made a subtle shift in tone.

"I am, Aldonzo. I truly am."

They stopped at the bottom of the gangplank. No movement was apparent above. Aldonzo reached into his pouch, withdrawing the ring, once again his.

"He said I could give him something he wanted *and* something he needed. I know he needed information . . . but what did he *want*? And how could he have gotten anything if he had killed me?"

Unable to answer his own question, he shrugged, then took a step onto the gangplank. But before his foot landed on the cross tread, Elaetha grabbed his arm. "Wait, Aldonzo. There's one other thing I need to know."

"What is it?" he asked, but he noticed her face once more became a mask, neutral of any thought or intent.

"Why were we part of the bargain?"

Aldonzo was taken aback. "How do you not know?"

"And how *would* I know?"

He nodded. She was right, of course. "It was that night with the Hounds, when I swore to protect Fainche," he said with a firmness that surprised even him. "To protect her with my life."

"But that was Fainche. You swore no oath to me."

"What kind of a nobleman would I be if I broke up a family?" Aldonzo stated, allowing a smirk to touch his lips—an expression that appeared to irritate her, if only in small measure. "But you are right. We must rectify that before we take journey."

He dropped to one knee, took her hand in his, and summoned his most dramatic voice.

"Lady Elaetha!" he began, but as he went on, the drama dissolved and a surprising sincerity took its place. "Inasmuch as I have made you a fugitive . . . inasmuch as I have wounded you with mine own blade . . .

and inasmuch as I have blatantly lied to good people for the sole purpose of ensuring your welfare—making you dishonest by extension"—his voice hitched and he caught himself placing his hand reflexively over his heart—"I throw myself upon your mercy and swear to ever atone for these sins. Please accept my humble offer until such time you shall deem the debt paid." He looked up at her from under his brows.

Elaetha scowled at him. "You are a scoundrel, Aldonzo of Septimania," she quipped, but she did not pull back her hand.

He stood, releasing her hand so as not to hold it too long. "Perhaps I am," he admitted. "But now I am *your* scoundrel."

Fainche could only stand by, wondering, as a one-time prince of the Visigoths offered a slave girl a slight bow and a rakish grin.

Elaetha rolled her eyes, but her own smile reached to her eyes, and for the moment Aldonzo was content.

Fainche squealed and jumped, pointing up the gangplank. A corpulent figure had finally appeared at the rail, silhouetted against the night sky, head cocked to one side as if trying to make sense of what he'd just witnessed.

Chapter Nineteen

THE ROAD BENEATH

A full day had passed since the revolt had been put down. At the end, Erik had been insane with undead hunger, egged on by rivers of flowing gore, such that it had taken all of Lucian's considerable strength and several of his followers to secure the young Briton. To his credit, Hypatius managed to retain his own wits despite everything he had witnessed, and once the Higher Dead had lashed the crate into a wagon, he navigated it out of the city before the sun rose.

Beneath the driver and inside that government-issued crate, Erik jounced along in a feral state. He hung by the length of the blade thrust through his chest and lodged into the stout planking against his back by the city's Higher Dead. The knight remained nearly oblivious to the day's journey and the passage of the sun into the west.

His flesh recoiled, however, when the wagon finally entered the holy ground near the stylite's broken column. For the whispered cries of the surviving harpies reached his ears, those damned creatures still seeking entry through the wards that surrounded the stylite's refuge.

The wagon creaked to a halt. Then, a moment later, there was the *thump* of a mallet. Wooden pegs squealed, and the side of the box opened.

"No!" Erik raised clawed hands before his toothy face, pressing his body against the remaining length of the blade to the back of the crate.

But the wooden panel fell open to reveal the dark column and its rickety ladder, the only pathway upward to the holy man.

Cassandra beckoned him to come forth.

"Please," she whispered. She held her hand out, not shrinking from the beast lurking in the darkness.

Erik shuddered but saw no other way to keep the curse from cutting through everyone that might cross his path. Regardless of not accepting the covenants offered by ancient gods, his own actions appeared to seal his fate. Peering through his splayed fingers, Erik's bloodshot eyes met hers. But her eyes remained steady—for all he had done, he believed she continued to trust him.

He lowered his hands to the spatha's hilt protruding from his midsection and wrenched the weapon free. He fell forward onto his face. Then the knight crawled to her, reaching up to take her hand. She drew him forth into the moonlight, where he planted his feet on the ground, taking the few halting steps to the ladder. The knight grabbed a rung and began the climb.

Erik struggled harder to harder to lift fingers, then feet, from one rung to the next. He leveraged his body against the ladder, stretching his limbs and grinding his joints for each step. The wound in his abdomen shrieked in agony. As he lifted his eyes upward toward the starry sky above, the stylite's form superimposed itself across the enormity on the edge of the broken column. A blinding light rimmed the monk's craggy features with a brilliance that caused Erik to throw a hand before his face. But his skin did not blister and burn.

Daniel's gnarled hand extended to him.

"No," Erik groaned. "I should not be here . . . I am unclean."

The stylite studied the knight's face for a moment, the crevices across his own features softening.

"We have need of each other most when we are unworthy, my dearest son." He offered his hand once more.

"I killed . . . so many, so very many," Erik murmured. "I am covered in their blood." With each word the wild teeth in his mouth slashed his flesh and ichor poured from the wounds.

The stylite extended his hand yet again, his dark eyes meeting Erik's. A vortex of veins and shadows swirled in the knight's orbs. Under the holy man's scrutiny, layer upon layer of his guilt peeled away to uncover afresh old wounds. Each was populated by those he had left behind, bodies torn, blood congealed, eyes clouded with death.

A gallant steed galloping beneath a clear, moonlit sky with a Briton knight straight in the saddle. Pirates off the Saxon shore, wicked men who took on more than they had bargained for. Innocent citizens that wanted nothing more than to be heard and dealt with justly.

Somewhere, buried deep beyond those layers of turmoil and shame, there supposedly lay an honorable heart and a noble quest. Yet the war horse now lay rotting in a forgotten meadow, the raiders' burnt remains long sunk to the bottom of the sea, and the citizens' blood yet stained his lavish surcoat. And that once-gallant knight now teetered on the brink of ruin, perched on a stick ladder within sight of the imperial city smoldering in ashes and ruin.

"Yours is a mission like no other," the stylite whispered to Erik alone. "It is neither fair nor right that this task fell upon you. Yet in the face of perils beyond comprehension, behold how far you have come."

The light above the stylite's head stung Erik's eyes. The knight's hands softened in a gesture of supplication, hesitant to touch the stylite's pale, wrinkled skin.

"I have no right to seek absolution," he choked.

"And I cannot offer you absolution, nor release," the stylite replied. "Neither are in my purview to grant. But I can extend a moment of respite if you will take it."

Erik grabbed his hand.

The stylite hauled him onto the column's broken summit, taking Erik's hands between both of his own. He murmured in slurred Greek that Erik could not understand. Nevertheless, a sense of peace washed over him such as he had not experienced since his earliest days in Caer Baen.

Through the inner darkness that suffocated him, a light burned, much as one from a lamp but whiter, purer. This sliver of brightness caused his dead body to take a breath.

Then, painfully at first, his extended teeth began to recede.

The stylite then withdrew the cup from its wrappings, filled it from a water barrel, and pressed it to the knight's lips. The water soothed the hunger that, until then, had been kept in check only by means of Thelwyn's elixirs.

"Take this," the stylite instructed. "You will know where it needs to be to fulfill purposes beyond either of us."

What followed that interview with the holy man was several weeks of travel by sea, then again in the back of a wagon. Antioch, the great city overlooking the Middle Sea, now lay far distant to the southwest. The crowded markets and fortified walls of that great city had been little more than a stopover affording temporary shelter for travelers departing into the bleak late winter for points beyond.

Now the wagon rattled on a rutted, narrow track through broken hills toward the highlands and mountains. Hypatius clucked under his tongue for the horses to keep up their pace, though he meant not to push them too hard. But the rattle of ruts and clucking to the draft horses allowed him distraction from his losses in the city that had smoldered as they fled. Now these long, lonely miles wore heavy on the man in their own right as he and the horses continued through the wilderness, even when the foodstuffs began running low.

Hypatius reached up and rubbed at his nose, protected from the winds by a woolen hood.

Inside the wagon, Erik's wooden crate bounced against the thick ropes that lashed it into place. Next to the box lay a pile of blankets and furs, crowded up against the driver's seat as a break from the weather. The bundle stirred, then the gray head of the fox rose above the tumble to scan the ragged spires. Round eyes swept the horizon with a methodical thoroughness not typically associated with the species.

When finished, the beast turned an accusing eye on Hypatius, as if reproving him for choosing to make their way over what surely must have been the roughest road in the eastern empire.

A hand reached from the blankets, slender fingers that tangled in the fur on the back of the beast's neck. With her other hand, Cassandra brushed back her hood, lifting her face to the gray that extended from the stone beneath the wheels up to the jagged mountains and toward the sky. Yet her focus was not on the barren vistas, but rather on the crate. She placed a hand against it. The knight remained inside yet had been quiet since the night they'd left the stylite's column.

Their destination drew closer, finally, at the edge of the empire. And after all the tribulations, she desperately wanted this trip to be done. Tartars and Persians fought the Romans here, had in fact for centuries, leaving travel a risky undertaking. She hoped the stylite knew what he had been about when giving Erik the means to continue his journey.

Hypatius cleared his throat.

"What is it?" she asked.

The old scholar traced a finger across a wrinkled map on the bench beside him, squinting to match the chart with the land. "We should soon see the ruins," he murmured.

She lowered her hand. "Mary, mother of the One God, hear me— please keep us from the evil in our hearts."

⚬⚬⚬

Erik sat hunched in the crate as the wagon jarred over the ruts and holes in the dirt washboard. He held the worn and unadorned cup, turning it over for the thousandth time. After months trekking over land and sea, pushing through storms, urban markets, and winter-ravaged hinterlands, the knight now sat in darkness, tracing the contours of the cup that Daniel had left in his care.

It was not particularly heavy or ornate, having come from some humble tradesman. But with each fill from the stylite's barrel, the water within had seemed to seethe with power imbued in the hammered metal from centuries of carrying the Blood of Christ.

396

The wagon lurched, then halted. Someone banged on the box. Voices spoke. He plunged the cup back into his worn travel bag. Then he extended his mind into that of his familiar.

Outside, Cassandra argued with a handful of horsemen clad in heavy exotic armor. Through his familiar's eyes, the knight saw the long, wickedly barbed lances with which the Persian cavalry had for a century dueled the Romans across the frontier. Erik's spatha lay near at hand, but the sun still rode above the horizon. And the wagon carried no pitch or canvas that could be improvised into suitable coverage. The war horses danced nervously, blowing steam from their nostrils like mythical coursers of exotic heroes. Their nervousness was written palpably across their long faces.

Cassandra stood behind the driver's box, hands raised before her. Hypatius followed suit. When she spoke, her words were unfamiliar, but the warriors responded readily enough with gestures toward the track ahead, where a fading hint of mist lingered near the ground. Cassandra offered a measured, deliberate response. One of the warriors doffed his helmet, regarding her with a critical look. His face, darkened by sun and weather, was framed by a thick dark beard and long locks. He spoke in broken Greek.

"No . . . there is no life. No life . . . all death."

He elaborated further in Persian. Cassandra translated for Hypatius and by proxy Erik as well. "They came with pilgrims—no, seekers of curiosities—to see the ancient gates. Some of them entered to find what was in the darkness but never returned. The soldiers will not bar our way. But they said there is death—death along this path."

"Then we best carry on," Hypatius replied in a low voice. "This is likely our goal—the destination of pagan soldiers wishing to reunite an emperor with his sword."

From his perch atop the wagon, the scholar offered a bow to the Persian troopers. He grabbed up the reins, slapping them against the horses' flanks. The wagon lurched forward, Cassandra bracing herself against the rail.

"God have mercy on us all," she whispered.

She slid back down into the furs, but the familiar remained upright, watching the riders recede into the drab landscape under the weeping, overcast sky.

The wagon rolled along with creaking wheels and clattering hooves. The path twisted around a last sloping hillside of gravel and rock before opening to a row of broken columns jutting up to a great porch that had once provided shelter to pagan pilgrims. Beneath the stone pillars heaved floor pavers, oddly angled under a heavy mist.

Hypatius pulled the horses to a halt, grabbed a document from his pack beside him, and jumped down. He stretched his joints, then opened the scroll.

"This necropolis is not a widely known place like Hierapolis," he muttered. "But during the time of Magnus this would have been a place where Theodosius' agents may not have searched for his loyalists. A remote place in a disputed border zone, it would not attract the casual visitor."

Cassandra wrapped herself in her blanket, jumped down from the wagon, and alighted after Hypatius. She surveyed the ruins, the entirety fallen to ruin since Rome had outlawed the pagan rites.

"Where are the gates—the actual gates?"

Hypatius studied his document, then pointed to an area at the far end of the ruin where the mist bubbled more thickly over the floor.

"The entrance would be there. A path that not many of the living would dare to place their feet upon."

The sun had barely made way for the shadows when Erik thumped on the crate. Hypatius pried it open with a crowbar and a mallet, loosening the pegs holding it together until Erik could kick it open.

Cassandra stood guard nearby while the Albion knight rose, stretching against the overcast sky that hid the stars. The fox crept from the pile of blankets to attach himself as a shadow to the knight's heel. Erik stood still as death itself, the spatha on his hip, customarily a sign of imperial service and martial devotion. The lady had seen that sword brutally deployed for sinister purposes. She had witnessed the curse rise within him, had seen the shadows reach out in his wake, and had stood by in terror when the living died at his passing. Her view of him was conflicted—an odd mixture of fear and comradeship forged from a strange alloy that bound them together. And that bond had been smelted in the catacombs of Rome, hammered at the anvil in the wealthy districts of Ravenna, and tempered in the Imperial Palace itself. Yet here she stood, not knowing what the next few minutes or hours would hold but trusting that he would not unleash his hunger upon her.

"The gate is indeed there," Erik confirmed.

He set out immediately for the ruins, and she trotted alongside to keep up.

Gases roiled near the edge of the temple complex. Inside the outer circuit of columns, stairs descended deep into an unroofed lower chamber surrounded by stone benches. Here and there the bleached bones of animals and men appeared within the mists, momentarily visible, then hidden once more by the swirling vapors. Ironwork gates stood at the far end, where the gases bubbled up from the hot spring deep within.

The gates were ajar—just enough for a lone man to pass through.

"This appears to be the place," Erik observed drily.

"And the gates—" Cassandra began.

"The doorstep to the underworld," Erik finished for her.

Hypatius built a sputtering fire near the wagon, away from the lurking gases. In deeply blackened iron pans, he prepared cakes and sausage over its glowing embers. When Erik and Cassandra returned to the circle of light, he handed the girl a portion, but Erik stepped past them to drag his pack from the wagon.

He froze.

He heard a sound, faint enough he couldn't pinpoint its origin. But when he moved, the creak of his harness chased it away. After a long moment, he shrugged and bent back to his task, rummaging in his pack for the gear needed for this journey. The armor given him by Belisarius he would wear with his spatha. But most of the kit he had borne from Albion was no longer serviceable and ended up in a pile on the wagon.

"Much of that has served you well," Cassandra noted, standing next to him now.

Erik ran a hand across the scars and welded seams in the steel plates that memorialized his journey from Birkenshire to this distant place.

"All that remains of what my father passed on to me," he said.

He knelt over his canvas pack, settled in a length of rope, a spare dagger, a woolen cloak, the cavalry helmet, and some small sundries, then shoved the rest back into the crate. He whistled, and the fox appeared near his feet. Erik gathered him up, handing him to Cassandra.

"I've no wish to lose another valiant comrade."

"Is that so?" she asked with a wry smile. "Then you need to offer him to Hypatius."

"Hypatius? You cannot come. There are dangers yet undiscovered. Hypatius can find you a ship back to your family."

"He could. If I asked him to assist me," Cassandra replied. She shrugged her own travel pack onto her shoulders.

"This is not your fight," Erik insisted.

"I do not accompany you because of the fight," she said, looking him in the eye. "Surely you have learned this in our travels together?"

"Did you not hear the soldiers?" he snapped, jabbing a finger at the mists. "There is nothing but death down there."

She reached into her pack, pulling forth a bright-colored scarf. "The finest samite. From imperial stocks," she said, wrapping the shimmering fabric around her face three times. "This is sure to keep out the smell."

His hand reflexively tightened on the pommel of his spatha.

"I cannot keep you safe," he whispered. "From those vapors, not even from this curse. You must not accompany me."

"And *you* cannot forbid it," she said, her face flushed. "Oh, Erik, do you not see? I have sought these things since I was a little girl—

things that rationality and understanding cannot explain! Sacred pilgrimages, mystical texts, rumors of miracles. How can you of all people not see? We are spiritual but fallen beings, living in a world where the mortal and the divine intersect. I want to go with you, to see what you see."

She placed her hand on his shoulder.

"To the end," she finished with the promise.

Hypatius rubbed his tired eyes. "Such companions are a rarity in an uncertain world," he observed, standing to offer his hand. "You, sir, gave me purpose when everyone I loved was lost. Now you go into dangers of your own. I hope you find what you seek. I will remain here until you return."

Erik took his hand.

Hypatius released the knight's hand with a cautious smile. He then bent near the fire, lifted an oil lamp, and checked the wick to ensure it was trimmed. With a burning twig, he lit it. Once the lamp ignited, he handed it to Cassandra.

"Let us hope it is an uneventful hike and nothing more."

The fox squirmed out of Cassandra's grip, leaping to the ground to wrap itself around Erik's ankles. He gathered it into his arms, then dropped it into the top of his pack.

"I suppose I will have to keep you safe as well," he murmured, scratching at the creature's ears.

He cinched the pack tight, hoping the hemp lining would protect the woodland beast. Without another word, they set off for the iron gates.

At the edge of the mists, Cassandra adjusted the layers of cloth over her face. They descended the steps to the beclouded floor, crossed to the spring, and stepped in with a hushed splash. The knee-deep water was hot and stank of brimstone and death. Beyond the spring lay a cave that appeared to be carved from the rock by the watery mists swirling with each of their steps. Within the entrance, the stone walls immediately sloped downward into the earth.

Erik put a hand on the wall for support, then stepped cautiously onto the slick surface. Cassandra ducked her head to follow.

The lamplight was dim, the footing treacherous, and the sides of the passage overspread with stone protrusions. Both stepped carefully to keep upright in their progress downward until Erik halted. Cassandra grabbed his pack to keep from sliding into him.

"What is it?" she hissed, raising her other hand to the cloth over her nostrils to hold it in place.

The air was thick, each breath noticeably painful to draw into her lungs.

Erik remained unmoving and silent while she counted the pulse of her heart.

"Something is here," he finally replied. "I can hear it. Feel it as if it were within my own bones."

After a few more of her heartbeats, he resumed the descent. Cassandra pushed after with renewed effort against the increasingly leaden weight of her legs.

The passage opened into a cavern, which, while larger than the channel they followed, remained a confined space. Noises chittered through dripping stalactites. Erik picked up his pace through the alien landscape. Cassandra fought to keep up, but her body slowed and her lungs suddenly spasmed with a cough.

The oil lamp flickered, the flame shrinking with an oily smoke trail. Then something moved in the shadows.

Erik forged ahead into a tunnel at the far end of the cavern. Now Cassandra's lungs burst aflame, leaving her gasping for air. She held the faltering light before her, catching at the wall with her hand. Something moved again, this time behind her. She spun around, brandishing the lamp, but nothing appeared in the shrinking circle of light.

"Erik?" she called into the shadows.

But the darkness did not respond to her entreaty.

The inky black surrounded him like a cloak in the already oppressive confines of the subterranean path. While Erik could make his way easily enough in the darkness, the finer features of the stones were lost to him. Not that it mattered—he was drawn unrelentingly onward by the sound that had transformed into a jarring melody echoing through the bones of the earth. A song without a recognizable voice or timbre of any instrument, but that nevertheless lured him onward. His feet slipped on the slick stone, but he quickly adjusted his steps and kept up pace, drawn further and further into the eternal depths.

A woman's scream tore through the tunnels, yet his senses were engulfed by a haze that muted even that desperate sound. Something in his pack began scratching at him. However, Erik could only respond to the siren call, for it consumed him with desire to find its source.

Then he heard another call, almost like a melodic scream. More frantically, the fox dug at the inside of the pack.

Erik remained still. The melody grew more forceful in its rhythms and notes, entwining with the hunger that had accompanied him every minute of every hour for these last many months.

There was a third scream, and a revelation pierced the haze.

Erik balled his fists. With great effort he lifted a foot, taking a step in the direction of Cassandra's voice. His teeth ground together until he thought they would crack, then he took another step. With sheer force of will, he tore himself loose to take one halting step after another until he broke the siren call. The knight scrambled back into the cavern, where his companion lay.

Gaseous mists swirled around her struggling form. The lamp lay nearby, sputtering a barely visible flame.

Something clattered against the stone. Before he could drag his spatha from its scabbard, a massive force crashed into him, driving him into the cavern wall like a battering ram. Stone shards cut at his face and his armor crunched, grinding into his back. He grabbed at what felt like thick horns rising out of coarse hair. He heaved against them. The creature slid off balance, scraping across the slick stone floor. Erik wrenched the horns sideways. The beast stumbled but then jerked itself upright, throwing Erik once more against the wall.

A bellow echoed through the cavern with the beast looming high over him. It had a man-like shape but was extraordinarily large, and crested like a giant Rus gladiator. Yet the creature was not of the living—the stink of decay overpowered the brimstone stench of the vapors.

Spatha finally in hand, Erik gathered his feet beneath him and leapt away from the wall.

"Cassandra! Cass—"

Hooves clattered across the cavern floor.

A broken horn caught him in the side, flinging him into a stalactite. He counterattacked with the blade's long edge. When the steel lodged in bone, it was wrenched out of his hand.

The beast threw him across the cavern again. Erik hit the floor, sliding through bones and debris. Again, the creature bellowed, and Erik now realized he was facing a myth risen from the dead. The knight scrambled away, determined to keep from the creature's reach. He cast about with his cursed vision until he found her, a blot of fading warmth under the mists on the far side of the beast.

Pulling out his dagger from the scabbard at his belt, he hefted it in his fingers, then made a dash for Cassandra. The minotaur's movement was hard to track, having no pulsing lifeblood. But the air pushed before the great beast when it lunged, like the bow wave of Kulo's old corbita. Erik ducked under the slashing horns and swinging arms and slid the last few feet to Cassandra. He snatched her arms, dragging her along with him into the tunnel.

Behind him, hooves crashed like anvils with cavern-shaking fury. Erik pivoted against the tunnel wall to make his stand. Yet the melody kept calling with hungry urgency, boring into his head. It snared his thoughts and desires, fluid notes and flourishing crescendos all clutching at his faculties.

I will stand with you, Cassandra had assured him above the gates.

She had trusted him. Erik focused on that trust—focused on their companionship and on the quest that had drawn him to this pit.

You shall draw power from your desire to remain worthy, the stylite had said when the graal passed into Erik's hands. *Even when you don't believe you are worthy.*

Erik threw himself into the fight once more, for he was a knight of Albion. Though he had soaked his garments in blood, the youth had not drunk of it even when surrounded by buckets of the tempting ichor. While Marianna had left him with a hellish curse, this burden

406

did not define him, and neither would this siren song, as he now recognized what it was.

The minotaur's horns drove into his armor, pinning him to the wall. His dagger rattled to the ground. Erik braced his feet against the wall and pushed, his arms knotting like a thick-wound coil. He lifted the horns from his body, then twisted them to the side. The minotaur stumbled. Erik wrestled atop it, knees on its chest. His expropriated spatha grated against the stone. The creature let out a bovine wail when he grabbed it, wrenching it free. The knight forced the blade to its throat, fully intending to strike off its head.

In the guttering light of the lamp, the beast fell calm, its milky eyes unflinching.

An unexpected cry from another quarter in the cavern ripped through the toxic air. A shadowy form, erratic and fluid, rushed in, clawing at the darkness with hooked fingers and trailing a thicket of hair and tattered shreds of fabric in her wake.

Erik threw up his free hand.

"I have no quarrel with you," he declared. "We only need pass this place."

The harpy ignored the knight. With motions that flashed, jumped, and stuttered, she rushed to the minotaur's side. Her face was seamed with wrinkles, her skin gray and mottled. The harpy snarled, pulling her lips back from feral teeth.

Then she placed her hands into the minotaur's chest, itself an open wound of decayed flesh and exposed bone. The beast shuddered, its mouth twitching to release a guttural moan. A ruined hand rose toward the apparition, but as the harpy tried to take it, her grasp only passed intangibly through the beast's flesh.

Erik rose, pulling his blade away the minotaur's neck to a guard position.

"Please. Let us pass," he said.

"She dies," the harpy screeched, pointing to Cassandra. "It consumes her!"

"The sky . . . the day and the night . . . only there is freedom," the spectral apparition cried, with a longing desire that nearly brought tears to Erik's own undead eyes.

She reached out to the minotaur's face, but her wretched fingers were unable to caress the ragged cheek. She moaned again, her form losing substance with the effort to communicate.

"Lost . . . lost . . . she will be lost . . ." the harpy hissed.

Erik gathered Cassandra into his arms. Her body was still, but life still flickered deep within her.

You can save her—the words sounded quietly in his mind in a cruel, familiar voice—the voice of a god far removed across land and sea. *Accept the covenant . . . become one with Death.*

Become my creature.

"No!" Erik spat.

But the apparition stood now in front of the knight, her face wriggling like worms cut from the soil by the sharp edge of a spade.

"Trapped . . . caught by the song . . ." the harpy shrilled. "No escape . . . only . . . only . . . *oblivion!*"

"Show me," Erik demanded.

But she was already away, bouncing through the cavern with all the sense of a mad firefly, trailing dying tendrils of energy. The harpy rushed the mouth of yet another tunnel that was choked with bones, weapons, and armor. Erik hefted his pack. The fox stirred within.

Assured at least of its safety, he dashed after the harpy while Cassandra's life began to wane.

Erik stepped carefully through the subterranean lichyard where weapon furnishings in everything from steel to bronze lay corroding in the dank brimstone vapors. Each step brought the wordless melody closer, the harmonies becoming darker, twisted, more dissonant. Confusion invaded his thoughts, drawing him into a web of notes, power, and chaos.

The harpy shrieked, shattering the magic. For the moment, Erik was freed. He took a slower, more deliberate step, then another, then another. He strained to focus on his task—to keep moving under his own control and to find someplace he could nurture the last struggling ember of Cassandra's life back to full flame. While he pushed deeper into the caves, the temperature rose, the way steepened, and water bubbled more freely from the walls. Pinpricks of light clustered on the rivulets, each step taken to keep apace of the erratic apparition fading and reappearing ahead.

A shape undulated from the shadows and flowed through him, cold and biting for a moment. Then it was gone.

More shapes swirled about, some human, others fantastic as the minotaur. Erik was attuned to the life force in them, but their touch was as chilling as the mists of Albion. The melody continued, the intricate dance finally laid bare to reveal the snare entangling the ghosts. The subterranean air became denser and more chaotic, anguished faces flashing into view. The mash of apparitions then vanished, to be replaced by others even more pained. Erik adjusted his hold on Cassandra, waving with his other hand to clear them from his vision, but his flesh simply passed through them.

There was a small, feeble rattle in Cassandra's chest.

"No!" Erik cried out.

But he could do nothing to stop her spirit from joining all the other souls clogging the passage. He howled. Down and down and down he chased after the harpy. The glittering illumination of the damp walls grew, the soupy throng of souls about him congealing. Their sheer coldness stole his energy at each step, Cassandra's dead weight dragging on him like an anchor. A vortex of pebbles skittered back and forth along the track in time with the music's ebb and flow.

Suddenly, in the narrows before Erik, the souls parted to reveal the source of the siren's song.

There, the harpy hovered over a desiccated corpse clad in Roman armor that slumped with arms outstretched. Erik carefully lowered Cassandra to the ground, settling his cloak over her, then dropped his pack. The fox poked a nose from the depths but quickly retreated from the melody.

Beyond the cadaver's hands lay a sword upon a moldering cloak. Erik knelt beside the weapon, eyes straining for focus against the song that roared through his skull. He clapped his hands over his ears, but that did not dim the notes soaring through the horde of souls and trilling through these very tunnels.

He had seen this blade before, in a vision.

The rubied pommel pulsed deep crimson. The furniture was exotic, etched with symbols that moved of their own volition. Gold filigree wound around the grip in a spiral to a cross guard attended by opposing fire-eyed serpents. The long blade was elegantly shaped in a dire sort of way, like a nightshade's leaf.

"You must . . ." the harpy hissed near his ear. "Please . . . please . . . take it."

The sword of the Magnus—*Demonbane*, Thelwyn had named it. The very weapon borne generations ago by the Spaniard when he had marched on the Eternal City. The same weapon Thelwyn had bidden him to take up to kill the god of Death. And now, after all the struggles, after the long months of this odyssey—now this young knight knew fear. The path ahead led unavoidably to more death—if not Arawn's, then his own. And he had seen enough these last months to know that death was not the end. There were destinies more horrible than any sputtering monk's ravings about fire and brimstone.

Everlasting darkness lay in wait with ragged flesh, the loss of sun, sky, and the simple beauty of a sparrow in orange fall leaves. When he reached for the sword, he could not close his fingers around that exquisite hilt.

"You must . . ." the harpy intoned once more. "Please!"

In the corner of his vision, Cassandra's form remained slumped against the damp stone. She had trusted him, had walked beside him, and had even driven onward when he could not. Beside her, the travel pack quivered with the fox reacting to his doubt. Of course, her sacrifices were not the only ones to bring him to this mystical juncture. Hypatius waited dutifully far above. And the stylite perched on his broken column in rags and filth, who likewise had urged him to remain true to his quest.

He squeezed his eyes shut.

"Saint Michael . . . if there was ever one in need," he whispered.

He stretched forth his hand, taking hold of the hilt.

Voices thundered through his head. Erik threw up his free hand to ward off the unseen foe—a massive jumble of spirits, drawn through this subterranean nightmare when the clutch of stalwart soldiers sought vainly to return the blade to the only underworld they knew.

Yet, one by one, they succumbed to the vapors in this lonely and forgotten place. Heat coursed through Erik's fingers. A warmth he had not experienced in a very long time exploded through his body. He screamed when long-dormant energy—all from the souls that had been consumed over centuries—flooded into him, revealing the sword's power. That power blazed in his veins before receding to lurk in the shadows of his mind like a stalking predator. Surely such a force in the hand of a mortal man would be overpowering. But for Erik, this unholiness made him feel vibrant, near alive—and dangerous.

The melody abruptly transformed.

The sword howled, etched runes glowing through the accumulated dust and mold. Erik swung the flat of the blade against the wall. Centuries of crust scattered into the air, along with the thick swirl of souls that blew deeper down the tunnel.

The harpy fluttered above Erik, her eyes kindled with a steely glow that shone through the supernatural, windswept tangle of hair and wrinkled, desiccated skin.

"Quickly!" she hissed, then flitted after the rush of faceless dead.

Erik slid the sword into his belt alongside his father's spatha, then snatched up his pack and Cassandra. Even though the apparition was not wont to tarry, he would not leave his companions like Magnus' legionaries, abandoned to die in this darkness.

After a length of time, the tunnel opened into an immense cavern where the floor spread like a plain to the edge of a turbid river blanketed by a thick layer of sulfuric vapors. The banks buzzed with the milling souls, now free of the siren call. The harpy swept through their numbers to the water's edge. There, she gradually transformed—the ruined visage of the ancient harpy giving way to youth and humanity. Her face smoothed and softened, hair deepening to a lustrous flow rather than tangled chaos.

Near the woman reborn stood a solitary shade, while the multitude of lost spirits now crowded a ragged stone dock some distance upriver.

"They call to her," the woman said, sweeping her arm to the bluffs rising beyond the far bank, where an imposing shadowy form stood. "*He* calls her. Not in malice, but you must act quickly!"

The knight laid Cassandra's lifeless form on the strand. From her body rose a form, a shade that held the young woman's form. That apparition rose into the air—even as the pulse in her body slowed.

"What must I do?" he begged.

"The cup!" the woman urged.

Erik unslung his bag, dumping the contents. The fox tumbled limply out onto the smooth stones. Erik reached past his familiar to grab the cup. There, in the darkness, the vessel began glowing at his touch—a gentle light that brought color to Cassandra's pallor. A light that drew her flat eyes back to him.

But her gaze did not linger. She drifted toward the dock, where a bent, hooded figure deployed a long pole to guide a barge up against the stones.

"Hurry. Fill it!" the woman cried. "Before she crosses the river! Else she is lost to you!"

Erik stumbled to the river's edge, plunging the cup into oily waves reeking of death and finality. By the time he returned to Cassandra's body, the contents had transformed into a crystal-clear draught that rippled and bubbled with its own effervescence.

"Water from the Eternal River," the specter hissed in a low tone. "She must drink!"

He lifted Cassandra's head, pressing the cup to her lips. But she did not drink. He pressed at the muscles of her throat, rocked her head back and forth, yet she did not swallow. The knight became desperate for some method to make her at least sip from the cup. Cold air rushed about him, parting the noxious fumes and bearing the scent of a distant spring emerging from the frigid grip of winter.

The fox stirred weakly and lurched to its feet, coughing. The apparition reached down to Cassandra's breast, and, in Erik's supernatural vision, her life spark sputtered. She convulsed, gagged— and swallowed.

At the dock, Cassandra's shade stepped up to the boat. But before she could place a foot on the deck, the ferryman held up a hand in a gesture that demanded obedience. As if emerging from a deep sleep, Cassandra opened her actual eyes.

"Where . . ." she began, but her lungs spasmed in a coughing fit. The knight clapped her back, then held her until the coughing broke.

"I know not," Erik murmured near her ear.

The boat scraped off the dock. The ferryman leaned against the pole, propelling the shallow barge across the currents to the far side of the river. Then Erik lifted his eyes to the visage of the woman who, by now, glowed brightly.

"You have my thanks, and my apologies for your companion."

When her eyes met Erik's, they were no longer the inky pools of the void, but rather a warm walnut.

"Rhoen was drawn to the pits by the sword's song," she shared, her voice bearing a promise of budding leaves and chattering birds. "Yet he kept me company, protected me when madness fell upon me."

414

"I will take the sword far from here," Erik assured her.

"Yes," she agreed. "It belongs elsewhere, for it is a foul thing—a weapon that has tormented so many. For the endless years since it was left here at the gates of the underworld."

Cassandra's eyes drifted to the figure standing on the distant bluffs, overseeing the souls streaming off the ferryboat.

"I must go . . ." she whispered. "I must go . . . away."

She struggled against Erik's embrace.

"A stone," the reborn woman demanded. "A river stone—give it to me!"

Erik snatched a brown-and-black-striped rock at random, pressing it into her now solid hands. She cupped it between her palms, murmuring words in a dialect of ancient Greek that Erik did not understand. But her incantation was brief, and she then pressed the stone back into his hand.

"This will bind her soul to her body," she said, "so that you may cross the realms of the dead. She must keep this with her. For she was lost, and her spirit continues to be lured to Elysium's haunted fields."

Erik grabbed Cassandra's hands, firmly closing her fingers over the stone. Her eyes returned to Erik, and she screamed.

"I must go," she panted. "Please. Please, let me go!"

"I cannot," Erik countered, brushing dark tangles of hair from her face. "You do not belong there yet. You are my companion. We must finish this journey."

He lifted her to her feet. "We must return to Hypatius," Erik said. "He awaits us, my lady."

Then, like a statue thawing from an eternal sleep, the imposing figure across the water lifted its arm to point downriver.

"No . . . no . . ." Cassandra said. "We cannot go back . . ."

"I must return to Albion. There is no other way to fight Annwyn."

"No, Erik . . . this way . . ." Cassandra murmured, her distant eyes now turned downstream.

The dark waters of the river tumbled away, beyond the souls trudging past the gatekeeper toward another cave roaring with hidden rapids.

"It appears your destiny lies upon the waters of the underworld," the woman observed.

She reached out to touch Erik's shoulder, and that touch blossomed through him like spring sunshine and refreshing rain.

"I cannot go—" Erik started.

"Trust me," Cassandra interjected in a serene whisper.

"Hypatius," he reminded her. "He awaits us. The cup. We must return it to its resting place—"

"Have you considered," the woman noted with a wry smile, "that your destiny may lie on a different path?"

The river burbled, splashing against the shore. Underworld vapors spilled over the banks. Above it all, the solitary man continued to point downriver, and though Erik could not see his eyes, he believed that they watched him.

"I was traveling to my mother's homeland," the woman whispered near his ear, "when the melody of the sword ensnared me. I must continue that journey before I return to my beloved. My way is to the surface. Allow me to return the cup to this man who is your friend."

Cassandra nodded, her eyes strangely animated. "Hypatius must take the cup," she said. "Our road lies on that river. Oh, I know things now. Please believe me, as I believe in you."

Her final words struck Erik's heart. Trust was not something that had come easily for him since Marianna's betrayal on that strand of beach.

"The cup of Christ—the stylite gave it into my hands."

"And Hypatius traveled with us for a purpose," Cassandra countered. "Now we must trust that he will attend to the relic."

Erik hefted the cup.

The relic had saved Cassandra twice and had brought Erik back from the brink of the abyss after the bloody revolt in the Hippodrome. The contents, the very Blood of the Christ, had been stolen from it long ago to provide divine power for the Grey God's machinations in the mortal world. It was a precious treasure to kings and kingdoms, and he had carried it to the gates of a hellish underworld, far from those who had been entrusted with its care at Canterbury. And now that he was to take up the sword of the Magnus, the cup's purpose no longer lay upon his path.

"He is a good man," Erik whispered.

"We must go down the river," Cassandra urged.

Erik climbed wearily to his feet, facing the woman that hovered above the shore like a beacon.

"Give this to Hypatius with a charge—though it's empty, he must return the cup to its resting place. He must swear upon his very soul that he will protect it. Serve the righteous purpose of God's blood . . . if it and the cup are ever reunited."

She nodded solemnly, taking the cup in both her hands. "I will take it to Hypatius and lay it to his charge as you require."

Erik offered a hand and Cassandra took it, tucking the river stone into her belt pouch. The fox brushed through her legs, face upturned, tongue once again lolling out of the side of its mouth.

Erik grabbed his travel bag and, with Cassandra's hand in his, set off toward the dock where the souls continued congregating for the ferry ride across the river. At that waypoint of the dead lay the means for them to continue their journey.

The ferryman had just moored his craft when the companions stepped onto the cold flagstones. The dead scattered—whether from Erik's cursed flesh or the murmuring sword at his side, he couldn't tell. The ferryman cut a tall figure, albeit hunched over by centuries of toiling on the waters between life and death. His skeletal-framed black sockets dripped with wriggling worms and weeping mist. A wry, thin-lipped smile exposed ancient yellow teeth.

"You would take my boat," the creature mused. "I have not been separated from this damned old thing for a very long time."

Erik's hand fell to the sword, and a burst of dark energy thrummed up his arm.

"I have a need—" he began.

"All have *needs*." The ferryman chuckled with a raspy crinkle. "All who arrive here have *needs*. And I've carried each one across to the eternities, their *needs* be damned."

He laughed outright at his own pun, then sobered. "But where you desire to go, I cannot take you."

"Please, sir, we need your boat," Cassandra said, a tremble in her voice.

The ferryman turned his vacant regard on her. "I nearly brought you to the other side—you but delay the inevitable, daughter," he said, placing a thin finger alongside his nose and grinning horrifically. "Do not lose the stone."

He turned back to Erik. "This vessel has made the crossing for centuries on end. The only vessel of its kind. You cannot take it."

Steel rasped from its scabbard, a horrific melody spilling into the vaporous air. The length of steel flickered from the infernal light within.

"No time for argument," the knight said. With his chin, he gestured across the waters to the figure still pointing downstream. "Your own god commands us."

"I do not serve the Lord of the Dead," the ferryman hissed. "His power does not reach beyond the far bank. I serve these—the dead themselves."

Erik raised Demonbane's burning steel to the ferryman's chest, the sword's cruel chant crashing in his skull, demanding violence.

The ferryman disappeared in a puff of smoke—to reappear behind Erik's shoulder.

"There is always a price," he choked in the knight's ear. "Always coin that must be paid for my services. Take this vessel but know that price will be required of you before you face the gates of Annwyn."

Erik swung the blade, but the sword screamed only through empty air. The milling dead swayed back and forth like grass in a field swept by an unseen breeze, but the ferryman was gone. Erik extended a hand to assist Cassandra into the boat. Then he cut through the cords that lashed it to the pylons, grabbing the long pole that lay in the stern. The ferryman once again stood on the dock, standing with arms crossed among the souls crowding the edge. Erik poled the craft out into the current.

The rushing flow grabbed the vessel, twisting it through the mists while Erik fought to keep their heading. Behind him, on one side, the dark figure still presided, while on the opposite shore the angelic woman raised her hand in farewell. Erik thought he saw a patch of green bespeckled with colored sprouts beneath her.

The river surged madly over broken rocks and boulders into the dark maw ahead. Erik bent on the pole to keep them away from the clutching reefs until darkness consumed any remaining light and the river fell out from beneath the ancient keel.

The boat dropped into the void.

Epilogue

INQUISITIONARY

The elven ship, with sails trimmed to slow her speed, descended majestically between the trees to the still water of the lake. During the lengthy journey, Thelwyn had carefully eavesdropped on his captors at every opportunity. Many of the fae crew expressed regular frustration with sailing so far afield to fetch him. Their recent route had doubled back east to west, then back again before focusing on what had to be the only unfrozen lake in the area at this time of year.

Had finding this body of water taken any longer, some of the crew whispered that charting a course toward the southern continent or simply sailing all the way back to the west would be their preferred course of action.

But eventually they found open water, nestled among the vales of the salt-mining Nori tribe where they now made their approach. The helmsman displayed considerable skill in this maneuver. The craft settled until the lowest point of the gracefully curved keel just touched the water, sending out a single ripple.

Fae crew dragged Thelwyn from the hold onto the deck, his wrists and ankles bound in iron manacles. Elves hated the metal's touch, but controlling a skilled mage was a challenge unique to the fae, for which the poisonous metal was well suited. Fortunately, the Romans had been fond of manacles and had left many behind when they abandoned Albion. These elves had seen the value of procuring such equipment.

The captain leaned over him, shaking his head pitifully. "You should have dealt with us," he said. "There would have been no need for this kind of treatment." He gestured to Thelwyn's escorts onto the rail.

They hauled the mage to a gangplank propped out over the water. Stars wheeled above in a cloudless sky while the ship's master scattered a handful of tiny leaves onto the lake's surface, muttering an incantation in the melodic dé Danann language.

The captain stalked through the crew to the aft deck. An escort of armed warriors marched Thelwyn out to the gangway's end, then forced him to his knees. One of his guards, a burly sort who was large even compared to men, held his head with a meaty hand and violently wrenched his face toward the water.

Thelwyn did not wait long.

The fluctuations from the leaves settled once more into a mirror. An ancient fae stepped toward the surface—white-haired, bearded, with emerald eyes that narrowed dangerously. Richly appointed guards flanked him, bearing staves topped with curved blades that were at once graceful and wicked. This aged creature likely stood over a pool of his own in some distant land and gazed into it to examine Thelwyn.

Behind him, bright blue sky and clouds nearly blinded Thelwyn, with dizzying effect.

"Oberon," Thelwyn breathed. The very king of the fae stood before the magicker.

"Thelwyn." Oberon's voice was smooth and relentless, like a glacier. "We have found you at last."

He did not appear pleased, particularly when his eyes fell upon Thelwyn's captors.

"Had to rebuild old bridges, did you?" Thelwyn observed.

"I have had much on my mind of late. Smithies and forges. Eldritch blades of great power. Wayward apprentices. And, of course, keeping my people safe from prying eyes. And you," he thundered, stabbing a finger at him, "seem to be at least one focus of this grand ellipse!"

Oberon squatted closer to the pool.

"Now. Where would you like to start . . . *son?*"

About The Authors

Mike has wanted to write since he was very young. His earliest memories are of carrying a battered old notebook around full of illustrations and stories that he would often transpose those ideas on his grandmother's old typewriter.

While in college at BYU he was inspired by professors and visiting writers. Literary classics such as *La Chanson de Roland* and *Inferno* were often in his backpack. Chapter 3 of *Annwyn's Blood* was written during this time as a short story.

He now lives in Northern Virginia with his wife, Lori and his wonderful children, and dreams of one day driving in his old Defender to Alaska with his family.

Steve grew up on a farm in Northeast Ohio where he spent his free time reading Burroughs, Lovecraft, Zelazny and Tolkien, and his earliest writing efforts were creating adventures for his Dungeons & Dragons group. A veteran of the Army and the Navy, he currently lives near his childhood hometown with his family, two dogs and two cats. He has won awards for his writing in collaboration with Michael Eging on *The Silver Horn Echoes: A Song of Roland.*

Ingram Content Group UK Ltd.
Milton Keynes UK
UKHW040624150623
423495UK00001B/37